Since securing the top prize in a widely publicised UK writing contest, **Anouska Knight** has become an international sensation with her debut novel, *Since You've Been Gone*, hitting both *The Bookseller* and Heatseekers bestseller lists and securing praise from the likes of Jackie Collins and Jenny Colgan.

A former bakery owner, she has gone on to wide acclaim in her native England and now writes full-time.

Anouska lives in Staffordshire close to the countryside where she grew up, with childhood sweetheart Jamie and their three growing sons.

When the storylines are a little darker, Anouska writes under the pseudonym Erin Knight.

CW01496246

Also by Anouska Knight:

Since You've Been Gone
A Part of Me
Letting You Go

Writing as Erin Knight:

Perfect Strangers

Love in Pieces

ANOUSKA KNIGHT

ONE PLACE. MANY STORIES

HQ
An imprint of HarperCollins*Publishers* Ltd
1 London Bridge Street
London SE1 9GF

www.harpercollins.co.uk

HarperCollins*Publishers*
Macken House, 39/40 Mayor Street Upper
Dublin 1, D01 C9W8, Ireland

This edition 2025

1

First published in Great Britain by HQ,
an imprint of HarperCollins*Publishers* Ltd 2025

ISBN: 9780008180256

Set in Sabon LT Std by HarperCollins*Publishers* India

Printed and bound in the UK using 100% Renewable
Electricity at CPI Group (UK) Ltd

For Mena,
who never really left

Chapter 1

Mostly the dream is the same. Months go by without a single echo, and then a flurry, as if making up for lost time. But when they do come, the dreams, almost always they are the same. When Nancy wakes and replays them, which she always does, only the endings have ever strayed, but they never stray far. The core facts remain, steadfast, accounted for. Always in their right order, coursing their unwavering path even through the anonymous landscape of sleep. These are those facts, repetitive, hard, like worry beads on a string: urgency. Movement. A dirt track that has to be known by heart to be driven in the dark. A car too fast. Legs shaking with enough adrenalin to jump their own feet clear from the pedals. Skidding. Stones. Glass. These are the truths Nancy's brain will not bend.

Sometimes there is snow caught in Clarence Ludlow's hair. Sometimes not. His expression is changeless, and he doesn't change anything. Clarence is always a spectator under the sycamore tree. Sometimes he sees, sometimes he looks away.

The heaviness is no different in Nancy's bones when she wakes. It's worse when he looks away, she thinks. Clarence knows what she has done. What she has not done.

On the nights the car explodes against the trunk of the sycamore, there's a sweet whipped-up relief when Nancy wakes. She tries to swallow it down into herself before it can dissolve on her tongue. Sometimes, it is the tree that explodes and the car charges on, unfaltering, unstoppable. Another chance to get home. But Nancy never gets home. She never makes the end of the furlong. The dream cracks. She wakes. She lets the sting bore deeply down, wills it deeper still, it knows the way. She will not wish for a happier ending.

Last night had been dreamless.

At first, it was just the feather. The only oddity when Nancy opened her eyes. An imposter in the bedroom. Pristine white thing, materialised from nowhere, apparently, peculiar in its perfection, sitting just an inch from her nose. Nancy blinked at it. It seemed to be waiting for her to wake up, to see how they'd both come to find themselves down here together, on the floor, in the silence. Only her childhood pillows had been stuffed with feathers. Not since then had she fallen out of bed either. *Why am I . . .* The thought pushing its way in, stopped, half formed, interrupted by what came next.

Pain.

A searing reached through Nancy's chest. A hot, urgent claw, angrily snatching her breath and the last sweet remnants of sleep clear away. She heard the air leave her, watched the feather waft indifferently away. An invisible pressure moved through her ribs then, as if trying to squash her to the floor. As if trying to *kill* her. Then, just as abruptly, it eased.

Nancy caught her breath, reached for the bed frame above, tried to pull. A familiar image of a colossal sycamore swam giddily through her mind, a goliath alone and shelterless in a sweeping valley, thrashed mercilessly by the wind. She knew this tree. Knew its footings and fingerholds. An impossible climb. *Climb, Nancy* . . . she thought she heard. She pulled again at the bed frame, but another wicked tightening moved through her chest, blanching her thoughts colourless.

Panic started to climb her throat. She thought of her mother then. How Annabel would stand on the doorstep and wait for them both to get home from school, even when they were teenage girls walking fifteen minutes apart. One home safe, then the other. *Two for joy*, their mother would say. Nancy pictured the house, the family home Annabel still clung to like the splintered hull of a shipwreck, the noise and chaos that used to live there with them, sounds suddenly tangible in her ears. She could smell the coal and wood ash in their living room burner, the musky scent of cigarettes and perfume in the hallway when their dad would come home late from work. The leaves that blew in off the doorstep the morning he left for good. How they'd clustered in the space beneath the stairs and lived there awhile with the laces and buckles of forgotten shoes.

Nancy lay in the quiet of her apartment. Her brain suddenly hyperfocused. She didn't like it, how it was making her heart race. The pressure was instantly there again, pinning her to the rug. Nausea swept through the parts that didn't hurt. The purple suede roller boots with the glittered

3

toe stoppers she'd treasured as a child popped into her head, then evaporated again with a short, sharp stab in her diaphragm. She looked down at her silently rampaging body. *Dreaming? No. Febrile? Was this what a stroke felt like?* Her mind raced. She'd woken up flat out on a floor she definitely hadn't fallen asleep on last night, a sweaty, breathy mess in the middle of a pewter hand-tufted statement rug that really was too good ever to be sweated upon. And now her chest was *burning*. Should she call someone? She tasted an echo of last night's birthday treat to herself, a second falafel eaten hastily over the kitchen sink. Was killer indigestion a legitimate reason to bother NHS Direct when there was a perfectly good bottle of Gaviscon in the kitchen she could probably crawl to?

Another crushing pain stilled her brain. Nancy pictured her sister, spinning a sycamore helicopter in her fingers. *Make a wish, Nance.* She wished her body didn't hurt. She was definitely in it at least: didn't you leave your body when having a near-death experience? Was that what was happening here with the purple roller boots? Her life, small as it was, flashing before her eyes?

Nancy groaned, an invisible force conjuring strange sounds from her body. There were more pressing things to consider right now than the ins and outs of purported near-death experiences. And yet for a few fleeting seconds, squeezed between the mysteries of waking up down here and the spiteful tightening twisting through her body, she found herself wondering what her sister's take on *flashing lives* might look like. Molly, with her notably more impressive rap sheet. She had been born the spring before Nancy had

4

turned four in the autumn. Three and a half years between them. But Molly hadn't let being the younger sister slow her down. Everyone had had their own anecdotes to share at Mol's leaving party. In just under twenty-seven years she had single-handedly rampaged her way through two high schools, either side of one expulsion, a half-finished university degree, four long-term relationships (anything over the six-month mark), short-term versions running into the double figures, two engagements, one with a ring, the other a late period; a blue period, a hippy period, an emo period, three piercings, one tattoo – remarkably only one – every colour hair on the spectrum and brief dalliances with balalaika lessons, community service and pescatarianism. But these were other people's memories. They probably wouldn't even rank on Molly's Top One Hundred Life Flashes if it was Molly lying down here now all sweaty and reflective. Mol's most memorable milestones might look different entirely, a whole other mountain range of noteworthy peaks and troughs, knocking spots off Nancy's dull recollections about sycamore helicopters and roller boots.

It was a generally accepted rule in the Woods household that they were perhaps best off not knowing the full extent of Molly's misadventures. And yet Mol's escapades were suddenly all Nancy could think about, lying here alone in the early-morning gloom, a long two-hour drive and lifetime away from the bedroom they'd once shared back in Mistleton.

Nancy snatched a breath before anything hurt again and rolled her head towards the balcony doors. Her cheek met the feathery touch of the rug. She let her lungs empty, slowly. Nothing of her own life was flashing before her eyes any more. *Good. Unless* . . . She let the thought percolate. Maybe she didn't have enough interesting bits to draw on.

A pang of doubt flooded her, as if she'd been rolling along with an old joke for years and had just realised she was the punchline. *Busy fool.* She tried fending off any more useless, unhelpful trains of thought while the light of another brand-new day continued its inevitable invasion through the drapes, an unapologetic diffusion of warmth picking out first the outline of sleek bespoke built-in wardrobes, then the studding on the ottoman sitting squat at the foot of her bed. She'd paid too much for the apartment probably, but the investment was still sound. That was what you were supposed to do, wasn't it? Knuckle down and cough up. Work hard, climb the ladder. Single file. How else did anyone ever climb a ladder? Not in twos. Never in twos. The opportunities would come later, to slow down, maybe find another climber to enjoy the view with. Or just someone who'd peer over the edge of the bed and offer to go grab the Gaviscon. It didn't matter that she was alone now. *Now* was fleeting. *Now* never lasted.

The apartment seemed suddenly huge from down here. Barren. A bead of sweat rolled down Nancy's neck. She scrunched shut her eyes while another spasm of something wicked zipped behind her ribs. Indigestion on turbo. Had to be. Outside, the reassuring sounds of a city waking stirred. Buses pulling off, a crossing in use, familiar noise pressing in over the balcony where the silence of the apartment was giving way to another late-August morning.

Nancy's mobile phone peeked down at her over the edge of the bedside table. She reached. It toppled onto the rug beside her. 05:47 blinked back through the twilight. She swiped it open and scrolled through her calls, *Recents*, past Molly's name, and their dad's, past Haima's and the direct line to the office, until she got to Annabel's landline at the bottom. *Mum & Mol.* Her mum would know what to do, Annabel had a gift for knowing the best over-the-counter remedies on the market, but Nancy wouldn't call Annabel. Instead, she glanced across the apartment towards the kitchen and its promise of antacids. The fragments of crystal were still strewn across her rich hardwood floor where she'd left the mess and ruin beneath the island last night, an obliterated cake stand and the birthday cake it had been elevating like a prize until their demise over the edge of the worktop. Nancy didn't want an award for reaching another birthday, for successfully slaloming the obstructions that might've prevented her from getting to thirty-two.

She'd been working late when her mother's home-made cake had arrived on the apartment doorstep two days ago. Annabel had pulled out all the stops this year, arranging pear segments petal-like, sticky and sugar-glazed, into a flower formation on top of a rich chocolate torte. So much effort. As if either of them needed reminding that time stopped for nothing and no one and definitely not the Woods family. Nancy pictured her mother, alone in the corridor outside. A four-hour round trip nearly, for thirty seconds outside a closed door.

Something ominous reshaped itself, moving through Nancy's body. NHS Direct would run through her symptoms. Besides the nasty pinching behind her ribs, what was there? Some breathlessness lately, a few aches through her neck and back, probably from falling out of bed. There were the flutters she'd felt in her chest last week, after her run around Chortley Park, but she was getting older. Bodies only had to work harder if they wanted to be faster. And she would be faster, if it killed her. She unstuck the hair from her forehead with her knuckles. Did NHS Direct bother much with sweating? Probably not. She'd never been much of a sweater before, though, not on a gruelling ten-miler or under fire in Deep Dish's boardroom. That was why Haima liked to send her into battle: apparently Nancy had a gift for keeping anxieties out of view. So the sweating was definitely new. She rolled onto her back. Hot flushes? Was that what this was? Was she about to crash into early menopause, right here on her favourite rug? She let the thought roll around her head like a marble, waiting to see where it came to rest. Haima had flashed her an article on early menopause in *Marie Claire* on their flight to the Stockholm office last year. It happened all the time. Wasn't thirty-two a bit too early for *early*, though?

Another trickle of sweat tracked down her hairline. She teased her pyjama vest from her midriff. It stretched obediently over her other elbow, then her shoulder. Another careful pull and she'd freed herself. The effort was exhausting. She used the vest to wipe the sweat from her lip, then let her fingers fumble towards the place where ribs met to suffer the tyranny of underwire and rubbed at the storm there. *Get up*. Deep Dish had a big day ahead. The whole agency was Saturday brainstorming this morning. She had to *get up*. Haima would be in at seven, champing at the bit, vaping her heart out while the rest of the team pinballed ideas on the coveted festive ad campaign they'd somehow nailed down despite the big boys over at Mason & Muster's tendering this year too. Deep

Dish had finally done it, the big one, *the* Christmas ad was theirs, and now there was a rumour Macca's people were in talks with the sound department. Haima had confided there'd already been a handbell version of 'Pipes of Peace' doing the rounds in some very inner circles, but nothing official. Yet.

'Get up, Nance.'

She snatched a breath and nearly made it up onto her elbows when some survival instinct, the same thing that told her not to walk down certain alleyways or eat particular prawns, told her firmly to STOP. It said *Do Not Move*. There was a sudden seriousness. Something like real fear. Or relief. It was hard to call it.

She whispered into the vacuum of her apartment. *One hundred . . . ninety-nine . . . ninety-eight . . . ninety-seven . . .* She did this all the time now, the quiet counting-down. It distracted her heart and lungs from firing too fast when she pushed herself too hard around Chortley Park. It steadied her. *Ninety . . . eighty-nine . . . eighty-eight . . .* Another bead of sweat trickled down from her hairline towards the back of her neck. She let it go and sent a silent apology to the rug. She was waiting for something, she realised then. Something deep down in her body she might've been expecting for some time, something she wasn't able to control. *It's just a hiccup, kiddo*, Annabel would say, soothing Nancy's fever with a damp flannel or fixing a scuff with a plaster. Everything a hiccup. Short-lived. Survivable. But a flannel and plaster didn't cut it any more. And Annabel didn't come inside the apartment now, not if Nancy could help it.

Nancy swallowed and pushed Annabel out again, safely back to Mistleton, where she herself would be waking soon, ready to fight another day with busyness and routine and counting down from one hundred.

She looked at her phone, then tapped out a text message.

I ate my food too fast and now it's trying to kill me. Thought you'd find that amusing xx

She pressed send, waited for the three dots to appear from Mol's end. No dots came. Different time zone.

Their dad had raised the toast at Mol's leaving party. Molly was embarking on her next adventure, alone. And like everything else, she had organised it all her own way. Everyone had wished her bon voyage before their dad pressed play on John Denver's 'Leaving on a Jet Plane' and kissed their mum on the head while she'd pretended not to cry, pretended not to be a party pooper. And then Mol was gone.

Nancy gave the column of blue unanswered messages another second before shutting off the phone.

In the apartment next door, Dr Peter Buckley's day was getting off to a more predictable start. The well-versed sounds of him unlocking his own balcony doors floated in through Nancy's. Pete was an oncologist and a wealth of dismal information. Actually, that wasn't fair. He'd only ever shared the dismal information after Nancy had asked. Elevator small talk. She imagined him to be a good doctor to his patients, to the families who clung to his words searching for any snippet of hope, any tiny fingerhold. A kind man with an open face and perennial half-smile who Nancy now went out of her way to avoid being cornered with in the lifts. In the small pockets of private life he'd managed to ring-fence from his work, Pete was a creature of habit, fortunately. He liked an espresso on his balcony each morning, forty-five minutes Peloton, shower, work. Nancy waited for the routine sounds to give away his position now, the sliding-open of his door, the pulling of a chair from under its dining set, the clink of a saucer against tabletop. She set her phone down and realised her arms were trembling. She pulled the rug over her naked upper body. Her voice sounded pinched and pathetic when she finally called towards the drapes.

'Pete? It's Nancy . . . next door.'

Pete's bistro chair scraped urgently along his balcony. 'Nancy?'

Bad idea. This was the only thing she felt any certainty about. *Get up and stop being such a wimp then*, Molly would say. If she was here. But Molly didn't come to the apartment now either.

'I'm inside, Pete,' croaked Nancy. 'Sorry, I was just wondering . . .' The effort was suddenly obscene. So too the sweating, the tightness, everything. 'Any idea if indigestion can kill?'

Chapter 2

*M*inor. Nancy let it sit on her tongue, wondering how it might sound if she said it aloud. Whether her own voice would bend it differently in some way to the doctor's. An affable junior cardiologist with a calming face and prematurely greying hair had fought his way in through the cubicle curtain earlier. There'd been a steady stream of nurses and consultants before him, sweeping in to observe and document the information promised by the monitors stationed beside the bed. But unlike them and their quiet, efficient note-scribbling, the doctor with the greying temples had given up something Nancy could work with. *Minor*.

He'd come to talk about the angiogram they wanted her to have. They wanted to flood her with some sort of ink and then take X-rays of the parts she'd gathered still weren't making sense to them. He was in training, shadowing the brisker chap who'd insisted on the repeat ECG. He didn't have all the blood work back yet, didn't have any answers at all, but minor, he thought, if he were a betting man. A *minor* heart attack. You could hang a lot on one word, they did it all the time at Deep Dish. Clients loved to sit in preliminary briefings and give them one word to work with. Invariably words like *aspirational. Inimitable. Seductive.* One word on which to balance their whole year's campaign budget. Never, ever had *minor* walked into the boardroom. Minor was not going to impact her life. Minor wouldn't dent a work diary already heaving for the rest of September and beyond. No one blinked at *minor*, least of all Haima, which was integral to how the rest of today was going to pan out.

Nancy shifted herself carefully against the pillows, rubbed at her dry lip. No, Haima definitely didn't do *minor*. Deep Dish Creatives would never have grown legs without Haima pushing for *major* all the way. There had been write-ups. Great write-ups. Nancy had kept them all to show her dad the times he had chance to swing by, and she'd sent the odd one home to her mum through the post sometimes too, poor compensation for all the months that went by between visits, but Annabel understood. Deep Dish was a rising ad agency with young blood, twice featured in the top ten 'people to watch' as compiled by industry insiders, Nancy a dependable Robin to Haima's Batman, delivering on all the whizzes and bangs asked of them. Big brands cornering their markets – heavyweights in sports apparel and pet-care chains – names every household knew, these were the clients finally starting to come knocking on Deep Dish's doors for their next two and a half minutes of screen gold. And they all wanted the same thing: fresher, louder, punchier than the competition. *Major* impact. It still took Nancy by surprise that somehow she'd proved she could lead her own small but perfectly formed team. A finely honed and reliable cog in a greater, shinier machine, where you didn't have to be the most gregarious or colourful character in the room, your impact could be made in other ways, from the shadows.

She pressed herself into the hospital pillow, eyed the ward corridor, took a deliciously deep painless breath. Haima absolutely was not going to baulk at *minor*.

Despite reassuring herself about this since first handing over Haima's number to the nurse with the lovely lowlights, Nancy's stomach churned. Haima would come. Her arrival was imminent. They spent a lot of time together, at the office or Garfield's boot camps. But this was different. Haima was going to be here on the *other* side, in that part of life that was underneath and tucked out of view. She was going to get another look at the belly of the boat, the side that sat beneath the waterline while everything else took place somewhere overhead with better light and sound. Nancy sensed the danger ahead. Haima invading her private life. You couldn't share a thing and not utterly relinquish control of it. Sharing and loss were two wheels on the same bike, and if you didn't want to wobble off, best not to get on in the first place.

The lady across the ward lifted her plastic jug of iced water, shakily pouring it into a beaker. Nancy didn't have a beaker or a jug. The nurses had said to call for anything. There was a buzzer clipped to the bed here somewhere; she fumbled around for it, but there had been very set views on such things back home. People wasting NHS time, nurses running around fetching and carrying when they should be left to nurse, to dish out desperately needed pain relief or reset the drivers that would bleep incessantly for hours, keeping their patients awake until someone just had a sec to hang up another bag of chemical warfare and disarm the relentless alarms. Nurses were not waitresses.

Nancy took her thumb off the orange button with the nurse pictogram, worn by a thousand more deserving thumbs before her own. The sound of tap water sloshing away down a basin gurgled along the corridor. Then a snatching of paper towels from their dispenser. A pedal bin squeaking open, clattering shut. She fiddled with the plastic bracelet on her wrist. *Nancy Woods Hospital No: X05121986.* She pulled her gown sleeve over it.

The top of Haima's unmistakable glossy ebony head bounced past the windows to the bay. *Shit.* Nancy's pulse hitched. The monitors gave nothing away, continuing their reassuringly monotonous patterns. The squeak of Haima's pumps faded as she strode purposefully down the corridor towards the nurses' station. In an ideal world, they wouldn't have called her, but it wasn't an ideal world and they'd pressed for a number. *Is there a partner or parent we can call, Nancy?* And, *Is there someone who's going to start wondering where you've got to?* She had to give them something. She gave them Haima before they dug anyone else out. Like Pete from next door. In fairness, Pete had earned his excellent neighbour badge, clambering first onto his own balcony furniture before swinging a loafered foot onto Nancy's. Incredibly, he'd done this without breaking anything – bone, bistro set or even a sweat – while Nancy had lain there swimming in the stuff like a wet moth in a shower tray, thinking how much hotter it was having pulled the rug over her boobs and how irresponsible she'd been all summer long, sleeping with her sliding doors ajar so the city's sounds and any opportunistic deviants with good upper-body strength and grippy loafers could limber their way in if they so fancied. The paramedics had swapped the rug for a blanket, wheeling her out past the broken crystal they'd inadvertently trodden from the kitchen floor all through the place. Nancy had caught a parting look at her decimated birthday cake on the way past while the female paramedic with the cold hands had lamented, *Your poor cake! Isn't life rotten sometimes, my lovely?*

The corridor linoleum heralded Haima's squeaky approach. The woman in the bed opposite rolled onto her side as if taking cover. Nancy tried sitting more upright. The last of the cubicle curtain whooshed to one side. Haima's eyes widened. Nancy intercepted her.

'What, no fruit basket?' she rasped, betrayed already by her own voice. She hated her body all over again. Haima set her keys and bag down on the bed tray, marvelling at the machinery. 'Don't ask me what they're all for.'

Haima's perfectly manicured eyebrows hit the giddy heights of incredulity. 'They're keeping you bloody alive. What the *hell* have you been doing?'

It was a foregone conclusion, the drama. Haima would do what she was paid a lot of money at the agency to do on a daily basis and turn the mundane into pure theatre.

'They're not keeping me alive. They're just checking I'm OK. Which I am, by the way. Thanks for asking.'

Haima leant forward and kissed Nancy's forehead. 'Sorry, doll. How are you feeling?'

'Fan-bloody-tastico!' Exhaustion washed over her.

Haima's eyes were steadfast. Great brown buttons of scrutiny. 'Did you know? What was happening? Have you been ill? I said you looked run-down, you told me you weren't. You've been overdoing it, haven't you?'

'No?' Nancy half laughed, but daren't see it through in case. There was still some residual discomfort, a little bit, sitting between her shoulder blades like a bandit's blade, just letting her know it was there. 'It's not that big a deal. Apparently, lots of people—'

'You've had a fucking heart attack, Nancy.' Haima prodded the air violently, pointing specifically at Nancy's left boob. 'This is your *heart* we're talking about. It's a big fucking deal.'

'Shh!' Nancy winced at the curtains next to them. 'These people are ill, you have to behave.'

'*You're* ill!' Haima leant back for a look at the other ward-dwellers, frowned, trying to make sense of Nancy's new context. 'You've had a—'

'Suspected,' whispered Nancy. 'And *minor*. A suspected minor . . .' She couldn't say it. Old men had heart attacks. Chain-smoking, heavy-drinking, overweight old men. 'They're still looking at scans and things.' The ECGs had not been brilliant. The bloods might be better, the bloods might get her a pass, maybe there were so many allowances before a fail? Like a driving test. Or mortgage application.

Haima's voice was low, unbudging. 'They're treating it as a heart attack, they just told me. This is serious, Nance.'

'You're not about to have one, are you, Haima? Your neck's getting awfully red.'

'It's not funny. Why didn't you tell me something was going on?'

On this, Nancy could offer the truth. 'There's been nothing to tell.'

'Bullshit. You're always plugged in, listening to your stats at the gym, it's not like you don't know your body.'

Haima didn't realise, though, mostly the headphones had been a ruse. A buffer. Not everyone needed workout apps to push their body until it screamed for mercy, Nancy did that herself, willingly. She'd been slow. Now she was fast. She would *always* be fast now. The exertion pushed the other stuff out too, left less room for it. And music? It was a double-edged sword, wasn't it? Stoking white-hot memories. Taking you places you didn't always want to go back to. Places you couldn't always fight your way out of. She'd stopped listening to music when Molly had stopped returning her calls. But the headphones, they'd stayed. People didn't engage when you wore headphones.

'You'd think,' conceded Nancy. And she had thought she'd known her own body. How to push it, how to trick it. How much it could take. But this morning had been . . . a curveball.

'Well?' Haima was still waiting, wide-eyed.

'What?'

'Was there a warning?'

'No.' But Nancy was more educated on such things now. 'I didn't think so. There might've been a few flags, nothing obvious.' Until Dr Pete had stacked them all up nice and neatly for the paramedics' arrival.

'Like?' Haima pulled a brown paper bag from her Karl

Lagerfeld. Then a carton from the brown bag. Rice tumbled onto her lap.

'You've brought sushi in here?' Nancy's stomach rolled again, nausea, not nerves, this time.

Haima manoeuvred a temaki roll into her mouth. 'I have to eat, doll. No vaping on site. It's one or the other, you know that. Bite?' Nancy passed. Haima chomped on. 'Well? What did you miss? Talk to me.'

Eating had become a private ritual, over sinks and the like. It felt intimate watching someone else do it. Nancy looked away, at her hands on the sheet, pale and listless like bleached driftwood. 'Just some discomfort . . . not like in the movies.' Hardly surprising really. TV lied. 'And then last night . . . I thought there might be something wrong with the apartment, couldn't stop *sweating* and my head was banging. So, you know, I thought *carbon monoxide*, but . . . I paid enough for the intuitive air con not to be poisoned, right?'

Haima stopped chewing. 'Jesus.' For an atheist, Haima liked to reference Jesus quite a lot. God too. 'Thank God that weird guy next door saved you.'

The thought was excruciating. '*Saved* is a bit much. He called the ambulance. They whizzed me in here, hit me up with a few drugs and . . . straightened me out.'

'Now here we are,' said Haima flatly.

'Here we are.'

'All straightened out.'

'Yup.'

She needed to google what an angiogram might turn up. What exactly they were looking for. Haima chewed the last of her sushi slowly and wrapped the rest away. She liked the sustenance, but not enough to put in an extra half-hour at Garfield's boot camp. Nancy drummed her fingers against the bedsheets. Haima set her hand over them, speaking between swallows. 'The nurse thinks you'll probably be in for a while.'

'What? They haven't said that yet.'

'Of course you will, Nance. Even though you do look reasonably alive. They have to monitor you here first. Then you'll leave coronary care for the other ward. For hypochondriacs and shirkers.' She grinned.

Nancy smiled too. 'Did you go in this morning? Noah's using the weekend to get a head start on his outline concepts. I need to go over them with him, I should be at the office now.'

Haima dipped her chin to her chest. 'About work, Nance. The nurse, she said two weeks at least.'

'Two weeks! Absolutely not.'

'I agree,' blinked Haima. 'I agree.'

Nancy nodded. 'Way, *way* too long. We have the Christmas campaign in now and . . . my lifestyle is mostly excellent. In a few days—'

'No, Nance. Two weeks is too *soon*. You've just had a major life event. Another one. Don't be an idiot and play this one down too.'

Nancy accidentally flicked the oxygen monitor off the end of her finger. It slid off the bed onto the floor.

'Don't go blowing it up! I'm not a bloody project, Haima.' Her voice had climbed but she'd missed a trick. She should've said *fuck. I'm not a fucking project, Haima!*

Haima liked *bloody* but she preferred *fuck*. 'Look. They've already said I'm not overweight. Non-smoker. I just need to get my blood pressure down a little and . . .' And there was the small issue of her heart's rhythm that Dr Grey Temples had also mentioned. This erratic heartbeat she'd developed at some point since her last full medical for the company insurers. 'I'll take a long weekend. Concentrate on our ideas pitch next week. Their brand managers aren't going to reshuffle meetings because one of us let a few palpitations get out of hand.'

'I knew you'd do this, Nance.'

Nancy tucked her hair behind her ears, an affronted teenager. 'Do what?'

'Let's talk about it later. When's Mama Bear getting here anyway? Poor woman, I bet she's panic-stricken. And speaking of Annabel, why did you tell the hospital I'm your next of kin?'

Nancy hurdled the questions. 'Talk about what later?'

'You're not coming to the meeting.' Haima was smiling. Bad sign. Very bad.

'Why? Haima, this . . . *this* isn't even a *this*.' More smiling. 'OK. It's a *this*, but only a small one. It was a warning. Consider me warned.'

'And?'

'And . . . I'll go steadier. Ease off the exercise. Sleep more. Drink less. I guess.' They'd also said something about axing sixty-hour weeks, but Haima was on a need-to-know basis.

Haima shook her head, her face softened. 'I can't get my brain around it. How can a woman your age, your build, your lifestyle have a heart attack? How is that even possible?

21

Will you have another? Is it congenital? Hereditary? What do they think caused it?'

The same questions had been on loop in Nancy's brain since they'd wheeled her in. A nurse was coming back later to talk about family history. Nancy was younger than they liked for any cardiac event. There were tests they could do, checks for relatives who might also be susceptible. Minesweeping, sort of.

Nancy shrugged. Haima searched her face for an answer. 'Stress then. It has to be stress. Well, no wonder.' They sat in quiet contemplation awhile. Someone on the ward began snoring. Lucky them. 'Have you told them? About Molly?'

Nancy swallowed, could feel a distant echo of it behind her ribs. The churning, tickling sensation that wasn't funny, and behind that, the great gaping black hole. They didn't talk about the black hole; Haima was usually more careful.

'There's nothing to tell.' Mol had always fallen in love easily. It wasn't a stretch to think of her falling in love with another part of the world, living and loving there instead of here, where she belonged.

'You pile through everything we throw at you at work and keep going, and I did think . . . it must help?'

One hundred . . . ninety-nine . . . ninety-eight . . .

But Haima was relentless. 'We're friends, aren't we? Not just colleagues? I don't think I've ever seen you cry, Nance. Never smashed anything! But now this . . . I'm worried here. Tell me you understand that?'

Haima had forgotten the company Audi. Headlights smashed to hell, caved in on themselves like two vacant eye sockets. And she hadn't seen the mess back in the apartment, a billion fragments of cake stand, splintered to oblivion. Unfixable. Fucked.

Nancy gave a placatory smile. 'I understand. But honestly, boss. I'm good.'

'That's what you said last time. And I let you beat me down because you said you needed *normal*. But . . .' Haima glanced across the ward at the other, older patients, white-haired and snoozing in their bays like cribbed infants. 'You being here can't be any sort of *normal*, Nance. You tried to outrun it, didn't you? And now it's caught you up.'

Nancy laid her head back, shut her eyes, shut Haima out. One thing had nothing to do with the other. This was bad luck. Something she'd inherited off a great-grandparent somewhere.

'You took one week off, Nance. *One*. And you've been a hundred miles an hour ever since.'

It suffocated her thinking about being back there, in Mistleton. Visiting home before Molly's hiatus had been strained enough. Going back there afterwards had been impossible, watching Annabel not knowing whether to stand or sit, boiling kettles she wouldn't pour, making sandwiches she wouldn't eat. And all around them, everywhere they looked – the shoes by the door, magazines in the rack, shampoo bottles in the bathroom – Molly. Everywhere and nowhere.

'It's been . . . how long?'

Since Nancy had last spoken to her sister? 'Nearly two years,' she answered.

'I don't think you've stood still in all that time.'

It was a long time not to hear from someone. No texts.

No calls. People stopped returning messages for all sorts of reasons. Sometimes they were just too busy. Busy working, busy playing, busy finding themselves. And sometimes they went off on adventures travelling the world and simply didn't want to keep in touch with strait-laced big sisters who always knew better. Sometimes they needed space, and you just had to wait. And then one day, they turned up again and everything was reset. Until then, you had to avoid looking at all the things left behind waiting for them. Shoes and shampoo bottles and mothers who couldn't sit still. Let the days pass, taking you with them, into new weeks, then months. And sometimes years.

'I can't stand still, Haima.'

'I know.'

'I need to work.'

'I know. But I'd quite like you alive while you do.'

'I'll take the fortnight off.'

'Nope. You'll never be off the phone, pissing everyone off.'

'I'll rest.'

'You need to go home, Nance. Home home. To your mum.'

The suggestion was like a pebble to the head. 'I'm not ten years old, Haima. I haven't skinned my knees.'

'No, you're thirty-two and your heart's not working properly. And now you're going to do what's right for it, and take it back home to your mother, who maybe *does* know what it needs. And who knows? Maybe it will be good for her heart too. When was the last time you visited her?'

Nancy glanced down at herself, deposited in this bed by strangers. All control gone. She couldn't even drink a beaker of water without buzzing for it. The sensation was suddenly there, ominous and uninvited. She shut it down immediately. Crying was pointless. Possibly the most pointless thing of all. 'Annabel doesn't need *this*.'

Haima slipped her hand back over Nancy's. 'How do you know what she needs, doll? If you're never there?'

Chapter 3

The afternoon moved in like cold treacle. There was an infection on the ward. Something respiratory they didn't want Nancy picking up too, not when her chest had been so well behaved so far this morning. They'd offered her a side room. A familial history specialist was going to stop by later for a chat, talk about family members who might benefit from investigations. Having a side room would give them more privacy, the nurse said. To discuss causal links, risk factors and shared genetics. The invisible, irrevocable ties spanning space and time between generations. Binding parents and children. Siblings.

Nancy stared at the ceiling tiles, pondering who they might invite for screening. The nurse's brother had been alerted to his arrhythmia by a younger cousin who'd collapsed on the football field. One minute here, the next . . . gone. It had led to a pacemaker for the brother and a calling to cardiology for the nurse. *Hasn't slowed him down any. Do you have brothers?* she'd asked, pumping Nancy's arm for a pressure reading. Nancy had told her, just a sister, but Molly was travelling way across the other side of the globe. A gap year, sort of, that had bled into two almost. Such was the pull of warm cerulean coral reefs by day and overarching unfamiliar constellations by night. Molly had wanderlust. She'd given in to its call and was enjoying a spell totally off-grid. Who could blame her? Not the nurse, who'd smiled wistfully about taking a two-year holiday someday, constantly moving, beach to beach, time zone to time zone. Nancy had smiled too. When her sister did touch base, of course, Nancy would encourage her to get checked out before cardio catastrophe could hit Mol too. But there wasn't much point giving the hospital her details before then, she had explained, not her contact number or last known address, email . . . any of the usual channels Nancy still used to reach out to her, to ask after the weather, to ask for forgiveness, to never, ever receive anything back. Nancy didn't share that part, though. Or that two birthdays had passed since Molly last called home. That since she'd stopped calling, no one knew where she was, not even Annabel, who'd always shadowed Mol so devotedly she must now feel like a kite cut adrift from its hand. Groundless.

A familiar pattering fluttered beneath Nancy's ribs. She needed to get back to work, this was what weighted her, work was what she tied herself to, so she wouldn't drift away too. She needed busyness. Tasks. The nurse had left a pad to make a start on names. Persons of interest. It would do. Nancy scrawled a heading. *Usual Suspects*. Would the specialist want to talk about her maternal side? Paternal? Both? Where were the weak links? Where were the threats? Who had passed down this defect and where might it next pop up? And what now? What was she supposed to tell them? The listees? They weren't a close family, at least not close enough to drop a bomb in each other's laps with an apologetic *Sorry, but you might want to check your ticker too*. She went to write her mum's name, then stopped. Annabel was the last person in the universe she was about to drop genetic fault lines on. For Annabel, there could be nothing worse than this.

Richard Woods, wrote Nancy. *Father*. He was still young for a heart attack. Young enough to deserve a warning. She'd thought about calling him already, he'd be here, come from wherever he was, she knew that. A bustle of energy, light-footed about the bed, jangling his keys, going over the plan for Nancy's swift and linear recovery. Her father was no stranger to a quick jaunt about, a flit from here to there. He was well suited to his life along the marinas, the dampened gravity of the water, the constant promise of movement. Currently, that was where Richard Woods belonged, along the Great British coast, somewhere along the south for now. In another few years he'd be somewhere else. But never back inland, always safely away at the edges.

She could call. But it was a lot, to invite a person to your bedside vigil. Self-indulgent. And he had things to do, maintenance to complete on his sailboat. He'd found a stress fracture after a summer of cruising along the coast. His card had come in the post, accidentally signed *Richard* but amended to *Dad* followed by a playfully apologetic exclamation mark. Did Nancy mind if they rain-checked her birthday dinner, he'd asked, just for a while? This was his pattern, Richard Woods. His cycle that sometimes spun closer on its axis towards his previous life, his previous wife and two daughters, and sometimes further away. But he would come for her, for Nancy, if she called him. And he'd be able to help navigate all this with Annabel, if they had to tell Annabel at all.

Nancy was still thinking of Annabel when *Ginny* emerged scratchily from her pen. *Maternal grandmother*. Did she need to know about genetic testing? Or would she delight in telling Annabel? Ginny was always floating somewhere on Nancy's mum's periphery, a distant but constant threat of thunder and lightning, moving in and out of striking distance when the whim took her. Nancy's pen hovered over her grandmother's name, the innocuous roundness of the *G*, the benign double *N*s, softer letters belonging to softer beings, softer words, like *bunny*. It was more than Grandma Ginny deserved to be given ink, a line, thought time. She'd had years enough already, the constant futile appeasements, trying to say the right thing, be the right grandchild. Molly had never pandered to Ginny, Mol pandered to no one, but it had taken Nancy much, much longer to catch on and let the divide widen. One day, Molly said, Annabel would manage it too.

Nancy struck through Ginny's name. No. The likelihood of any coronary issues in her grandmother's medical background were slim given the distinct lack of anything heart-like beating in Ginny's chest. And she would only wield this information over Annabel, look for fault, as if anyone could spare their own children the rogue genes inside them. As if the power was ever Annabel's. Nancy could protect her mother from this at least.

A knock yanked her thoughts back into the room, to the

two figures already slipping inside. 'Hello, I'm Dr Clem, one of the senior cardiologists here. You've already met . . .'

The nurse who'd given Nancy the pad saved the doctor the task of remembering her name. 'Ally. Yes, we've met. Nancy was telling me about her sister's adventures in Bali. The incredible temples and puppet shows there, the Way . . . what did you say again?'

'*Wayang kulit*,' swallowed Nancy. She'd got carried away.

'Bet we'd all rather we were there right now.'

Nancy fiddled with her pen. 'I've made a start. My dad's quite healthy, fit for his age, but—'

Ally cut Nancy off too. Ally was not a nurse with time to waste.

'Actually, Nancy, Dr Clem has some interesting findings he'd like to discuss with you. He's not here to talk about familial screening, we don't think you'll benefit from that service now. So no need to interrupt your sister's sunbathing at least!'

The nurse smiled over, the doctor didn't. 'How's your Japanese?' he asked solemnly.

Nancy frowned. '*Konnichiwa*?'

The nurse smiled again, turning her ear towards an alarm on the corridor.

'*Takotsubo*,' said Dr Clem. 'It's the name given to a Japanese pot, a trap, for catching octopus. Shaped like so.' He brought his palms down to a slender neck, then rounded them outwards again as if shaping an invisible bulbous-bottomed vase. 'Takotsubo cardiomyopathy. So called when the left ventricle of the heart becomes enlarged and shaped similarly to . . . well, a Japanese octopus pot.' Nancy stared at him, waiting for something to make sense. 'The results of your angiogram have ruled out a heart attack, Miss Woods. But the echocardiogram has shown some enlargement, which would explain the symptoms you've been experiencing.'

Not indigestion then. Not even Japanese indigestion. Right. But not a heart attack either. *Tako* . . . She tried to form useful words instead. 'What does it mean?' What would it mean for Annabel and her heart?

'It means the heart muscle, your heart muscle, has been shocked in some way. Weakened. As a result—'

'Shocked?' said Nancy. 'As in, electrically?'

His smile was quick, short-lived. 'No, not electrically. Shocked as in . . . it met with something overwhelming it didn't much like. Extreme strain. Emotional strain. Brought about by significant stress usually, or in some instances even significant joy.'

'So winning the lottery, for instance,' the nurse offered brightly. 'Or, the other culprits, job loss, bereavement . . . divorce perhaps.'

'As a result of the apical ballooning,' continued Dr Clem, 'your heart isn't pumping blood as it should, which resulted in the episode you experienced before admission. Takotsubo presents much the same as acute coronary syndrome, or heart attack in layman's terms – palpitations, shortness of breath, chest pain. Even your ECGs were telling us that you'd suffered a myocardial infarction, but that's now ruled out. Have you been experiencing heightened stress lately, Nancy?'

'Or won last night's Euromillions rollover?' added the nurse jovially.

31

Nancy tried to laugh along, but nothing came. *Shit*. Vital organs and blood. He was serious.

'Can you treat it?'

Dr Clem rocked back on his heels. 'Yes, and the good news is that Takotsubo usually does resolve itself. But equally, it can recur if the underlying cause isn't addressed.' He glanced at the nurse before continuing. 'So we would benefit from getting to the bottom of things by understanding what might've triggered it. And might potentially re-trigger it in the future. What we don't want is for you to go on to develop chronic heart issues. Tell me, can you think what might've contributed to this episode? Are you under undue pressure at work, or at home?'

'No.'

'Because ultimately, we are looking at this from the angle that it's stress-related. So it's absolutely imperative that we work out how to reduce the strain on your heart so that it can have the best chance of recovery and avoid any more incidences of Takotsubo, or indeed, longer-term damage.'

Her throat was almost too dry to choke out the words. 'What sort of long-term damage?'

'Subclinical cardiac dysfunction. Persistent heart failure.' He shrugged as if it were a foregone conclusion that her heart was buggered, or that she should've seen it coming, perhaps. 'So we're going to keep you in for a few days, keep an eye on things. Start you on a course of medication to help ease the load on your heart, make sure the blood's moving around your body nice and steadily. And see where we go from there.'

'But where *do* we go from there? What happens when I leave hospital, when can I go back to work?'

He was looking at the nurse again. 'It's going to be crucial over the coming weeks that you take your foot off the pedal. We'll get you booked into our cardiology clinic for your ongoing appointments, follow-up echoes so we can monitor any further changes in the ventricle, and there'll be an opportunity to discuss additional psychological therapy sessions that might . . . help address any underlying issues that may have contributed to your condition.'

Nancy cocked a smile. He wasn't serious. 'Psychological therapy?'

'Talking has proven to be a very effective tool with this particular form of cardiomyopathy.' So, what, she was going to be able to talk herself out of it? To a bunch of strangers? Excellent. 'But in the meantime, so that we don't have any repeat incidences, it's all the boring, common-sense advice, I'm afraid. A heart-friendly diet, limiting alcohol intake, gentle exercise, and most importantly, the big one, avoiding any extreme physical or emotional strain.'

The nurse glanced at him, good cop/bad cop. 'Have you ever experienced anything like this before, Nancy?' she asked softly. 'An incidence of heightened stress perhaps, making you feel very unwell?'

A darkened room in a service-station Travelodge pushed its way out of the place Nancy had tucked it away for forgetting. A frantic check-in, a long night alone in a starchy bed, listening to the cars on the motorway rushing to or from homes suddenly, catastrophically, unlike hers. Homes still obliviously intact. Her body remembered that racing, panicked feeling from almost two years ago. It wasn't the same as this morning's, but a close cousin. No chest pains, just the tightness then. Everything a too-tight cord leaving not enough room for a full lungful of air. She'd thought it was a panic attack. That she wouldn't make it back to the city and couldn't turn back to Mistleton. That Barry Manilow on the radio could *not* be the last thing she heard before hyperventilating behind the wheel and careering off the road. That Annabel would never see her like that, breathless, out of control.

'No,' swallowed Nancy. 'Never.'

Chapter 4

'OK there, kiddo?' Annabel glanced over from the driver's seat. A smudge of foundation sat just beneath her nostril. Nancy had clocked it when she'd first climbed into the passenger seat of their old blue pickup, a truck that had survived every pothole life had thrown their way and seemed destined to outlive all else, potholes and people.

'You don't need to keep checking, Mum. Thanks, though.'

Annabel smiled and nodded over the steering wheel. Haima had a lot to answer for. She'd left them last night with an obscene fruit hamper of biblical proportions and platitudes to *Come back when you're ready, doll. Bright-eyed and bushy-tailed.* Instead of saying, *But I'm ready now . . .* Nancy had smiled along, imagining herself stuffing kumquats up Haima's nose.

Her heartbeat skipped at the lost opportunity to talk Haima round. Or perhaps it wanted to thump its way out of her chest and bounce itself straight to Deep Dish for a reckoning. A weak reflection challenged her from the passenger window.

No it doesn't. Women like Nancy didn't do confrontation. Not when you could let the thoughts rage inside your head instead, settling, compacting over time into sedimentary layers, hardening past the point of redress. She rolled down her window just enough to lose her reflection. Her thoughts shifted back to Annabel, coming all this way, and before that, putting on her foundation this morning. Did she pick out make-up for herself in Boots or at the supermarket now? Now that Mol wasn't there to drag her around the MAC counter on payday. They'd sprung a surprise shopping trip on Nancy once, an odd couple loitering in the Deep Dish lobby, Annabel holding onto her own elbows lest she get in anyone's way and Mol donning a pair of embellished flip-flops, great big silk sunflowers the same unnatural shade of yellow her hair had been at the time, each one poking above her sparkly polished big toes like a satellite dish.

'How's the travel sickness, Nance? Surviving my driving?'

The warm afternoon sun beat in on them. Nancy closed her eyes, let it warm her lids.

'It's gone now, thanks.'

She let out a long, silent breath towards her window. They'd survived nearly a whole afternoon together in her apartment yesterday, after the hospital had finally given her their marching orders. Nancy had wrangled one last night at home, to steadily pack essentials – clothes, toothbrush, phone chargers. Work laptop, had Haima not confiscated it. Three days on the ward had given Haima enough time to mastermind this SAS-style extraction from the city, everything organised, Annabel prepped. Annabel had been toing and froing for days, but not to the apartment. No time. Molly's dog didn't do well in kennels and Annabel wouldn't go against Mol's wishes, so kennel-phobic Fig had been stuck home alone in Mistleton with an absorbent pad on the kitchen floor while Annabel had been commuting to and from the hospital.

The silver lining to this gas-guzzling routine had been that until yesterday, Annabel hadn't set a toe inside Nancy's place. There were things in any thirty-something's home they wouldn't want their mother tidying around. Things Nancy didn't want to have to explain. But then Annabel had walked straight slap-bang into it, the sticky, sparkling devastation all over the kitchen floor. Nancy had watched her hesitate, then pick through shards of crystal cake stand and her own glazed pear and chocolate torte with quiet efficiency. Nancy had sat on the balcony, inwardly going insane trying to figure out how she'd fill weeks – *weeks* – back in Mistleton, while Annabel had buffed every surface to within an inch of its life, calling out offers of tea and triangles of toast as she polished. Now here they both were, a new day, with their small talk and sensible driving and not a single bolt of sunflower yellow to shake things up.

'Been a while since I last drove you along these roads, Nance.'

The breeze through Annabel's window sent wisps of her auburn waves whipping against her face. The auburn was greying now, just below the clips she'd fixed above each ear to keep all those curls pinned in place.

'Yeah, it's nice to be chauffeured.'

'It's nice to be chauffeuring.' Annabel gave her another quick smile from the driver's seat before setting eyes firmly back on the road. It was jarring, Nancy thought, that her mother was approaching sixty. It wasn't old old, not these days. People were living longer, so the statistics said. Grandma Ginny seemed dead set on bolstering that data at a healthy and unrelenting eighty-two.

Nancy breathed in a lungful of familiar air. The landscape rolled by like an old record. Mistleton must've seemed a forgettable town to anyone passing through. For an ex-native though, the forgetting wasn't coming as easy.

'Not far now,' Annabel finally chirped, hands braced on the steering wheel. Annabel drove the way she spoke, the way she'd always spoken – to teachers, other parents, bank cashiers, their dad's secretaries – carefully and quietly, with more caution than confidence, but always polite commitment.

'Home soon,' agreed Nancy.

She gave the cling-filmed bowl of fruit salad nestled in her lap another check for leaks and settled her head against the window. Annabel hummed near-silently beside her. This was something they had in common, the ease of settling into the spaces between conversations. The quiet refuge. Annabel liked to avoid crowds, but large gatherings of strangers beat road trips for two. You could be comfortably marooned in a crowd.

A shadow whooshed past Annabel's window. 'Blimey. Slow down.'

A people carrier with a *Baby on Board* window sticker sped ahead.

'Maybe it's an emergency,' said Nancy. And not just someone wanting to get home before the turn of the decade.

Annabel chewed her lip. 'I was just thinking the same thing.' She held the steering wheel tighter. 'I'm glad I won't be driving this road again for a while. Six weeks' paid leave, Nancy, isn't that something? Haima's been so wonderful.'

'Sure has.'

Annabel checked her mirrors again. 'Boxing Day. Must've been.'

'Hmm?'

'The last time you drove these roads. I was just trying to think. Time flies by so quickly now.'

Nancy counted the months since her last visit home. *Nine.* A lot changed in nine months: tiny humans were conceived, carried and born, concepts at work taken from the drawing board through test audiences and out into the viewing world in much the same way. Annabel could have a six-foot silver-haired hunk back home with his feet under the table. Nine months was long enough for all sorts of fundamental changes to be afoot back in Mistleton. Only they wouldn't be. Mistleton would be exactly the same, unchanged, set in time, like those villages they sometimes discovered entombed in volcanic ash. Nancy gave the silver-haired hunk theory another few seconds' thought. There was something likeable about this fantasy, far-fetched though it was, given that Annabel had been going it alone since she was thirty-five years old.

Thirty-five. Nancy's breath caught. Three years . . . that was all she was off hitting her mother's divorce age.

'There have been lots of changes since Christmas.'

Nancy looked over at her mother. Was Annabel about to surprise her? Say she'd switched the bedrooms around . . . thrown out some of the perfumes left behind on Mol's dresser? She'd said it herself, you couldn't keep even the nicest things for ever, they all spoiled eventually. Sometimes it was the loveliest things that went first.

'A boy racer took the roundabout near the memorial too quickly in his mother's smart car last week, completely squashing the WI's display. Betty Hollins is incandescent with rage, I heard.'

Nancy looked back to the horizon. 'I thought Mrs Hollins was only ever incandescent with sherry.'

Annabel chuckled over the wheel. 'Don't ever let anyone hear you say that, Nance. Betty's a pillar of the community.'

'And?'

'She swears she's teetotal.'

'Doesn't everyone?'

'Maybe.' Annabel shrugged.

In polite company, the recycling box had been an eye-opener. Pete had seen Annabel struggling by the lift. He'd taken it down for her, making a second journey for the last of Nancy's empty wine bottles. Bin collections were every fortnight. Six bottles, fourteen days. Could've been worse. And it *had* been her birthday week, so. *You've had friends over*, Annabel had beamed. Nancy hadn't corrected her.

Nancy let her window down the rest of the way and propped her elbow on the ledge. The air whipped in warm and earthy. It had rained here earlier this morning, dark grey patches clung rash-like to the kerbside. The view rolled by as familiar as an old song, the lyrics coming back one landmark at a time. At the outskirts of Mistleton, open views became punctuated by pin-stick trees jostling for solitude along hedgerows cutting and splicing a land long since beaten into submission by generation after generation of the same farming dynasties. Nancy relented, allowing the petrichor to fill her lungs, and the shifting scenery to call them home. Mistleton was a continual cycle of new growth, harvest and emptiness. Acres and acres of emptiness.

Annabel straightened her arms out against the steering wheel. 'Whittackers have had some super weather for the crops this summer. I'll bet it's been humid in the city?'

'Oh yeah,' smiled Nancy. 'Stifling.' Annabel's bedrooms would be as they'd been last Boxing Day. Mol's spoiling perfumes still waiting. For something to happen.

A bang crackled through the distance. Annabel ducked for a better view of the treeline ahead. Whittacker was always scaring something off his land, birds, children, whatever he wanted shooing off. Not everything had needed chasing away.

'If you get too hot at night, there's the desktop fan in your sister's room.'

'I'll be fine, really.'

Annabel bothered at the steering wheel. 'I wish the circumstances were different, Nance, but I am glad you'll be home for a while.'

'Me too.'

'And I'll try not to fuss. I know . . . you like your space.'

The sounds of Whittacker's gas guns backfilled the silence. Nancy couldn't remember ever telling her mum not to fuss. It was possible she'd given off some sort of don't-fuss signal somewhere along the line, emitted it like a pheromone she could neither detect nor control, Annabel respectfully obeying, but mostly she just hadn't wanted to get in the way. Annabel

41

had always had more than enough plates to spin. Even before the black hole had opened wide. One moon could not orbit two planets.

The first road sign for Mistleton whistled by. Fittingly, Annabel clipped the edge of one of its famed potholes.

'Blast it!' she said.

The fruit salad in Nancy's lap sloshed violently, syrup leaching its way down the outside of the bowl.

'Sorry, Nance. No wonder you'd always get tummy ache when we used to drive to Gran's. I'm not the best behind the wheel.'

'That wasn't travel sickness, Mum.'

Annabel's mouth formed that same one contour Nancy had never been able to decode.

'And you're her favourite too.' Her face softened again, as if warmed from within. 'Remember your sister locking herself in the car? Refusing to budge?'

A staring contest. Molly's eyes, too astute for a child's face, fixed on their grandmother in her doorway. *Witch*.

'I remember.'

Ginny with her thin lips and whispered advice. But some kids were harder to fool. Nancy blinked against the sun skimming Whittacker's hills. Ginny was in sheltered accommodation now, forty miles south, where the climate better suited her allergies and Uncle Jules could shake her down for his drip-fed inheritance.

'Have you heard from her lately? I spotted a birthday card, in your recycling, I mean. I wasn't prying, they were just all there and . . . Did you know you'd accidentally thrown a ten-pound note away?'

42

Nancy looked out of the window and spoke passively. 'Did I?'

'Well . . . that's nice of her anyway. Isn't it?'

'Uh-huh.'

Nancy thought of her mum trying her best to be helpful around the apartment, privy to things usually kept behind closed doors.

'About the cake, Mum . . .' She should've said something already. 'I'm sorry I said I'd taken it into work. I felt bad about knocking it over and . . .'

She'd taken down the crystal cake stand from where it lived authoritatively next to rows of lesser glassware. It had been nowhere near the edge of the counter, at no risk of being knocked off at all. Nancy had sat with her Merlot and beautifully elevated cake, imagining Annabel in her rubber gardening clogs nudging ripe Conference pears free from where they hung lightbulb-like from their bearings, sitting them in the sling of a tea towel so they didn't bruise. She'd pictured her mum's face in quiet concentration, deftly skinning the fruits for poaching in sugar before cooling and slicing each one into perfectly uniform slivers. Nancy had pictured all these things as she'd reached across the countertop, let her fingers trace the decorative relief of the crystal stand, the beaded edging and slender stem, all the way down to its fluted base. And then, she'd pushed. Until all that loveliness had disappeared over the edge of her perfect, clean-lined, aspirational kitchen island.

'It's all right, love,' Annabel soothed. 'I've done it myself, only takes a careless elbow. I'll make another, you can help.'

They made a right at Beckitt's Pottery Barn on the river

and drove on into town, the sun beginning to dip again now, splashing the road with long shadows and dying light. Annabel drove them through the high street to show Nancy all the changes since Portland's fishmongers had sold their car park to another housing developer, and what was left of the WI's Community in Bloom display. They passed Pickering's Bookshop, its window display untouched since Mr Pickering's wife died, some twenty years ago. The same CLOSED sign had hung in the door ever since. When they were kids, they'd make up stories about what had really happened to Mrs Pickering, because simply dying, as people so often did, wasn't story enough.

At the end of the high street, literally the end of the road, Bartram's Funeral Directors stood with a strange cordial finality. Cordial thanks to the oddly carnival-style window signage that Nancy had thought garish and inappropriate but Molly had felt stonkingly fabulous. Bartram's were the only funeral directors in Mistleton, Mol had argued. *They can stick bald monkeys with nipple tassels in their window if they want, business is guaranteed.* Mol's was a rebel heart, and Mistleton her town. Not Nancy's. Every brick, every bush they passed seemed to shout it. But did its inhabitants still pray for her, for Molly, as they'd promised? Or had they already moved on?

Nancy zipped up her jacket all the way to her neck and tucked her chin inside. Something was waking inside her, clambering from its hiding place. Tentacles unfurling. *Relax.* She reminded herself that the hospital had given her enough leaflets and pills to stave off any repeat hiccups. What they hadn't given her was a strategy to get through the weeks ahead. Weeks. Here. She'd been booked into a cardio rehab group, the only opportunity to get back to the city, but that was a fortnight away. As if a heart could be rehabilitated anyway.

Annabel drove them past Benedicto's and all the other family businesses still holding their steadfast positions along the high street, aligned like old organ bellows trying to keep air in the lungs of this fusty old town. Then, pavements gave way to hedgerows again and eventually she made the turn at the Jackdaw Inn. The Jack's canal-side beer garden shrank away in Nancy's wing mirror as the smooth ride of worn roads gave way to unevenly beaten lanes beneath them. Woodland crept alongside the hedgerows here. All those trees and not a single yellow ribbon to be seen anywhere. Nancy liked to fall asleep thinking of it some nights. A town ablaze with yellow, calling her sister safely home. That the pull of enough voices might be enough. That Molly could still be found.

'Whoo-ey,' huffed Annabel jovially as they pulled onto Mountford Road, overlooked by a gathering of watchful semi-detached cottages. 'Home sweet home.'

The houses along their road looked strangely unremarkable. Not new enough to be modern, not old enough to be traditional. Theirs was the fifth house in from the end of the lane, like its companions a pale, squat building with dark slate roof standing sentry over its own tiny kingdom. This was the home Annabel had made for them. Worn, but not worn out. And still neat as a pin.

They rolled to a stop. The street was lined with rowans and damson trees, clusters of red berries and purple fruits all the way down the road. There'd be some terrific shades of bird shit all over the cars this time of year. The prospect of having no car here suddenly crashed home. Nancy rolled up her window, shutting out the sounds of Molly's bamboo wind chimes hanging from the front porch, clunking their hollow welcome.

Annabel shut the driver's door, then shouted at the glass. 'Why don't you go stick the kettle on and I'll get your cases?'

Nancy climbed out. 'I'll get them. You need the loo.'

'Cripes, you're right, I do. Just hang on there a sec, OK? It's in your pamphlets, no heavy lifting.'

Nancy peered into the back of the truck. 'They have wheels.'

'Then I'll lift them down, and you can wheel one to the house,' heaved Annabel.

Complying was easier. Nancy took one of the cases through the gate and down to the front door while Annabel brought up the rear. *You Again?* asked the doormat. The script was faded now, imperceptible almost where once black lettering had worn back to bristles. A Secret Santa gift for Annabel, Molly's little challenge to their mum's perennial politeness, something to make Annabel's bottom clench every time someone knocked, but that would go out on the doorstep anyway because a gift was a gift.

Annabel jiggled for the loo, slid her key into the lock. Movement stirred through the stained-glass panes.

'Brace yourself, Nance. I did shut her in the kitchen, I knew she'd go ruddy wild.'

Fig wasn't shut in the kitchen any more. Annabel fought her way into the hall, the smell of logs and potpourri from the lounge same as always. Then another smell, the tang of Fig.

46

The barking was immediate. Annabel tried to take her by the collar. Nancy stood still, watching the struggle.

'You can let her go, Mum. She'll calm down.'

'Fig, settle down!'

'Careful she doesn't pull you over.'

'Already has!' yipped Annabel. 'More than once . . . Second thoughts, I'll just put her back in the kitchen while we get ourselves in.'

There was a clammy film on Nancy's palms. Fig didn't frighten her exactly. No more than any other feral creature with plenty of teeth and defiance in its eyes. Annabel closed the kitchen door on the dog, who got straight to trying to claw her way out again. Nancy found her bearings with a quick look around. Hallway dresser. Shoes stacked under the stairs. A couple of Annabel's scarves hanging from the dark wooden newel post. Everything in its place.

'Fig, just a minute, *please*,' sighed Annabel, reaching an old shortbread tin from the dresser drawer. Nancy watched her in the mirror, taking a whole handful of dog treats, bunching them in her palm. Annabel carried her age in her hands. Pronounced creases and the looseness of the ring she'd worn in place of her wedding band since Nancy had stumbled across her father's happy secret and skipped it straight back into this very hallway and her mum's lap like an Acme bomb.

Fig clawed feverishly at the kitchen door.

'I'll let her in, Mum. She's just excited. You go to the loo.'

Annabel thrust the treats into Nancy's hand. 'Try these.' A couple of the biscuits slipped between their fingers.

'Won't one do it?' They weren't heading into a performance at Crufts.

Annabel whipped upstairs. Nancy crossed the hallway tiles to the kitchen door. *Step on a crack and you'll fall and break your back.* Her feet were too big for superstition now. All that stuff was best left to the believers out there. Nancy believed in other things, like cells and synapses, even when they faltered.

She reached for the door and found her hand was still clammy. Molly's theory was that Fig knew Nancy didn't like her. No kidding. At the time, she'd just apprehended this animal behind the sofa happily chewing the corners off her iPhone. Fig was intuitive, apparently. Maybe even psychic. It hadn't been entirely clear if Mol was joking about her faith in the dog's abilities. But her love for her was beyond doubt. And yet, here Fig was too. Left behind.

Nancy eyed the doorknob. Turned it just so. Fig wasn't psychic. A psychic dog would know there was no chance of this door being opened more than a crack until she calmed down. And if she was even remotely intuitive, she'd have known to lie on Molly's bed for the weeks running up to her departure, instead of the weeks afterwards, when Mol had already gone.

A thud. Then, a feeling. Nancy staggered backwards. A familiar, unpleasant fuzziness bloomed outwards across her face. Fig didn't care and scrambled up Nancy's legs, thick, heavy claws digging into her thighs. She dropped the dog treats, heard them bounce over the tiles, Annabel galloping back downstairs. 'Down, Fig. Down! *Basket.*' Annabel threw another fistful of gravy bones towards the kitchen, Fig skittering after them. 'Good Lord, Nancy! Are you OK?'

She'd been hit in the nose with a tennis racquet once at

an office fundraiser. Same drill. Stinging face. Watery eyes. That feeling in the back of the throat similar to putting your head out of a car window and trying to breathe. 'Ruddy hell, Nancy. You're bleeding! And *you*, you bad girl!' This to the dog, Nancy assumed. She blinked the tears away, back whence they nearly came, while her mum fished a tissue from her sleeve and pinched it over Nancy's nose. The shock of Fig in the flesh, so much flesh and fur, was almost as jarring as the door slamming her in the face. Fig had always been a handful, an untrained, unresponsive, overindulged dog. A pungent one. But she'd never *looked* like a monster. Until now, the monstrosity had all been on the inside.

'Mum . . . what happened to Fig?'

'I'm sorry, I should've locked her away. I knew she'd misbehave.' Annabel's eyes glazed over. She tipped Nancy's head back gently and blinked up her nostrils.

'Mum, it's fine.'

Annabel stopped. For a second, Nancy thought she might cry, but she held Nancy's face in her hands, taking it all in, searching for injury or some other answer Nancy wasn't sure she knew the question to. Annabel closed her eyes and pressed a kiss to Nancy's forehead, then rested her cheek against the spot she'd just kissed, while the rest of the hallway and everything in it seemed to hold its breath. There had been some light hand-patting in the hospital, a squeezed arm in the apartment. Very little touching until now. There wasn't a lot of touching in Nancy's average day. Casual contact, perhaps, but . . . nothing intentional. Intimacy brought with it a feeling that reminded her of the time she'd slipped off the school climbing frame onto her side and thought, *Hey, that could've been worse*, and then lifted her arm to find it looked to have an extra elbow. Relief and resignation all in one icky hit.

A cold, wet nose nudged between them. Annabel broke her hold. 'I think she's found everything that was on the floor.'

'Saves hoovering at least,' replied Nancy, eyeing up her assailant. Fig used to look like a sturdy fox with a big, solid head; now she looked like the dog that had eaten that big, sturdy fox. Nancy wasn't the only heart-attack risk then. 'What happened to her? Is she sick?'

'No, not really.'

'But she's so . . .' Molly had run Fig over Whittacker's fields religiously, unless the sheep were out. Fig was a mix of red Labrador and something else. Something that needed running. Half Lab, half menace, and mostly capybara now.

Annabel fidgeted with the cases. 'I know. It's just, I can't walk her for long enough. She pulls so much, she's so strong. She tries to take me off on the same routes your sister . . .' Her voice trailed. 'The vet said go easy on the treats, but she won't always do what I ask without them. Or with them!'

Nancy looked down at the animal waiting for Molly's return too. Did dogs know? When to wait? When not to.

She rubbed at the pressure starting in her right temple. 'If she's too much for you, Mum, we can think of something.' Exercise equalled escape. It had been nine days since Nancy's last run. Fig had twice the legs, she must be borderline insane. 'Mistleton's big enough now that someone entrepreneurial must be offering dog-walking services? They'll just need to be built like The Rock and have a hard nose,' she tried gently. Fig let out a half-hearted howl for no particular reason. Belly wobbling with the effort.

'She's not too much for me, Nancy . . . she's Molly's.' Annabel's voice was low, quiet. Charged like the air about a storm.

They hadn't made it out of the hallway yet and Mol was already there, all around them. The hurricane that would never blow herself out. Fig deemed that a reasonable moment to fart into the silence.

Chapter 5

'My grandpa says only plonkers put missiles up their nose.'

Nancy startled. The voice had come from her right. She dropped the bag of frozen butter beans into her lap and flicked away the clod of tissue from her nostril in one smooth motion. A child's head, just above the fence line. Staring, through too-long hair.

'A plonker is another word for an idiot,' he continued.

Nancy blinked at the boy. She should've left the garden chair up by the house, insulated by neighbouring hedgerows, but the open view of the Whittacker's fields was uninterrupted this side of Annabel's fruit trees.

'Hello,' she said finally. Politely. He didn't return the smile, though. Nancy resumed her watch of Whittacker's fields, waiting for the boy to lose interest.

'Why's your dog so plump?'

Nancy let out a long breath, kept her eyes on the fields. The quiet of the garden was easier than the quiet of the house.

Until the boy. 'You shouldn't really look in other people's gardens.'

'You shouldn't really poke missiles up your nose. My grandpa says the NHS spends millions of pounds every year removing things from people's noses. Batteries, Lego, sweetcorn. You might be next.'

'Thanks for the warning.'

He scratched his ear and surveyed Annabel's plot. 'Is this your garden?'

'No.' The boy shook the hair from his eyes, watching her. She cleared her throat. 'It's my mum's.'

'Is your mum Mrs Woods?'

'Sure is.'

'Can I give your mum's dog one of my blueberries? He looks hungry.' Fig had ignored Annabel's pleas to stay in her basket and taken up a spot at Nancy's feet instead. She hauled herself onto four paws at the promise of *blueberry*. Maybe she *was* intuitive.

'He's a *she*. And not really, no.'

'Why? Blueberries are good for dogs. My grandpa grew it in his allotment. It's organic.'

Why? Because Fig was overweight enough? Because she didn't deserve an organic blueberry? Because she was a strange dog and shouldn't be fed over fences by even stranger children? 'Dogs can be unpredictable,' Nancy said with conviction. Fig bobbed her snout to the air like a great grizzly bear cub. A ginger one.

'She looks friendly to me. Here you go, girl.' Fig trotted over to the fence. 'Good girl, Pig. Does your mum call her Pig because she's quite chubby?'

Nancy raised an eyebrow in Fig's direction. 'It's Fig. Like the seedy things they make rolls from.'

'Figs are a fruit.'

'I know.'

He lolled his head. 'Then why didn't you say *Fig, like the fruit*? Instead of *the roll that's made from the fruit*? It takes longer.'

All the tiredness of the day rushed her then. Finally undone by one boy in need of a shorter fringe. And higher fence.

'What's your name?' he asked.

She hadn't much experience with children, or animals. Neither entered her world regularly and no experience today, with child or beast, was shaking the positives.

Reluctantly, she gave it up. 'Nancy. Shouldn't you be getting back to your mum now, it's nearly dinner time?'

She began thumbing through her phone. One crisis at Deep Dish was all she needed and *beam me up*. But . . . no. Nothing from the mothership.

Another blueberry sailed over the fence in Fig's direction. 'My mum's at work at the garage. She sells the petrol and overpriced convenience goods like pasties, key-ring torches and travel-sized toothpaste. Sometimes she has to stay late so I come and stay here for a sleepover. It's just me and Grandpa this weekend.'

'Oh.'

'Aren't you going to ask what my name is now?'

'I'm a stranger.'

'My grandpa says your mum is too shy to be friendly and talk to him very much. Are you too shy to be friendly too? Offspring copy their parents. It's called mimicking. My grandpa says I'm like my dad in some ways. And like his first pet ferret in other ways. And like myself in other ways.'

Unfriendly? She'd been friendly enough not to tell him to bugger off.

'Not wanting to talk to strange boys, or strange grandfathers, over the garden fence does not make you shy or unfriendly. Now run along. I know all the teachers at your school. They'll want to know you're being good.' Eugh, she sounded sixty years old.

'My teachers know I'm good. Some of them are nice, but I'd still rather stay here with Grandpa. He makes me go to school, though. Every day.'

Nancy scanned her emails in case Haima had made contact there instead.

'Good. School's good for you. It's not healthy to stay home all day. Work is good.'

'Why are you here then? Jobs take longer than school. Shouldn't you still be at work? Have you been sacked? People get sacked for being unfriendly.'

'I'm not unfriendly!'

'You are unfriendly. And my grandpa's not strange. He's my best friend. And he knows everything about growing vegetables and he can make brilliant things in his shed and . . .' The boy's face had changed.

Nancy held up her hands. 'I didn't say your grandpa was *strange*.'

'Yes you did. You said *strange boys* and *strange grandfathers*.'

'I didn't mean strange as in bad. I just meant . . . we don't know you. I should've said . . . *unknown*.' The grandfather would be out any second. Confrontational sort? Annabel hadn't mentioned him.

'Unknown?'

'Sure. Unknown.'

'Like the megamouth that marine biologists classified in 1976? That was unknown until one got tangled in a naval ship's anchor in Hawaii and in one single second it became the coolest and most interesting shark discovery in *ages*.'

Moisture leached across Nancy's lap. The butter beans were melting. 'I guess?'

'Nobody cared about the megamouth while it was unknown. Everyone cared about it a *lot* though once they knew its name.'

Nancy relented. 'What's *your* name?'

He straightened up, skinny shoulders just visible above the fence. 'Ray Ernest Robinson. Ernest like my grandpa.'

Nancy threw a lacklustre wave and held the beans against her nose again. 'Beyond pleased to meet you, Ray Robinson.'

'Are you staying here long?'

One of the problems with small towns like Mistleton was there was always someone peering over a fence somewhere, wanting to know more than they needed. But this, at least, was a question she did have the answer for. 'No, Ray. I'm not.'

Chapter 6

Mist clung to the mirror over the bathroom sink, betraying the lines of Annabel's last assault with her squeegee. Nancy could hear her downstairs, still pottering around the kitchen, straightening chairs, rinsing and re-rinsing the dishcloth. Always in motion. Nancy gave the mirror a quick wipe with her towel, wrapped herself inside it again and gave her nose a sideways check in the mirror. No asymmetry, no puffiness. Everything run-of-the-mill.

Fig's welcome had given them something to talk about over dinner at least, besides the second pruning Annabel thought next door's roses were in dire need of, particularly if the neighbour had his grandson staying over. Annabel couldn't believe how much he was letting the horse chestnut tree in his front garden run away from him either, but she wouldn't ever broach with him how it was affecting the light in the front room. If he did cut back his roses, the grandson would have more fence to hang over. But Annabel was more worried about thorns than privacy, she'd said, nudging a second course Nancy's way, a light lemon cheesecake with a side of fruit salad and a great dollop of squirty cream on top. Nancy didn't buy squirty cream. Hadn't even seen it for years. Hadn't wanted to eat any more, but when she'd slipped into the bath afterwards, the fullness of her stomach had moved through the rest of her body like a dull anaesthetic, weighting her to the water, tugging her down while the night had closed in outside.

The quiet had bothered her at first, lying there with water up to her nostrils and nothing to listen to. No sirens or beeped horns. But then the cry of a fox reached over the meadows behind the house, reassuring her, *You are not the only restless creature here.*

Nancy gave her nose its last test and sniffed her arm. Her skin smelt faintly of mandarin now. She pushed the bathroom window open a fraction, looked out into the darkness over the meadows, listened for the fox. Blackness blanketed the landscape. She couldn't even see the stream meandering down from Whittacker's hills, cutting its course through the grassland right behind their back garden, but it was there. It would call to them both when they were still young enough to hoick a leg over the back fence and go looking for adventure with the other kids across the meadows. To the sycamore tree. Their sycamore tree. Hours spent in its branches. But that had been before the Fear had kicked in. At some point, maybe while her arm had been healing after the climbing frame, she'd developed a sudden aversion to heights. To any danger. Molly had called her boring. But why do a thing twice, if it had already hurt you once?

58

Nancy exhaled deeply towards the mirror. She *was* boring. It was there in her reflection, unremarkable and undefined. Molly had got the adventurous streak, and the best of the genes, with Annabel's bright eyes and high cheekbones, while the dark hair and plain features staring back at Nancy now were from their father. She opened out her towel and looked at the rest of her reflection. A body just as unremarkable. A small bruise sat just inside her groin from the angiogram, another on her wrist. She turned her arm out for a better look, but the evidence was already waning. Other than these missable clues, there was nothing at all to show for the catastrophe that had erupted within her, back on her apartment floor. Her body looked the same as it always had, pale and unexceptional.

Cautiously, she set her hand under her left breast and felt for the beat, imagined the angry red muscle there, doing its best . . . or plotting its next revolt. *You're one of the lucky ones, Nancy*, the cardiographer had told her. *Looks like you got the warning tremors instead of the full-blown earthquake.* Yes, lucky. She'd been lucky before, too. *Lucky you broke your arm and not your neck*, her class teacher, Mrs Dutard, had marvelled when Nancy had taken in her X-ray for show and tell. And then Grandma Ginny, too. *Lucky we had your eyes and ears, Nancy, or your poor mother would still be bumbling around, clueless.*

Nancy wrapped herself back up and stepped out onto the landing past Annabel's bedroom door, Molly's door safely across the landing. She pushed into the spare room. This room, the largest of the bedrooms and overlooking the street out front, had been the only room big enough for both of them, the room they'd shared before Mol had moved her stray bras and chaos into the box room and, eventually, Nancy had moved out altogether. She left the light off and sat on the bed. The sheets smelt floral, freshly changed for her, the duvet thick and marshmallow-like. Moonlight and shadows pressed in through open curtains defining the edges of a simply furnished room, walls neatly papered, except for one. The memory was a good one, cemented in place, signposted. Wanting to be found. *It's your room, girls, and I want you to make it your own. So on this wall here, I want you to use these special pens and turn this blank canvas into a great big piece of Nancy and Molly artwork, OK, my darlings?*

The box of markers Annabel had handed them had been brand new from Buster's Art Emporium. Every colour, like the maypole ribbons they'd danced with.

Nancy towelled her hair and studied the wall Annabel had basically allowed her two children to deface with their own candy-coloured cave markings. Even in the gloom, the wording was still legible, faded but there. *Nancy and Molly's Room.* Bubble letters full and rounded like a child's expectations. *Draw nicely like Mum said, Molly.* She'd been so bossy, Molly still pliable enough then to listen and follow. They'd drawn a snowman they were going to build taller than their house, the pumpkin heads they wanted to leave on the driveways of Freddie Blumfield and Simon Marston for blowing spit bombs at them from Simon's mum's car on Jubilee Day. Silly doodles of all the things that had been so important.

Nancy took it all in. At the centre of their mural, thick

brown felt tip and acid-green leaves plotted the sycamore nestled at the bottom of Whittacker's valley. The real thing was so much bigger than they'd drawn it. A tree that in childhood had seemed so endless, they'd been certain it might eventually grow tall enough to reach heaven itself. But even children couldn't clutch at straws for ever. When it had become harder to convince themselves that heaven really did lie up there somewhere, they'd consoled themselves with another nonsense about the millions of helicopter seeds growing on the sycamore each autumn and how if you spun a good one, made your wish turn quickly enough, you were as good as made. Years later, bickering teenagers and too old for helicopter wishes, Annabel had made them flip for the bedroom and Nancy had struck lucky again. But there had been a caveat to keeping the biggest room. Mol and all her crap would go, but their wall art stayed, Annabel decreed. For ever.

Nancy pushed herself off the bed. Her body felt heavy and lethargic. Waterlogged. She folded her hair towel, set it over the radiator. At the window, she reached for the first curtain. On the street below, peeping through the swaying boughs of next door's runaway conker tree, the porch light over at Birdie Ludlow's house came on. Someone stepped out of Birdie's door. In the city, this wouldn't have caught Nancy's interest, not at eleven at night or in the morning. People didn't always know or care what was going on next door. It was wonderful. But this wasn't the city. Eleven here was like the middle of the night and everyone knew Mrs Ludlow only left her house when there had been an intervention of some kind and she needed looking after for a little while at the hospital.

Nancy watched. Birdie's hospital stays didn't happen that often now, she didn't think, but often enough when they were kids that the boys at Mistleton Comp would dare each other sometimes to get all the way up to the Ludlow house and bang Birdie's windows for a reaction. They called it *Lucky Dip*. But Birdie always bit, always gave them a prize. Depending on how things were going for her that day, whether the brandy had made things worse, she would either go on out and shout at them in her dressing gown, or appeal to their better nature. Sometimes she went back inside and played her piano all night long, sometimes she stayed out there. One time, after the hammering, Birdie had tried coaxing the teenagers into an impromptu music lesson, playing her accordion right there on the driveway as they sniggered from the kerb. Clarence had calmly walked out there in his high school uniform, coaxing his mum back inside with gentle words.

The figure standing at Birdie's door now wore a backpack slung over one shoulder, that much the porch light was giving away. Nancy studied him through the swaying boughs of next door's tree. He locked the front door and walked to the van at the end of Birdie's drive. Clarence was Birdie's only child. No siblings. No dad. A year older than Nancy, he'd been sitting one row behind her, cross-legged on the gymnasium floor, the day of the nativity when Mrs Ludlow, as they had to call her in school, had been standing in for the regular pianist. Birdie hit the high note in 'The Twelve Days of Christmas' and threw up all over the keys and the backs of her own fingers, right there in front of the whole school and parent audience. Nancy had never forgotten it. *Five gold rings* and bammo. Purple vomit like they'd never seen.

There was a time, a sacred time, when this had been the first thing she had thought whenever Clarence's name had resurfaced down the years. Clarence Ludlow – purple piano vomit. Like Tom and Jerry. Apples and pears. But not any more. Clarence had slipped free of his moorings, his place in Nancy's world had moved. And she couldn't move him back. When she thought of him now, she had to force him back there, concentrate on it, Clarence stepping around the other pupils in their shepherds' tea towels and narrators' dickie bows, trying to get over to where his mother, still singing and covered in vomit, was being ushered from the school hall. That was where Nancy tried to keep Clarence Ludlow now, eleven years old and firmly fixed in the gymnasium of Mistleton Primary, weaving around other shell-shocked children. She kept him there so that she didn't have to think of him standing on a country lane in the snow, a grown man with red cheeks and haunted eyes, hands upturned, softly asking if she wanted him to call somebody.

Despite the memory of that night, the cold and dark already pushing its way back, Nancy found herself shifting, adjusting, watching him for just a little longer from the window. She gently pressed her thumbnail against the part of her fingertip where the feeling had never fully returned after accidentally stabbing it with a fish hook in her youth. Still nothing.

The bedroom light suddenly blazed on around her. The backpacked figure glanced up at the window. Nancy snatched the curtain shut. 'Mum! What are you *doing*!'

'Hi,' came a throaty whisper from the bedroom door. 'What are we looking at?' Annabel's eyes followed Nancy's hand where it now sat over her thundering chest. She looked suddenly horrified. 'I didn't mean to make you jump. I'm *sorry*.'

Nancy breathed steadily. 'I didn't hear you coming.'

'I thought you were still in the bathroom. Is everything all right?' Outside on the street an engine rumbled to life. Annabel stepped around Nancy's cases to the window.

'I just thought I heard something. A fox.'

Nancy sat back on the bed, began picking through the first travel case while the pulse in her neck subsided. Clarence was in Mistleton.

Annabel peeked through the curtains then neatened them again. 'Probably. Betty Hollins caught me in the post office last week: Harold lost five chickens over the bank holiday weekend. *Not the goddam cockerel, though*, Betty said.' Annabel smiled at that. She straightened the towel Nancy had laid over the radiator. 'Betty says they need a dog. A big old hefty one like Fig. I didn't tell her Fig'd likely run the other way if we ever had a fox come over the back fence.' She watched Nancy briefly. 'You'll get used to countryside noises again. And Clarence would've scared anything off out there. He's been leaving about this time for the last few nights.'

Nancy gave a small nod, as if this made perfect sense. Perhaps his band was playing somewhere local. A late-night intimate venue in Clarence's home town.

Clarence's name hung in the air. Nancy tried to conjure the school nativity, Birdie knocking back the mulled wine, but her thoughts were already changing course, fast-forwarding through time, sliding towards the collar of Clarence's jacket pulled up high over his ears against the snowfall two winters ago, the rosiness in his cheeks from all the New Year's Eve alcohol he'd drunk and the long walk back from town through biting cold. Their paths had crossed on the furlong. So much colour and life in his face, she couldn't help but scream in it.

She pinched her eyes, tried to bury Clarence completely. Boy and man.

'Poor Clarence,' said Annabel, scanning for other things to straighten. 'Going out working this late. Who'd want it? Even with the warm nights.'

'Clarence is *working* in Mistleton?'

'Didn't I say?'

'But . . . why?' Clarence had been the one. Not *the one* as in unrealistic romance novels, but *the one* as in the one from town who'd made it, who'd turned out to be destined for bigger things, fame and fortune, or well on his way at least. Clarence had chased every teenager's dream and caught a hold of it, so Nancy had heard anyway. 'I thought he was taking the world by storm?' By world she meant a growing number of small but notable venues up and down the country. No one was talking Glastonbury or anything, but Clarence's band was doing OK.

'I'd have thought you know more than I do, Nance. Don't your generation all keep tabs on each other with your Facebook-ing and TikTok-ing?'

'Not really.' But word about Clarence's rising star had still filtered through.

'Birdie hasn't been home for nearly two months now, I think. I'm sure I told you?'

'Oh. Maybe you did . . . but not that Clarence was home, I don't think.'

'Of course he's home. She's his mum. You know how good he is with her.'

Nancy concentrated on the contents of her suitcase. Comfortable sweatpants, comfy knickers.

'Clarence came home months ago. Goodness knows Birdie's always needed looking after, and that boy's done a better job than anyone could, but there's only so much you can do sometimes. Sometimes even love . . .' Nancy's eyes sloped up towards her mum, 'just isn't enough.'

Nancy chewed at her cheek. 'That's too bad. For both of them.' And it was. Nancy liked Birdie Ludlow, despite the infamous nativity incident. Birdie was like the prettier curiosities Grandma Ginny had kept in the display cabinet of her old house, unusual and not what you'd find in your own home but familiar and intriguing and in some odd way comforting to revisit from time to time, to touch and feel the weight of. When Birdie was well, they would spot her sometimes sitting on the bank of Saxon's Hill watching them play. Molly had spent nearly a whole month barefoot one summer because Birdie liked to walk the river with her sandals in her hand and she reminded Molly of Annabel's *Ophelia* print hanging over the downstairs toilet, with her long hair and sodden dresses. Mol had her first tetanus shot that summer after standing on a hawthorn. Nancy stared down into her suitcase. She tried to picture Molly barefoot now, dragging her case along white sands somewhere the other side of the world, too busy having the time of her life to pick up her phone. To sort through her perfumes. To walk her own dog.

'It is too bad,' agreed Annabel. 'Clarence was doing so well too. It must be every boy's dream to have people buy tickets so they can listen to you play interesting music.'

'Interesting music?'

'You know what I mean. They're not mainstream, are they? It's not like a rock and roll band.'

'Alternative folk pop.' Nancy had seen a clip.

'Any good?'

'I guess. If you're into that melancholy acoustic sound for sitting on hay bales writing love letters with fountain pens.' That wasn't fair. Clarence's achievements weren't trivial. One of his solos had made her chest ache so much she'd shut her laptop and slid it under the bed. 'They are good, I mean. If you're into that genre.'

Annabel frowned with this new knowledge of a boy she used to make sandwiches for when his mother wasn't up to fixing dinner. 'I can't think he's playing much music now, not unless the harvesters have radios.'

'Harvesters? Clarence is working for the Whittackers?'

Annabel shrugged. 'Anyone who disappears off with a packed lunch this time of night is usually working the fields. Whittackers have been cutting for the silage, it's been so hot through the days, you can't blame them. You might hear them later. Betty Hollins said there have been complaints, mainly from the new estates. She says they're not country people and don't appreciate that it makes sense to do it at night while it's cool and the rest of us are sleeping. Speaking of which, I should let you get some rest.' She bent down and kissed Nancy's damp head. 'Need anything?'

'No. Thanks.'

Annabel nodded. 'You'll get used to being home. The sounds. Even the revolting ones Fig makes from time to time.'

Nancy saluted. 'Roger that. And yuck.'

Annabel dug around in her blouse pocket. She pulled a milky pinch of fluff from it, reshaped it, set it in Nancy's hand.

'What's this?'

'It's yours. I found it in your room, back in your apartment. Nearly lost it to the vacuum. Isn't it a beauty?'

Nancy regarded the feather. 'What's it for?'

Annabel smiled lopsidedly. 'For safe keeping. Just in case.'

Nancy was missing something, but Annabel was already on the move, tucking herself behind the bedroom door. 'Goodnight, love. See you in the morning.'

'Goodnight.'

It wasn't the sounds of Fig's flatulence that woke Nancy, or the heavy machinery in the distance, she didn't think, even though the gentle thrum was all she could hear now. She lay in the darkness, wondering if she'd slipped into a proper sleep at all. This was not new, this rippling of tension that woke her in the night. The adrenalin coursing so close to the surface of her body it felt as though, if she scratched herself, it might all flood out onto the sheets. She kicked them back to cool down, sounds of Whittacker's harvesters and foragers floating in from the fields, anchoring her. *Mistleton. Home. Stuffy August, not freezing December.* A skinny memory of a dream came back to her, beaches and sandals with sunflowers on them. A lightness stirred in her stomach, then the sinking again. Exhaustion weighted her. In a couple of hours, when it was true morning, a coffee might be enough to shake off the worst of the tiredness that had blighted her lately. It was as if sleeplessness had taken up residence in her bones at some indecipherable point and was refusing to move on. She closed her eyes and tried to get back to the sunflower sandals, feeling around for them in her mind, but she was already thinking too clearly, the wrong side of subconscious to get back there. *Fine*, awake then. She sat her body up in retaliation. The feather sat on the bedside table.

'We meet again,' she whispered.

Thankfully this time, her skin felt normal, no sweats, no tightening chest. But she was too hot. She left her bed, crossed the room and lifted the window latch. The air was different here, it carried the musk of newness, fresh starts, a day untouched by exhaust fumes or goods baked early for commuters. Nancy sucked it in. A van crawled onto Mountford Road, engine rumbling low. Its headlights were on but the night had already surrendered, the pale blues and yellows of morning invading inkier strongholds of sky. Clarence Ludlow pulled onto his mother's driveway. Nancy tilted her head to compensate for next door's chestnut tree and hung back in the shadows. The headlights died. Clarence stepped out of the van. She watched as he arched his back, rolled the tiredness from his shoulders, tucked the loose waves he'd inherited from his mother behind his ears on the walk up towards Birdie's porch.

They'd laughed at Clarence. Not so much when they were still too young to understand it better, but later, when their bodies had changed and voices deepened and they'd learnt how to identify and pick at another's weakness, a speech impediment or a parent different to their own. They'd all laughed at Loopy Ludlow's kid. Nancy watched as he let himself into his mother's empty house. *Clarence*. Back now, working the land in Mistleton. And he'd so nearly gone and shown them all.

Chapter 7

Morning doll flashed mid screen. Nancy perched on the end of the bed, moisturiser in one hand, phone in the other, a thrill in her stomach. She slung the moisturiser. Haima talked a good game, but she buckled easily. There'd been a glitch somewhere, a problem to unpick.

Morning doll, just checking in! Everything's fine here. Quiet. Send over any juicy gossip: it all goes on in the sticks, right? H xx

A battery warning flashed and Nancy's phone suddenly, inconveniently died. The phone followed the moisturiser. Gossip? With who? She gave a few seconds' thought to the friends who'd remained rooted here. Beth Whittacker had married and brought her husband back with her. Why wouldn't she? The Whittackers had more acres to enjoy here than anywhere. Emma Clayton was another with a family business, a hair salon, inherited from her aunt, a powdery woman with downy cheeks and her own unique perfume of perming solution and Marlboros. One good

71

whiff each time she leant forward to snip away at you. Nancy had liked having her hair done. Lathered or just teased and brushed. She'd loved the feeling of someone's hands moving purposefully over her scalp. Even her grandmother's bony fingers. *You've such beautiful long dark hair, Nancy. Not ratty like your sister's.* Ginny liked to plait hair. Twisting and tightening things together into forced orderliness.

Molly wouldn't let Ginny anywhere near her head, but Nancy had been duped, for years, the ceremony of being allowed to sit in the special chair, holding Ginny's special mirror, being made a fuss of. All the while Ginny quietly twittering over her shoulder, a steady stream of soft, subtle opinions that hadn't seemed relevant, the same way the rising temperature of water didn't seem relevant to a lobster until it realised it'd been boiled.

Nancy stood at the window and faced the new day waiting outside. Three birds sat on the phone wires stretching across the street. They bobbed their tails, rebalanced. One flitted away.

Downstairs, markedly less graceful than a bird, Fig raised an eyelid where she lay sprawled at the bottom stair.

'You look like a ginger walrus.' Fig flopped her tail against the floor tiles, but didn't move otherwise. 'What, no attack mode this morning?' Nancy stepped over the furred form.

Fig rose lethargically to her feet. She brushed past Nancy on their way into the kitchen with just enough contact to leave a clod of wispy dog hair on the leg of Nancy's blue lounge pants. Annabel straightened up from the Aga, pressing her hair back into place with her wrist.

'Morning, sweetheart. How did you sleep? Did we wake you? Pop back up for a lie-in if you'd like?'

It was nearly 8 a.m. The hours had dragged since Clarence had rolled down the street with the dawn. She could not spend any longer up there twiddling her fingers, looking at three blank walls, one abstract childhood mural and now a dead phone.

'Oh no. Today we are *carpe diem*-ing, thanks. Morning.'

'Seize one of these instead,' said Annabel, sliding a tray of fresh croissants from the oven, at least a dozen, each as perfect as the next. Croissants were usually reserved for birthday breakfasts and Christmas mornings, and board meetings.

'I fluffed my quantities, there's enough here to feed the street. Hopefully they'll freeze. Or I've yogurt? Or granola? I could fix you an egg? I thought maybe a full English might be too heavy just now, small meals they said, didn't they? Nice and light. Pastry is about as light as you can get, I thought. But if you did fancy a full English?' She smoothed her hair again, face flushed.

'You made these fresh? Wow.' Nancy slid her hands into her pockets, the smell of warm buttery pastry waking her stomach. 'They look delicious, Mum. We'll get through them.' Fig whimpered next to her leg. The leg still free of dog hair up until that moment.

'She's been waiting for you.'

'I don't know why. She hasn't flattened me yet.'

'Oh good. What are you looking for?'

'Did I leave my charger down here last night?'

'On the shelf there, by your candle holder.'

73

Annabel filled the kettle. Nancy crossed the kitchen and inspected the two lumps of crumbled clay held together by a smattering of fibres and sorry sequins.

'This thing? I think you're being generous with *candle holder*, Mum. If I move that, it'll disintegrate.'

'It's perfect. I love it. But yes, don't touch, just in case.'

Nancy teased the charger out from behind the crumbling clay and plugged in her phone. Gave it a minute. No more notifications appeared.

'Everything OK?'

She scratched her eyebrow and propped the phone on Annabel's cookbooks. 'Shall I just throw it away? You don't need to keep it, it's taking the whole corner of your shelf.'

'What is?'

'The crumbly lump.'

'It's a candlestick holder and you made it when you were six. It can take as much of that shelf as it needs. Tea or coffee?'

Nancy lifted a glass from the drainer and pulled on the fridge door. 'Coffee, please. I could just use some water first . . .' No integrated water filter. She looked into her glass.

'We still get our water from one of those silver things there,' chuckled Annabel.

Nancy held her finger up as if remembering such technology and headed for the cold tap.

Annabel nodded at the cupboard. 'Your tablets are in there.' She'd always kept the family medicines there. Calpol, plasters printed with cartoons. And later, anti-sickness pills and painkillers heavy-duty enough to kill a horse. 'You left them on the side with your charger, I didn't want to lose them.

Or Fig to eat them. Anything's possible. She ate a pair of my reading glasses last month. That was interesting later on.'

The medicine cupboard was neatly ordered, and still well stocked. Nancy's newly prescribed beta blockers were up front, flanked by collections of drugs not in her name. *Domperidone. Cyclizine. Molly A. Woods.* Mothers were hoarders, of one kind or another. There wasn't much a mother couldn't find room for. Surplus medicines, disintegrating candle holders. Unlikely keepsakes, but who was to say how a parent should keep her children in the home they were both so indisputably absent from?

Nancy grabbed the box with her name on and shut the cupboard. The hallway phone rang. Annabel was already off. Nancy popped a tablet from its blister pack. Her dad had been helping another *friend* move house when Annabel had emailed him. He was going to let Nancy get settled, then call to arrange a visit, when everyone knew where they were.

'Hello?' said Annabel in the hallway. Nancy spooned the coffee. A treat for Annabel, to have a drink made by somebody else. 'How are you?' Annabel went on. Nancy half smiled. Her dad pretended not to worry about things, but he did, that was just his way. Nancy waited to be summoned. 'She's OK. Yes, of course I will . . . Oh, now? She's just about to have breakfast . . .'

It wasn't her dad. Annabel had a quiet contemplation about her when it was him. Nancy stopped listening, finished the coffees. Gulped her water, sloshed the last down the sink. Annabel moved into the doorway. 'Nance? It's Gran.'

In the hallway, a pale reflection stared out from the dresser mirror. Nancy lifted up the receiver and faced the stairs instead. There was nothing in her washbag for dark circles. 'Hi, Gran. How are you?'

Ginny's tongue clucked disapprovingly against the back of her teeth. 'You never mind me, my darling, how *on earth* are you?' Nancy smiled for Ginny's benefit, tried pushing it into her voice, but Ginny didn't wait for her reply anyway. 'Good Lord, I've been worried *sick*. Just when I was starting to get over things, just when I thought life might be settling down again . . . *this* comes hurtling at us. Darling, your poor heart. It's too much to bear.'

Nancy stared vacantly at the newel post. 'Everything's fine, Gran, back on track now.'

'You've been working yourself too hard. You always were the hardest worker over there, always trying to get ahead. Trying to get *on*. Your mother never had the stomach for getting *on* much. Manning phones at the eye clinic was never going to lead to a career. How's she performing now? Encouraging you to go private, I hope? It's not like you're limited to the NHS. Let's face it, you've more resources at your disposal than your average young woman.'

Nancy imagined herself slamming down the receiver. Yanking the cord from the wall. Slinging it all into the street. 'The NHS have been excellent, Gran.' There was no reason to go private. And nothing average about the young woman Ginny might be comparing her to.

'I'm sure they have, darling! Anyway, you're a clever girl, you don't need an old stalwart like me telling you. You might want to mention at your next check-up though how tender-hearted your mother can be. She was a nervous child, forever flustering, these things are passed on, aren't they? That's probably something to do with it I'd say, wouldn't you? Now then, have you heard from your father? Or is he too busy off gallivanting somewhere? You'd have thought he'd put his back into it a bit now, *fatherhood*, it's not as if he's overly stretched. But then, leopards and spots, I suppose.'

An old nausea churned in the pit of Nancy's stomach. The inability to stop her grandmother in her tracks, ever. To feel anything but complicit. No. Leopards did not change their spots. And Nancy was no different.

The factory had scared her after shutdown, but she'd been braver back then. Brave and bored. When Ginny had sat in the car park all that time after collecting Nancy, instead of driving her home to Annabel and her sister, Nancy had felt the boredom seeping into her in the back seat. But her grandmother hadn't been bored. Ginny had been preoccupied. Uncharacteristically uncertain, drumming her fingers on the wheel as if trying to make up her mind. A mind that was usually, rigidly, preset to its course. And then, flustered, she'd sent Nancy in. The factory had felt like a ghost ship after the workers had gone home, she'd worried for her dad up there in the office alone. But the thrill of being allowed to run back to him, by herself, had thrashed the competition of sitting in the car park any longer. Ginny had lost something important. Nancy was tasked with retrieving it. She was to nip back into her dad's office, without deviation, without disturbing him, and find the glove Ginny was certain she'd left behind. *Like a game*, Ginny had said. *Quiet as a mouse.* Nancy had liked to play games, she used to be good at sliding her body into hiding places, limbering into unreachable branches, sparring with her own fear. But she'd learnt.

When she'd first crept out from behind the water cooler, her father had smiled strangely at her, clambering around his desk, pulling her into a strange cuddle. A sort of panicked bear-hug, hulking around her eight-year-old frame. *What are you doing here, honey? You shouldn't be in here, I thought you'd left with Grandma?* Nancy had liked his secretary. Liked her name, Hazel, like the gnarly trees curled along the park railings. She'd liked the shoes Hazel had worn under her desk, open-toed and high-arched and nothing like their mother's sandals. Her shoes had been off, of course, when Nancy had crept back in there, quiet as a mouse. Difficult to have your toes kissed with shoes on.

'Hello, Nancy, can you hear me?'

Nancy glanced down at the space beneath the stairs. At her mother's shoes, neatly paired. No leaves there now. 'Sorry. Yes. What did you say?'

'Has your father been in touch?'

Nancy turned her back to the kitchen. 'He's calling later.'

'I should think so too.'

The words sat on the back of Nancy's tongue, where they always sat, sedentary, slobbish, knowing their place. *SHUT UP, Ginny, you spiteful, interfering old troublemaker.* But she was the wrong granddaughter for that. 'Actually, Gran, I'm quite tired.'

'Of course you are. Put your mother back on and go and get yourself settled, go on.'

Annabel was leaning against the sink, hands braced

behind her, watching the wall opposite. Away with the fairies, or maybe she'd floated off to one of the many subtropical beaches Nancy liked to visit at night when sleep eluded her. Just in case, Nancy decided not to pull her away.

'Mum's just taken the dog out, Gran. I'll get her to call you.'

'I won't hold my breath. She's nearly always out when I ring, at this club or that. I hope she's squeezing at least one of us into her hectic social life. I'll call her.'

'Bye, Gran.' Nancy replaced the receiver, pressing it down hard into its cradle.

She walked back into the kitchen. Annabel snapped back from wherever she'd been.

'OK, love?'

'Yeah.'

Annabel spotted the two mugs of coffee as if they'd just appeared by magic. 'Your gran's called every day since I told her what happened.'

'That's nice.' Ginny hadn't made it to Molly's send-off. She'd read *rowdy going-away party* in Mol's plans somewhere, decided it wasn't for her.

'Gran says you've been hard to get hold of lately. Always out. That's good.'

Annabel blew over her cup. They took their coffee the same way. There weren't many common denominators between them, but unexpectedly here was another one.

'Just a few hobbies really. Nothing to write home about.' Annabel sipped her drink. She'd mentioned the clubs. Nancy couldn't remember them all.

'So what's the current tally of memberships?'

'Umm . . .' Annabel held her cup in front of her mouth.

'Flower-arranging?'

'Yes, yes, that's one.'

'And?'

Nancy should remember the clubs. They'd been a lifeline for them both. At first, she'd called home every day. The same conversations asking the same questions – *How are things today, Mum? Is there anything you need?* – and the same responses – *Keeping busy . . . No, nothing at all.* And then Annabel had tried out the calligraphy club, then something else at the community hall, and Nancy's calls home had become shorter, less frequent, until *Fine* and *Trying to stay busy* became *Not a blummin' minute to myself* and *Flat out, Nancy, flat out.* There had been a shift. Knowing Annabel wasn't staring into space every day had been a green light. So Nancy had put her foot down and floored it.

'Wasn't there a baking group?'

'You're thinking of the artisanal bread workshop.'

'Oh. I thought you'd mentioned cakes.'

Annabel nodded over her mug. 'That's the cake and conversation meet-up. At the old people's home.'

'You bake for the old people's home?'

'Oh, no. Everyone just takes a cake in and, you know, shares them out and has a chat with the residents. It's nice.'

'Oh, nice,' smiled Nancy.

'I mean, you can get a lot out of talking to older folks, can't you? They know a lot of interesting things and I suppose they know a lot about people too and . . . they make for nice company, don't they?'

'Sometimes.'

Nancy pushed back against her dubious experiences with Ginny. There had been heated bunkbed debates down the years, whether the glove was ever lost, why their grandmother had never been lopped off the family tree like a diseased bough, something you knew wouldn't take your weight when you needed it to.

'Your gran thinks I should spend less time out of the house and more time in it, sorting through things.'

Nancy swallowed too much coffee. It burnt bitterness down her throat. She tried shutting the conversation down. 'It's your house, Mum.'

'Our house, Nancy. It will always be *our* house.'

The croissants were going cold, temporarily forgotten.

'I was thinking,' Annabel said brightly, 'we could go to Beth's anniversary party? I saw her invitation in your recycling, with your birthday cards . . . but as you're in town now, I thought you might like to catch up with some of your friends? Beth was a good pal to you girls and . . .' Annabel gave a resigned laugh, 'not everyone makes it to ten years of marriage without catastrophe.'

Nancy picked a croissant from the tray, turned it over in her hands. The birthday cards had gone from envelope to bin in one smooth action. Beth's invitation had followed on nearly as fluidly after a second read. Beth was Nancy's school friend, but Mol had never quite managed to appal Beth the way she had Nancy's other friends. For a while, they'd been a solid threesome.

'And Beth came to Molly's party. She even knocked back those dreadful woo-woo shots your sister made us buy.'

When Molly had been gone a full year, and the reality of

her never calling home had begun to slowly set in, Beth had sent a card. *We'll see her again, Nancy. I know we will. I feel it in my bones. She is not gone. She can't be gone.*

'But I haven't spoken to Beth for a long time, Mum.'

'She'd love to see you. If you felt up to it? I wasn't planning on going, parties aren't really my scene, but if you could be tempted by an evening of live music in one of Whittacker's barns, we could . . . both go?' Annabel did not have a soft spot for socialising, but she had a soft spot for Beth.

Nancy filled her mouth with warm pastry, chewing slowly so she could pick her words. 'It'll be crowded. And I've already RSVPed. They'd have needed numbers for catering.' She gulped down a mouthful of croissant and excuses. Annabel nodded. The conversation wouldn't be pushed. Annabel never pushed. This would be their dance for the coming weeks. One of them treading tentatively forward, the other taking a careful step back. The Woods family cha-cha.

Annabel offered a plate for Nancy's croissant. Fig monitored the movement of hands.

Beth had written a note with the invitation. *Please come, I miss my homegirls. Mol would NEVER shirk a shindig xx*

Nancy had replied by text. *So unfair! Away with work. Ten years of bliss though, Wow! Xx*

Annabel dolloped honey next to Nancy's croissant. 'You're right. We'll stay home. Your grandmother's got a point. I should make a start sorting upstairs, and as you're here . . . you could look through it all first and—'

'No.' Nancy jerked towards the French doors with her plate and coffee cup. 'We'll go to Beth's. I'm just going to eat this outside, it's a nice morning, isn't it?'

Annabel looked dizzied. Nancy wanted to undo the harsh *no* but she already had a hand on the door handle, balancing her mug on her plate. Fig made her move. Nancy snatched the plate away, forgetting the coffee. Hot liquid sloshed down her leg, the cup landing at her feet, cracking open its wet mess.

'Fig, basket!' yelped Annabel.

'Sorry! I was trying to save the croissant.'

A flash of hopelessness passed over Annabel's face before she could hide it. She blotted a tea towel against Nancy's leg. 'Go on, you go outside before she has that off you.'

Nancy's heart had already seized its opportunity, lunging ahead. An urgent tempo in her chest propelling her away. It wasn't the dog. It was this place. All of it. The *weeks* ahead, trying to avoid conversations wrapped inside other conversations. But there was no forwards here, only backwards. Everything an echo from behind that couldn't be properly heard. She felt vicious, stalking between the rusted garden chairs, cutting beneath the pear tree, thumping her plate onto the fence post. She wanted to sling her breakfast to the birds, smash the plate against a tree, *God*, she wanted to smash something. To scrunch and tear and obliterate a thing with her own hands. *This place.*

She heard a voice then, clear as day. Deep in the pit of her.

For God's sake, Nance, it's a party. Not a funeral. Get on with it.

The pumping in her chest answered whatever call it had just heard. She felt the adrenalin coursing through her. Fight or flight. Run. Stay. *Act.* Do a thing. Say a thing. She was losing the plot. She would go mad here. She knew it. She looked out over the fields, listening, but nothing else came.

Her breathing slowed as calm seeped in. She held onto the fence, felt the quieting of her heart. She watched the grasses bending to the breeze awhile, then spoke clearly towards the meadows and the universe beyond, in case by magic or miracle Molly might somehow hear her voice too.

'You said you would wait for me, Mol.'

Chapter 8

The world map still clung to the back of Annabel's downstairs toilet door. Nancy perched on the loo, studying it, its edges curled now but each continent still stuck with her drawing pins. So many pins. Each one like a barbed lie.

She'd travelled with work but never stayed long enough to let a place seep into her. The trip had been her idea. Molly had shared her news and a bomb had gone off, things instantly dislodged and dispersed. In the chaos, something inside Nancy had scrambled to the surface and taken over. The world had seemed suddenly present, *a* present, to be grabbed by the scruff, gotten under their fingernails. She was going to take a sabbatical, Molly just had to say when she was ready and they'd get it booked. They were really going to do it, get out there, together. A rock-solid plan. They'd get to know each other again, properly, under the haze of foreign skies, backpacks strapped to their shoulders, make up for the years their lives had split off like two branches of a river.

The map glared down at her now, paper thin as her plans. Nancy couldn't take her eyes off it, the destinations she'd blindly punctured, or the stickers Molly had added, colourful dots stuck among Nancy's pins. Cambodia's ruins of Angkor, Bora Bora's crystalline lagoons, British Columbia's glacial rivers and ancient forests – these had been Nancy's, but Molly had other ideas for their dream trip. Some further afield, like the town in Ohio renowned for its giant doughnuts, and the place in South Dakota famed for mashed-potato wrestling, but the rest closer to home. *Best of British*, she'd said. Nancy let her eyes coast over the dots. A blue sticker on Gloucester, the neck-breaking cheese chase down Cooper's Hill. Another blue sticker on Shetland, an effigy-burning ceremony? *No.* A burning boat? The yellow sticker sat somewhere she couldn't make out but was for the Nutters' Dance, she remembered that much. *They clog-dance for twelve hours, Nance, over seven miles! Bet they don't do that in the Angkor temples.* Molly thought a Tour de UK would be fun. But Nancy hadn't wanted to watch clog dancers, she'd wanted to show Molly the sun setting over Santorini, hike along the Plitvice Lakes in winter. *Rolling cheese?* she'd winced.

A shadow arrived at the gap beneath the door. Then the end of a snout. Nancy shuffled her trousers back up and pulled the chain. Fig whimpered. For the long daily walks, or fusses, or other things her life was lacking now. 'She's not here, Fig,' Nancy said quietly to the door. 'She's on a catamaran somewhere in the Indian Ocean.'

Annabel was standing in the hallway, getting herself ready to leave, plum chiffon scarf draped loosely around her neck, a cautious sweep of mascara. Paper crafting club.

They were learning to quill. Nancy had politely passed on the opportunity.

'All set?' she asked.

Annabel held up a confused black form, something vaguely recognisable even in mangled arrangement. 'I found it in her bed. I didn't know she had it, love. I'm so sorry.'

'She's eaten my pump? I haven't brought any others!'

'I'll replace it. We could go into town now? I don't think Coco Chanel has come to Mistleton yet, though.'

Nancy closed her eyes and exhaled. Those pumps were so comfortable she could weep. Fig trotted through from the kitchen, wagged her tail and sat on her haunches.

'Say something, Nancy, I feel like you're about to hulk out or something.'

Fig on the other hand couldn't give two shits. An unreasonable swell of rage surged through Nancy from nowhere, collapsing in on itself just as suddenly, demanding she give up and sob for her lost shoe. Her shoe!

'It's only a shoe!' she yipped. 'I'll order something online, next-day delivery. No big deal.' Except she had sod-all else to wear in the meantime.

Annabel was tentative. 'There are pumps upstairs, Nance. It's up to you, I mean. You don't have to borrow them.'

Nancy shut it down. 'I'm a half-size bigger, so . . .'

Annabel hesitated. 'She went up a size on the wellies so she could wear her festival socks with them. Her Hunters are by the utility if you need them.'

'No. Thanks. I don't need to leave the house.'

Annabel nodded. She checked her wristwatch. 'I'll see you girls later then.' Fig whimpered, pressing herself between

Annabel and the front door. 'You know where the treats are.' Annabel gave Fig a quick ruffle of the head and gently pushed her back. 'Go on, be a good girl. I'll walk you when I get back, promise.' But Fig wasn't swallowing any of it. She began barking, frantic yaps. The routine must be driving them both insane. Annabel slipped through the front door, closing it behind her. Fig huffed and trotted to the dresser. She nudged her snout to the treat drawer. Nancy decided to test the psychic dog theory, staring hard at the animal, thinking very slowly and clearly, *You are fucking joking*. She sat down on the bottom stair just as the front door opened again. Annabel rubbed her forehead nervously.

'I'm just going to say it. Not because you don't want to borrow her shoes, or for any other reason, but . . . but because if I don't, I know I'm not doing my best for you, Nancy. So I'm just going to say it.' Shit. Nancy grabbed around for it, anything in her brain she could hold onto: a catamaran, a tiki bar, a passport full of stamps. Annabel looked at her hands, then around the hallway, anywhere but at Nancy.

'You don't have to talk about her if you don't want to. But if ever you do, I'd like that. And if you don't want to talk to me, that's OK too. But talk to someone. If it will help.' And then the door closed again and she was gone.

Fig scratched the door after her. Dogs did not grasp the concept of *goneness*. And it was just too vast for a mere mortal to explain. Nancy waited for the sound of Annabel's truck rolling away before unlatching the door and letting Fig into the front garden to go and see for herself. 'See? *Gone*.'

She felt tired. Heavy-limbed. She walked absently into the lounge around the oversized footstool her mum liked to rest her books and tea tray on, sitting herself on the beaten leather sofa Annabel affectionately bookended with velvet cushions the shades of wax crayons. Nancy felt a pang of guilt at this brave splash of colour. In her own quiet way, Annabel wanted to be heard.

Ginny's hideous pair of Staffordshire dog figurines peered down from the mantel as if there was an argument to be had. No one in the house had ever liked them. But Annabel was a good daughter and this was what good daughters did, they found a way to safe-keep the treasures of their parents, despite their ugliness. The ugliness of the treasure or the ugliness of the parent.

Nancy sank into the sofa, scooped up the remote and flicked something on the TV. She pulled her phone out, shoes . . . express delivery.

When she woke, the last thing she remembered was switching over from a nature documentary on some disturbing species of huge-headed stork that knowingly singled out one of its chicks to survive the other. She lifted her head from the sofa arm, brought the heel of her hand to the edge of her slackened mouth.

The clattering of the door knocker sharpened her. She tried to get her bearings on her way into the hall. Daytime TV was a revelation. Drug-like. Gentle and sedate. How did home-workers get anything done?

She opened the door. Gentle and sedate was now standing awkwardly on Annabel's *You Again?* doormat.

'My grandpa says there's something of yours at our house and can you please come get it quickly but also not to rush you.'

The light had changed over Mountford Road. Nancy stifled a yawn and blinked at Ray Robinson on the doorstep. His face was clear and serious despite the hair in his eyes and a reluctance to look anywhere but at the flaking paintwork on Annabel's door frame. Nancy leant against it, trying for direct eye contact. *You again?* she wanted to ask.

'Hello.'

'Hello,' he mirrored.

The bumbag was an unusual accessory to pair with sheriff's dress-up, but what did Nancy know about youth trends? The bumbag resurrection she did know something about at least. They called them *hip packs* now, Noah liked to wear his slung across his shoulder like a pageant sash when he biked into work. Nancy had seen a teenager hawking cocaine from one behind Garfield's gym.

'Nice hip pack, Ray. I used to have one.' They both did, two daughters, two bumbags. For the safe keeping of hair bobbles and contraband bubblegum while they'd rollerbladed for hours up and down Mountford Road until their ankles ached.

'Bumbag,' said Ray.

Nancy smiled. 'What do you keep in yours?' The spectrum of possibilities spanning bubblegum to cocaine was huge.

'It's quite important,' added Ray. 'My grandpa said you need to come around and get it as soon as you can, please. But not to make you rush.'

Nancy frowned. 'There's something of *mine* at your grandfather's house?'

Ray nodded at the paintwork. 'He said not to say what it is because you might be eating your dinner and then you might think you have to come around straight away and let your dinner go cold.'

'Right . . . Makes sense.'

Ray made no sense whatsoever. Something of hers? She cast her mind back pre-nap. Losing at *Countdown*, texting Haima, trawling Google for footwear. Sending Mol a text too, letting her know there'd be a bill in Fig's name heading her way. 'Right. Well, I have absolutely zero idea what your grandfather has around there.' She looked at her socks. 'Can it wait until my mum gets home?'

The light hung low in the sky behind Ray, early evening pressing in. Nancy cast her eyes down the street for any sign of Annabel's blue pickup. She'd expected her home by now. Perhaps paper-crafting had run way over. Should she be worried? What time was too late for your mother to be out until? Past teatime? Nightfall? Midnight? What were the rules?

'She shouldn't be too much longer,' said Nancy. She wished she'd just agreed, said she'd look through the shoes upstairs. Pretended.

Ray sighed as if he'd been sent to summon the village idiot. Nancy puffed out her cheeks. She *was* an idiot. She should've humoured Annabel.

'Are you eating your dinner?' asked Ray.

'Hmm? No.'

'Then you can come now, I think my grandpa would like you to come now.'

'Well . . .' She looked back over her shoulder at Annabel's shoes under the stairs. Her tiny feet. 'I don't actually have any footwear . . .'

Ray strolled straight into the hallway, bent over Annabel's shoe rack and pulled out a pair of size 4 rubber gardening clogs. Bright orange things, like two great baked beans. He offered one in each outstretched hand.

'You can use these ones. Come right now, please.' He thrust them into Nancy's hands.

'Ray! Hang on, these won't fit . . .' but Ray didn't hang on and was already on the move.

Nancy quickly ducked into the lounge, then into the kitchen, looking for an alternative. Molly's hot-pink wellies stood waiting by the utility door. She hesitated, then pulled them on and clumped back through the house out to the front.

Ray had left his front gate open for her. Nancy shuffled through it and down the path towards their porch. A window sticker welcomed her. *We don't like cold callers, but our dog sure does!* Excellent. She knocked on the door and rocked back on her heels. The wellies felt foreign and conspicuous. Walking in somebody else's shoes was nothing like borrowing a scarf or a pair of jeans. She wasn't about to be eaten barefoot at least. She knocked again, impatiently. Nothing. She could hear their dog though now, barking somewhere around the back.

'Ray!' Her own voice startled her.

'Round the back!' came a reply.

Nancy followed the path around the side of the house towards the agitated barks. Her heart started to patter. Another gate stood open for her. She crossed her fingers Ray's dog was old and gummy as she stepped around a huddle of plant pots into a reaching garden, packed with colour and movement. She stopped dead in her tracks. Ray's grandfather, a sturdy man with an impressive greying moustache, sat on the edge of his garden shed roof, two streaks of blue war paint on each cheek, a familiar red furry mass lying in wait for him on the lawn.

'Fig! What are you *doing*?'

'She's trying to chase back the resistance,' grimaced Ray's grandfather. Fig barked at him. He shifted anxiously. 'Ray wanted to play cowboys, you see. I think she thought I was hurting the lad.' He smiled sheepishly, blue face paint bending over his cheeks. 'I wasn't really scalping him, of course, but he was squealing and making a hullabaloo and . . .' He motioned to tip an imaginary cap. 'Ernest. Robinson. Very relieved to meet you, miss.'

There was a flush of embarrassment beneath the war paint. Ernest's voice sent Fig bouncing around the corner of the shed, fixing on him like a squirrel up a tree. Ray watched from inside, nose pressed against the glass of patio doors. 'Your red friend here seems to quite like our Ray,' added Ernest from his lookout. 'Ray's not so keen on the noise, though, so I told him he could go on inside the house after he'd fetched your mother.'

'Fig!' barked Nancy. 'Oh my gosh, I am so sorry, I don't know, I don't know what she's doing! She's not mine and I . . . I'm only visiting . . . Fig, you *bad* dog, how did you get around here?' At that, the barking ceased.

'Oh, don't be too cross with her,' said Ernest from the roof. 'She was actually rather impressive to watch, not what you'd expect to see flying towards you over a hedge, not that I'm particularly aerodynamic myself, but, as I said, I think she thought I might be hurting the lad.' He blushed again then, his skin turning a deep pink above the grey of his moustache. 'You must be thinking what feral neighbours your poor mother's stuck with.'

'Feral?' Nancy half laughed. 'You think you're the feral neighbours? After meeting my sister's dog?'

Sister sat on her tongue. A forgotten flavour. As soon as she tasted it, she wanted to take it back and swallow it down again. She wasn't usually complacent about Molly, not now. She didn't let her out into the open like an everyday comfort, she didn't keep her in the room the way Annabel did, anchored to the here and now with anecdotes and school macaroni pictures and wellies by the back door. Nancy kept her somewhere else, safely tucked away. Where nothing else could happen to her.

Ernest cleared his throat. 'Oh, yes . . . well I'm afraid I didn't meet your sister before . . . Well, what I mean to say is . . .' But people never were really sure what they meant to say. Nancy held her breath while Ernest gave it another run-up. 'I realised the day I moved in that you were, um, having a family gathering. Normally I'd have introduced myself, I wanted to say sorry, what with the removals men making all that commotion and you having so many guests to accommodate and, well, I'd have stopped them from knocking on your mother's door if I'd had the chance . . . told them to just park the blasted van further up the road, but . . .' Nancy hadn't heard Ernest's removals men knocking. She'd just heard Annabel asking three of Mol's workmates to move their cars from the front so the men in overalls could park nearer to Ernest's gate.

He cleared his throat again. 'I tried calling around, in the end. I left it a fortnight then . . . It was the curtains, you see. They were closed a lot. So I thought I'd leave it.'

Nancy felt her throat tighten. 'Did the move go well?' she asked brightly. A stupid question, given he'd been living here now for nearly two years. One year and seven months, to be exact.

'The move? Oh, yes! They say it's one of the most stressful ordeals a person can endure, don't they? Moving. But there are worse things, I know. And we can't all stay still for ever now, can we? We aren't trees.'

Fig had taken up position on Ernest's patio slabs, motionless but poised in that way working dogs, even overweight ones, lay ready to explode into action.

'I'll talk to my mum about a taller fence. Fig, let's go.' Nancy turned for the gate.

'Blimey, hold your horses, you're faster than our Ray with his holster.' Ernest turned his back, tackling the precarious business of manoeuvring himself earthwards. His foot felt around blindly for the tiered metal shelves he must've previously scrambled up.

'Mind the plant pots, Mr Robinson.' He was going to break his neck. Fig sniffed at Molly's wellies. Nancy grabbed her collar.

'Mr Robinson?' he chortled, clambering down. 'You make me sound like one of those giant old tortoises our Ray likes to read about. I'm only sixty-eight. That's barely older than an egg in giant tortoise terms.' He planted a foot on the metal racking. It wobbled under him. Nancy gritted her teeth. Any second now, gravity would undo him. 'Nobody calls me Mr Robinson other than my doctor, and only when she's coming at me with her gloves on.' He pretended to shudder. His foot made a successful landing and Nancy exhaled again. 'Call me Ernie, please. So . . . have you got a name, young lady?' He grappled for a handhold on the corrugated roof. 'Now then, how did I get around this bit?' His right foot reached lower and . . . *touchdown*. Hallelujah.

Ray called from the patio door. 'Her name is Nancy. She's been sacked from her work like Mum.'

Nancy gave a weak smile. 'I haven't been sacked from work.'

Ernest nodded and ran a finger over his moustache. 'Neither has his mother.' He gave his corduroy trousers a quick pat-down, then for Ray a double thumbs-up. 'He doesn't mean to offend. He's a good lad, our Ray. What you might call *outside the box*. But a smashing lad, no doubt about it.' Ray watched them watching him. 'I wish he'd make more friends, but he seems to put them off before they'll give him a proper chance. He's an only child. Has a different set of skills to most. All kids learn to make friends eventually though, don't they?'

Ray's forehead was pressed against the glass. 'I'm sure he will,' smiled Nancy.

Ernest let Fig sniff his wide knuckles. 'I knew she didn't really want to devour me.'

Fig got back to snouting Molly's wellies, trying to make sense of the wrong signals travelling from her nostrils to her brain. If she'd been a threat before, she wasn't a threat any more.

'Can dogs be fickle?'

'I believe they can!' rumbled Ernest.

'Come on then, Fig. Let's get you back before you do any more damage.'

Ernest jabbed a thumb towards the nearest greenhouse. 'Could I offer you some of my prize courgettes? By way of thanks for your excellent hostage negotiation work?' His moustache widened with his smile. Despite a decent effort with the face paints, he looked more Grizzly Adams than Sitting Bull.

'You definitely do not need to thank me for anything. I was the one who left her outside.'

'I insist! They're all ready to go. I picked a few things for a soup before my lord and master leaving nostril prints on my glass over there talked me into more exciting endeavours involving pistols and feathers.'

Ernest was already walking into his greenhouse. Pete from the apartment next door had offered Nancy some of his salad leaves earlier on in the summer. Just a few cuttings from his window-box lettuce, he'd said. She'd seen him over her balcony, tending to troughs of soil week after week. And then the greens and deep reds and purples had steadily appeared. Nancy had politely turned them down. She wasn't sure why. She liked lettuce.

Ernest emerged with an apple crate laden with the promised courgettes and other things destined for his soup. 'How about that little lot then, miss? Aren't they beauties? You've got bell peppers, some lovely cherry toms, celery, garlic and a beautiful summer squash. I've spotted your mother's herbs up by the house, so you'll be right for a good bunch of thyme if you wanted to rustle yourselves up a soup with *real* pizzazz.'

He held out the crate, a shock of colour and goodness.

Nancy let go of Fig then, certain she'd follow Molly's wellies, and took hold of the apple crate instead.

'These look incredible. Thank you, Ernie.'

He nodded his big, bushy face, blinking a smile. 'You're very welcome, Nancy.'

Chapter 9

'Don't think I don't know what you're doing. With the eyes.'

Fig nosed the dog lead again, hanging from its hook. She'd happily followed the wellies home straight into Annabel's kitchen, then realised her mistake. Nancy moved a vine of cherry tomatoes from sink to drainer and looked down at the boots. Moving her body had felt good. The fresh air had felt good. The footwear did not.

'Once around the block, that is *it*. Capisce?' She was supposed to wait for the rehabilitation clinic before any meaningful sort of exercise. 'And no funny business.'

She finished rinsing the bright yellow bell peppers and set the last of Ernie's produce out on Annabel's draining board where she'd see it. Then she dried her hands and grabbed the dog lead, clipping it to Fig's collar.

The last warmth of the afternoon was just leaving the air as Fig pulled them both down Mountford Road. The coolness felt good on Nancy's arms, and floating on that, the smell of warm pavements and farmers cutting fields, the sweet mossy scent of early evening. As she walked, she felt the first steady endorphins in weeks trickle through her. It had been a long time since she'd last *ambled*, moving on foot slowly enough that she could see the rowan berries fallen between cracks in the pavement. She hadn't walked this stretch of Mountford for so long. A familiar rush of well-being moved through her, the same as it always had along this stretch of pavement, on their rollerblades, skateboards, backies on each other's bikes. There were forty people in the Deep Dish offices. Mountain-bikers, climbers, outdoorsy types and fellow fitness devotees, but not a single one of them *walked* for pleasure, she didn't think. Walking was for the undriven. Or the lost. The self-assured moved quickly. Leave a place, get to the next. She'd forgotten this part, though, the part in between. The getting from A to B along familiar pavements. Until the pavement stopped.

The old farmer's track lay at Nancy's feet. A barrier. An invitation. Over the street, the bottom end of Mountford was lined with squat family homes. Conservative driveways and neat gardens all along the left there, but on this side, the view opened straight out into the rolling acres of Whittacker land, nothing but landscape and sky. Other farmers had sold, of course, like Beckitt and Lane. New-build estates swallowing up the land one bite at a time. But the Whittackers would never sell, Beth said. Nancy hoped they wouldn't. And it took her by surprise then that she still cared.

Fig yanked for the farmer's track, the *furlong*, the locals called it. Only Whittacker's tractors were supposed to use it. Only the old locals knew it could still make a handy cut-through for any drivers prepared to take their chances with the potholes and windfall, people who had to get their labouring partners to hospital, or other emergencies. Nancy looked to where the furlong shrank from view. There was a prize hidden just beyond this first field, where the land steadily dipped into the valley and cradled that one spot all the village kids had held sacred, their ultimate meeting point summer after summer after summer. She pictured the sycamore tree. A halo of helicopter seeds carpeting the ground beneath.

A murder of crows skittered skyward in the distance. Fig yanked towards them and the open fields Nancy's mind had already run ahead to. An ache started beneath her collarbone.

'No, Fig.' That way wasn't for them. Whittacker's sycamore belonged to someone else now, other girls and their sisters and school friends, still in their dungarees and alliances, spinning their helicopter wishes.

Fig gave up on the fields. Nancy let her pull them both towards the junction of Mountford and Lower Brook. She hadn't noticed walking through the hazel trees until they were already inside the park. It seemed claustrophobic now, smaller. Overgrown rhododendrons reaching around the lake like a protective parent. They'd added a log cabin-style refreshment hut over the bridge too. The same bridge Molly had thrown Freddie Blumfield's bike from into the slick of algae that still sat on the water there.

Fig followed the railings around the water. A jogger Nancy hadn't seen coming was suddenly there; she tried pulling Fig off the path but the runner had already done the work, running wide around them. The walk had made Nancy buzzy. She felt the ache Fig had put in her shoulder, the tightness that

101

hadn't left her collarbone yet since the mouth of the furlong. The doctor's words of caution swam back into mind. She'd sit then, just for a minute. She made the nearest bench, tied Fig to the arm, just in case. *One hundred . . . ninety-nine . . . ninety-eight . . .* She blew, slowly, steadily. Focused on the railing, the lake, the willow touching the water. Fig panted beside her, lips pink and flaccid.

'Nancy?'

The figure standing behind their bench stared down from beneath a baseball cap. Curls of dark hair escaped from its underside but the evening sun cast his face in shadow. Fig yanked at her lead so she could investigate his trainers, then got back to lying and panting, which was a sod because she looked half dead and, now that Nancy had just realised who was standing there, they should really get going. As in, *now*.

'I thought it was you.' His voice wrestled past the exertion.

Heat flushed up Nancy's neck. She felt around in her pocket for her earphones.

'Hello.'

She'd left them. She hadn't thought about *people*, hadn't meant to walk this far from the house.

'How are you doing?' The light caught the edges of his face, his cheeks were flushed again, a red warning like on the furlong, but not. Clarence was like a lighthouse that didn't know itself, pushing Nancy away with his helpful glow. *Come no closer, or break yourself on the jagged secrets I keep.*

Nancy looked back to the lake. 'Good, thanks. You?'

Her voice was even, her hands already working to unknot Fig from the bench.

'Hey, Fig,' said Clarence. Fig was up again, straining

against her lead for the fuss already promised. There was no undoing the lead until it slackened again. 'I'm good too. What are you doing back home?'

Nancy hesitated. The more she tried to think of a lie, the more the possibilities slipped from her, like bobbing for apples.

'Spending some time with Annabel?' he ventured. Nancy nodded. 'Mind if I sit?' Nancy looked at the empty end of the bench, breath stalling in her chest. 'I felt my hamstring going about half a mile back. If I get it in time, it might not give me hell tomorrow.'

In the absence of any other ideas, Nancy smiled.

'Sure.' Of course he could sit. She didn't own the bench. She shouldn't even be on it, or in the park, or out of the house. She should've stayed put, washing vegetables.

Clarence sat, pulled his knee to his chest, manipulating the back of his thigh.

Nancy's skin prickled. They were on the cusp of conversation and its infinitely perilous potholes, but there was nowhere to go and so she'd have to make small talk just to lead it around in one big circle so she could make her excuses and leave.

'You should ice that. The pressure sleeves are good too.'

Clarence drove his thumbs into his muscle, the contours of an athletic thigh bending to the will of his hands. 'You run, right?'

His familiarity sat like a hulking being between them on the bench. Nancy tapped the toes of Molly's wellies together.

'Not today.'

Clarence took off his cap, tucked the edges of sweat-dampened curls back over his ears. A deep pink imprint tracked across his forehead where the hat had sat. He looked like his ten-year-old self, a ghost from a past that didn't feel like it belonged equally to Nancy any more. They'd grown up together, they'd been the three kids from Mountford once. Clarence loved Molly. He'd always loved her, came calling for her, hung around the Jack waiting for her to finish her shifts and walk her home. Sometimes he'd turned up at the pub when Mol wasn't working, realising with crushing disappointment, no doubt, that the wrong sister was waitressing that night. Perhaps he'd never been brave enough to ask Mol out, or Mol had said no, but Clarence had loved her. Which was why Nancy could not share this bench with him.

She cleared her throat, but he beat her to it.

'Guess who was here yesterday, frisbeeing bread slices to the ducks?'

'What?'

'In the park, feeding the ducks. I'll give you a clue . . . predilection for cloche hats and *epic* storytelling.'

Nancy brightened. 'Mrs Dutard? Is she still alive?' Mrs Dutard had been credited with some of the high points at Mistleton Primary, and sobering Birdie in the staff room after Birdie's last ever piano solo on school premises.

'And kicking. I hadn't seen her in years and *years*, she hasn't changed. It was weird bumping into her, just standing there like she'd found her way through the mists of time and should still be . . . tucked away in our childhood or something.' Nancy smiled to herself. 'It's weird, isn't it? How easy it is to freeze people where they were when you last spoke to them?'

An old invisible weight tugged Nancy downwards.

Clarence's eyes narrowed briefly as if he'd felt it too. He looked away to the lake. Had Clarence frozen her to the furlong too? It was the last time they'd spoken, two New Year's Eves ago. A night that occupied such a deep, dark pocket of Nancy now, buried and immeasurable, she wondered if it might be growing like a disease inside her, eating away at the healthier parts around it. Clarence's universe had shifted that night too, but there was nothing else he could've done. *Should* have done. It couldn't be so profoundly visceral for him, to think of those few shared moments on the furlong. He couldn't know how many times the same night had chased Nancy back to consciousness through the trickery of her dreams, or how often he'd played spectator in them . . . standing there on the furlong watching her, the lights of her company Audi smashed into a state of blindness, snow falling around them both as the rest of world celebrated a new year with fireworks and drunken kisses.

Nancy swallowed back the nausea surging upwards through her, Clarence silent beside her. They hadn't spoken at Molly's leaving party the following month, Nancy had made sure of it. When Clarence had gone out into the biting January sun to help Ernest's removals men reshuffle the cars, he hadn't asked for the keys to the Audi, sticking out like a sore thumb out there with its headlights fixed and shiny again, as if nothing had ever happened. Nancy had stayed inside, offering party nibbles on paper trays shaped like pineapples. *Salmon blini, anyone? Beef Hula Hoop?* No one had been surprised by the catering options. When Clarence had been given the nod to fire up his mum's accordion in the lounge, and he'd managed an even chirpier rendition of 'Always Look on the Bright Side of Life' than even Eric Idle had mustered, Nancy had taken two piña coladas into the downstairs toilet and necked them both. *Don't be a party pooper*, Mol had made her promise. *It's MY day*. But promises were brittle things.

Clarence dropped his leg. He set his elbows on his knees and leant forward to look out over the lake. Nancy suddenly wished he would say something, anything, so they could complete their loop of chit-chat and go their own ways. But Clarence wasn't a bringer of noise and chatter, he was steady by nature, the gentle antidote to his mother's mayhem, the willing ear to Molly's husky laughter, the guiding beat to his bandmate's melodies. Clarence played from the back, and would wait for Nancy to lead.

She concentrated on the sunlight catching the gnats' wings over the water. Ethereal flecks of light rising and falling with no rhyme or reason. There were so many mistakes she wished she could go back and change, but she couldn't. This was it. This was all there was.

Clarence fussed Fig behind the ears, she pressed herself into his fingers. Nancy quietly cleared her throat, Clarence mistaking it as an invitation.

'Gasps a lot, doesn't she?' he asked.

'She's out of shape.' They would talk about the dog then. Nancy could chortle about her boshed nose anecdote, then get up and leave with a *Cheerio, Clarence.*

'She's not alone.' Clarence smiled boyishly. 'I'm trying to find my feet again, but the trails over Saxon's Hill are a killer on these glass ankles.'

'Mind the badger setts,' she added conversationally.

'Mrs Dutard said that. Said she'd tried telling Mol too, when she saw her exercising Fig here over the back hills, but Mol was never keen to stop and talk. Mrs Dutard reckons she was still sore at her for sending her home with blue hair that time.'

Nancy swallowed. The first pothole underfoot. She tiptoed around it. 'Well . . . her love for troll dolls peaked in Year 5 when she found Mrs Dutard's art cupboard key.'

Clarence smiled to himself. Nancy caught a flash of teeth before he closed his lips again, tendons tensing in his jaw.

'She asked me about you too, Nance. As if I'd see you around, or something.'

'Mrs Dutard did?'

'Sure. You realise she attributes your success to her English lessons, right?'

Her success? *Her* success? Clarence was the big music star, rising star anyway.

'She's probably giving us both too much credit.'

Fig licked the side of Clarence's calf. The salty reward of runner's sweat.

'She thought I needed reminding what a *bright little girl* you always were. Imaginative, she said. And how she likes to think all those *wonderful stories* you used to come up with in your creative writing book paved the way for the *inspired* work we all get to see now on our living room TVs.'

'She said that?' But it made Nancy uncomfortable, as if Clarence's default was to handle her with care, to remind her of the path she'd picked, that it was justified to have let it take her so far away from source. English had been her favourite, though. Sitting up front in class, trying to be the model child.

Who didn't cause trouble for her parents. No more ripples of any kind. It had been easy for Mrs Dutard.

'She was fun,' said Clarence. 'A good teacher. Kind to my mum. Knew how to get the best out of us too, I think. I used to think she was crazy. All the times she'd *implore* us in class: *Give me more, children! Give me adventure! Give me excitement! Give me deep perilous oceans and vast starry skies!* Remember that, Nance? She was so cool.'

Nancy kept her eyes on the lake. She remembered. *Give me something better than reality, Nancy*, Mrs Dutard would demand. *Give me fiction! Lie to me!* It was a role Nancy had perfected through work, playing with a narrative, giving the beholder what it was they wanted to behold. And always, *always* a happy ending.

'Yeah,' continued Clarence, 'I liked her, a lot. She said she was sorry not to get to say goodbye to Mol, said she had a small surgery or something. She'd heard about it, though . . . asked me how everything had gone.'

Nancy swallowed. She felt glandular. Clarence was looking at her, pale eyes staring back out of a face already affected by long hours working hot fields.

Her voice sounded tight, barbed. 'What did you tell her?'

The swell had started, growing, pulsing, rising. She didn't want to count it away, she wanted it to surge upwards, crash through her body, steal her breath, wash away again taking her completely and utterly with it.

Clarence looked caught out, the other side of a fatal move, a collapsed bridge. 'What should I have said?'

Nancy felt her breathing quicken, but Clarence wouldn't look away, wouldn't read the signs and give her half a chance.

'You should've given her what she wanted, Clarence.' As if this was obvious. 'You should've told her that Mol's party was standing room only. That it went exactly the way she wanted, with music, and cheese and pineapple on cocktail sticks, and troll-blue cocktails.'

The thudding had begun. A metronome deep in Nancy's chest. This was what the pills were supposed to stop, but medicine didn't work. It did *not* work. Her hand wanted to find its way up to her ribs, to rub there, calm the thing inside. She sat on it instead, fingers pressed to cold bench slats. *Breathe.*

'Are you OK?' Clarence had sloped off the bench without her noticing, and now he crouched in front of her, one hand still on Fig's scruff. 'Do you need to put your head between your legs?'

'What?'

'You look pale. Are you all right? Are you . . . asthmatic?'

Nancy pulled a deep, steady breath in through her nostrils. She refused to have another cardiac event here on this bench, with *Clarence*.

'Do you have a puffer or something?'

'A what?'

Clarence seemed magnified, point-blank range. She could see how his eyelashes clustered together, the creases where his lips parted. The morning's stubble, coming through again. Nancy closed her eyes and lifted her face to the sky, waiting for her lungs to steady.

'Sorry.' She kept her face to the clouds, willing a miracle to lift her up, up and away from Mistleton.

The seconds stretched silently between them. Clarence's

voice changed, low and serious. 'I didn't mean to upset you, Nancy. I've been on the road a lot with a bunch of heathens. I guess you forget how to speak to people . . . what to say . . . or not say.'

It wasn't Clarence's fault. *This place*. She couldn't breathe here, the air was too thin, like living at altitude.

'How's your mum? I see her from time to time, Nance.'

It was more than Nancy had managed. She bit her cheek, looked down at herself, waited for the answer to find her. How *was* her mum?

The gnats over the pond were still floating about their business, oblivious.

'Deep perilous oceans and vast starry skies?' she asked.

Clarence turned himself around and sat back on the bench beside her. He looked out over the water. 'If you like.'

'Then she's fine. My mum is great. She's unbelievably busy with endless fantastic hobbies and friends and is just waiting for Molly to take five minutes off having an absolute whale of a time and call home. She's still backpacking around the southern hemisphere, but you'd think she'd pick up a phone occasionally. We're all eager to hear what she's been up to all this time. Snorkelling, mountain-climbing, kayaking over waterfalls . . . who knows? There's just so much out there for her to see and do. Nineteen months is a long time not to hear from her, but then she's lucky to be globetrotting and not stuck here doing the old nine-to-five, right?'

Clarence absorbed this information and sat with it awhile. He picked something small off the floor, threw it over the railings into the lake while Nancy fought to keep the muscles around her mouth from moving.

'I'd like to think of her doing those things too, Nancy. With bright-blue hair, a bottle of JD in her rucksack and those massive sunglasses she loved on the end of her nose. I miss her. Everyone must miss her. No wonder . . .'

Nancy forced the words out. 'No wonder what?'

Clarence held another pebble in his hand, felt its weight. 'No wonder half the town went to her funeral.'

Chapter 10

A column of blue sat before Nancy, message after unanswered message, charting the path like digital breadcrumbs back through nearly two years. She'd sent the first text from the Travelodge. When there'd been no one else to tell. She remembered how it had calmed her, just long enough to get her through the night, check out, the rest of the journey back to the apartment. She wanted to send another, now, to feel the fleeting relief of a message just dispatched, the possibility of a reply, that skinny space between the two where her sister might still be reachable. But Clarence had moved all the parts. Sitting next to him at the park, she'd felt herself solidify, from the inside out. She hadn't cried, she would not cry. She would not. But the ache had bored all the way down inside her from her heart to the rubber soles of Molly's wellington boots and straight through them, down into the earth, a thousand leagues beneath her like the anchor of a ship.

'A lot of people wanted to say their goodbyes to her,

huh?' Clarence had offered. 'She was somethin' else, Nance. A firecracker. People are drawn to warmth. Burns, though, doesn't it? For those closest.'

Nancy had nodded. Hoping that it would be enough. But Clarence wasn't done.

'Did you manage to say yours?'

She'd looked a question at him.

'Your goodbyes?' he explained.

That was the point of funerals. To say goodbye. Farewell. A bon voyage party, as Mol had sold it to them. One last huzzah before getting on with it. You had to accept death. It was part of life, and all that bollocks. Accept and move on.

She'd given Clarence the straightest answer she could. 'Not yet.'

Nancy pinched her face between her hands and tried to root herself to her surroundings here in their family garden, and not back at the park with Clarence. She concentrated on the cooling of the evening air, the very slight breeze, the birdsong quieting around her. There was still no sound of Annabel's truck rumbling down the road. Nancy rocked gently on the garden chair beneath the pear tree, watching the dusk sink over the fields, a darkness separating this curve of the earth from the next.

Molly was not the other side of this darkness. She was not the other side of the earth. Not stirring from her sleep into the light of a new day as Nancy watched this one ebb slowly away. She was not walking barefoot along white sands, not sipping flamboyant cocktails at the end of a tiki bar, sea salt crusted to her hair. She had not met someone in a taverna, an airport lounge or on a museum bench. She had not fallen in love, got married in a village chapel with daisies over her ear, she had not been welcomed into a new family and forgotten her home. She had not had babies, not gifted them her green eyes and quick laughter, not held them through the night, let them suckle from a body that was strong and invincible, that would remain invincible for long enough that they would be kept warm . . . safe . . . loved fiercely until they could follow their mother out into the great blue world and have adventures and babies of their own. Molly was not missing. She would not turn up one day with a heart-stopping story about how she came to be gone for so long.

Molly could not be in any of those places, be living any of those lives, unless Nancy stayed away from this place. From the city, her possibilities were endless. Here, in Mistleton, there was only one life for Molly, and she'd already lived it.

Across the field, a pheasant made a leap from the tall grasses, disappearing again into the last patch of ground the light lay dying on. Annabel would surely be home soon. She would see the soup ready on the hob, the peeled remnants of Ernie's kindness in the compost caddy. She'd ask how Nancy's day had been as they sat eating together, and Nancy would explain, she had to go home, tomorrow, back to the city. A work emergency. Annabel wouldn't put up a fight.

Nancy's eyes followed the line of rushes giving away the route the water had chosen across the land, the changing light through Annabel's fruit trees, all that sky above them. You didn't get big sky in the big city, you got park benches without conversation. Clarence Ludlow had sat himself down and it was as if Molly had sat down too. Not the Molly who had danced on the bar at the Jack every New Year's Eve, but the Molly whose weight had dropped to a child's and who could barely rise from her seat.

Something panicky was sending its first warning shot. Nancy heard it, loud and clear. She tried to focus. A catamaran. A beach. Toes in the sand. Mol was travelling. She was travelling. Nancy pulled the phone from her pocket, messages, Molly . . . a blue cursor patiently flashing. But her thumb wouldn't play along.

What are you doin, Nance?

Nancy swallowed. She wasn't sure whose voice was in her head. Her own, perhaps. It didn't matter. What *was* she doing? Alone in their mother's garden at thirty-two, playing make-believe.

She closed her eyes, felt the balmy evening warmth on her face, and Molly there at the edges, waiting to be let in. The last time they'd sat down here together, just two sisters shooting the breeze, there had been no warm evening sun. No fruit hanging overhead. It had been a biting December afternoon. Icy paving stones and frozen grass crumpling under their feet before they made their way to the end of the garden to sit awhile, away from the house and Annabel inside.

Nancy stopped rocking in her chair. And let it all in.

'Right, one hot chocolate, squirty cream and a nip of Baileys. Hurry up and drink it, Mol. If Mum finds out I've laced it, she'll throttle me.'

'Thanks, Nance. Fig still can't be swayed then?'

They'd been sitting here together at the end of the

115

garden, sharing the view, for almost an hour. Sitting. Watching. Plumes of breath rising into the hazy winter air around them. The fields and birds and sky beyond the fence, everything as far as the eye could see in winter's chokehold. *She should be inside,* Annabel had fretted while Nancy had made the hot chocolates. *As if she'll listen. It's been bitter since Christmas and every day, out she goes, hoping for snow. As though if she shivers long enough . . . she'll be rewarded!*

Fig had been smart enough to stay by the fire while Nancy had brought the drinks outside and their mum had gone back to trawling the internet for breakthroughs: clinical trials, foreign technology, stem cells. Anything to hang their thinning hopes on.

'The Baileys won't interfere, will it, Mol? With any of your other jungle juice?'

Molly smiled at the view, blinking lethargically. 'Let's fucking hope so, Nance.'

'Mum asked if you need the other hat . . . the one with the furry bits? To keep your ears warm?'

Annabel hadn't asked, she'd told Nancy to take it out and staple it to Molly's bald head if necessary.

'No, I'm good.'

Molly tried to reposition herself, but the effort was more than she had going spare. Nancy took the hot-water bottle from under her arm and swapped it with the one already gone cold across the toes of Molly's wellies.

'No complaints,' she said firmly.

She moved her chair closer, trying to offer some tiny added

116

protection against the cold. A silly thing. Protecting Mol from the winter was easy, but it wasn't the threats outside her body that were coming for them.

The clouds had paled yellow where the sun was losing its battle to warm this little spot on the earth. Molly watched them with interest. Nancy watched Molly, trying to trace everything by heart for later, when it would be most relied upon: the shape of her nose, the difference in her eyes without eyelashes, the roundness the steroids had left in her cheeks. But the exhaustion in her sister's expression threatened to crack Nancy in two, right down the middle, so she looked away to the white frosted fields again.

'It's so beautiful here, Nance, isn't it?' Molly pulled off her glove and reached a pale hand over to Nancy's. 'We're so lucky. You know that?'

Nancy's voice was feeble. 'Yeah.'

'I'd really like to see the snow again.'

'Well maybe if you'd do as you're told for once and stay inside in the warm instead of coming out here freezing us both half to death, I might go find you a decent helicopter to spin for it,' said Nancy sternly. Better, much better.

Molly smiled, mischief in the usual places around her eyes, the corner of her mouth.

'Then I'll behave myself, Nance. I'll do as you say.'

'You will? Since when?'

'Now. You're my big sister. It's about time I started listening to you. So . . . I'll stay inside, safe and sound.' She squeezed Nancy's hand. 'I'll stay until you come and tell me I'm allowed to go.'

Nancy swallowed. Molly squeezed her hand again, hard. She believed in what she was offering, and Nancy believed it too.

'You promise? You'll wait, you'll be able to?'

'This is my party, Nance. Ever known me to leave one before I'm ready? I promise.'

'Well something smells delicious!'

Fig let out a startled bark. Nancy snapped from December back into August again. She swung her head over her shoulder. Annabel stood in the back doors, marvelling in the direction of the Aga. Fig bounded up the garden to her and greeted her.

'Good day?' Annabel called, ruffling Fig's fur.

Nancy pushed herself up from the chair. Fig charged back to the bottom of the garden then slowed, obediently shadowing Nancy's feet back up to the house, as if best behaviour might persuade her to stay. Nancy reluctantly followed her mum inside. In the kitchen, Annabel was setting the lid back on the soup.

'Hi, love.' She bustled around the kitchen table, pulling the plum-coloured scarf from her neck, setting down various items, car keys, drinks flask, packets of pocket tissues and other things that had sustained her through a full day of paper-crafting.

'You've been gone ages,' said Nancy.

Annabel blew the hair from her face. 'Basket-weaving is not as simple as it looks! Let me tell you!'

'I thought you were quilling?'

'Did I say that? I meant basket-weaving.' Nancy scanned the worktops for a newly woven basket. 'This smells home-made, Nance.' Annabel peered over the compost caddy. 'Have you been to the shop? I didn't think I had this much veg in?'

'Compliments of Ernie next door. After Fig nearly ate him.'

'Who? Mr Robinson? He sent soup?' Annabel planted her hands on the back of a chair. 'What about Fig?'

'Never mind. Yes, Mr Robinson, *Ernie*. He sent the soup . . . in its deconstructed state. I've just done the chopping and added the water. And some of your herbs.'

'Well it looks and smells amazing. Shall we get stuck in? I'm famished.'

Annabel already had the salt and pepper in hand. She dug around the cutlery drawer for spoons. All day she'd been gone. Now she was home again, a whirlwind of busyness, which would make leaving tomorrow easier.

Nancy opened her mouth, lined the words up ready. *Mum, I'm going back to my apartment.* Where she could breathe. Where Molly could be something other than just . . . gone.

'Are we going to bother with bread? I might have a few rolls in the freezer.'

'Sure,' answered Nancy. As she spoke, she spotted a small glass jar on the very top shelf, one up from the crumbling candle holder. A jar for the safe keeping of Annabel's white feathers. Nancy gave it a few seconds. They both had their rituals. And Nancy needed to get back to hers. 'Mum?' Annabel looked up, offering an expectant smile for her daughter. Nancy felt clammy and disjointed. A nervous tension between her shoulder blades, too much saliva in the back of her mouth. 'I just need to nip upstairs, freshen up.' Sit on the bed for a moment. Count back from one hundred.

119

'Hurry up then, love. I'm starving.'

The phone rang out in the hallway as Nancy made the top of the stairs.

'I'll get it!' hollered Annabel. 'Hello?' she said brightly. 'Oh, hello, Mum.'

Nancy sat on the end of her bed and dropped her head between her knees. Her carry-on suitcase peeked out from under the bed. She'd pack it after dinner, book a taxi for the morning. She listened out for her mum downstairs, but it had all gone quiet in the hallway. Nancy heard the lounge door click shut. Annabel had taken the phone in there like she used to do when their dad called from work saying he'd miss dinner.

The bedroom phone sat on the chest of drawers like an invitation. Molly had perfected the earwigging technique. Lift the receiver slowly enough at an angle and there was no click on the downstairs line to give the game away. There wasn't much that had gone on in this house that had slipped past Mol. *Dad's just one big excuse, Nance. I don't know why you still put so much faith in him, does he ever earn it? Really? He's just one big no-show. Mum should've told him to shove off years ago, but she never stands up for herself, to anyone. Always ready to accommodate folks who don't deserve it. Even now. And Gran . . . God, she's even worse. She walks all over Mum, you should hear her on the phone. She's a real bitch to her at times, when she thinks no one's listening. Always poking and picking. One day, though, Nance. I'm telling you. One day Mum is going to find her voice.*

Nancy pulled open the top drawer, fished out a fresh long-sleeved tee. She changed her top, waiting for her mum's

120

voice to rise through the bedroom floor, but Annabel wasn't saying much down there. Nancy put a finger on the receiver. Hesitated. Lifted it the way Molly had perfected. She held her breath, set a hand over the mouthpiece and gently pressed the other end to her ear.

'... was telling me about those vacuum bags you can use to store clothing and the like, although as I tried telling you earlier, Annabel, it's charity bags you need. There are plenty of people out there in need of extra clothes, although you'll have to be more cut-throat with some of the more outlandish items Molly used to walk around in. I can't see those being sold at the Red Cross, can you?'

'I'll order some. The vacuum bags. That's a good idea, Mum, thanks.'

'Was Nancy all right today? On her own all day?'

'I think so. She's made a lovely soup. We're about to eat.'

'If she's well enough to cook, she's well enough for visitors, surely?'

'Soon, Mum. I'll let you know when she's feeling up to it. You'll be the first to know.'

'I'm no fool, Annabel. Why did you come and visit me today, when you could have been home, making *soup*?'

'I just thought . . .' Annabel said she'd been paper-crafting . . . or basket-weaving. Nancy could hear her own breathing. She tensed her diaphragm and tried to respire quietly. Annabel took a breath too. 'Nancy could do with a break from me, that's all. And that it would be nice to come see you for the afternoon, of course. We had a nice lunch, didn't we?'

Ginny's voice was acidic. 'You thought you'd cut me off

at the pass. Go visit your mother so she doesn't come visit you, am I right? I hope you're looking after her properly, Annabel.'

A shot of adrenalin zipped straight through Nancy's heart.

'I am looking after her.'

'None of this *standing-by* business while she decides what treatment she does and doesn't want this time. Children always think they know better than their parents. Look at Molly, deciding what she did and didn't want. You're too soft, Annabel.'

This would be the last time Nancy ever eavesdropped.

'Nancy knows what she needs. She's smart, independent. She prefers when I don't . . .'

Annabel's point of their telephone triangle fell silent. Nancy swallowed. She'd chased her mum back at every turn. Every offer of a shopping trip around the city, or a show, or lunch . . . they'd all fizzled away to a promise of looking through a busy work diary, a less hectic month in the future. Vague points on the calendar Nancy never quite committed to. It was just easier to keep moving forward when you didn't have any fellow passengers. Easier if you didn't have to keep looking over to see how the journey was working out for anyone else.

'I don't want to suffocate her,' said Annabel quietly.

'I should think being in that house is suffocation enough, isn't it? How will it ever be anything but? Nancy's more like her father, isn't she? Not suited to small-town life. I understand why you feel compelled to make a shrine of the place, Annabel, and I don't mean to sound harsh but . . . not everyone wants to be reminded.'

Nancy's heart was thudding now, she wanted to put a hand over it to steady the thrum before they heard it, before Annabel felt its reverberations from the room below, but she couldn't move.

Ginny's poison trickled on. 'It was dreadful watching your father leave this world right before my very eyes, but at least he was in the hospital. At least I didn't have to picture it every time I went into his bedroom. Watching Molly give up like that, at *home*. She should've been in a hospice, or the hospital at least, like your father. I told you this at the time. I *tried* to guide you.'

Grandad James had actually wanted to die in his fireside chair or propped on his piano, Annabel said she'd heard him say this many times. Nancy wanted to hear Annabel say it now, to put Ginny right. And she wanted her mother to say that Molly hadn't *given up* at all, not in any way. She'd fought with every last scrap of courage until her broken body just couldn't do it any more.

She willed her mum to snap, to scream down the phone and defend her life, their life as it had been. But Annabel sounded weary.

'I don't regret honouring Molly's wishes so she could be here, Mum, in her own bed, with us. I only regret that Nancy wasn't there. But that's my fault, for not calling her sooner, and something I'm trying to learn to live with, every day.'

'Yes, and so must poor Nancy. She couldn't have done any more. We're lucky she wasn't killed, trying her best to get through those lanes in such *horrendous* conditions. She might've had a fair chance, getting to the hospital in time. Now she has to be reminded of it every time she visits home,

I shouldn't wonder. Do you really think her being there is going to prove to be the rest and relaxation that girl needs?'

Conversation bubbled in Ginny's background. Someone vying for her attention.

'What's that? Annabel, I shall have to go, it's bridge night downstairs in the lounge. Make sure you take care of my granddaughter, would you? It wouldn't be a terrible idea to skip one or two of your WI meetings and so forth, would it? While your daughter's at home?' Annabel didn't answer. 'I'll telephone again in the week.'

Ginny ended the call. Nancy held her breath and listened for the telltale click of Annabel replacing the receiver on its cradle, but it didn't come. Until Annabel put the phone down, Nancy couldn't either, or Annabel would know she'd been eavesdropping. Instead, they remained silently connected to each other this way, Nancy barely breathing, Annabel preoccupied and unaware. A one-way understanding until finally, Annabel took a sharp intake of breath, let it out again slowly, and hung up.

Chapter 11

Nancy rolled over in bed and blinked at the window, the dawn starting to beat back the darkness out there. Sleep had come easy, just as her mum had predicted. Annabel had chattered happily over last night's soup, no trace at all of her phone conversation with Ginny, or the day she hadn't really spent basket-weaving or paper-crafting or at any one of her many hobby clubs. Nothing had given her away and Nancy had watched carefully for it, monitoring her mother throughout dinner with forensic interest. Annabel hadn't mentioned Ginny, and Nancy hadn't spoken of Clarence, sticking to the safer topics of just how lovely the park had looked in the evening sun, how well Fig had walked, how good the fresh air had been.

We could walk together sometime? Annabel had offered brightly. *Any time you like . . . I could easily rejig my workshops, no problem at all. But if you'd rather walk alone, don't worry about me. There's a new concrete craft club I'm thinking of trying, I've seen some beautiful plant pots they'd made. Gives you a bit of peace and quiet if I'm not under your feet all day, doesn't it?*

Annabel's poker face was faultless. She'd cajoled a step-by-step of the soup recipe, but the more enthusiastic she'd become about roasted root vegetables, the more a feeling had grown inside Nancy that she couldn't shake.

The same feeling stirred along her skin now. She lay still, let her eyes focus. The sun tracked across its morning course. The bedroom was filling like a bath with soft morning light, the dawn pressing in first through the boughs of Ernest's conker tree and then Annabel's cotton curtains. Nancy listened to the clock downstairs in the lounge, tick-tocking as if the house had a tired heartbeat of its own.

Something creaked out on the landing. Nancy rolled her head on her pillow to face the door. Annabel was out there. The floorboards only creaked up this end of the landing, a handy warning for the days Annabel used to come and make sure they were asleep. Nancy listened, half expecting a knock on the bedroom door. They were both early risers, had she disturbed her mum? Was Annabel coming to check on her?

She waited for the gentle knock, but Annabel's footsteps moved away across the landing. The clock ticked on downstairs and then Annabel's bedroom door clicked shut.

Nancy pinched the bridge of her nose, which already felt like an old bruise. She yawned, threw back the duvet from her feet and planted them squarely on the carpet. Her phone said nearly 6 a.m. She traipsed lethargically onto the landing. Annabel's door was shut tight, but across the hall, Molly's was ajar. Molly's door had been closed last night when Nancy had gone to bed, closed the entire time she'd been home.

126

Nancy would like to close it now, but it jammed and needed a good loud slam, the result of years of teenage melodramas and fights over stolen belongings loosening hinges. She stood in her own bedroom doorway.

Something had drawn Annabel from her sleep, something in Molly's bedroom. Something Nancy wasn't sure a better daughter would want to be in the dark on. She stepped across the carpet, avoiding the creaking parts, let her fingers find Molly's doorknob. And heard her. *Mum will struggle, Nance. You'll have to keep an eye on her.*

Nancy took her hand away. Could see Molly saying the words, plumes of icy breath rising over them in the garden on a frosty December afternoon. She put her hand back on the doorknob, pushed on the door, just enough to see. Molly's slippers were still at the foot of her bed. Nancy concentrated higher up instead. The curtains were closed. Not all the time, she would've noticed from outside. Annabel must open and close them each day, even now. Nancy rubbed the sleep from her eyes, leant against the door frame. Bar the curtains, everything seemed undisturbed. Normal. Pillows plumped and neatly placed beneath the duvet, the duvet immaculately laid, untouched. A warm trickle of relief set in. Nancy felt her body soften. Annabel hadn't been sleeping in here. Of course she hadn't. It would be absolutely OK if that was what she wanted to do, but she'd have said. Of course she would have. People did those things in the early days, didn't they? Not years later. Time was a healer, and all that. The idiosyncrasies of grief were supposed to subside with time, everyone knew that. There was even a model by some academic, Cube-something? Kubler? Signposting all the stages a person would inevitably roller-coaster through – denial, depression, anger and other fun stuff – before their hellish white-knuckle ride came to its eventual end. Good old academics. Some claimed a year made the difference, others put the magical number at two years, four max in case a person worried the misery might actually last *for ever*. Everything was going to be fine in the end, so long as you weren't suffering from *complicated grief*, in which case you were royally stuffed because even the Kubler-Something model couldn't map you through years *and years* of utter shit before finally spitting you out somewhere in a slightly less bleak future.

Nancy pushed her hair back over her head and took in all of Molly's bedroom, all it kept safe. *Complicated grief*. What a load of old tosh. As if grief could ever be anything but complicated. Of course it was. Life was complicated. Death was complicated too. Everyone just had to muddle through, that was all there was. No models, no timescales, just muddling. And more muddling. Yes, Molly had made Nancy promise to look after their mum. And no, Nancy hadn't been home as much as she should have been, but Annabel was doing great. *Really* great. She had clubs, and now Nancy knew more about Ernie next door and what a nice man he was, and Annabel's life . . . ticked. Probably much better actually without Nancy here creating issues for her, drawing Ginny's attention like a pair of search lamps sweeping across a prison yard. But other than that, Annabel was muddling on brilliantly. Nothing to see here. No siree.

Nancy gave Molly's room a last look over, everything ready for Molly to walk straight back in at dawn and collapse on the bed, fall asleep with her Doc Martens still laced up her shins. But Nancy's brain wouldn't let her hold onto this picture, it traded for Molly in the garden again, pale, cocooned in blankets and woolly hat, chunky knit scarf over the line they'd stitched into her chest, a plastic umbilical for the poison that would fix her. Nancy tried to shake it. But Molly shook back. *Stick together, Nancy. Please.*

'We are,' whispered Nancy. But she tasted a lie.

To prove or disprove it either way, she pushed further into the bedroom. *Stick together?* Fine. She would make sure Annabel was behaving herself, no big deal. She knelt by the bed and slipped her hand beneath Molly's duvet. The warmth of Annabel's body lingered there like a memory between the sheets. Nancy felt her heart fold in on itself like a piece of origami. *See?* It was impossible to tell Molly's voice from her own, which one was berating her, which one was demanding to be heard. She left the bedroom, pulled the door to, slipped quietly back into her own room, her own space. She climbed into bed, pulled the duvet over her, thought of the suitcases beneath her, under the bed, waiting to be needed. Thought of their mum across the landing, sneaking back into bed after a night in Molly's, waiting to be needed too.

Chapter 12

The post office queue hadn't moved in eight minutes. Not an inch. Nancy slowly craned her head to see if the same elderly gentleman was still standing three people ahead at the Plexiglas being served by the same smiley lady with the too-long too-white fingernails. Yep. She was still trying to count out foreign currency using just the side of one taloned thumb. Nancy idled in the queue. A holiday abroad seemed like all sorts of wonderful: sunshine, ancient ruins, museums stacked with the mysteries of civilisation. She thought of turquoise water, lapping her sister's tanned ankles, but it didn't bring its usual release. A pang of guilt rooted in her gut. *Cheese rolling*. She'd scoffed at the idea. It had been too much of a stretch, spending hard-earned holiday time watching lunatics breaking collarbones in the downward pursuit of giant Babybels. Nancy tapped her thigh impatiently with her phone, thoughts ambling away from her. Even in her fantasies, she'd forced Molly to foreign shores, when Mol would've been happy as Larry sitting on a grassy bank cheering for crazy Englishmen.

The post office offered its distractions. She reread the posters for travel insurance. Ha. Who'd insure her now? Her and her defective heart. Who would she travel with anyway?

'Next!' came an authoritative voice. The queue shuffled forward. The tooth of a new blister bit into Nancy's heel. The comfort of Molly's wellies yesterday had been short-lived. Serendipitous and welcome evidence that Glastonbury would've been a nightmare, hobbling around with raw skin all weekend. So Haima had been wrong, actually. Poking fun at her for ditching a girlie weekender with Mol's mates for an extra weekend in the office.

As if conjured from the ether, Nancy's phone began vibrating in her hand, Haima's face on screen.

'Haima, *hey*.'

'Hi, doll. How's it going?'

'Good. Thanks. How's everything there?'

'Yeah, good, good. All under control. We've been getting some heat about the *watertightness of our outfit*, can you believe that? I guess that's what we can expect going forward, if we're going to play with the big boys.'

'The Christmas campaign? They think Deep Dish is an IP risk?'

'Nance, given what they're paying for the product, and five times that on promotional broadcasting once we've given them that product, *everyone* is a risk to their intellectual property. Legals are just wading through non-disclosures now, you'll have to sign one too. I'll email it over once they're in.'

'Yeah, sure. Send it over. Can I do anything?'

'You can rest. Come back to work fighting fit. How's that going?'

'The resting?' asked Nancy, scoping the queue again. 'Restful.'

'Cool. That was the other reason for my call, actually. You don't know what Keith did with the key to the plant room, do you?'

'No. Don't the cleaners have one?'

'It's Saturday, Nance. They don't come in on Saturdays.'

'No, you'll have to get it off them Monday.'

'Yeah, but I need it now.'

'Why do you need to get into the plant room today?' Maintenance didn't work Saturdays either.

'The barbecue and cool box are in there. The team have worked so many weekends lately, they deserve a thanks. We're having a few beers on the roof later. Before the summer's gone completely. I was thinking, if you're up to it, I'd send Rupert to come pick you up for a few hours? I know you'll be desperate to hear what's been going on, and if you promise to chill and take it all in without interfering too much, Rupe said he wouldn't mind running you home to Annabel again afterwards.'

'Rupert would come all this way?'

'It's an hour and a bit, Nance. You aren't the other side of the world over there! And of course he would, he's got a newborn at home, he's powerhousing through the days as it is. Anyway, we all would, you're a valued member of our tribe. We miss you. We want you to be well again.'

Nancy smiled into her phone. She kept her mouth pressed. Her voice was an arm that wanted to reach up, part her lips and throw gratitude out into the open, just for being reminded that in some place, some *other* place, she was not useless.

132

'*I* wouldn't drive you all the way home again, though, and miss out on the drinks. Sorry, doll, but I need to unwind too. It's been a fucker of a week.'

'Thanks, Haima. And thank Rupert too, I am really *really* tempted but . . .' She gave Mistleton a chance. Looked around at her surroundings, a world away from the Deep Dish rooftop. She scanned the shelves lining the walls. Safety pins. Playing cards. Fray Bentos pies. Elastoplasts. The mind boggled. Actually, she wanted some plasters for her heel. She also wanted to go to the rooftop barbecue. And she wanted to get back to the house and check on Annabel. Check she wasn't in Molly's bed. '... I can't. I have plans.'

'Ooh, plans doing what?'

The queue moved again. The clerk with the long nails was persevering, this time navigating her way around a book of stamps. How did women with such huge nail extensions get anything done? How did they prepare vegetables, or put an earphone in their ear? How did they tickle their children?

'Nothing much. We need to take Fig somewhere off lead. The exercise might kill her, though, if you believe my mum. Which I'm not sure I do.'

She would stay just a bit longer, and while she was here, she would be useful, genuinely useful, and ease things for Annabel where she could. Even if it was only to get Fig a little exercise.

'What do you mean?'

Nancy scratched her eyebrow and looked down at Molly's wellies, wondering what it was she did mean. 'Nothing. I think maybe it's just easier for my mum to say, *Don't overdo it, you might kill the dog* instead of *Don't overdo it, you might kill yourself.*'

Haima was clunking around the office, looking for her missing keys. 'She's allowed to worry, Nance. You're just not used to seeing it up close. How is Mama Bear, anyway?'

Nancy thought of Annabel curled up in Molly's bed the way Fig had curled up on it in the first months, waiting for her to come back.

'Yep, she's fine. We're going pottery shopping later.' Haima snorted down the line. 'Thought you'd be impressed. I need a new cake stand, the place down the road, they have these earthenware ones . . .' Crystal was too fragile, un-stick-back-together-able. 'We're having lunch too.'

She'd waited for Annabel to finish her toast this morning before suggesting a mooch around the pottery shop. Annabel had stopped chewing, spoon hovering just above the honey jar while she'd processed the invitation. *You and me? Like a girls' day? I'd love that*, she'd blinked. But Annabel had also said she'd got into bed last night, shut her eyes and not moved again until morning. So there was no telling really whether she would love to go pottery shopping or if it was another fib for Nancy's benefit.

'Nice,' said Haima.

'Yup.'

'So pottery shopping. Was she keen?'

'Yeah, she was actually. Really keen. I'd half expected her to be too busy, she's signed up to all these clubs: the traffic-calming committee, litter brigade, knitting . . .'

'Well you obviously got it from somewhere, Nance, you don't stop either. And of course she's keen, why wouldn't she want to spend quality time with you? She's your mum!'

'Yeah, I guess.'

134

The clerk was whipping through them now. 'I've got to go, I need to find my order details on my phone.'

'OK, doll, well . . . enjoy pottery shopping. And dog-walking! Don't kill it!'

'Don't tempt me. See you later.'

'Later, doll.'

Nancy swiped off the call. The man in front was just punching his pin into the card reader on the counter. The door rattled open behind them. Nancy glanced over her shoulder.

Clarence Ludlow stepped into the post office, looking down at a scrap of paper in his hand. Nancy whipped her head back around to face front. She scrolled to the order information on her phone, tried to think of something natural and unnoticeable to do with the rest of her body, before Clarence came and stood right behind it. But he didn't. He ambled around the post office shop, picking things off shelves. By the time he moved towards the queue, he had an armful.

Nancy's hand moved of its own volition. She wasn't sure why, but it was already lifting her phone back to her ear. She spoke into it before Clarence took up his spot behind her.

'Yep, definitely. No problem. Uh-huh. Uh-huh.' She was suddenly struck dumb, her blathering mouth functioning autonomously. 'Yeah, me? I'm just . . . in a queue, about to be served.' But the clerk had come a cropper again and was having to pick her way around a paper clip with ten talons slowing her up. 'Yep, at the post office. Yeah.'

The man in front frowned at Nancy over his shoulder. Maybe for the paper-clip trials, or for Nancy's extremely boring *yeah*s and *uh-huh*s. His expression said he knew she was yapping away to nobody, making up all this winning conversational gold. But then he looked over her head.

'Hello, Clarence, hotel supplies?' He nodded at Clarence's armful.

Brilliant. Now Clarence knew she knew he was standing right there and pretending not to see him.

'Something like that,' said Clarence.

'Shouldn't your rock 'n' roll roadies be doing your shopping for you these days? Hey, no throwing television sets into any swimming pools, you lot,' joked the chap in front. Nancy didn't recognise him, but Mistleton was full of strangers now. She looked at her feet instead.

'No, sir,' said Clarence.

Clarence's friend continued his business with the counter clerk. Nancy's phone was still clamped to her ear. Could she be any more ridiculous? she wondered. Unlikely. And then she pictured it ringing in her hand. *God.*

'OK, bye then!' she trilled.

Clarence cleared his throat behind her, quiet but she heard it.

She shot him a quick smile over her shoulder. 'Hello, Clarence.'

'Hello, Nancy.' Something fell from his armful of provisions, settling at the heel of her wellie boot. Nancy bent down, scooping up a disposable toothbrush. She slid it back into the other items Clarence was holding onto, toiletries mainly, and a copy of *Compers News.* Then she turned back and waited her turn. Again. Clarence was close enough that she could smell the field work on him. Sweet grass and diesel. She fumbled through her phone again for the collection barcode, but her brain and fingers wouldn't coordinate.

Something barely brushed past the back of her neck. She swung around. Clarence was all elbows, trying not to drop his things, but in his fingers he was holding something up between his face and Nancy's, an explanation for the touch, another imposter, another small white feather.

'It was in your hair,' he said apologetically. 'Sorry, I didn't mean . . .' He held it out for her. She looked at it. Took it from him before he dropped anything else.

'It's fine,' she managed, stuffing it in her front pocket. Another one for Annabel's jar. Now what? She nodded at his *Compers News*. 'Hotel reading?' she asked light-heartedly. 'Something to pass the time once all the TVs are in the pool, right?'

A smile broke across Clarence's face. He dipped his head, soft dark waves falling over hard blue eyes. 'No, that's for my mum. I'm more of a *Woman's Weekly* kinda guy.'

Nancy felt the beginnings of a smile. She hadn't asked him on the bench, hadn't even thought to. 'How is Birdie? Mum said she's been a little under the weather recently.'

Clarence opened his mouth to answer.

'Next,' yapped the clerk.

Nancy jumped. Clarence smiled and retreated. He nodded a goodbye to the old chap as he passed.

Nancy approached the counter. 'Click and collect, please.'

The clerk tapped a fingernail to the countertop. 'Do you have any ID on you, my love?'

'Yep, sure. It's right here . . .' Nancy presented her driver's licence. The clerk took it, inspected the photo, then Nancy's face, then dug around on a shelf beside her. She put the box into the chute on the counter. 'You look different with shorter hair, older. You might want to get that updated. Every ten years, or you're risking a fine.'

Nancy took the package. 'Thank you, will do. Bye.' She turned and smiled a goodbye to Clarence too without looking any higher than the collar of his plaid shirt. She was halfway down Mistleton high street before she heard him calling her.

'Nancy, hold up!'

She was just about to cross the road to the bench over there outside Benedicto's Sicilian, get the new trainers straight on, but she slowed by Scorlucci's Ice Cream Parlour so Clarence could catch her up.

'That's an impressive power walk,' he said, jogging the last few steps towards her. In the daylight, his skin looked darker against the white of the tee beneath his shirt. Nancy realised he looked tired, but without the shadows of his face, his eyes were softer, and the mouth that never had said very much, less serious. 'You left your licence at the counter. Don't want you getting into trouble next time you're behind the wheel.' He seemed to regret his word choice. Nancy took the licence from his fingers and slipped it back behind her phone.

'Thanks.' She looked about herself, the wooden bistro sets on the pavement outside Mr Scorlucci's place, the giant ice cream cone standing at the door.

'Anything nice?' he asked, gesturing towards her package.

Nancy looked at the box as if it had just appeared in her arms.

'Just a pair of cheap trainers.'

'Yeah? Well expensive isn't always better. I guess I must've inspired you yesterday?'

'Yesterday?' Yesterday had been awful.

'My fine performance through the park. I'm going tomorrow too, if you wanted to break in your new trainers? I run better when I buddy up. How about you?'

Nancy angled herself to cross the road. 'Thanks, but I'm not really home to run.'

'Yeah, I didn't get a chance to ask properly yesterday, how come you're back?'

Nancy glanced across the street. The bench had gone now, an elderly couple were just sitting down on it, the husband helping his wife take her seat, finding his place beside her. 'Um . . . my mum needs me to . . . help out with a few things. Around the house. Decorating.' *Decorating?*

'Well if you need any heavy lifting, shifting furniture, I've got this piano dolly that moves just about anything. I'm usually home most afternoons.'

'We're fine. Thanks, though.' She'd answered too quickly.

'Got it.' Clarence didn't push. He'd always been adept at quiet retreat, knowing when to pull back, when to wait, when to try again. Skills Nancy had seen resurface on those videos of him online, fingers drawing gentle melodies from piano keys. The same way he'd been with Kenning's horses when he'd been their weekend stable boy.

Nancy puffed out her cheeks. 'Nice day,' she tried conversationally, looking to the cloudless sky. She'd never done well with horses. They were too powerful, unnerving. No matter how much she'd wanted to be like the other girls, she'd never gone with them to hang over Kenning's fences

139

to giggle at Clarence, feeding apples to his charges, stroking velveteen noses. The risk had never been worth the reward. Moving too close, touching them, trusting them . . . No matter how much she had wanted, they were always something that made the sweat prick her neck. Something that would knock her off her feet eventually.

'A belter,' replied Clarence. 'Summer's nearly over too. Soon be sycamore season, huh?'

Nancy smiled. Her neck felt clammy. She glanced over the signage hanging above the ice cream parlour beside them, pastel lettering in ice cream shades some thirty years old and polished to perfection. 'Can you believe this place is still going?'

'Nope.' Clarence squinted through the shop window. 'Are you *kidding*?'

Nancy frowned. 'What?'

'Go on. Take a look, at the far wall.' Clarence nodded towards the door, a golden-scripted *OPEN* sign hanging the other side of the glass. 'Look what's on the menu, Nance.'

Nancy hadn't set foot inside Mr Scorlucci's since she was a teenager. Couldn't remember the last time she'd eaten ice cream. She stepped around one of the bistro chairs and leant into the window pane. Above the back counter, the same menu board boasted the same flavours they used to pick over and ponder with their weekend pocket money. *30 Different Flavours!* Next to the menu, an updated version of the Famous Five-Scooper Knickerbocker Glory leaderboard, the names of those who'd managed it without throwing up, and those who hadn't.

'Mr Scorlucci's Famous Five-Scooper Knickerbocker

Glory, Nance. Still going and making grown men cry with brain freeze.'

Nancy felt herself stepping back in time. 'Oh my goodness . . .'

'Yep. Joyful tastebuds, bellyache and humiliation in thirty different flavours.'

Nancy let her eyes coast over the words. Their favourites. The highlight of so many Saturdays.

'I might try them out again sometime. Never did manage the Famous Five. How about you, Nance? Fancy your chances?'

Nancy stepped back from the window. 'I have to run, Clarence, sorry.' She didn't know where he was going with the ice cream thing, but she couldn't go there with him. She was here for Annabel, just for a while. Then she was going home, back to her own life. 'I promised my mum lunch at Beckitt's.'

Clarence smiled at his feet. 'Got it,' he repeated. 'I'll see you around, Nance.'

Chapter 13

Beckitt's Pottery Barn wasn't a barn at all, but the old water mill the Beckitts had hung onto after selling off the rest of their land for housing. They'd turned this place into a nice enough hub on the edge of town so people with an appreciation for quaint tableware and olde-worlde tea rooms could kill an afternoon. The afternoon currently being killed was slipping away more easily than Nancy had anticipated.

Annabel was like a child in a sweet shop. They'd just about moved through the best of it now, aisles of egg cups and milk jugs festooned with bunting and chalkboard sale signs.

'I haven't been here for years,' she said. 'They have some lovely things, don't they? And the lunch was just delicious. Didn't you think? I'd never think to put horseradish in egg mayonnaise. I'm so glad I asked the waitress.'

'Let's not mention the waitress, Mum.' Nancy picked another egg cup out of a display and turned it over in her hand. Yep. Same as all the others they'd looked at. But lovely enough.

Annabel straightened a bunch of silk flowers in their milk jug.

'You were only trying to be friendly. I did think she was expecting too.'

Nancy cringed at the memory, tried to dislodge it by picking up a mug covered in beagles. It was the way the girl had patted her middle protectively. *How much longer do you have to wait?* Nancy had asked brightly. The girl's lips had made a strange shape as the hot tang of embarrassment had filled Nancy's mouth with a rush of saliva, reminding her why it was she didn't inhabit this world. *Wait for what?* the waitress had replied. *Until the end of your shift*, Nancy had gabbled, *you look rushed off your feet*. Haima called it 'calm under pressure'. But if felt more like con-artistry. Calmness only ever found Nancy when she'd pounded at least six miles of road and the endorphins brought it in. She put the mug back on the display and found herself looking for one painted with a dog more like Fig.

'Are you all right, Nance? You're not feeling tired, are you?'

Annabel had applied a light dusting of make-up for the occasion. Her eyes looked bright and warm, she suited the pottery barn with its practical, pretty offerings. Annabel was an attractive woman, who'd been alone for ever. It seemed suddenly likely that Nancy would be alone for ever too. Genetic. Genetically adrift. An egg cup waiting to be noticed.

'Nance?' smiled Annabel. A tiny fleck of cress sat at the edge of her front tooth.

'I feel good, Mum. Absolutely fine.' Nancy pointed at her own tooth. 'You have a little cr—'

'Oh no,' whooshed Annabel.

Nancy glanced across the displays. 'What?'

'By the cake stands. The two ladies, the one in green used to play bridge with Gran – every Thursday until she moved to Dorset.'

Nancy spotted the white-haired women, the cake plates behind them. 'Ah, there they are. Why are you whispering? Don't you want to say hello?'

Annabel slipped her arm through Nancy's, gentle but solid contact, a feeling that pushed as much as it pulled, for reasons unfathomable. Nancy forgot about the cake stands and concentrated on trying to not feel so stiff, to be more tactile for once, make her shoulders fall, loosen the crook in her elbow.

'How about we call it a day and go and get a cup of tea in my new mugs?' Annabel's arm slipped free.

'Sure. Sounds like a plan.'

Nancy followed her to the tills, watched as her mum unloaded her wares onto the counter. Annabel had gone for a simple geometric design that would go with absolutely nothing else in her kitchen.

'No, just the three, thanks,' she said to the boy serving. He tried explaining why buying in pairs worked out better value while she dug around her purse. 'Thank you, love, but four's too many. I don't need four. I haven't really room for three.'

'Do you even need three, Mum? Why not just take two and get the better discount?'

Annabel stopped fishing for her bank card. She looked at Nancy and shrugged one apologetic shoulder. 'I can't. I, er . . . I can't not buy three.'

'We'll take three,' said Nancy.

She hung back from the counter while the boy boxed them up and handed them over to her mum. Nancy gestured towards the doors leading out onto the garden terrace and the car park beyond.

At the exit, Annabel pushed the door first but her escape was blocked by an odd pairing, little and large, a *Star Wars* T-shirt, a dickie bow. Ernest Robinson stood aside, instinctively offering Annabel safe passage.

'Oh, hello there,' he rumbled. 'I was in a world of my own for a second, it was all Yorkshire puddings and real gravy dancing around my head!'

'Hello again, Ernie,' smiled Nancy. Annabel shifted, holding her bag of mugs in front of herself, body armour of sorts. 'Come to buy a new egg cup? There are thousands to choose from.'

Ernest patted down his waistcoat and sank his hands into his trouser pockets. Then he took them out again and fiddled with the face of his wristwatch.

'Oh, no . . . I, er . . . No shopping. I must admit, I'm a little lazy when it comes to cooking at the weekends. I like to bring Ray here for a break. We like a good Sunday roast in the afternoons, don't we, Ray? It doesn't have to be Sunday. You like the ice cream afterwards, don't you, lad?'

Ray hovered behind his grandfather, chunky vintage sunglasses covering most of his face.

'Hello, Ray Robinson,' said Nancy. 'Nice shades.' Ray stuck the toe of his trainer in the gravel. 'Everyone in the city is wearing Ray-Bans this summer. It usually takes a while for the smaller towns to catch up, you're ahead of the curve.'

'See, I told you they were hip, Ray,' added Ernest.

Annabel was doing an excellent job of remaining invisible. She had a knack for stillness when it suited. Ernie noticed her again and blushed despite Annabel not glancing up from her shopping to either see or warrant it.

'We've just had a lovely lunch, haven't we, Mum?' Annabel's eyes snapped back towards the group. 'But you were saying, weren't you, that the soup we made last night with Ernest's veg was going to take some beating?'

Annabel blinked at her. She reminded Nancy of the fish they used to pull out of the canal. Wide-eyed and yanked from their natural environment.

'Oh yes,' she agreed. 'Really lovely soup. Thank you for the vegetables. It was very kind of you to send them round with Nancy.'

'And kind of Ernie not to report Fig for antisocial behaviour too, wouldn't you say, Mum?' Ernie was getting redder. Annabel more fish-like by the second. Nancy smiled while no one was looking. It was so much easier, this gentle social sparring, if you got to be the umpire and nothing more. Her mum deserved to be surrounded by good people, and Ernest Robinson was a good person, Nancy was sure of it. His feelings sat on his face, bold as his moustache. An open, honest man. Someone her mum might forge a friendship with over their shared boundary, spend some of her endless energies on if only to talk veg, instead of spending whole days heading off an elderly mother who had never really shown any great fondness for her.

Annabel fidgeted with her mug boxes. 'Nancy did mention I might need to get a taller fence. I am very sorry. I hope you managed to get back down from your roof without too much difficulty?' She chewed her lip. The cress was still there, Ernie didn't seem to mind much.

'Oh, no bother really. I'm up and down there all the time anyway. No harm done.'

Ray cocked his head. 'You said your life flashed before your eyes, Grandpa. That's why you had to have a drink of whisky before it got dark, to help your jangled nerves unjangle, you said.'

Nancy smiled at Ray, then down at her feet. Annabel bothered at something on her cardigan. The sound of water cascading off the mill wheel filled the silence until Ernie found his voice again.

'No, er, no, that was when you were coming at me with your pistol, our Ray.' He looked at Annabel then. 'I wouldn't blame you if you wanted a taller fence, to keep us heathens at bay. But please don't go putting one up on the dog's account. She was only looking out for the lad. And anyway, truth be told, I'd hate not to be able to see your evening primroses, Annabel. I've never had much luck with them myself.'

Annabel seemed to have solidified. Nancy gently took the bag of boxed mugs from her hands, just in case.

'I guess we'd better stop holding everyone up, Mum, and let these chaps get to their lunch.'

On that cue, Ray walked straight between them and in through the door to aromas of warm meats and roasted vegetables. The Ray-Bans were too big for him: Ernie's once, Nancy suspected. Definitely retro. Or perhaps they were Ray's dad's. Perhaps he was a weekend father, or an every-other-weekend father. Or just an occasional father who liked to leave the odd souvenir of his presence, like a pair of sunglasses, or a trip to the ice cream parlour.

'Hey, Ray?' she called after him. 'Ever been to Scorlucci's in town?' Ray shook his head, the glasses slipping further down his nose. 'If you like ice cream, that's the place to go. Take your grandpa. They sell whisky flavour. And *twenty-nine* others.'

Annabel came unexpectedly back to life. 'Nice seeing you both.'

She held out a hand stiffly. Ernie took his chance and gently shook it in his own. Hands like shovels, hands for getting jobs done, digging earth, lifting grandsons, Nancy thought. Not office worker's hands like her dad's, neat and nimble for typing reports, delegating, cradling women's feet.

'A pleasure to see you, Annabel,' said Ernest.

Annabel jangled her car keys. 'Yes, you too. Come on then, Nancy.'

Chapter 14

'I can't remember the last time anyone took me out for lunch. Feels like a lifetime ago that we last ate out. Hospital canteens aside,' said Annabel, setting her elbow on the open window. She propped her head on her hand like a teenager, no bracing the steering wheel, no double-handed iron grasp. The breeze whipped playfully through her hair. 'I've been trying to work it out. Three years . . . must be, since the three of us were last at Benedicto's.' Nancy looked out of the window. Annabel had taken the slower route home along the lanes behind Saxon's Hill. 'I miss their delicious cassatelle,' she continued, her free hand migrating back to the steering wheel. 'I miss the special occasions.' The truck fell silent. Nancy did not miss them.

The autumnal light on the town's outskirts sent afternoon shadows chasing down the sweep of Whittacker's hills in a final show of defiance, catching the undersides of the trees and the wings of weightless creatures drifting about them.

It was criminal really, driving back when the walk would've been so beautiful. Even with a healing blister.

'Maybe we shouldn't have stopped going there for special occasions, Nancy? I don't think . . . well I don't think she would've wanted that. She really loved it there, didn't she?'

More than anything, Nancy wished she'd walked. She laid her head back against the headrest and watched the trees roll past. 'I'm fairly certain Mol preferred Sicilian when I wasn't there spoiling the fun, Mum.'

A hesitation, and then, 'What on earth would make you say that?' But Annabel didn't turn her face when she asked, squinting towards the low sun instead.

Nancy fixed back on the world outside the truck, its wheels rumbling steadily beneath them.

'I was hideous that night. It was her birthday and I was a complete idiot.'

'You are not and have never been an *idiot*, Nancy.'

Nancy smiled emptily at the view. 'Thanks, but we both know I was.' She'd meant it to sound motivational, to encourage Mol to aim higher than waitressing at the Jack and the other piecework she liked so much, that was all. But it had come out wrong. Patronising. Snobbish. Idiotic.

'I can't really remember,' lied Annabel.

'Yes you can.' It pushed its way in. Nancy held the door open for it. 'I told her she was wasting her life. Having *too much fun* with her friends, instead of taking life more seriously.' Setting goals. Planning ahead. Pensions. *Pensions.* Jesus. They hadn't known then what was to come and tear through their lives and punch a black hole straight through the universe before they could even find something to hold

150

onto. The trip planning had come later. It had been something to aim for, a celebration once the treatments finished. Nancy had gift-wrapped the atlas, the box of maps and stickers and pins, taken it into the hospital. But the treatments didn't finish. They barely started. Lasted just long enough to plot a journey they would never take. Months. That was all it took. An ache, a scan, a plan. A blink and gone.

'Don't say that, Nancy. Please.' Annabel braced the steering wheel again. 'Don't do it to yourself. No good will come of it.'

Nancy swallowed. 'Do what?'

'Pick through the ashes looking for spent matches. We have to look for the treasure. Or we'll have nothing to save.' Annabel took a long breath and blew it out over the wheel. Her hands relaxed again just enough that the pinkness returned to her knuckles. 'Sisters fall out, Nancy. It's as normal as normal gets. You were there for her in every way you could be and she knew how much you loved her. That's all anyone can ever hope to have in this life, and it's all anyone can ever give.'

The rest of the slow drive home through the back lanes had been an unexpected reminder of what else was still here, some of the near-forgotten parts that still felt familiar and good, places Nancy could disappear into for an hour's walking if she needed to, while the snow was still safely months away and the landscape didn't threaten its New Year's secrets with a knowing nod. Annabel didn't have all the facts. But she'd awoken a need Nancy had buried so deeply only its thin edge now pierced the surface of her, a tiny corner she wanted to sweep the grit and muck from, to buff with her sleeve and hold tightly in her palm. She wanted to look for the treasure that sustained their mother. To be able to think of her sister without the drop, the heavy impossibility of missed chances. She wanted the proof that their sisterhood had been more than its end.

When they pulled up outside, the house looked different, a hand unclenched. Annabel took straight to rinsing her new cups before even de-scarfing herself, then on to scribbling notes in her recipe pad for *Jazzy Egg & Cress Sandwiches with Horseradish*, telling Fig about their lunch and all the reasons Ernest's evening primroses might not be doing so well.

Annabel seemed different too. Watching her move around the kitchen was like seeing a penny at the bottom of a fountain, an animated version of itself, reminding the beholder of its existence, its value, right there, just out of reach.

Later, they'd sat down together in the lounge and unravelled the mysteries of the iPad login Molly had set up for Annabel two birthdays ago without ever writing down the passcode anywhere, just in case one day the unthinkable happened and Mol wasn't here to tell her.

'How the Dickens have you figured that out?' Annabel asked, staring at the iPad.

Nancy sank into the sofa cushion and crossed her legs like a child. Tiredness sucked at her. 'There are harder things to break your way back into.'

Annabel's eyebrows rose. 'You sound like your sister. She thought breaking in through the utility window was easy enough too, easy if you're like you girls. Brave. And bendy. I've never broken my way in anywhere. Ever.'

Brave? Annabel was confusing her daughters. 'I've never climbed through the utility window, Mum.'

'Your sister said you had.'

'She would.'

'Yes, she would.'

'Maybe it's easier if you're drunk,' suggested Nancy. As Mol tended to be before breaking and entering.

'Maybe.'

'You need to fix that, Mum. Before you get burgled.' Now that no one would be clambering through it any more, drunk or not.

'I'll get around to it.' Annabel tried out the iPad passcode again. 'I can't believe you've made this usable. Bravo, Nance.'

'Why don't I set you up with your own Pinterest account? We use it at work. You'll like it. Might give you some ideas for your next hobby . . . if you can squeeze any more in.'

'Yes please,' yipped Annabel.

It had taken minutes to get Annabel logged in and signed up and then she was off, like a child wobbling down the road on their first bike, head filling with all the online inspiration she could take back and share with her hobbyist pals. Nancy watched her go, expressions of awe and concentration taking their turns over Annabel's face. The afternoon had been nice. Had felt *good*. This had been the overriding feeling Nancy had felt, sitting there in the lounge, sipping tea from one of the new mugs under the watchful gaze of two ugly china dogs, Annabel swiping and tapping away. *A good afternoon. With Mum.* It seemed sensible to quit while they were ahead.

'I might go up for a nap, Mum.'

Annabel sat upright in her chair and laid the iPad flat in her lap, its inner marvels instantly forgotten.

'Are you OK? Have we done too much today? Do you need any of your medication?'

'Mum, it's *fine*. I probably won't even snooze, just look at my phone for a while. You stay put.'

But upstairs, there hadn't been anything attention-worthy on her phone, not even the glitzy American reality TV she secretly indulged in sometimes, impeccable families opening their homes to the world, the cut-throat realtors selling the dreams. She'd tried her emails too, skimmed the background info Haima had sent through on the non-disclosure wrangles, but that hadn't held her interest for long either.

She gave up on her phone and pulled her foot up onto the bed, peeled back the plaster from her ankle and inspected how the healing process was working out for her blister. Skin took a day or two to harden up, heal over. Skin knew what was good for it. Nancy lay back on the bed with her hands rested across her middle, the body she'd honed and exercised and fed kelp shakes to now back to square one, slow and useless. Feeling instantly restless again, she looked down to her feet.

'You will run again, feet. You will learn to be fast enough.'

Deep orange sunlight mottled the bed where her feet were, warming the bedclothes. She crossed her ankles, remembered her mum examining those sandwiches, so much enthusiasm for just an inspired dollop of horseradish. Right on cue, Annabel let out a yip of wonderment in the living room below. A muffled voice followed up through the floorboards.

'That is *ruddy* genius!'

Nancy smiled at the ceiling. She closed her eyes and tried lying still awhile, concentrating on Annabel's online odyssey, but the buzz had started in her head. The sort that grew the more you tried to settle it down. A wasps' nest of thoughts. She tried lying on her side. The mural opposite stared back at her. Their dubious artwork saved by Annabel for posterity like bizarre cave-markings, only more primitive and candy-coloured. Nancy looked at the sycamore drawing and felt the day's unknotting re-weave itself. They'd loved that old tree. It took eleven minutes to run home from Whittacker's sycamore if you cut across the first field to the break in the hedgerow, scooched through the gap without getting your hair snagged and then followed the millstream all the way back behind Mountford Road. Kids had to know that kind of thing when there were curfews in place. Eleven minutes. And you could shave almost three minutes off if you were going to hop over Annabel's back fence onto the pear tree and straight into the garden, but you couldn't always guarantee Whittacker hadn't let the cows into that field and you didn't mess with cows, not even for a three-minute save. So, calving season aside, the general rule of thumb was eleven minutes, trunk to door. But that was when you were twelve years old and could still move like water. At thirty, in falling snow, in the dark, with lungs that wouldn't fire right and legs heavy and useless, it had taken longer than eleven minutes. Too long.

There was a memory of it, a physical memory rooted into Nancy's body, into her heart. How unfit she'd been, how it had caught her out. Her brain had tried to filter it but her body was doing its own thing, it wanted to remember, it

155

wanted Nancy to remember too. *You were too heavy, too slow, too selfish.*

Too late.

The problem that had first awoken her on her bedroom rug reminded her now that it was still in there, waiting, in the thrum of her chest, the unstable cocktail of panic and adrenalin suddenly firing through her again. She'd disturbed it and now she could feel it coming back to life, wanting out. She looked away from the sycamore tree they'd scribbled onto the bedroom wall. *One hundred . . . ninety-nine . . . ninety-eight . . . ninety-seven . . .* She should've kept driving straight past the sycamore, should never have stopped on the furlong, never tried to explain it to Clarence. All those precious extra minutes, wasted. As if they'd been hers to squander.

Nancy drew in a sharp breath and held onto it. *Eighty-six . . . eighty-five . . . eighty-four . . .* The pattering carried on relentlessly. Her mother's face as she'd sat waiting at the bottom of the stairs hadn't often chased through Nancy's thoughts. She'd managed to block it, somehow, as if she had a choice on how any of it played through the darkness of her recollections, which parts landed at her feet. This memory of Annabel waiting for her other daughter to get home didn't follow on when the dream played out and Nancy relived the moments driving along the furlong, seeing Clarence in the snow, trying to get back home to Molly on foot because the car no longer had lights to see through the dark. The dream never carried Nancy in off the furlong, never as far as the house, the door, their mother at the bottom of the stairs. But she remembered now, Annabel's face, pale and empty, waiting.

The air had gone from Nancy's lungs, from their home even, when she had reached it, but still the lie had crawled out from her lips and sat in their mother's lap. Nancy's lie. A fox cutting in front of her on the furlong . . . skidding in the snow . . . broken headlights . . . *undrivable, Mum, I had to run*. But Annabel hadn't been listening anyway.

Nancy closed her eyes now, remembered her mother's hands, warm and trembling at Nancy's frozen cheeks. The same need moved its fingers through Nancy's chest, pinching and twisting her now as if she was back at the foot of the stairs. The need had never left her, for Annabel to not say the words. *She's gone, Nancy. Our beautiful girl is already gone.*

The bedroom door opened.

'Quick question,' beamed Annabel. 'How do I upload a profile photo?'

Nancy's heart galloped, a thundering animal wanting free of her. She wanted free of herself. She wanted to tear herself open and climb out and flitter away on the air like a piece of litter, gone and forgotten and good riddance. She rubbed a knuckle across her mouth while the galloping raged inside. 'Sorry?' Her voice sounded wiry and tight.

'A profile . . .' Annabel frowned. 'Are you all right?'

'Sure,' managed Nancy. 'A . . . profile picture.'

'Nancy? Your eyes are like saucers, sweetheart, has something happened?' Annabel spotted the mobile phone on the bed. 'Work OK? It wasn't the hospital?'

Nancy got a hold of it, dragged the oxygen in, smiled as she let it out, *in . . . out . . .*

'Everything's fine. Just yoga breathing. One more minute . . .' Sixty precious seconds.

'Oh. Good. Yoga breathing. You had me worried!' Annabel looked at the mural opposite, her expression shifting again as old thoughts trailed away, new ones elbowing their way in. 'If only you girls had got to the world before Banksy, hey?' She stepped further into the bedroom. 'I can still picture your faces when I asked you to do all this. You probably wouldn't remember, but you kept on asking if I was *sure* it was all right, as if I'd change my mind and tell you off, as if I'd set a trap or something. Your sister didn't need telling twice, obviously, but I practically had to force your hand, Nance.'

Nancy watched her mum cross the floor for a closer look, set her fingertips against the colours on the wall, what was left of the fainter parts faded over time. Annabel's head lolled to one side over her shoulder.

'I remember, Mum.'

'It was so unlike you,' said Annabel quietly. 'You'd always liked taking charge, but you were so . . . uncertain. As if you might do something terrible or irreversible with just a packet of colourful pens. I guess there were a lot of changes going on at the time. After your dad . . . Well, you know.'

Everything had changed after he'd left. After he'd decided he wanted to spend more time with his friend from work and her children, instead of his own.

'I think your sister took full advantage of your reluctance that day.' Annabel grinned. 'She didn't half go to town on this poor wall. Are those satsumas? I can't remember.'

Nancy blinked at the orange blobs on the mural. 'Pumpkins.'

'Ah, yes. A revenge plot, if I recall? Something to do with getting Simon Marston back for something?'

'Something like that.' Though it had been Freddie Blumfield Molly hated most.

'Goodness, she was fearless, wasn't she? Even as a little girl. She faced everything head on . . . even when it terrified her. I would do anything, *anything*, to be half so brave.' Nancy watched her mother's shoulders fall, her face unwavering from Molly's markings. 'Maybe one day. One day I'll do something brave, and make her proud.'

Annabel traced her fingers over Molly's sketches on the wall and Nancy knew she was surplus to the journey now, Annabel tracking back through the years to her little girl. Back to Mol. She touched the outline Nancy had drawn around Molly's small hands, pressed her hand flat against the wall where Molly's had been more than twenty years before. She opened her mouth, then closed it again, her voice and memory in gentle conflict. Nancy waited to see which one would triumph.

'I miss her,' Annabel said finally.

The thing inside Nancy stilled. As if it knew there was something else, something bigger and hungrier to hide from. The room and her heart quieted in tandem.

'I know.'

'Do you think we'll ever see her again?'

Nancy didn't have an answer to that. No one did.

Annabel stared at the marks her younger child had left behind, as if staring alone could shorten the thread of time stretching between them now.

'It's so hard, some days . . . not having anywhere to lay flowers for her. But then on other days, I'm so relieved she's not buried in the earth. I *ache* with relief. That we're doing what she asked. Nowhere and everywhere.'

No burial, Molly had said. No headstone to permanently anchor them to Mistleton churchyard lest they ever fancied emigrating or joining a cult. Her ashes were to be scattered far and wide. Everywhere that had meant something to her, anywhere that might mean something to Annabel and Nancy in the future Molly wouldn't accompany them into. But everywhere had had to wait. Annabel had had to wait. No ashes had been scattered. No fitting locations spoken of. Nancy didn't even want to think of places that might be good enough: there weren't any, there couldn't be. Molly's plan was flawed. *Everywhere* was impossible, and *nowhere* was more impossible still.

'Me too,' lied Nancy. She hated it, and you weren't supposed to hate the last wishes of someone you loved. Molly said they'd know where to find her. The places that hadn't been about plasma transfusions and lung aspirations and chemotherapy flushes. Places that had nothing to do with her rest, or recovery, and absolutely nothing to do with dying. Places where she had *lived*. One of those places winked at Nancy now in shades of green and brown from their mural. A place they'd known by heart. But she'd sullied it. She'd panicked when she should've been stronger, faster, better. She'd made the sycamore on the furlong something else, *somewhere* else, that didn't belong to them in the same way now.

'Mum?'

'Yep?'

'I'm going to pop out for an hour. Do you mind?'

Annabel turned and smoothed down the cuffs of her

cardigan again. All neat and tidy. 'Of course not. Do you need a lift?' She checked her watch. 'It's nearly five thirty, I was thinking I might run an RSVP up to the Whittackers, I could drop you anywhere you like? On the way? We are definitely going to Beth's party, now, aren't we? Just to show our faces?'

Molly's worldly possessions were all still waiting for the big sort-through. Beth's party, still the lesser of two monsters.

'Sure. Looking forward to it. I don't need a lift, though. Thanks.'

'OK. Don't go too far then, save your energy. You never know, you might fancy a dance when you get there next Saturday!'

Nancy smiled along. 'Unlikely. But you never know, *you* might.'

Their sycamore painting peeped over each of Annabel's shoulders, calling its invitation. 'I'd better get going then. Just want to break my trainers in a bit. Won't be long.'

'OK. Well, where are you headed? Anywhere in mind?'

'No.' Another lie.

Chapter 15

The light rested over Saxon's Hill like bronze gauze, waiting to be reached up to and touched. A pleasant tension sat in Nancy's calf muscles, the trees lining the lane curving overhead, cooling the air beneath. She'd walked for nearly half an hour without any effort, coming about in a great sweeping arc that would take her the rest of the way to the top of the furlong and eventually back onto the home strait of Mountford Road. Her breathing hadn't changed at all since she'd left the house: no hideous exertion, no hideous anything, and the fact both buoyed and niggled her. It was all so fragile, so changeable. And completely uncontrollable. One minute you could be pushing your personal best on the treadmills at Garfield's, the next a sweaty mess on a hospital gurney. People were too many things at once, she'd realised on the walk here. Why couldn't it be simpler? Why couldn't a person be just one thing at a time? Happy or sad? Healthy or unhealthy? Everywhere or nowhere.

At the stile, she made a left, clambering over the timber

steps, and stood at the top of the furlong, where the view opened out before her like an outreached hand. She watched the wind move down through the valley in front of her, calling the way. The trees lining the hedgerows down there fluttered and bowed as one before righting themselves again. She let her eyes drink it all in. From this end of the furlong, it was all downhill. A gentle decline into the natural basin of Whittacker's lower fields, the sycamore nestled at the bottom of the valley like a pearl in a clam. There was an urge in her legs to run. They were warmed and ready, knew their job. But she was in no rush to get to the sycamore. To face the thing that followed her through her sleep.

Nancy lifted her face and let the sun find her eyelids. She inhaled a lungful of air, sweetened by the tall grasses surrounding her. She pulled it all in, tried to fill herself up with it so there wasn't room for anything else, but she felt it. The shadow moving through her. Haima's voice whispered in her subconscious. *You tried to outrun it, didn't you?*

A winter's night followed Haima's voice in. A New Year's Eve, and a landscape bathed in darkness and the ghostly blue-white hue of new-fallen snow. Clarence had been shortcutting across the fields, merry from a lock-in in the Jack. He would've been happily staggering home, minding his own business, when Nancy had driven down the furlong here, straight towards him. No idea he was even there. She could almost feel the groan of the car under her when she'd jammed her foot into the brake pedal just short of the tree, the tree she'd later tell their mother she'd skidded straight into.

Clarence had seen it all. The skidding, the braking. The

waiting. The staring over the steering wheel while the thoughts had collected in her head, sticking themselves together, cobweb thin. He'd have seen her get out of the car and dig around to find something that would do what her nerves and accelerator foot had almost managed by themselves, until her survival instinct had kicked in without her.

It had frightened her, how easily she'd almost hit the sycamore, how easily she'd almost jeopardised her own obedient body when her sister was less than a mile away, trying to survive her own. But it had frightened her even more that she'd been so desperate to run towards the precipice waiting for her at the house. After the car had skidded, screeched to a stop intersecting the furlong, it was as if any courage inside her had unbuckled itself and stepped shakily out of the car. So Nancy had followed it.

In the ice and snow, the rocks had sat proud of the white, strewn about the bottom of the sycamore by ploughs and other heavy machinery. She'd lifted one, big as her fist. It had felt like a solution in her hand, the weight of extra time, if she could just wield it right and make a crack in the night closing in around them. She'd brought it down onto the first headlight until it gave, then the second, knocking out the last of the light between them before she'd even realised Clarence was standing there. Clarence Ludlow had quietly watched her do these things, huddled against the cold, snow in his hair, before speaking calmly through the darkness.

'Nancy?' Clarence stood like an apparition, appeared from thin air. 'Are you OK?'

    The phone rang again through the car. It had started to

164

ring near-constantly as she'd driven into Mistleton. She let it ring out again now, the panic rising in her.

'Can I call someone for you?'

She weighed Clarence's question. Who would he call for her? Everything she knew was in a house that was burning down. Nancy looked at him through the snow, pale flecks falling like white feathers between them. Like the ash that drifted back to earth after a great destructive fire. Something apocalyptic, changing the world for ever.

'Call who?' she asked.

Clarence stayed where he was, hands upturned. Voice steady and calm. They'd seen him this way since they were children, handling grown adults like skittish horses, slow and steady, no sudden movements. Birdie Ludlow had taught her son how to behave around the unpredictable.

'Is Annabel home, Nancy? You look unwell. I could call—'

'You can't call my mother, Clarence.'

He'd stolen another look at the broken headlights, a powerful car suddenly lame and fit for nothing.

'Then I'll walk you home. It's nearly two a.m. You shouldn't be here by yourself.'

But she wasn't going home. She was staying there. Between what was behind and what was ahead. Molly would wait for her. Molly did things her way, only ever her way, and her way was the three of them together. The Woods girls. That was what she'd said. If Nancy didn't go home, it wouldn't happen. Molly would wait.

Clarence pushed gently. 'Does Annabel know you're here?'

The phone rang through the darkness again. Annabel had called just as the first snow of winter had started over the city, drifting down onto the apartment balcony. She'd been following the weather report, wanted Nancy to sit tight, drive back the next morning after the rain had cleared the roads again. Molly was sleeping anyway, there were too many drunk drivers on the road New Year's Eve, leave it until they were all nursing their headaches, the roads were always clear on the first day of a brand-new year.

But as the last fireworks had died over the city, she called again. Her voice cracked and urgent, reaching out to Nancy as if she could do something.

'Nancy?' Clarence stepped towards the car, the snow tinted a cold blue now without the headlights to warm it. He moved closer, gently freeing the rock from Nancy's hand. 'Nancy, your phone is ringing. Should I answer it for you?'

She looked at him then and wondered why it was their lives all played out in the ways they did. What they each must've done to be dealt their own very specific hand.

'No,' she said calmly. 'It's going to be OK.'

'You don't look OK. Let me help you?'

The sycamore they'd played in as children hunkered over them like a hand that would come down on them at any minute, snatching them back into the earth. It was all so fragile. So pointless. So much stacked against them. Against Molly.

'You can't save everyone, Clarence. Go home to your mother.'

He'd stepped away from her then, snow melting on cheerfully pink skin.

'I'll call Mol. I'll wait with you until she comes. Where is she, partying?'

'You can't call Molly, Clarence. Molly's . . .' But even the rage couldn't carry the words to him.

'What?'

His fingers had found their way around her arms. Clarence was suddenly there, holding on. They'd all believed what Molly wanted them to believe. People plumped for hope. No news was good news. Wishful thinking was part of the human condition, from children spinning helicopter wishes to young women receiving bleak oncology results. It'll be OK, Nance. Mol hadn't wanted anyone to know that it might not.

'She's at home, Clarence. No one can help her now. Not the doctors. Not even Mum.' Annabel, who'd fought almost as hard as Molly to beat the odds stacked against her.

Clarence sobered, squeezed Nancy's arms. He spoke softly and slowly, delivering each word with precision.

'Then why are you here?'

A crow cawed above Nancy on the hillside. She looked up for it, but the sun was too bright, slanting across the land here like a slap. The echoes of New Year's Eve sank back into the void they'd spilt from. Whittacker's sycamore stood like a lighthouse ahead, calling her on through the sea of wheat parted straight down the middle by the furlong at her feet. Gravity did most of the work here, Nancy let it pull her further down into the valley. She looked for anyone cutting across the far meadows again, ready to stumble across her the way Clarence had. But there were no signs of life around other than the sheep Whittacker was grazing two fields over. She wondered if the local kids still knew to stay out of there before Whittacker could wave his rights and his rifle at them.

Perhaps they didn't play in these fields any more. Perhaps kids didn't even want to climb trees now, now that they had Xboxes and iPhones and all the other distractions companies like Deep Dish were helping peddle to the masses with catchy marketing and memorable straplines.

Her feet slowed as they reached the sycamore, stepping into the edges of its vast shadow. Fallen helicopter seeds carpeted the earth beneath her trainers, unspent wishes, trodden underfoot now. The sun couldn't break through all the branches above; goosebumps rippled over her arms. She set her hand against the tree trunk and let in the memory, the cold in her fingers, digging around in the snow. *Just one wish*, she'd wanted to take for her. One helicopter wish for Molly. Otherwise she wouldn't have driven along here in the first place. But as soon as she'd turned onto the furlong, something dark had slipped into the passenger seat next to her, telling her she couldn't go home to them. It was as if her senses had left her, replaced by the fear that stopped people diving into icy water, or putting their hands into open flames. The voice of self-preservation telling her, *It will hurt*. Going home to them would simply hurt too much.

She leant forward, setting her head against the trunk of their sycamore, and felt the overwhelming roar of tears that would come if she let them. The world was full of cowards of one sort or another. Molly knew that. She knew Nancy was not brave like her. And Clarence Ludlow knew it too. This was just what she was, what she did. She pretended. *Molly's on a dream holiday, travelling the world, bound by nothing!* And she hid. *The fox, the snow, I'd have been here if I could, Mum.*

The breeze moved through the leaves above her, agitating the branches. Nancy made a strange noise against the tree trunk. A whimper at first, then a wretched, frustrated, breathy sound like the noises they'd taught her to make in t'ai chi. She closed her eyes and let it out past the tightness already there in her chest, pressed her hands into the bark, speaking as if it could pass on the message somehow.

'I'm *sorry*, Mol. I'm sorry. If I could have the time again, I'd be there. For all of it.'

But she couldn't have the time again. Time didn't care about anyone. You got your allowance, and that was it. How you wasted it was your business.

The breeze whipped up, sending a whoosh through the branches. Sounds sharp and soft, tussling each other. She heard it then. A creaking above, then a dull crack. She stepped back instinctively just as a form thudded to the ground the other side of the trunk. It landed hard, groaned and rolled over onto its backpack.

Nancy flinched. 'Fucking hell!' Her heart pounded through her ribs.

The form listed like a boat capsized, groaned again and assumed a foetal position. Nancy hung back as a voice whimpered from the floor.

'My grandpa says people who swear can't think of anything interesting to say.'

'*Ray?* What the bloody hell are you *doing*? Are you all right?'

'You scared me,' groaned Ray.

'I scared you! Are you kidding?' Nancy stared up into the boughs. 'You just fell out of the tree, Ray! You could've

169

killed one of us!' There was a chance he still might if her heart didn't settle. Ray was not nearly as adept at rapid climbing as her pulse.

'It's your fault. You started saying weird things, to a *tree trunk*, and I forgot to hold tight. You put me off,' he said, clumsily making it to his elbows.

Nancy scanned the branches, then the meadows, checking for anyone Ray might've brought with him. 'What are you doing hiding in trees in the first place? It's dangerous.'

Ray inspected his knee and winced. 'Waiting.'

'For what?'

'My friends.'

'Oh. Right. Well. Do you see them?' They had a near-perfect 360-degree view across the valley from here. There wasn't another lookout like the sycamore in all of Mistleton.

'No.'

Nancy let the worry slide from her voice. 'Are you playing a game or something?'

Ray shrugged. 'I don't really like their games. They always make me count. I've been looking for them for ages, but they aren't in their usual places.' He jabbed a thumb up at the tree. 'I thought I'd see them better from up there.'

Nancy held out a hand. Ray took it, heaving himself to his feet.

'Don't you have other friends? Who'll take it in turns?'

'Yes. But these are new friends and I've got to make the effort. My normal friends live near my house. My grandpa says I should try to make friends with the boys from my school who live by his house too because I'm spending more time at his house now because Mum can't just work in the daytime at the petrol station, sometimes she has to work afternoons or teatime and I have to stay with my grandpa on those days.'

'Gotcha,' said Nancy. Ray rubbed his elbow. When she and Mol were Ray's age, there wouldn't have been anything less appealing than being regularly dumped at Ginny's, something Annabel thankfully had never inflicted upon them. Ernest was different, though.

'Nice that you get to spend so much time with your grandpa though, right?'

Nancy scanned the fields again, where Freddie Blumfield and his cronies had chased them after Molly had lobbed his new BMX into the duckpond.

'I don't think your friends are here, Ray. Isn't it getting late for boys your age to be out by themselves? What time did Ernie say to be home?'

Ray stamped his feet, swatting the detritus stuck to his shorts. 'Six thirty. But Oliver took my watch.'

'Somebody took your watch?'

'Oliver did. So he knew I was counting for the exact right time.'

'Didn't *you* need your watch to know that?' Ray shrugged. 'How long has he had it, Ray?'

'I gave it to him at five twenty-five p.m. exactly, after I gave them the cakes my grandpa bought for us all from the bakery at Beckitt's Pottery Barn. We got cream horns for everyone.'

'Nice.' A cream horn apiece and they'd ditched him anyway. Nancy brushed a twig from Ray's shoulder. She looked up into the canopy of the sycamore, pictured two little girls up there, hiding from another bunch of mean boys. 'Come on. If we go now, you'll be back before your grandad starts worrying.'

She helped Ray to pick up the few bits of loose change his pockets had given up on his way earthwards. She picked up a couple of helicopters too, force of habit, and slipped them into her own pocket. Ray found a swishy stick on the way to the hedgerow and took to swatting the wheat as they followed the trail home.

As Ray walked and swished, Nancy looked for signs of injury. A limp or an arm not hanging quite right. Ray was a sturdy child, but the ground was sturdier. James Chadwick had cracked three ribs falling from the same spot. If Ray had cracked anything, it wasn't showing. He swished his stick again, taking the head clean off a wheat stalk.

'Why were you talking to the tree trunk?'

Nancy plucked a cornflower, weighing it in her hand. 'It's complicated, Ray. Sometimes . . . people just do strange things.'

'Yeah, they do.' He shook his head disapprovingly. 'My grandpa does strange things all the time.'

Nancy smiled to herself. 'Oh yeah? Like climbing onto his shed roof?'

'No. Like when he washes up the things on the draining board even when they've been washed already. I tell him he's cleaned them already and he says, *Oh, I'm just making sure they're done properly like Nanny used to wash them.*'

Nancy let her hand coast over the tips of the wheat as they walked. 'So he washes everything twice? Every single time you guys do the dishes?'

'No,' said Ray, swishing. 'Only when your mum is in her back garden. That's why it's strange. Because if my grandpa just stopped looking out of the kitchen window and concentrated, they would definitely be clean enough and he would only have to wash them once, wouldn't he?'

Nancy glanced over at her unlikely companion traipsing along beside her. She thought of Ernest, looking out at her mother. Then what it had been like to be Ray's age, naïve and unable to see what the people around you really wanted.

'I used to play in these fields, Ray. When I was your age.'

'You're on a trip down memory lane then, I suppose,' said Ray.

'Yes.'

'I thought Memory Lane was an actual lane, but it's not. Or a road. Or even a real place. It's an idea.'

'That's right, Ray.'

'So people can remember nice times from before now. What was the nice time you thought about on your trip down memory lane today?'

He'd caught her short. She hadn't really had time to think of an excuse for being there before he'd scared her half to death.

'We used to lie under the sycamore in the autumn and wait for the wind to blow a massive cloud of helicopters down to us. That was really beautiful. I'd forgotten about it, actually. Until you reminded me.'

'How did I remind you?'

Nancy smiled at her feet. 'It's not every day a Ray-shaped sycamore seed almost drops on your head. Thanks for the new memory, Ray.'

Ray looked in her general direction through his too-long hair, and frowned.

'Did you play hide-and-seek with your friends here too?'

'Sort of. With my sister mostly, but I had some nice friends too.' She nudged him with her arm. 'Some not so nice.'

'Please be careful,' said Ray. 'You just bumped into me.'

'Oh. Sorry.' She felt her face flush.

After a few more swishes, Ray asked, 'Which friends weren't so nice?'

'Hmm? Oh, um, Freddie Blumfield was a real toad. And like all toads, he found himself squelching around a pond.'

'The park pond?'

Nancy nodded. 'Freddie liked to pick on people. My sister showed him what happens when plucky girls fight back.'

It came back to her as she spoke, so clear and vivid that she could even remember how weeks of rain before the first warm April days had kneaded the fields from bell metal back to a softer clay. How it had felt running over them.

'Wait for me, Nance!' Molly yelled across the meadow.

'No way!' Nancy squealed back, a mass of dark hair across her face when she'd turned to check Mol was keeping up. Her feet had wobbled on the changing earth but she'd kept running, kept panting, kept looking back for Mol.

'Hurry up, Mol! The others'll be here soon!'

Nancy sent up a fast prayer. Dear Lord, please make Freddie think we've run straight home. *Straight to the sacred refuge of their mother's garden gate. Just the thought of Freddie Blumfield with a dripping wet bike and a score to settle made Nancy's body feel like it wasn't her own,* boneless and slow. Mol looked over her shoulder to where the boys would enter the meadows from the park end of Mountford.

'Look where you're going, Molly. Don't fall!'

'I don't think they're coming!' Molly panted. 'Climb up and have a look!'

Nancy had never beaten Molly to the tree. Never taken the lead. She always let Molly win, always watched her from behind. Look after your sister, Mum said. But only ever to Nancy.

Molly called ahead, 'Hide, Nance, in case they're creeping up on us!' A nervous giggle in Nancy's tummy gave her a stitch as she reached her knee up onto the first branch. The bark bit through her jeans but she pressed against it and scrambled for the next branch above. Moments later, Molly was at the trunk too.

'Why are you laughing, Molly? He's going to kill us.'

Molly set her knee in the same spot, took another look over her shoulder for the boys, then threw her head back and laughed, a short, sharp, triumphant cackle.

'Served him right,' she said, hauling herself up. 'I told him if he said it again, I'd do it. I bet that stupid walkie-talkie on his handlebars won't walkie-talkie any more. Fart-head.'

Nancy shuffled along the second branch to where it forked off and crouched there, looking through the first unfolding leaves of spring for Freddie and his posse. They were their posse too, Molly and Nancy's, but when Molly had bolted through the park gates, only Nancy had bolted after her, and so two informal sides of a battle had formed. Nancy hated Freddie Blumfield. Hated his big fat head. And if they made

175

it out of this alive, she was going to give Mol her best bead
bracelet for shutting Freddie up for once.

'Why didn't you like him, though?' asked Ray as they walked.
'What did he do to make your sister throw his bike in the
duckpond?'

Nancy shrugged. 'It sounds silly now, but he was just
mean. He said mean things, about our dad, mainly. Just stuff
like that.'

The prospect of starting high school had been looming
over her that year, and thanks to Freddie, she'd been in the
foothills of some irrational anxiety that once at Mistleton
Comp, she'd be confronted by even bigger boys saying even
meaner things about girls whose dads didn't want to live with
them any more.

Ray trailed his stick behind him. 'A boy from my class was
saying mean things about my dad once. My grandpa said to
ignore him because people who talk about people they don't
even know have got mashed potato between their ears.'

'Sounds like good advice.'

'I don't even like mashed potato, so I stopped listening to
him straight away. What did your sister do after she climbed
up the big tree? Did she get away?'

Molly hung her arms over the higher branch and sagged
against it while she caught her breath.

'Nance? Do you think Fart-Head was telling the truth?
Do you think Dad really left home because we aren't pretty?'
Freddie hadn't said that, though. What he'd said was,
Everyone knows your dad ran off because he thought you

and your mum are so ugly. *But even Molly didn't want to hear it out loud again.* 'I bet he did say it. Mum always says we're pretty, but then they always choose the blonde girls to be angels in the nativity. Last year, I had to be a tree. I really hated Miss Dutard for making me hold my arms out for a *whole* hour. My armpits ached for a week.'

'That was your fault, Mol. You shouldn't have cut your hair with Mum's scissors. Angels have long hair.'

'How do you know angels have long hair?'

Nancy thought about it, then lifted one shoulder. 'Pictures.'

Molly rubbed her nose with her hand.

'Well I think it's because I'm not blonde. If I was blonde like Emma and Beth, I could've been an angel as well.'

'Mol, you'll never be an angel.'

'Even if I grow my hair?'

'You're too naughty.'

Molly jabbed a thumb skywards. 'What about when I go up there, to Heaven?'

Nancy looked up through the sycamore branches. 'I'm not sure. I'll go up there first. I'm the eldest.'

'You can make sure they let me in then. If my hair's not long enough.'

A threat of colour peeped along the hedgerow across the meadows.

'Look!' squealed Molly.

Five children, a couple of bikes. Freddie running as if his legs were made of wood, wet clothes clinging to his body.

'You have to go higher, Nancy. Come on!'

Molly clambered up to the next branch she sometimes sat on if she was careful, but she was standing on it now.

177

'Molly, Mum said not too high.'

'Freddie won't get his big fat butt up there,' she said, pointing at the bough above her. 'We'll be safe if we go up. Come on!'

'It's too high, Molly.' They should've gone straight home. But Molly didn't listen.

Molly's foot slipped and Nancy felt her tummy roll while her sister reclaimed her footing. Nancy tried to follow her up there, but the fluttering in the leaves and in her heart made her arms feels like sponge cake and the branches around her like the papier mâché sculptures they'd made for Mrs Dutard, flimsy and prone to disaster.

'What are we going to do, Mol?' she asked shakily. 'They'll see us. Freddie is going to kill us!'

Ray stopped at the hole in the hedgerow and lobbed his stick away into the grass. 'Of course they would see you once they got close enough,' he said. 'Or did she have a plan? She sounds like Chloe in my class. Chloe always has a plan. I bet your sister had a plan.'

Nancy held the thicket back with her elbow so Ray could scramble through into the next field.

'Sort of.'

'Nance, I've got a plan. When he comes up here after us, we can throw our shoes at him.'

'Then what? We only have four shoes, Mol!'

'I know! We'll tell him we're going to pee on him.'

'You can't do that, Molly, we will really be in for it!'

'I'm only going to say that we'll pee on him, Nance. He'll

believe me now too. That bike was completely underwater, just like I warned him.'

Molly ruptured with laughter then. And it jumped completely unexpectedly down a branch from her to Nancy. Nancy held on tighter with her arms in case the giggling made her fingers forget. The others were coming, cutting across the field now.

Molly was turning clusters of fresh pale green leaves over in her hand.

'What are you looking for, Mol?'

'Just a couple of wishes. In case I run out of pee.'

'But they won't grow for ages yet!'

The tiny sycamore helicopters wouldn't appear until the flowers had died back, Molly knew that. They couldn't send a single decent wish spinning through the air until the summer holidays at least.

'I know what I'd wish for right now,' said Nancy, their fate sprinting towards them across the field. 'I'd wish you'd never thrown Freddie's bike in the duckpond.'

Molly groaned and ducked for another look across the meadow.

'You know what I'd wish for, Nance?' she said, pulling off her pump. 'I'd wish you weren't always such a wimp.'

Ray kicked a stone into the grass.

'I don't think that boy would have cared very much about your sister throwing her drink down at him. Not if he was already soaking wet from getting his bike out of the pond.'

They made it out onto Mountford Road. Nancy had held back the peeing part.

'Maybe. But he didn't want to tangle with Molly any more anyway. She was a good shot with a shoe.'

'Did they say anything else mean about your dad?' asked Ray.

Nancy shrugged. 'Not in front of us. What about you, did your friend with the mashed-potato brains say anything else unkind to you?'

'Nah. It was ages ago. Before my mum changed her job and I started seeing my grandpa more. My grandpa says that people who say things to make others feel bad probably feel bad about something themselves.'

The grassy verge thinned as the pavement widened. They walked along the street, shooting the breeze like two school friends.

'Your grandpa's a smart chap, Ray.'

'I know,' said Ray, sinking his hands into his pockets. 'My grandpa knows a lot of stuff. My grandpa says your sister is in Heaven now.'

Nancy resisted the urge to look over her shoulder at him. What did little boys know about Heaven? It wasn't her place to get into the specifics of *nowhere and everywhere* with someone else's child. Not that she had any idea what those specifics were.

'I hope so, Ray.'

He scratched his nose and began dodging the cracks in the pavement as he walked. 'Maybe she knows my dad now. He's been up there a while.'

Chapter 16

'We'll only stay for an hour, Nance,' said Annabel. That made three times so far, each sounding less convincing than the last. 'And it makes a nice change from cooking and TV, doesn't it? Not that I've been doing much cooking!'

Nancy idly jabbed her straw into the ice inside her tumbler and took in the soft amber glow of Whittacker's cavernous barn, the roof space and rafters lit up by hundreds of light bulbs strung in great glowing laces for Beth and Stuart's anniversary party. They dripped star-like above a crowd of faces Nancy could pick only the occasional familiarity from.

'Well it beats peeling veg,' Nancy said amiably over the music. Or watching any more reruns. There was every chance boredom would kill her before her enlarged heart valve could. Perhaps sensing this over the course of the week, Annabel had reluctantly relinquished some household duties into Nancy's semi-capable hands. The sum total of productivity this last seven days had been a daring maiden voyage into shortcrust pastry while Annabel had popped out to her Gardeners' Guild club. And every other club. 'I'd have thought you'd already interacted with enough humans this week, Mum. Knit & Knatter, flower-arranging . . . I'm starting to wonder if you're a closet party animal.'

'Me? Party animal? I don't think so, Nance. I'm just trying to, you know . . . keep the cobwebs at bay. Anyway. We won't stay long if you don't want to. We'll just say hello, maybe have a cocktail sausage, and then hop off home for a cup of tea, deal?'

Nancy nodded over her mocktail and tried to loosen the neckline of the blouse she'd borrowed from Molly's drawer.

'Deal. One hour and a cocktail sausage.'

Things would be in full swing now on the rooftop at Deep Dish, cold beers and sunset over the city. Barbies two weekends on the trot. Kicking back and letting the ideas percolate. Some of their best campaigns had been born on that rooftop.

'It's busy, isn't it?' asked Annabel.

'Yep.' Beth's barn throbbed around them. It was an eclectic gathering, easily more than a hundred people. Plaid shirts, baker boy hats, sparkly evening dresses. Kids darting through the dancers in the middle of the barn, clusters of adults talking animatedly over their drinks.

Annabel stiffly rewrapped her shawl around herself.

'OK there, Mum?'

'Yes thanks, you?'

'Yep, good.'

They both sipped from their glasses, hunkered into their spot between the bar and one of many stacks of hay bales set out around the place for flagging guests. There wasn't any sign of flagging yet, the place was just getting swinging to a live band dressed like trendy Amish folk.

Nancy found herself giving each of the three men at the front of the stage a quick appraisal. Maybe it was their waistcoats all buttoned up neatly, or their sleeves rolled over forearms flexing with the movement of the music, or the deft play of hands over acoustic instruments, but she felt some quiet part of herself begin to stir. She slurped on her straw and tried not to feel like a raging pervert. It had been so long. She tried to pinpoint the last time she'd even been in touching distance of a man's clothing. His buttons, or forearms. Haima had warned her about this. *We're meat-eaters, doll. We're not built to live on salad. Celibacy – intentional or not – is like trying to live on salad. Fine as a side, but a woman cannot survive on lettuce alone. We need the bacon sarnies too.*

Nancy cleared her throat and took another sip from her drink while Annabel fidgeted with the turquoise earrings they'd picked to match the embroidery on her dress. She looked really lovely tonight. Attractive. Was it possible that Annabel still thought about bacon sandwiches, or was that it now? Salad only from here on in? She'd tried to swap the earrings for *something less look-at-me, Nancy*. But they made her neck look slender and had been non-negotiable, or Nancy was going to wear her trainers instead of Molly's kitten heels if everyone was choosing their own outfits tonight. Nancy gave the kitten heels another look, down there on her feet. Brand new, never been worn. Too nice to be left in a box in a wardrobe.

183

Someone nudged her on their way to the cocktail bar. Nancy smiled and shuffled automatically out of the way.

'Mum, leave your earring alone or you'll pull it out and we'll never find it in here. It will literally be like looking for a needle in a haystack.' Annabel smiled and did what she was told. Nancy leant in so she could be heard over the laughter at the bar behind them. 'You look lovely, Mum. Just relax. We're enjoying the change of scene, remember?'

Molly lived for this. The noise and the lights and the people. She wouldn't have been holed up in the corner like they were now, she'd have been on the dance floor, kitten heels slung off somewhere into the periphery, elbows and hips letting it all go wild. Nancy stole another look at her mum and wondered how much of Molly might be in there. It must've taken a momentous push for someone like Annabel to get out there and join her clubs. To try new things, meet new people. Meeting new people was like climbing trees. Nancy remembered how much she used to like both. She remembered how easy it used to feel after the first uncertain steps, how the footholds began to open themselves up to you. And then suddenly there you were, shaky-legged but with a stomach full of exhilaration and a changed outlook over everything before you. Horizons shifted and expanded if you picked the right tree. If you picked the right people. But then it had all changed and her survival instincts seemed to grow exponentially with the years. The fear of the fall if you picked wrong.

Annabel circled her glass with her drinking straw then got back to surveying the room with the same polite smile she'd worn since they'd arrived. A smile worn like armour. A smile that suddenly widened.

'Look, Nancy . . . At the back, on the piano! Goodness, he's quite nifty, isn't he?'

Nancy peered over the top of her bramble fizz at a fourth band member, the only one not donning Amish chic or interesting facial hair. Clarence was in jeans and plain shirt instead, clean-shaven, hunkered down and utterly focused on the sheet music while his hands bashed away at the keys.

'Yeah, he is.'

He didn't look nearly as stiff when he was playing for his own band. He was looser with a guitar, his weapon of choice on most of their YouTube videos. The warm flush of embarrassment crept up Nancy's neck. She looked down into her glass, as if there were people in this room who might possibly know how she'd caught the odd glimpse of Clarence playing online over the years, or had memorised the way the water had clung to his skin in the river as they'd tried to retrieve his fishing tin that last summer after college. She'd only been sitting up there on the bank to say her goodbyes to the river before heading off to uni and what had felt like a momentous shift in the cosmos. She'd watched from afar, hadn't expected him to return, not with a chance of Freddie and his mates still hanging around upstream somewhere. They'd thought it hilarious to skim stones across the water, tiny stones, just close enough to scare the fish Clarence was minding his own business trying to catch. It hadn't mattered that Birdie was there, trying to learn. She wasn't like other adults, she didn't count to Freddie. If anything, Birdie had been the cherry on the top, getting her dress wet trying to pick out the bright feathery flecks of Clarence's fish hooks from beneath the water that wouldn't hold still for her, Clarence battling to keep her feet from standing on any of them. Nancy had caught the tail end of Clarence's reasoning, that flies weren't like breadcrumbs, that his mother didn't need to scatter them to bring the bites back after Freddie's stones. But Birdie hadn't listened, opening the tin, sending the lot about her.

Nancy pressed the tip of her finger, still no feeling. She fell into the memory of reaching for something shiny on the riverbed, knee-deep as Clarence came back to the shallows.

'I thought you'd gone home.' Nancy half smiled. Molly was usually around to help the conversation along, the dry jokes, the light bullying of either one of them.

'I didn't want to leave them for anyone to stand on.' He hadn't bothered to roll his trousers up like Nancy had.

'Well I've found two,' she offered. 'How many went into the water?' Freddie was such a moron. But Birdie, Birdie was a mystery.

'Five, at least,' said Clarence. 'She was pretty keen to catch something today.' He wore an expression Nancy couldn't place. Clarence was changing, he looked like a man now, broader through the shoulders, more angled, stuck somewhere between Birdie's little boy and the adult who might go and catch up with the idiots who'd just helped spoil their afternoon. Nancy watched him for a second, the shape of his eyebrows as he searched the riverbed for colour, mouth set firm, his barely moving body. Water trickled down his skin. She turned back to her task. Something glinted, but she hadn't been concentrating. Made a foolish grab. The barb stuck her finger before she'd even reached the promised prettier part.

She yanked her hand away, looked at the imposter sitting in her fingertip, straight through, one side to the other, blood already snaking back down the wet of her hand.

Clarence took her hand before she could say anything. He pulled something from his back pocket. 'Count to three.'

'Huh?' But she saw the pliers and did what he said. 'One . . . two . . .'

Clarence squeezed, flicked his wrist, tugged the barb free. He led Nancy's hand to his ribs, wrapping her bleeding fingertip into his wet T-shirt, and held it there, bandaged for the moment.

'Ow,' said Nancy. A little bit stunned she hadn't fainted already.

'Best not to look at it yet. Think about something else.'

'Like what?'

'Like . . . uni . . . You're going, aren't you?'

Nancy swallowed. 'Yeah. You? You deferred, this'll be your first year too, right?'

Clarence puffed out a long exhale of air. 'Maybe next year.' His brow furrowed, then relaxed again, as if it was his finger that felt like it had a hot skewer in it. He looked at Nancy then. She wanted to look away. To not always feel like her own skin didn't belong to her, on the few occasions they were in touching distance. She wasn't sure exactly what Clarence was. Friend? Sort of brother figure? Brother-in-law one day? It was disorientating. Knowing a person this long, and not really knowing them at all. It wasn't a corner she wanted to find herself in again. She wanted to see the signs her mum hadn't. Lest she fall down any of the same potholes someday.

'You're really going then?' he asked.

'Yep.'

'Three years? Just think of all the new people you'll meet.'

Nancy smiled along, but the thought terrified her. People. Thousands of them. Figuring out which ones would fall away again. Which ones might stick.

'Getting out of Mistleton . . .' he said, nodding to himself. He took a look at her finger. Nancy looked away. 'OK, I guess this is it then.' Clarence was formulating a plan of sorts, for the finger, she suspected. A cauterising of the wound perhaps, with a cigarette lighter or something. 'Ready?'

'Wait, no. What for?'

'Best not to look. Think about something else.'

'Again?' Oh God. Nancy closed her eyes.

'I'll count to three.'

She swallowed. 'You didn't get to three last time.'

'I will. Ready?'

She nodded.

'One . . . two . . .' Clarence pressed his lips to Nancy's. A short kiss, but a kiss. A kiss that held long enough to make her forget the sting in her fingertip. He spoke quietly against her skin. 'Three.'

He looked pensive when she opened her eyes, steadfast. Not how he looked when he called for Mol or waved a shy hello. But serious again. Certain of something. Nancy felt the cool of the river send goosebumps up over her legs, her entire body . . . felt her trouser leg fall into the water . . . Clarence letting go of her sore finger, her still holding it up there, uselessly between them. 'In case you don't come back, Nancy.'

* * *

188

An arm snaked around Nancy's waist and Beth Whittacker's perfectly made-up face appeared inches away.

'You made it!' Beth squealed. 'I can't believe you're actually here! You said you weren't coming! Then your mum said your plans had changed . . .'

She launched in for a kiss and squeezed Nancy so tightly she spilt some of her drink straight down the back of Beth's beautiful dress, which didn't slow Beth down any because she was already going straight in for a cuddle of equal ferocity with Annabel. Nancy grinned wildly as her pre-uni days along the river and memories of bleeding fingers evaporated back to the decade they belonged to.

'I'm so happy to see you both!' Beth said this locking them in a double-armed embrace, more drink sloshing over Nancy's open toes.

'Goodness, it's lovely to see you too, Beth,' managed Annabel. 'Thank you for inviting us to your wonderful party. The flowers are just *beautiful*, aren't they, Nancy? And the sofas and rugs, in a *barn*. So inventive! And, oh, all the lanterns, Beth . . . It's like stepping into a dream.'

Beth's face hardened. 'Annabel, you would *not* have been saying that this afternoon. The caterers were late, we warned them about the postcode and satnavs but would they listen? And then the bloody band tried cancelling on us. With less than *three* hours' notice! The pianist has some sort of bug, but honestly, three hours' notice! Can you believe it?'

Annabel put her hand over her chest. 'Oh no, Beth. I can't believe it. What on earth did you do?'

Nancy leant in so she could hear over the noise of a barnful of people having a hoot.

189

'Well I panicked, obviously. You know me, Annabel. But thank God, Clarence Ludlow has been odd-jobbing for my dad, so Dad, completely sick of me in his ear, drove his John Deere over to where the boys were working this afternoon and asked Clarence to step in. Thank the Lord Birdie made sure he knows his way around a piano. And that he's back in town for a while to look after the house for her, or I tell you now, I'm not sure Stu and I would make it to our eleven-year anniversary. We've argued *all* day!'

Annabel patted Beth's arm. Nancy raised what was left in her glass.

'To Birdie Ludlow. Saver of marriages.'

'Absolutely,' said Beth, grabbing a tumbler of something orange and garnished from the row on the bar. 'To Birdie, poor love. Do any of us know how she's getting on? Clarence doesn't say much. Is she still in the hospital, do you know? Mum says she's a nightmare when they take her in, she's so awful to Clarence. But what's he going to do if she needs to be hospitalised? Sometimes she won't even see him, but it's not Clarence's fault he can't take the brandy in to her. Is it?'

Annabel sighed in the band's direction. 'I'm afraid we don't know much at all. But I think she is still at St Thomas's. I keep meaning to go over to the house, maybe offer Clarence something he can pop in the microwave when he gets in of an evening, but he always was shy about his mother's troubles. He was shy about everything.'

Beth grinned in Nancy's direction. 'Not with everyone, though.'

Nancy smiled and laughed along with the joke she wasn't in on. 'No,' she agreed.

Beth laughed throatily. 'Oh God, seriously?'

Nancy felt caught out by something she didn't know the shape of. She attacked it with another smile. 'Seriously what?'

'All the times Clarence knocked your door. Annabel, you obviously know, you're a mum. You see everything.' Annabel gave a soft non-committal smile. 'The *hours* he hung around the riverbank in the summer fishing on the off chance your daughters might go paddling instead of playing football with the rest of them in the park . . . and then sitting in the Jack, propping up the bar with Dodgy Roger on his weekends whenever Nance here was waitressing, instead of going into town with my brothers. Molly used to despair. But even she couldn't bully Clarence into just *asking*.'

Nancy swallowed. 'Asking what?' She'd never told anyone about the fish-hook incident. Well, she had about the fish hook, but not what had followed. How did you tell a story you didn't know the words to? It had been a silly nothingness, Clarence trying to nudge Molly into action with a bit of healthy competition perhaps. So Nancy had never said anything.

'You! To just go out for a bloody drink sometime like normal people.'

Nancy felt the collar of her blouse too close to her neck again and ran a finger along it.

'Clarence . . .' He was Molly's, mostly. Friend, or whatever it was they had or hadn't been during all those years in each other's pockets, bedrooms, cars. 'I think you mean he and Mol were close.'

'Well duh, of course they were close. He was in love with her sister, like, for ever. And you know what a sucker Mol was for a lost puppy. I guess it was only natural they'd become best friends: they both loved the same things.'

Beth swept her blonde waves over her shoulder and waved at someone across the crowd while Nancy mentally picked through each of her assertions about Clarence, dismantling them one by one. 'Well if I weren't so extremely happily married, Annabel, I for one wouldn't need asking twice if Clarence was hanging around waiting for me to notice him. Just listen to him tickling those ivories.' Beth nudged Annabel with a gentle shoulder. 'Show me a woman who doesn't melt in the middle at a ruggedly handsome fella playing the piano. Am I right?'

Annabel put a finger in the air. 'Now *that* I do know something about. And yes, I think I'd have to agree. My father was a beautiful pianist, when my mother was in the house anyway.'

'And when she wasn't?' Colour rose in Beth's cheeks from whatever was in that orange cocktail.

Annabel pulled at her earring. 'Well . . . when she wasn't home, he, ah, well he left the classical pieces alone and livened things up a little.' Her eyes shone. Nancy wondered if she'd handed her an alcoholic cocktail by mistake. 'He'd play all the crowd favourites from his army days then. The songs my mother thought were *crass*. But I just loved it. Sitting next to him, singing along like a cat on a stool.'

Annabel had shared fond anecdotes of Grandpa James. Not often, but they'd always floated from her when she lifted the bell jar and let them flutter out into the world.

'So you play too, Annabel?' blinked Beth warmly. 'I hope he taught you?'

Annabel seemed to shrink in on herself. 'Oh no. Not really. Children and pianos are noisy things together. Best kept apart, I suppose.'

Her voice had almost disappeared beneath the music, but Nancy knew what she'd said, they'd heard it hundreds of times at Ginny's house. Don't touch the piano.

'One day I might surprise myself, and learn something beyond "Chopsticks",' said Annabel brightly. She knocked back the last of her cocktail and pressed the back of her hand to her mouth. Definitely the wrong drink.

'There's always time,' beamed Beth. She nodded over at Clarence doing his best with the band and then looked back at Nancy. 'There's always time,' she repeated. 'Now then, where's my darling husband? I was rotten to him earlier and he deserves a kiss for putting up with me. Thank you so much for coming, really. It means the world. Molly would've loved tonight, I know she would. Please stay? Have fun! We'll make sure you get home all right if you want to ditch the teetotal stuff, Nance, and get stuck in?' Beth launched in for another hug then. 'Dad's doing a trailer drop-off if you fancy a merry tractor ride home in style later?'

'Thanks, but . . .' Nancy shook her glass over Beth's shoulder. 'I'm on a detox, kind of.'

Beth held her at arm's length and gasped towards Nancy's midriff. 'You're not, are you?'

Nancy laughed. 'Oh no. Definitely not. Just a detox.'

'Oh, well send me the details, would you? You're looking fabulous, Nance. You're clearly doing something I'm not. Better still, we'll get together properly? Soon please. You can share all your clean-living secrets with me then.'

'That sounds wonderful,' chimed Annabel.

Nancy could tell Beth the magic fix right now. *Dodgy heart. No alcohol. Beta blockers. Small meals low in saturated fats.*

'Sure. That would be nice.'

Beth squeezed Annabel's arm and planted another kiss on her cheek, then Nancy's, and disappeared into her sea of guests. They watched her snake through the bodies to her husband, a broad-shouldered Scandinavian-looking chap with one of their children balanced on his hip. He kissed Beth and buried his face in her neck while she brushed something off their son's chin with her thumb. Beth couldn't be right. Molly had thrown her off the scent, that was all. Deflected the gossip. Clarence had loved Molly in *every* way, Nancy was certain of it.

'They do look happy, don't they?' said Annabel.

Nancy stole another look at Beth's blonde unit. They did look happy. It was easy to feel happy for them.

'They do.'

Annabel's smile was back in place. 'I'm just going to pop to the little girls' room. Will you be all right on your own?'

'Sure. Did you want me to get you something to eat? I could join the queue for the hog roast. Or there's the crêpe and ice-cream caravan thingy outside? Or the buffet?' Something to help soak up some of the alcohol Annabel had just knocked back.

'Nance, just *relax*. You're making me nervous. I'll meet you over by the big buffet table in five minutes, OK? Won't be long.'

'Don't forget to wash your hands,' Nancy called after her.

Annabel held a thumb up over her head like a teenager so

Nancy could see it. The alcohol was already doing its work, loosening Annabel's knots. For a fleeting second, Nancy considered just a small quick glass of wine, or something off the bar ready-to-go while her mum was in the bathroom. But the warnings flashed before her with the disco lights. *Medication and alcohol. Blood-pressure drop. Dizziness.* Nope.

Another frenetic melody rose from the stage. Nancy caught a glimpse of Clarence, getting into it now; he knew this one well enough to ignore the sheet music and look over the dance floor instead. She watched him for a few seconds, then caught herself and headed for the buffet.

She wove through several seating areas set up across the barn floor, each mimicking an intimate lounge area with floor lamps and wing-backed chairs, making for the golden helium balloons, four of them calling *G R U B* along the far side of the barn. She joined an informal queue at the end of the first refectory table, picked up two plates and began the shuffle from savoury pastries to antipasti. Annabel loved pâté. Nancy went in with a knife just as another swooshed in from across the buffet.

'En garde!' Nancy pulled her knife away, hovering over the crostini instead. 'Woody? I have not seen you for *donkey's*!'

Her eyes slid from the crusty rolls up to the man grinning at her over the table. Only the pubescent boys at Mistleton Comp had called her and Mol *Woody*. Boys obsessed with all things penile, reminding them daily that their surname was a widely used byword for *erection*. She smiled back, not a clue which pubescent boy this one might've been before the manicured beard and impossibly white teeth had emerged.

'Hello.'

'How long's it been? You look great, are you still in town? Surely not, or I'd know. Just visiting then?'

'Just visiting . . .' She touched a sweet potato cracker thing she didn't want but was already committed to. She put it on Annabel's plate. 'You?' she asked. Still no clue.

'Definitely visiting. God, I couldn't wait to get away from this place. The high street never changes, does it? Remember that tacky little ice cream place? The old Italian guy with the greasy hair? It's still there, limping on. No, I'm just back for this thing. I manage a few interests for Harry Whittacker, you know? Technically we're family now so I'd have been invited anyway. It's hard completely severing ties with the place, right?' He leant in over the table towards her. 'At least we get points for trying though, huh, Woody? Not like these bumpkins.'

They'd loved Mr Scorlucci and his Teddy boy hair. Loved everything about his ice cream parlour, how he'd slip a bubblegum ball into the bottom of their banana sundaes and apologetically say to Annabel in his fantastic Italiano, *Too late-a now, Mrs W!*

The charmer with the Hollywood smile scrutinised a tray of stuffed peppers. He popped one into his mouth. Even perfect teeth couldn't hide the toad lurking within. *Fart-Head.* Freddie had filled out since their sycamore days, almost all of that sleek jet-black hair he used to scowl at them through gone now.

Nancy looked over her shoulder for any promise of a diversion, but Annabel was nowhere.

'So . . . you're related to the Whittackers now?' she asked.

'My eldest sister, Lizzie, married one of Beth's stepbrothers. The big bastard with the crooked nose.'

'Oh. That's nice.' She spooned something from one of the dishes onto Annabel's plate. Hummus.

'Not really, you should see him trying to fold himself into my roadster, makes my eyes water every time. The leather is hand-stitched, not iron-riveted.' Freddie nodded towards the barn doors. 'You probably saw it out there, cheeky little vintage Jag. Burgundy. Beautiful. 1951. I love her. Lizzie says the car's the only girl born before the nineties I'll ever take for a spin.' He laughed at himself, then reached for the crudités. 'I told her I'd stretch to the eighties, but no further.' Nancy watched him, crunching and laughing. Hate was a strong word, but Molly had hated Freddie Blumfield.

'Oh, the napkins are way over there,' she said. She smiled and started to make a break for it.

'I see Ludlow's still trying his hardest. Bit of a tumble from all the hype he was starting to peddle.'

Nancy gave Freddie the eye contact she'd been trying to avoid. He nodded across the crowd towards the stage.

'Peddle? I don't think Clarence has to peddle anything, to be fair. I think maybe any hype was from the people taking note.'

'Or just his mother,' snorted Freddie. 'Maybe she's the one buying all his crap. I mean, listening to that New Age folky junk, being pissed out of your tree probably helps, right?' He chomped into a stalk of celery and watched Clarence with curiosity. 'I don't know how he can even sit at a piano without cringing. Do you remember the nativity? The woman had no shame.'

Nancy pictured Molly slinging Freddie's bike into the stinking sludge and algae. There was a chance she hated Freddie too, but unlike Molly, Nancy wasn't built for battle. All she had to do was slink away and disappear into the crowd. Her shoulders turned but her feet didn't follow.

'Maybe there was more to it than that, Freddie. Birdie's a complicated person.'

'Well whatever there was to it, my dad got it all on video cam. He still gets it out every Christmas: it's as traditional as the King's Speech! Church, turkey dinner, and Loopy Ludlow's Twelve Chunders of Christmas.'

Nancy grabbed a few token spoonfuls of something in a bowl, piling it onto the plates with ratty dollops. There had never been any point trying to talk to Freddie. It was like talking to a stick.

'My mum's hungry,' she said, dolloping her last.

'Hey, Woody, just wanted to say . . .' He stopped chomping. His big loose mouth hung open while he fished something from his tooth with his tongue. 'Bad luck what happened to Mol. I mean, *cancer*. And nothing they could do? Talk about a shitter. Not that you can believe what anyone tells you, it's all about money at the end of the day, right? Big Pharma selling the drugs. Who's going to admit they can cure you for a penny if they make a pound off treating you with the poison? A shitter for sure, great girl like that.'

Nancy watched his mouth as the ignorance flowed out uninterrupted.

Fuck off sat on her tongue. Her mouth opened but the words were never going to come. *Wimp*, Mol would say.

Nancy couldn't even count the times Mol had stood up to bullies, instinctively, without even thinking about it. Freddie rolled on, unchallenged.

'Hit me hard, you know. When I heard. Felt terrible not making the funeral, but a colleague booked a long weekender to Vegas, and you know how it is for us corporates, gotta keep the bosses sweet. Can't always just click our heels and get back to Kansas. I hear you're heading up some big advertising agency now, that true? We should swap numbers.'

At the far end of the banqueting table, Ernest Robinson appeared like a beacon of light in crisp short-sleeved shirt, dickie bow and waistcoat. Nancy felt her whole self lift.

'Bye, Freddie.' She nudged around the bodies between her and Ernie.

'I'll look you up on LinkedIn then!' Freddie called after her. She held her thumb up over her head like her mum had on her way to the loo. Not easy with a loaded paper plate in the same hand. Flipping the bird would've been easier, but she was too wimpy for that too. And anyway, Ernest was watching, face lighting up as she weaved closer. The shape his eyebrows made triggered something warm and light inside her chest, the antidote to Freddie Blumfield's guff.

'Good evening, young lady. You're looking very lovely this evening, if I may say so?'

'You may,' beamed Nancy, rocking back on her kitten heels. 'You're looking pretty dapper yourself, Ernie, that's a smashing dickie bow.'

Ernest held his face up so she could get a good look at the tie. The underside of his chin was peppered with small red flecks where he'd shaved himself too enthusiastically. He was an enthusiastic kind of guy. Molly would've liked him immensely.

'We both made it onto the guest list then! Nice to be popular with the upper crust.'

'Are you kidding, Ernie? I think they've invited every commoner in the phone book.'

'Probably. I shouldn't feel too honoured then. Are you enjoying yourself, though?' He scanned the crowd. 'Here . . . by yourself?'

Nancy grinned. 'No. I'm with my mum actually. She'll be here in a second. And yes thank you, it's a great party, isn't it?' And it was. She didn't need to be into parties to see how much effort Beth had put into making it so lovely.

'You can't beat proper music. Fiddles and drums. Gets the old blood pumping!' But the live music in the background was dying back, changing to something mainstream over the speakers. A hand touched Nancy's elbow.

'There you are, Mum. I thought you'd fallen in.'

Annabel's cheeks flushed. 'Hello, Mr Robinson.'

Ernie put his plate on the hay bales behind him and stood up straight. 'Please, Annabel. Call me Ernie. I insist.'

Nancy held a plate out for her mum. Annabel stared down at it.

'Oh, lovely. A plateful of . . . sauerkraut? Oh no, there is something else under there . . . What's this, sweetheart? Hummus . . . one orange cracker . . . and a pound of sauerkraut. Thanks.'

Nancy looked at the two plates she'd sloppily loaded while Freddie had yabbered on.

'A woman after my own heart, Annabel. I do love

200

sauerkraut. Mind you, I very much enjoy pickled cabbage too. Well, any cabbage really. You can't beat colcannon, that's for sure. Especially with a beautiful piece of braised steak. I grow my own, in the allotment. The cabbage, I mean. Not the braised steak. For that I usually take myself off to the carvery at Beckitt's, as you know. But not this weekend, mind, our Ray's staying home with his mum this weekend.'

Nancy let her elbow softly graze her mum's. 'How is Ray, Ernie? I haven't seen him all week.'

She'd found herself looking out for Ray after *Countdown* when the other school kids got off the bus, hoping to see him walking along with them and not left behind like last weekend's game of hide-and-seek.

'No, well his mum's had a better shift pattern this week, so she likes him home when she's there to enjoy him. I miss the lad when he's gone. Miss our Sunday lunches at the carvery too. It's not the same when you're eating alone, is it?'

Nancy smiled but wasn't sure if Ernie was talking to her or Annabel. Annabel nibbled at the sweet potato cracker, soggy surely from the sauerkraut. Ernie ran a finger around the neck of his shirt.

'You should come over to ours, Ernie. Tomorrow. For Sunday lunch.' Annabel snapped her head around. 'We were saying just the other day how it's hard cooking a nice meal for just one or two, weren't we, Mum? Scaling down. You've got that big joint in the fridge. I'll cook. Ernie could bring one of his cabbages.'

'Nancy, you can't just go putting people on the spot like that. Mr Robinson might have plans, and you're not supposed to be eating red meat, you said, and—'

'I'll cook chicken too. I've been practising. Pastry yesterday. You can rustle up one of your famous pear tarts. Do you like pear, Ernie?'

'Oh, well, er, yes . . . yes I do, as it happens. Very much.'

'Super,' smiled Nancy. Annabel pinched her hip but she ignored her. 'Shall we say one o'clock?' Another pinch, harder this time.

Ernie put his hand over his heart. 'I would like that very much. If you're sure I'd be no trouble?'

Nancy looked at Annabel. Maybe it was trouble they needed. There had never been a deficit when Mol was around.

'Mum?'

Annabel was on to her earring again. 'No. No trouble. We'd be happy to have you. Ernest.'

Ernie beamed in Nancy's direction. 'Well there's an invitation I feel truly honoured to receive. Thank you, ladies.'

'Would you excuse us, Ernest. Nancy could you just show me where you found us those last glasses of punch, please, darling?'

Annabel waited until they were out of earshot of the buffet table before she started reeling off all the reasons they didn't know Ernie well enough to invite him for lunch. Nancy followed her through the party guests, hearing the tail end of sentences over Annabel's shoulder.

'And another thing, Nancy, people talk. They make assumptions about single men and single women. It shouldn't be that way, but it is!'

'We'll sneak him in round the back.'

'Ha-di-ha,' said Annabel. 'All right for you to joke, you'll be gone again soon. And I'll be left with the rumour mill. And a neighbour bringing me cabbages every Sunday! I don't even *like* cabbage that much.'

But Nancy was only half listening. Over on the stage, the band were just settling back down after their interval. Someone struck up a guitar. A few creaks of a bow drawn solemnly across a violin, the singer readying himself at the mic, and in the far corner from behind his piano, Clarence Ludlow looking back across the crowd to Nancy.

Chapter 17

Annabel rooted around in her handbag. 'Nance, did I give you my keys?'

Nancy took in a lungful of autumn night-time air, spilling like cold ink into her body.

'Nope? You put them in your bag.'

The darkness always hung heavier in the countryside. The city was eternally lit, but even Beth's richly illuminated party and torchlit pathways weren't enough to chase the night back outside the barns.

'I know, I know,' huffed Annabel. The air smelt sweet and charred, like the bonfire nights they used to spend sitting on Saxon's Hill watching the fireworks exploding over town, crackles of light reflecting in the river below. 'They're not in here, I must've dropped them inside, Nance. I'll have to go back.'

They'd already stayed longer than planned. But not long enough for a free ride home on Whittacker's trailer drop.

'Mum, they could be anywhere. Do you have a spare?

We can walk anyway. I think the first mocktail I gave you might've been alcoholic, maybe you shouldn't drive anyway?'

'No, but you can. It was definitely alcoholic. I had another after managing to go a whole song avoiding being trodden on by twinkletoes.'

Nancy smiled. 'Yes, it was getting a bit *Dirty Dancing* for a while there. Ernie can move, can't he?'

'It was a ruddy Horn Dance demo, Nancy. And not a thing *horny* about it.' Nancy grinned into the darkness. 'And the spare truck key's at the house, which we can't get into without the rest of my keys!'

'Oh.' They would have to do a Molly then. 'We can push the bin underneath the utility window.'

Annabel looked up at the stars. 'I need my keys. There are key rings and . . .' She trailed off. She didn't need to explain the worn, half-broken charms from Molly's old car keys, their hopeless irreplaceability.

'I'll text Beth, ask her to keep an eye out for them when they clean up. Someone will pick them up. No one's going to carjack our truck, are they? We'll sort it tomorrow. Come on, it's not far. And it's a nice night, we can walk it in twenty minutes, there's a torch on my phone.'

'We can call a taxi?'

'Or we could ask Ernie to run us back. That's his Volvo over there, isn't it? I'll go in the back, you two can sit up front, run through tomorrow lunch's seating arrangements?'

She shouldn't tease, but it was hard to keep away from it. Ernest Robinson had something that drew Nancy in, a campfire she could warm her hands on.

Annabel stalked towards the barn, earrings defiantly twinkling and swaying. 'No, I'll just find the blasted keys.'

Nancy called across the parked cars. 'Mum?' If Annabel wanted to warm her hands, she would hide them in her pockets, same as always. 'I'll just wait here then, shall I?' But her mum was already shoulders down in silent purposefulness.

Nancy walked around in a lazy circle, waiting. She dodged a pile of something pebble-like, and dubiously ovine. A little way ahead, a giggly couple were edging towards the beautiful ruddy-coloured vintage sports car sitting in the paddock with its roof down. They saw Nancy watching them.

'Just having a sneaky peek at how the other half drive,' smiled the woman over her cigarette. A grey plume billowed from her mouth. 'Is it yours?'

'Sadly not,' smiled Nancy.

She spotted the Jaguar on the bonnet, the cream leather interior and mirror polish on all those wheel spokes. Freddie had always enjoyed shiny spokes. His BMX had been the same. They were probably what had first caught Mol's magpie eyes when she'd been looking around the park for something of his to desecrate. Now he had four beautifully spoked wheels to bluster around being Freddie Blumfield with.

The couple put out their cigarettes. The woman smiled a goodnight as her partner took his phone out for a quick selfie with Freddie's car. Then they walked back to the barn, his arm draped around her shoulders, her hand over his hip, easy in each other's rhythm. Nancy turned back to the car, let her eyes run over the arch of its front wings. Freddie's beautiful trophy, pulling in the admirers. Second glances. Pats on the back. No wonder he looked so pleased, way up there above the little people with their regular cars and regular teeth. Freddie had always sneered down on people not like him. People whose fathers hadn't stayed, or whose mothers' crises had made for hours of comedy playback. Now he looked down on the people who'd never quite made it as far away from Mistleton as he liked to think he had.

A wave of shame washed over Nancy. Freddie had smelt it on her: another corporate, too big for the town that had raised them. Destined for better. Molly had poked fun at it, Nancy's *big rush* to get ahead, when there were so many roses to stop and smell along the way. But Nancy had known better. Live hand to mouth like Molly? Coasting from one week's wage to the next weekend's drinks with her mates? Oh no. Nancy wanted more, her own house, her own ISAs. She didn't want to be stuck when her husband eventually left her, didn't want to not have a healthy pot to fall back on, a contingency. She wanted safety nets, everywhere. Roses hadn't come into it, they'd come later. And then Molly had gone and blown that thinking clean out of the water, Molly had delivered the most brutal lesson of all. That not everything could be safety-netted. That *later* wasn't always going to be there.

The atlas had been an apology. A promise. A lesson learnt. They would follow it, together, Nancy would enjoy the ride, Molly would see the change she'd fostered. When she was better.

Freddie's words continued to uncurl themselves in Nancy's head. *Talk about a shitter.* As if what had happened to Molly had all been just a bit unfortunate. Nancy kicked at a mound of sheep crap. Another mistake. She stared at it, stuck there on the toe of Molly's pretty shoe. *Shit happens, Nance*, Mol had said after the first scan results. Shit happens. But it only happened to the best ones. The generous ones. The gentle-hearted, funny, beautiful, brave ones. The unforgettable ones. Freddie couldn't possibly fathom what he was talking about. *Talk about a shitter.* Like sarcoma was a missed flight. Or a bike in a pond. Something small happening to a small person. Not a person who had been big enough to fight back since she was eight years old.

Nancy pulled her phone out and shone the torchlight onto her feet, checking she'd done her best for Molly's shoe. The stars piercing all that darkness above made her feel small and insignificant. Freddie's flashy car didn't, though. Nancy snapped a picture and sent a message into the ether.

Any ideas? It's too big for the duckpond xx

Annabel emerged from the barn and stalked across the paddock. She swatted the air over her head.

'No keys, and no taxis until at least eleven,' she said breathily.

'We can walk,' repeated Nancy.

'What if it's too much for you?'

Nancy knew this landscape by heart. 'We'll be fine. I'll be fine. Will *you* be fine?'

'I'll be fine if we can get going before Ernest comes out here and tries to rescue us.' There was an edge to Annabel's voice. 'Sorry, love. I'm just annoyed at myself. For the keys. Let's go.' She started walking, then stopped abruptly. 'Are you coming?'

Nancy nodded towards the trees. Thick shadows beyond. 'It's this way, Ma. We're off-roading.'

Annabel hesitated. 'Shouldn't we follow the lane to the stile?'

'Nope. This way is quicker, just keep to the verge and watch the badger holes.'

Annabel followed. As they left the glow of Beth's garden torches, her arm found its way through Nancy's.

'Ruddy hell. Whose idea was this?'

'Partying in the middle of nowhere and losing the car keys? Yours, I think.'

'Yes, well . . .' Annabel sighed to herself. 'It wasn't my idea to invite old smiley-moustache around for lunch. Was it?'

The moon peeped through the trees overhead. The branched pendant light over Nancy's bed back in the apartment was a good impersonation, but nothing like the real thing. Some things Mistleton did do better.

'Ernie seems a nice chap, Mum. Don't you get the same feeling from him?' Nancy hated the thought of her mum turning down Ernie's offer of home-grown lettuce leaves one day, shutting him down the way Nancy had shut down Dr Pete.

They listened to the sounds of their feet over the track until Annabel finally answered.

'I get the *feeling* from him that he probably thinks there's a desperate old woman living next door who needs a man's company. And I don't, actually. Even when you're not here. I've managed this long.' She exhaled heavily. 'It's the only reason your sister bought me the blasted iPad, you know, to go *man*-shopping on dating apps. I much prefer Pinterest, I can tell you.'

Nancy thought about going home to the city, which she

would, eventually, leaving Annabel to navigate solo again. Before long, Nancy would be in her apartment, avoiding conversations with Pete next door, and Annabel would be avoiding Ernest.

'Can I ask you something, Mum?'

'Is it about Pinterest?'

'No. Sorry.' Annabel sighed again. Nancy took it as a green light. 'Why does Ernie make you . . . uncomfortable?'

'He doesn't.'

'He is kind, I think. And polite. And forgiving . . . of dogs anyway.'

'Yes, Nancy. He comes across as all of those things. But I'm just concerned . . . I'm just mindful that he . . . that he might . . .'

'Shimmy up the drainpipe and murder you in your sleep?'

'Don't be silly. They're made of plastic, not industrial steel. Have you seen the size of that man's shoes?'

'I have. He's a big-footed sort of chap.'

Annabel squeezed Nancy's arm where they'd linked. 'Yes, well, there is a Sasquatch-like quality to him, I suppose. His dancing was quite abominable.'

'I think you're mixing your monsters.'

'Oh, I know he's no monster. Of course he isn't. More like Yogi Bear.'

'Maybe you're underestimating him. Ernie's a big chap who bumbles around a bit, but you haven't seen him get up onto his shed roof when he needs to. The man can shimmy.'

Nancy grinned, but Annabel was watching her step in quiet contemplation. It wasn't fair to push in too much on her walls, but where was the sense keeping Ernie stuck outside them if there was even a small chance of something like friendship growing between the cracks?

'Big characters can be intimidating, I totally get that, Mum. But they can make for good friends too.'

Annabel halted on the track. Nancy felt her arm break free.

'I just don't want him getting ideas, Nancy. I've lived how I've lived for a long time. I'm not looking to complicate things now. I just . . .'

As the silence grew, Nancy regretted saying anything to Ernie. *Stupid*. Annabel didn't need curveballs, even lovely Ernie-shaped curveballs. Who was to say the loveliness even counted? Nancy's dad must've seemed lovely to Annabel once, and what had that counted for in the end?

Annabel hid herself inside her shawl and looked suddenly bereft.

'I don't even know if I have enough pears left on the tree to make a decent tart. And it isn't like you can just fill the gaps with apple: an apple is an apple. And there is nothing *wrong* with that. But an apple will *never* taste like a *pear*.'

She shook her head and started walking again. Nancy fell silently in line. Ernest had been so grateful, the thought of taking back the invitation was on a par with having to listen to Freddie Blumfield blather around a mouthful of crudités again.

'It's just lunch, Mum,' said Nancy softly. 'I should've asked, sorry. I'll do the work, nothing fancy . . . Forget the pear tart, I was just teasing. I'll run out and get a shop-bought crumble in the morning, no frills. Just a hot dinner, an hour's conversation about, I don't know, current events and home-grown veg, and a *see you around*. No big deal. You don't even have to be there. Go out if you prefer, I'll make something up.'

Annabel slowed. 'No, of course I'll be there, Nancy. He may be a terrible dancer but that's no reason to bruise his feelings.'

'Really?' smiled Nancy.

'Really. But no frills.'

'No frills, promise.'

'Righty-ho.' Annabel walked ahead without her. 'Then you won't think it's a big deal that I've invited Clarence too.'

Nancy's ankle went out from under her. She almost lost her footing completely, a sharp pain seared through her calf.

'*Clarence?* Clarence Ludlow?'

'Unless you know any other Clarences?' Which of course she did not. Bar Clarence the angel from *It's a Wonderful Life*, who they would all ring their bells for each Christmastime, and who was absolutely no help to Nancy now.

'When have you even *spoken* to him?'

'Nancy, you said yourself, it's no big deal. I asked him when he was helping me look for my keys. Clarence used the microphone to ask everyone in the barn to have a look around. Wasn't that thoughtful? Anyway, lunch is the least we should be offering, given his poor mother. *And* we know him an awful lot better than Ernest Robinson, who won't get the wrong idea now that he's one of a couple of neighbours invited around for a nice neighbourly lunch. So you'd better make it a big crumble from the shop. OK?'

A horrible little bit of grit had worked its way into Nancy's shoe, sharp and spiteful.

212

'But . . . I don't even know Clarence that well nowadays. We have completely different lives, what will we even talk about?'

'I hear current affairs and home-grown veg are hot topics.'

Nancy ignored her and hopped along the lane, trying to loosen the grit out as she walked.

'Did he say yes? I mean, confirmed?'

'Of course he said yes. Birdie's been in hospital for weeks. The boy's hungry.'

Nancy felt the prickle of panic. Clarence at the dinner table. Casually mentioning what he saw on the furlong. Annabel knowing that she'd been abandoned, again.

'But Clarence and I—'

'It's *just lunch*, Nancy. We'll cope.'

There was no rush to link arms now. After a few long minutes traipsing along the track, Nancy mentally berating herself for ever opening her big mouth, it was Annabel who eventually reached across the expanse and broke the silence.

'Clarence was always such a nice, quiet boy. Quiet like you. Molly thought you'd make a good pair. I suppose some folks thought *they* were a pair, with all the time they spent together. But I think she loved Clarence the same way she loved Fig. Which could only have been a wonderful thing for him.'

Nancy looked up at a million stars just beyond the black silhouettes of branches above them. Molly had liked lots of boys, but Clarence, it was turning out, she'd liked for different reasons. Reasons Nancy understood but had been forever behind the curve on.

'They used to bootleg, you know, Mum. Mol and Clarence.

On the canal bridge by the Jack. Clarence would skim Birdie's rum stocks and Mol—'

'Is that what the cola multipack phase was about? I did wonder.' They walked on through the dark.

'Ivy Spink caught them poaching her business from the beer garden. She was always soft for us kids, though.'

'Thank goodness. I don't think either of us believes that Clarence was the ringleader in that enterprise, do we?'

Nancy laughed quietly. 'Nope.'

'Clarence was like her shadow. I never worried about her when he was there.'

Nancy thought of him on the furlong. *Then why are you here?* Clarence had followed her all the way home that night, keeping pace behind her through the snow and dark until she'd reached the house, the front door, Annabel waiting on the stairs.

The darkness suddenly felt alien. Suffocating. Something to reach the other side of.

'It's getting cold, Mum. Can we walk a little faster?' Nancy felt her body straining to break free of her. She imagined breaking into a run, feeling the first resistance, then the stride, the reassuring euphoric repetition. All the circuits around Chortley Park had brought down her time, pushed her tolerance. Out she'd gone, even in the snow. *Especially* in the snow, when it had come to test her. Run after run, turning twenty-one minutes back into eleven.

Annabel's voice speared the darkness. 'I was glad he came back to say his goodbyes to her.'

Nancy had been walking too fast, Annabel a little way behind her, trying to keep up. Nancy stood still. Her body felt fuzzy, the possibility of being sick suddenly there at the edges.

'Did you see him? At the service? Clarence?' asked Annabel.

'No . . . only at the house.' Politely listening to other people he didn't know talking over their cigarettes and chicken drumsticks. Much of the conversation at the house had centred on the merits of the buffet. Normal observations about normal things, on the most abnormal of days.

'Me neither,' said Annabel. 'The service was a haze. I can't remember seeing a single soul there, but of course, they were. So many were.'

At the church, hundreds of faces had all blurred into one solemn mass Nancy had avoided looking directly at. It wasn't somewhere she wanted to go back to, but now Annabel was talking about it. Out loud.

'I thought Clarence had been in town already, from the New Year, but he'd driven all the way down from Gateshead the night before.'

'Newcastle?'

'I know. Miles away. He'd been playing up there. A radio station, I think.'

An owl hooted in the distance. Nancy swallowed. 'He's probably used to the travelling. Bands are always on the road, aren't they?' But she felt a gladness that Clarence had made the journey for Mol.

'He had to drive back up to Edinburgh the following day. But he still came for her.' The wobble in Annabel's voice tugged at Nancy, displacing that thing inside her body that wouldn't stay quiet. Annabel's hand found its way through the dark and touched Nancy's elbow, bringing them to another stop.

'People find a way, don't they, sweetheart? Even on two feet in the snow, if they have to.'

Annabel still believed it. She still believed in her elder daughter. Nancy wanted to throw up.

'It's not far now, Mum. We're nearly at Kenning's smallholding.'

'Oh. Right.'

Then they could join the road soon and worry less about rolling their ankles.

As soon as Nancy thought it, Annabel wobbled in the dark. She almost righted herself, then lost her footing again and stumbled forward. Nancy sent her arm out instinctively, half catching her.

'Ruddy heck,' yipped Annabel. 'Badgers, you say? I nearly fell all the way down that one!'

'Be careful,' snapped Nancy. 'You'll hurt yourself.'

Annabel wobbled again beside her. 'Whoops-a-daisy!'

Nancy's heart skipped a beat. 'We'll meet the road soon. Nearly there.'

'Don't worry about me, Nance. If I fall on my backside, so be it.'

'Don't worry about you?' said Nancy quietly. 'Okey-doke.' Like it was that simple.

'I mean it, you shouldn't. You should worry about yourself. Channel your energy into getting back on your feet.'

'OK.'

'No, I *mean it*, Nancy.'

'So do I! Look! I am on my feet, Mum. I'm fine, I just . . . stumbled. Like you in that badger hole just now.' Her voice had climbed too far.

'Sweetheart, you had a heart attack.'

'Minor. People have them all the time.' Except it wasn't a heart attack exactly. It was something else she wasn't sure how to explain. 'Everything will be fine, Mum. Look at me now! Night-walking! Strong as an ox!'

Annabel hesitated. 'That's just your body, though, love. Did the consultant say anything about maybe . . . I don't know . . . talking to someone? About anything that might be . . . putting extra pressure on you? Work or—'

'I do not need a shrink, Mum. I'm absolutely fine.'

'I know! I know. It's just . . . we've never been great talkers, have we? Apart from your sister, obviously. But everyone else . . . They talk about healthy bodies, don't they? But sometimes we forget to take better care of the rest of us. Minds are not always kind things. They play tricks on you. Make life tougher . . . especially for your heart.'

Something wet and leafy touched Nancy's head. She reached up to swat it away.

'So you do think I need a therapist?'

'No. No, of course not. Not necessarily.'

'Well, which is it? Of course not, or not necessarily?'

'I'm just worried about you, Nancy. I'm your mum, I worry about you every day.'

'Well I'm worried about you too, Mum, actually. Sometimes I am really, *really* worried.' There. There it was.

'About *me*? Why?'

'*Why*? Ha!' The tone of Nancy's voice said it was too late now. 'Where do I start!' She stood stock still and let the thoughts stampede haphazardly through her head. Thoughts she hadn't known what to do with, which box to stuff them into. 'You sneak around at night and sleep in Molly's bed, Mum. Don't you think that *you* might benefit from a little chat with someone? I mean, is *that* healthy? That you need to do that? That her room is still the same after nearly *two* years?' Her pulse had quickened to the speed of her voice. There was a mark somewhere that she'd just felt herself sail straight over the top of, but she couldn't stop herself, couldn't turn herself mid-air and un-jump.

Annabel turned to face her head-on, a barricade in the road. Nancy tried to swallow, but her mouth was suddenly dry. Her mum's eyes sparkled in the darkness. An immediate stab of guilt thrust straight through Nancy's middle. She was behaving like a child. Annabel had exposed a weakness, and in response, in retaliation, Nancy had gone and ripped open another wound.

'I have tried,' said Annabel quietly, 'to tackle some of it. But every time I go to move her clothes or sort through her make-up, I just think it's better left there for a while . . . until I know where she'd want me to put it all.' Her voice was small, a match flame fighting back the night. 'How can I get rid of her things before we've even scattered her ashes? I want to scatter her, but I can't do it without you. But you're not ready, are you, Nance?'

Nancy's heart was in her mouth again. She should have it surgically removed and save everyone the hassle. Annabel cleared her throat.

'I should sort through her things, I know that. I do wash everything in her wardrobe every so often to freshen it through, ready to send on. Honestly I do. They're always making charity collections. But I see the other bags left out there on the pavement, waiting for the collection van, and I think . . . what if it rains? On her things? Or a cat pees over them? So I wait for the van to come, so that I'm ready to hand the bags over fresh from the house. But then sometimes they don't look very friendly, or they're rough-handed, so I think *maybe next time* and it all goes back on the hangers again. And I feel better, Nance. Because they're the things she chose, they're Molly's things. And they're safe, because I can't just leave them out there in a heap.'

They should've got a taxi. They'd have been home by now, drinking tea and talking to the dog.

'I don't want that either, Mum.' And it was the truth. It was all safe where it was, Mol's belongings perfectly preserved in a room Nancy didn't ever have to go into if she didn't want to, Annabel the devoted caretaker of Molly's earthly footprint. And what was Nancy's role? A visitor to the museum, complaining about the displays. She'd left it all for Annabel to take care of, alone. Just as she'd stood in the snow, eleven minutes away, leaving Annabel to face Molly's final hours on her own, in a house with no heartbeat.

'I'm sorry, Mum. I'm out of order. I'm sorry. I just . . . find it all easier if I don't look at it.'

Annabel looked at her feet. 'And I find it easier if I do. And I'm sorry too, if that upsets you. I don't want to make it any harder for you to be here.'

'It's not hard for me to be here.'

'I know that it is. So . . . while you're home, I won't go in there.'

'No. No, no, you do not need to do that. Just ignore

everything I've said, don't even listen to me. I talk utter rubbish, all the time. Like, *all* the time.'

But Annabel wasn't listening. She stiffened, then moved suddenly closer to Nancy, focused.

'What? What's the matter?' Nancy felt the prickle of adrenalin. This was how the Fear used to get them down these lanes at night, teenage giggles turning into hyper-alert goosebumps. 'Mum?'

'Sorry. Go on.' But Annabel shuddered, then swatted her hair, sending Nancy's heartbeat up a notch.

'What is it? You're making me jumpy.'

'Sorry, sorry, love. It's nothing.'

'What is?'

'Has it been raining? I keep feeling something wet brushing over my head. Leaves or . . . Cripes, Nance, I hope there aren't any frogs about, they always come out in the damp. I ruddy hate frogs.'

'You do?'

'Always have.'

'Frogs? Like Kermit?'

Annabel huddled closer. 'Don't be fooled. I was walking out of the churchyard once, just closing the gate, when I felt something land on my neck. Tiny thing, a baby, must've scrambled up there waiting for a passing victim. It was on my *skin*.' She shuddered again. 'Just that one, fleeting experience, and scarred for life.'

There was a time Nancy wouldn't even wear gloves. For years after Ginny had sent her back into her dad's factory, she'd rather have frozen fingers than think about those stupid little garments, checking they were still paired, not left anywhere other secrets liked to hide. Just that one fleeting experience, like Annabel said. A glove. A froglet. Almost the same.

'A baby frog, though, Mum? Not even one of those dinner-plate-sized giant toads you see on the TV chowing down on mice and snakes?' Annabel almost heaved. 'A frog phobia? How didn't I know this about you? Did Mol know?'

'Of course not.' Annabel shrugged. 'Mothers are supposed to be strong. Brave. Why would I ever want you girls to know what I was afraid of?'

Bravery was unreliable company. Even for Annabel. Undone by a tiny amphibian, and yet Nancy could clearly remember watching her mother, on her own with two daughters, leave their home and walk straight over to the teenagers tormenting Birdie up the road, standing alone before a group of near-men throwing damsons at someone else's home.

'I guess we're all allowed to be scared of something, Mum.' Annabel smiled. 'The things that shape us, hey?'

She felt her hair again as they trundled on beneath the trees. 'The rotters love the damp. Why do you think I always enlisted you girls to help weed the shady bits?'

Another low branch brushed against Nancy's head. She ran her hand over her own hair where it had snagged, the light of her phone animating the branches above.

'Ugh!'

'What?' Annabel jumped.

'Urgh, Mum, what is that?' Something cold and wet on her hair had stuck itself to the underside of Nancy's wrist.

'What is it, Nance?'

Nancy moved her hand over her head again. Yuck, something had definitely been there, cold and slimy and just under the cuff of her jacket now. She shook her arm to get rid of it.

'You're pulling my leg!' yipped Annabel. 'It's not a frog? Oh my gosh, is it?'

Nancy felt her scalp tickle. 'Oh my God! What *is* that?' She swatted at her hair, the light thrown from her phone through the trees in panicked jerky flashes, everything around them sent into frantic shadow puppetry.

'Is it a spider? Nancy? Stand still! Tell me what to do!'

Nancy shook her head violently, smacking herself with her free hand.

'It's a worm, it's . . . it's some kind of wet worm! It's on my hand! Oh my God, is there another one on my head? Mum! Look with the torch, look with the torch!'

'A *worm*? Do you mean a ruddy leech? Oh Lordy, Nancy, hold still, don't *scream*! Give me the phone! Stand still!'

'*You're* screaming, Mum! Help me!' She felt the cold wet against her cuff again and jerked her arm violently. Her phone clattered to the ground but whatever had been on her skin had come unstuck. *Gone.* She held still and breathed steadily, blood thundering through her ears. *Gross wetness on wrist, gone. Creepy-crawly feeling on head, gone. Relax.*

Annabel picked the phone off the ground and shone it on Nancy's head.

'What just happened?'

'Do you see it? Is there anything there? It was cold and wet.' She wasn't going mad.

'Well . . . I can't *see* anything . . .' Annabel got bravery points for even looking.

'Are you sure? Get closer, Mum. It's not a baby frog, OK? It would've buggered off by now if it was, deafened by the screaming.'

Annabel was deep-breathing. She started to giggle. 'Well, sorry, but I didn't know if it was going to jump on me or not. Where was it first? On your head? Or your hand, did you say?' Nancy held out her arm, Annabel inspecting with the phone torch. 'I don't see anything, Nance.' She swept the flashlight over the floor. 'Is that it? Stuck to your shoe?'

Nancy peered down against her better judgement.

'What is that, Nance?'

'Ew. I don't want to know.' Whatever it was was pale and unmoving now. She'd killed it. She tried shaking it off her toe, but it wouldn't budge. 'It's not another bloody white feather, I know that much.'

Annabel hunkered over with the torch. 'It looks like . . . Is that *cabbage*?'

'What?'

Annabel snorted. 'It's . . . it's ruddy *sauerkraut*, Nance.'

'*Sauerkraut*?'

'Yes, look! How did you get it in your hair? Maybe when you were slopping a great heap of it onto my paper plate? You couldn't have left much behind on the buffet table. By the way, who were you holding your thumb up to? With your plate in the air? I was too far away to see.'

'Freddie Blumfield.' Never far away from someone's mess. One day, Freddie would have his own mess to clear up. Sooner than he might think.

'You know, I think I did see something in your hair, Nance. I almost said, but then Ernest didn't stop for breath and I

223

don't like to interrupt, then you volunteered me for the Horn Dance and, well, I forgot.'

'Oh, well thanks for that, Mum. Three hours that's been stuck to me.'

Annabel was stifling her laughter. 'Not a frog, at least.'

'Because fermented Baltic cabbage is any better.'

'There are worse things, love. Crikey,' Annabel tittered, 'my heart is galloping like Seabiscuit.'

'*Yours* is?'

'Are you all right, love? Do you feel *not* all right? Do you need to sit?'

'No, I need to get bloody home! This is the most ridiculous walk back ever.'

Annabel slipped her arm through Nancy's again. 'Are you sure?'

'Yes, Mum! I had a fright! It's normal! I'm not made of glass.'

Annabel was chuckling again. 'Come on then. Before we're attacked by anything else.'

Nancy closed the crook of her elbow around her mum's. 'Don't snigger, it's not attractive.'

'Sorry.'

'You sound like Molly when you snort, by the way.'

'Do I? Good. That is good.'

'And you should know, you had a clump of cress stuck in your teeth last weekend when we came out of the pottery barn.'

'When?'

'When we were talking to Ernie and Ray.'

'I *didn't*.'

''Fraid so. Not so sniggery now, are you?'

'Cress? In my teeth?'

'Yep. Big old clump.'

'Why didn't you tell me?'

'Ernie . . . doesn't stop for breath, does he? I didn't like to interrupt.'

Annabel tightened the link in their arms and shone the light of Nancy's torch onto the path ahead.

'Touché, kiddo. Touché.'

Chapter 18

She'd been trying to remember how she'd spent the first summer break after her freshers' year. The question had been there in her head when she woke up, sticking fast all through her shower. A mystery she couldn't solidly piece together. All she could place was what she *hadn't* done. She hadn't gone to spend the first weeks of summer scouting marinas with her dad.

Nancy thumbed the soft, perpetually numb tip of her index finger. Had she come back to Mistleton instead that year? The possibility swam away from her. No. Clarence's prediction had been right then. She must've stayed away, at uni. She'd thought the summers spent wiping down sticky bars and ferrying fried beige foods to other adrift students had started after her second year, but it must've been the first, when the alternative had been to come home and explain the last-minute change in plan, a plan Molly had never had any interest in, any faith in. Nancy hadn't needed to see the look, the *Well you already knew Santa doesn't exist* look.

She grabbed her toothbrush, slathered it with toothpaste and felt around the edges of an old disappointment. She'd heard one or two mentions of her father's friend Jane in the months before they'd first spoken, divorcee, one daughter older than Nancy, living at home but only temporarily. Between boyfriends, or jobs, Nancy couldn't remember which. How nice it would be for them to all meet properly when Nancy joined her dad, he'd said, before they set off by themselves to find the next leg of his coastal adventure. They could hang out, he had said, *as adults*! So weird! Molly had passed on his unexpected invitation, but Nancy had been ready to hit it head-on, spending the last weeks of the university term plotting their route along the south-east coast, the best-rated seafood restaurants, what the mooring fees might be in each of the spots their dad might want to drop anchor next.

Something's come up, baby.

When he'd rung, he'd made sure to drive home how much Jane had been looking forward to meeting Nancy, how lucky he'd been meeting a woman who lived so close to the marina, who took such good care of him, gave him a place to stay when it suited, a hot dinner, a soak in a bathtub. What a sod it was that they wouldn't get to try out those stuffed crabs together at the five-star family-run harbourside place Nancy had found, now that he was staying put for a while. But how Nancy should come meet Jane properly, soon. *But not this summer, honey.* Jane wanted a fortnight in Malta instead. And after that? Well, she'd be tied up helping her own daughter get back on her feet, probably. Or making space for some of his things, so Nancy's dad could move them out of storage. Again.

He'd put Jane on the phone, keen for Nancy to hear first-hand just how much this new lady was looking forward to getting to know his daughter. Bond. And between all the right noises that had come down the line – *Hope your course is going well. Your father's told me a lot about you. You mustn't worry about coming all this way, we can organise something closer to Christmas perhaps. Or Easter* – Nancy had heard what her dad didn't seem able to. It was there in the clipped responses. The eagerness to get off the line. The lack of any questions nudging into Nancy's world. *Stay away. We're not interested. I am not your family.*

Molly knew that summer. It would've been written all over her face if Nancy had gone back home to see it. Nancy had kept the faith, and got another lump of coal for it. And maybe swallowing their dad's promises had been childish, and not all that unlike still holding out hope for Father Christmas. But when you believed in a thing that not everyone else did, a lump of coal was not nothing. It was still proof of something. Something that might be better next time round.

Annabel was up to something outside. Nancy carried on brushing her teeth, angling for a better view through the bathroom window. Annabel had pulled rank last night, insisting she'd be much more relaxed about the whole Sunday-lunch situation if she could at least be in control of the cooking. Nancy watched her teetering in baked bean gardening shoes, fishing apples off the last tree furthest from the house. The boughs hung over the back fence, the ripest, brightest fruit always just out of reach. Nancy swilled, rinsed and took another look. The sleeves of Annabel's gypsy blouse billowed in the morning breeze. One of her turn-ups had unturned itself so she looked to have one leg longer than the other as she stood on tiptoes, making calculated grabs for the fruit. If Ernest was watching from his kitchen sink, washing and re-washing, he was getting a real show.

'Clever clogs,' said Nancy quietly, watching as Annabel reached with Fig's plastic ball-flinger to the branches hanging over the meadow, gently cupping the apples she'd otherwise have to go and fetch her stepladders or a willing, limber child for. But Annabel had mastered self-sufficiency. She'd perfected it: a small flick of the wrist and off came the apples one at a time, safely cradled. Just like that.

'That's the crumble sorted then,' said Nancy, dropping her toothbrush back into the pot. Now it was just lunch they had to get through.

Nancy was waiting for the toast to pop when Annabel brought her haul through the back doors into the kitchen.

'Hey.'

'Morning, love.'

Annabel moved to the sink, made a start rinsing the Bramleys. Nancy tried picturing Clarence Ludlow sitting at their kitchen table again, and not be waiting for Molly to fly downstairs and yank him from the house to walk her to school, or go watch a band or grab a beer and burger. He would speak about Molly. Clarence couldn't eat a meal here and leave her out. But how would Nancy keep the conversation light? And nowhere near New Year's Eve. She reeled through a few safer topics. *Beth's party. Ernest's greenhouse. Annabel's fruit trees. Annabel's hobbies. Birdie.*

Ray. No, not Ray. There was more to Ray than Nancy knew what to do with. She'd found herself thinking about him all week, for some reason. Worrying for him. She felt the worry come back to her now. Maybe they could walk Fig, or go for a banana sundae the next time his mum was at work. Ah! *Work*. That was a safe lunchtime topic. Safe as houses. She double-popped the toast, pushing it down again for an extra browning, just as the sinking feeling hit.

'Mum? We don't need to tell anyone today why I'm home. Is that OK?'

Annabel looked over her shoulder, slicing the apples blind. 'Of course.'

'No one needs a miserable conversation-killer, I mean, that's all.'

'You don't need to explain. It's private. You're just having a few weeks off.'

Nancy nodded, relief flooding her system. Clarence must've had enough hospital talk to last him a lifetime. They all had. She noticed the hazy ribbon of thin smoke hanging in the kitchen air seconds before the alarm blared to life in the hall.

'Sod.' She popped the toast, opened the back doors and grabbed Annabel's tea towel to waft the air. She smiled gingerly. 'Probably a good thing you're cooking today.'

Annabel carried on with the apples. Nancy sat down with two blackened squares and scraped butter across them. The first slice shattered as she took a bite.

'Mind your teeth.' But Annabel was being quieter than usual and Nancy felt fully responsible.

'Nifty work with the ball-wanger this morning, Mum.'

She nodded towards the drainer even though Annabel's back was still turned. 'I thought we agreed, shop-bought apple crumble?'

Annabel picked up a cloth and pivoted from the sink with it. She swooped in, running the cloth around the crumbs that had overshot Nancy's plate, then shook them into the sink.

'I can't give them bought apple anything when there are hundreds of perfectly good apples out there in full view. So I'm making a crumble, and a pie too. Crumble can be quite sweet, can't it? Better to have a choice.' The cloth came back in for another sweep.

'Why don't you wait for the crumbs to fall onto the table first, Mum?' said Nancy lightly, but the tension had thickened.

Annabel lobbed the cloth into the sink and turned, bracing her arms behind her. 'Sorry, love.' Her mouth was firm, expressionless. 'Just trying to keep on top of it.'

'One o'clock's still almost . . . *five* hours away.' Nancy risked another bite. The cloth came back in for another circuit. 'Should I just eat this over the sink?' But Annabel didn't hear.

Nancy gave the kitchen a once-over. She could smell it now, the furniture polish and Febreze fighting back the more agreeable scents of slow-roasting meats and morning coffee. Fig's basket was immaculate. Not a clump of red fluff in sight. She leant around the table and peered down at her black jeans, perpetual victim of the ginger shedder. But there wasn't a single stray dog hair stuck to her, yet. No nose prints on the glass doors either. Everything shone.

'What time did you start the great purge?' She hadn't heard her mum get up this morning, no bedroom doors clicking open and closed in the early hours. In fact, she hadn't heard anything all night. The walk back from Beth's party had wiped them both out. Capped off interestingly by Annabel's fear of the police turning up while Nancy had contorted herself through the utility window. She thought of Annabel's eyes darting everywhere, looking for trouble, and smiled behind her toast. Last night's exertions had bought Nancy her first night's rest in a long time. Nine blissful hours of nothingness.

'Not that early. Six maybe.' Annabel set to scrubbing something on one of the Aga lids.

'I thought we said no frills? You look like you're trying to destroy evidence, Mum. And two desserts?' But Annabel just nodded and scrubbed on, her back rocking with the effort.

Nancy gave up on her crusts. 'Mum?' The scrubbing stopped. Annabel lifted her head from the Aga and looked ahead at the tiled splashback. Her shoulders sank. 'If you want to cancel, they'll understand. Sometimes things come up.'

'Answer machine,' said Annabel to the splashback.

A red light flashed at Nancy down the hallway from the phone sitting on the dresser. The thought reinflated itself. Her father had called, he'd shoehorned some time to come visit, when Ernest would be here, of course. She pushed out her chair and walked into the hall.

You have one recently saved message . . .

Ginny's voice filled the hallway.

'Annabel! Out again? Well I hope you're off doing something necessary. And I do hope I'm not disturbing Nancy resting. You should turn the phone to silent before you hop off on your recreations so as not to disturb her. You probably haven't thought of that, so I'll make it quick. My wonderful friend Mrs Smithson has kindly offered me a lift tomorrow on her way to her son Harold's house. They're not far at all from you. Harold's agreed to drop me off, but I shall need someone to pick me up from town, I can't expect him to bring me all the way out to the house. I expect you still haven't got around to notifying the council about those potholes and I don't much want a bill for Harold's car repairs. But I shan't miss the chance to see my convalescing granddaughter, so I'll await your call back, Annabel. If you can fit me into your busy schedule.'

End of saved messages.

Nancy stared at the console while it exhausted its bleeps. Tomorrow. Brilliant.

'I didn't hear the phone,' she said, walking into the kitchen. 'We were at the party.'

'She called last night?'

'Yes.'

'So, *tomorrow* is *today*?'

Annabel pinched the bridge of her nose. '*Tomorrow* is in four hours. I'm supposed to pick her up at twelve. In Tesco's car park.' Like some hideous click and collect.

'But the truck? It's still . . . Shall I call Beth?'

Annabel stared at the garden. 'No. I'll send a taxi for her.' Her voice lowered. 'With any luck, it'll get five flat tyres.'

Fig waddled into the kitchen and nuzzled her nose into Nancy's hand. Nancy rubbed the scruff of her neck, fur slipping reassuringly between her fingers. Ernest, Clarence and Ginny. Fuck.

'It'll be fine,' Nancy declared brightly. 'They'll all

233

entertain each other, you and I can just hide out in the garden or something. With Fig.' Fig wagged her tail at her name. Annabel was deep-breathing over the Aga. 'Mum, it'll be fine. And there we were thinking it might be awkward!' She laughed half-heartedly, then picked up another cloth from the sink and squirted Annabel's Mr Muscle onto it. She gave Annabel's cloth a couple of squirts too.

'We'll be fine. It's just *lunch*.'

Chapter 19

The taxi hadn't gone down well. Nancy could sense her grandmother's disdain from the doorstep, swollen in the back of the cab, an airbag swallowing the space around her. Ginny emerged from the back seat, alert and with purpose, sweeping the residue of public transport from her clothes. Annabel hovered obediently on the kerb. Nancy fixed a smile on her face, in case Annabel needed it, so it was there ready if she glanced back for it.

Ginny was a fan of coats with more buttons than were necessary. She liked having the air of someone in charge, regimental, poised to pull someone or something into line. Annabel paid the driver and helped her mother to the house, where she greeted Nancy with a powdery cheek.

'My darling.'

'Hello, Gran. How are you?'

Ginny handed her bag to Annabel so she could get on with giving Nancy a thorough visual inspection for outward signs of defect. The gloves she held onto, clutched in her hand like a pair of strangled birds. Miraculous to think she'd ever managed to lose one.

'I've been better, my poor darling girl. But I'm not here to talk about me, I'm here to see my granddaughter is all right. With my *very own* eyes.' She wrung the gloves in her hand and looked about her, towards the living room, up the stairs, finally resting her eyes back on Nancy. She swapped her walking stick into the hand with the gloves, freeing the other to cradle Nancy's chin between long, authoritative fingers. 'Your uncle Julian is beside himself, I shall have to report back,' she said, inspecting Nancy's face. She let go then, as abruptly as she'd taken hold. A timer sounded in the kitchen and Annabel seized her chance. *Uncle Jules?* Nancy wanted to say. *Worried?* Uncle Jules only came out of hiding for weddings, funerals and will readings. He was like a pair of dress shoes.

Nancy led her grandmother into the kitchen.

'Well, you picked the right day, we're going to have a lovely lunch, Gran.' She said this to the sounds of Annabel ferociously mashing a pan of carrot and swede. 'Actually, we're expecting guests, so Mum's even broken the good china out, haven't you, Mum?'

Ginny sat herself stiffly at the kitchen table Annabel had attentively laid, first with the big dessert spoons, then without. *I need more spoons for all the serving bowls! Where are all the spoons, Nance? I must have more than this!* But there had only ever been three of them at full capacity, and so Annabel's thinning arsenal of cutlery had never been vigorously tested before battle.

'Crystal,' Ginny observed. 'My, my, what a difference a little effort makes. Did I not give you some of my silver cutlery, though, Annabel?' she asked, lightly touching a bony fingertip to one of the fork tines. She'd had her nails painted at the retirement village salon, a brownish plum colour, like chicken livers. 'Silver looks so much more discerning, don't you agree, Nancy? You have a sharp eye for detail. Perhaps something you've inherited from me?'

Annabel shook a jar of nutmeg over the saucepan and spoke without turning.

'Julian had the silverware. When you moved into Hollyfields.'

'Oh. You can't take everything into sheltered accommodation, can you, Nancy? I'm afraid I was forced to strip back to basics. Julian does have a much more formal house, though. More room. Better suited.'

Nancy smiled at her grandmother. Annabel bashed her saucepan again. There wasn't a drop of alcohol in the house, Nancy didn't think. It was only noon, and she was suddenly preoccupied with thoughts of a nice large glass of full-bodied red. Then another. In the absence of anything to dull the nerves, she got on with making everyone a strong tea while Ginny moved on to the day's *other guests*, surgically extracting what information she could about Ernest and Clarence, until their joint arrival with a jovial clattering of the door knocker. *Rat-tat-a-tat-tat . . . tat-tat*.

Annabel wiped her hands on her apron then shook them in front of her like a pianist preparing to do battle with a tricky melody. Ginny elegantly craned herself to look disinterestedly out onto the garden, grey bobby-pinned hair near-perfectly in place. Nancy looked from her grandmother to her mother, then rose to her feet.

'I'll just go get that.'

Ernie was standing back from the doorstep in another fetching bow tie and short-sleeved shirt. He looked like he was off to school. Clarence looked only slightly more relaxed in black shirt and jeans. No tie, good. It was already starting to feel like Christmas dinner.

'Good afternoon, young lady,' beamed Ernie. He held a bunch of mauve chrysanthemums at arm's length. 'From the allotment. I'll give them to you,' he smiled, 'but if you could put them somewhere the head chef can enjoy them?'

Nancy nodded and ushered them inside. 'Sure. Come in.' Clarence stood awkwardly in the hallway, one hand on the back of his head, the other wringing a bottle of wine by the neck. Nancy's stomach did something strange. One of them was wearing something delicious, woody and citrus. The sort of delicate aftershave that made fresh air seem pointless.

'Hello,' she said to Clarence. It was a start.

'Hello,' said Clarence. 'I, er, didn't know whether to bring red or white. Chicken or beef?'

'White's perfect,' she said, taking it from him. 'Chicken *and* beef, actually. Mum's covered all bases.' Clarence nodded, and it was as if they might be about to reach their first easy milestone in three decades. He rubbed his eyebrow again while Nancy turned the bottle in her hand and pretended to read the label.

Ginny's voice reached through from the kitchen. 'No one likes lumpy gravy, Annabel.'

'I'll show you through,' said Nancy apologetically. 'We have an extra guest.'

Despite the odd observation from Ginny – Annabel's high colour, the length of the grass, a blemished glass – lunch got off with all the usual choreography of strangers politely taking seats, offering and accepting drinks, sourcing a replacement knife when one fell to the floor. Clarence made easy conversation of the observable, nice, easy subjects like the universally appreciated aroma of baking fruit; the uninterrupted view of the meadows from the gardens this side of the street, the pylons chasing through the view from Birdie's garden stuck on the other side of Mountford Road. It was Ernie who raised the changing temperament of autumnal weather. They managed to get a good five minutes' discussion out of the seasonal climate, the fierce colours of dying leaves, the clothes it was sensible to wear tending an allotment, like Ernest, or working the fields by night, like Clarence. It was all easier than expected.

They were nearing the end of the main course when Annabel finally started to settle into the rhythm around her, talking more, laughing at a joke Clarence made, Ernie reeling her in with his expertise on inspired composting methods. Nancy watched her mum with interest, seated between her and Ernie. Annabel's mouth moved carefully as she spoke. She reminded Nancy of the hermit crabs they would find down on the estuary, tiny, timid things poking just the tips of themselves out of their shells, out into the open when it was safe to be visible again. While others talked, Ginny kept to chewing. Absorbing the conversation around her like oxygen.

Feeding a fire, perhaps. It wasn't until Nancy got up to start clearing plates that Ginny finally swallowed and put her teeth to better use.

'Nancy, darling. Sit. Let your mother get that. You're here to convalesce.'

Nancy hovered over her seat. It wasn't laziness that made her sit so obediently, or that Ginny was two glasses in to Clarence's Chardonnay. It was her own total lack of foresight knocking her smack down onto her backside. She hadn't asked, before going to open the door to Clarence and Ernest, that private matters remained private.

Ernie set his hands in his lap. 'Oh, been under the weather, have we, Nancy?'

'Ah,' spluttered Nancy. She batted a hand and felt the red burn through her cheeks. 'Not really. Fine now. Who's for pudding?'

'Under the weather?' scoffed Ginny. 'I'd say a heart attack was a little more than *under the weather*, wouldn't you, Mr Robinson?' Nancy felt herself solidify. A coagulation, travelling from her core all the way to the edges of herself. 'How many girls do you know have had a *heart attack*? Take note, modern life and all its pressures is not all it's cracked up to be.'

'Minor,' choked Nancy. Her voice sounded strange, stuck in her throat. *Minor* too minor a word to help. She should've said *cardiomyopathy*, not a heart attack at all . . . but she hadn't crossed Annabel over that bridge yet.

Ginny rolled her eyes. 'No. Such. Thing. Do you know how many women die each year in this country from heart attacks? I asked Julian to look it up. A *lot*. That's how many.

You are *twice* as likely to die from heart disease as you are from breast cancer! Did your doctors tell you that?'

Nancy balled her hands into fists under the table. There was no blockage in her artery, a bona fide heart attack would've meant a blockage, caused by lifestyle things or . . . biological things. Fixable things, potentially. But that wasn't what Nancy was dealing with. Hers wasn't a lifestyle or physical problem. It was a psychological one. An over-the-top emotional response. Stress hormones had raged through her, stunning her, *warning* her. But how could she tell Annabel that?

'They said everything's on the mend, Gran.' A weak attempt to shut Ginny down, but it wasn't a lie. The hospital had said she'd every chance of a swift recovery. So long as she didn't let it happen again. On that, the doctors had been very clear. *A recurrence would not be good, Nancy.*

Ernest's moustache didn't cloak his expression. He stared over it, eyes not knowing where to rest. Nancy's neck felt hot. Annabel stood, setting scrunched napkins onto plates, gathering them up with quiet efficiency.

'Would anyone like apple and frangipane pie? Or there's crumble? With ice cream?' she asked, ferrying plates to the sink.

Nancy swallowed, catching Clarence's eye before he set his sights safely back on his wine glass. So this was what Mol had meant. *They look at you differently, once they know you're dud. Try hiding the Big C after your eyebrows fall out. No one wants to argue with you any more. It's a real drag.*

Ernest smiled weakly at Nancy across the table, around

the great big elephant Ginny had just parked in the middle of the table.

'Annabel, perhaps allow your guests to finish chewing on that beef before you get to pushing the next thing into their mouths. Can't you see this young man is still eating?'

Clarence's jaw slowed like he'd been caught out. He held his hands up apologetically. Apologising for eating his lunch. 'No, I had finished,' he managed. 'Sorry, Annabel, I spotted a last bite of that spectacular mashed potato and cabbage.'

'Colcannon!' beamed Ernest, seizing the diversion. He linked his fingers and laid his hands casually on the table. 'A firm favourite!'

Annabel gave a quick smile and rubbed her hand across the back of her wrist. 'Take your time, Clarence, sorry,' she repeated quietly.

'How can the boy take his time with you hovering like a mosquito? Do sit down, Annabel.'

'Sorry. I was just going to take the crumble out of the oven.' Annabel hesitated, then pulled her chair back from the table to take her seat. Like a good little girl. Like Nancy, sitting to have her hair plaited.

'No,' blurted Nancy. Ginny's back straightened. Nancy could feel her words fleeing her. 'If you take it out now, Mum, it can cool, can't it? Before we all have some.'

Annabel blinked at her, then pushed her chair back under the table. Her face was blank, detached.

Nancy smiled at no one in particular. 'Anyone else for apple pie or crumble? It's making my mouth water. Big bowl for me, please, Mum. Either will be lovely.' She picked at her thumbnail in her lap. It was a race now, to help Annabel get them all fed and gone. Any silly notions about nurturing the fragile buds of friendship between her and Ernest would have to take a rain check.

'Me too, please,' said Clarence. 'Smells incredible.'

Ernie pressed a napkin to his mouth and smoothed his moustache. 'I'll say it does! Yes please for me *three*, Annabel. You choose.'

Nancy took a long glug of water from her glass, deeply regretting not going for the Chardonnay. Ginny held up her own glass then for inspection.

'This wine, Annabel?'

Clarence drummed his fingers on the table and answered for Annabel. 'Guilty as charged. A quick grab on the way over here, I'm afraid.' He tucked his hair back over his ear, only just long enough to stay put. 'Last night was a late one, I slept in this morning. Didn't quite have time to get into town, so I, er, was at the mercy of the local Co-op.'

Clarence slept? When did he sleep? He was always doing something, going off to the fields at night, presumably the hospital in the day. Finding the time to run, and shop for *Compers News*, and step in for missing band members in the hours left between. Nancy found herself trying to think of him curled up somewhere, features softened by rest, the tautness gone from his arms.

'Working, were you? Or living it up?' Ginny smiled at him like a cat amused by a lesser, feeble creature.

Clarence nodded into his lap. 'Probably more of the latter last night. But a bit of both.'

'Well I hope you weren't drink-driving your tractor?' challenged Ginny.

Annabel spoke then, from the sink. 'Clarence is also a musician. He was playing last night. Very well too.'

Nancy took another sip of water. Ernie picked up the gravy boat and said something under his breath about helping out. Ginny's eyes followed him to the sink, but she stayed with the conversation.

'Is he now? Not an easy arena in which to make any real gains, I daresay. Your grandfather would've told you so, Nancy, so heed the warning.'

Nancy caught a look at Clarence beside her. It was absolutely nothing to do with anyone how he made his living. Clarence widened his eyes at her, as if agreeing completely with Ginny's poison, then smiled into his lap. Nancy felt his smile jump over to her, settling onto her own lips. She took another sip of water.

'But your grandfather played for love, not profit. Broke my heart letting go of his piano after he passed. I shall never, *ever* forget having to relinquish it.'

Annabel dropped something heavy into the sink. The clatter set Fig off the other side of the utility door.

'That dog, Annabel! Honestly. How can you bear it? The noise and smell. Holes in the garden. Hair *everywhere*.'

Annabel didn't answer. Clarence puffed out his cheeks.

'They do make wonderful pets, though, don't they? Wonderful companions,' tried Ernie, taking his seat again along the battlefront. Annabel smiled over her shoulder in quick surreptitious agreement.

'You keep an animal in your house too, then, Mr Robinson? I take it you're still seeking companionship elsewhere, though?' Ginny's eyes sloped off towards Annabel, spooning volcanic-hot pudding into dishes on the side.

'Oh, er, not exactly,' Ernie said jovially. 'I have a grandson, Ray, keeps me company enough. He's like an animal sometimes. You're right about the holes in the yard. Although he doesn't shed much hair, thankfully.'

Clarence smiled lopsidedly. Fig cooled the disgruntled barking. Ginny tapped her wedding band against the stem of her glass.

'Yes, I should've liked a grandson, I think. Less fuss. Girls are more weepy.'

Nancy caught a look at her mum. 'How is Uncle Julian, Gran? Still with . . .' What was her name again? 'The air hostess?'

Ginny reached across the table and set a hand over Nancy's.

'Only just. I don't think she's right for him. But we'll see.'

It hung there in the air, waiting to be plucked. Nancy found herself reaching for it before she could make the risk assessment. 'Or . . . Uncle Jules will see. Figure it out for himself.'

Ginny smiled benignly in nobody's direction. 'One day you'll know for yourself, Nancy. It's very difficult, being a mother. Spotting the dangers your children can't. Or *won't*. Even when they're all grown up.' She dropped to a conspiratorial whisper. Nancy focused on her grandmother's hand, delicately clamped to her wine glass again. 'Sometimes you have to give them a jolly in a better direction, for their own good.' A jolly towards divorce, for example. The total devastation of a family unit.

Annabel set Clarence and Ernie's desserts down first and returned to the sanctity of the sink, drying the spoons she'd used for the veg and now needed for the pudding. Outside, the wind was picking up across the garden, the occasional yellow leaf giddily tumbling past the window, looping up and over the pear trees. Up, up and away.

'Does your uncle play the piano too?' asked Clarence. It was the first question he'd directed straight at Nancy, and a fair assumption given that Clarence's musicality had tumbled straight from the generation above. Nancy contemplated the other predispositions Birdie might've passed down to him, but Clarence had never been hot and cold, not manic in any way. He had always been a gentle, steady hand, with not much to hold onto.

'Um . . . No, I don't think so?' blinked Nancy. Clarence's eyes didn't falter. A blue deep as the sky before dusk, features as solemn as ever they were. 'Does he, Gran?' She swallowed.

'Julian? Play piano? Of course not. He *could've*. Far too busy applying himself to his books, though. You don't get to where he is without fully committing yourself. Well, you know that, Nancy. You've worked hard too. No, Julian didn't have time for *playing* anything. He's a go-getter.'

'Oh. Shame,' said Nancy.

'Why is it a shame?' Ginny's head was cocked, birdlike. Like one of those hideous storks Nancy had seen on the wildlife documentary last week, watching its chick peck its own brother to death, gobbling down baby crocodiles.

'Um . . . that no one else learnt to play. Mum was saying again just last night how much she loved sitting with Grandpa while he played. What happened to it?'

246

'To what?'

'Grandpa's piano. Did you have to sell it when you moved into Hollyfields?'

'Sell it? Don't you remember it? How battered and scratched it was? I wouldn't have got much for it. People don't pay for sentimental value or I could've asked a million pounds.'

A bowl of dessert arrived under Nancy's chin.

'Thanks, Mum.' Annabel slipped back into her chair, smiled at the table and began prodding her own ball of ice cream with the tip of her teaspoon. 'What happened to it, Gran? Shame we didn't have it here. As you liked it so much.' Nancy blew over her apple pie. 'It would've been nice at Christmas, in the front room. Even if we'd just hung our stockings on it.'

Ginny clucked her tongue and grinned, perfect dentures shiny as boiled sweets.

'Your mother hasn't the space. She certainly didn't back then, toys all over the place.'

Nancy bristled. 'We could've made room somewhere, couldn't we, Mum?' She bit into her pudding. It burnt her gum. The clinking of spoons on dishes pushed back a growing, stuffy silence. 'Where did it go then?' Nancy asked conversationally. 'If not to Mum or Uncle Jules? Or eBay.' Molly would've wanted to know, the fate of this piano their mum had treasured. And Nancy did too.

Ginny threatened her dessert with her spoon. 'I donated it. To a good home. It's what your grandfather would've wanted. Someone to appreciate it. Sarah was so grateful, she almost cried. It was very touching.'

Wasn't theirs a *good home*? A good enough home?

Annabel watched her ice cream slide off her spoon. 'It wasn't Sarah . . . it was the next one.'

'The next what?' snapped Ginny, already exasperated.

Clarence and Ernie had melted into the background, two underlings sitting silently at the grown-ups' table.

'The next girlfriend,' said Annabel. 'Sophie. Julian said she wanted a piano bar in her apartment. You gave her Dad's.'

Nancy tried to do the maths. The equation was usually simple, wasn't it? The inheritance side of death? The only simple thing about it. Family minus dearly departed equals worldly goods shared between loving relatives. Not transient girlfriends called Sarah. Or Sophie.

'A piano *bar*?' she asked. 'For . . . keeping bottles of tequila in?'

Ginny turned her soft, peachy cheek to face the garden and the skittish leaves beyond the window.

'It was no good you having it, Annabel. You'd have only upset yourself. You were upset easily enough back then as it was, and I know how you felt about your father, it wouldn't have done you any good feeling miserable every time one of the girls touched it with their sticky fingers, would it? And Molly with a musical instrument to create merry hell with? The din would've driven you mad.'

'Right,' said Annabel softly.

'Tell me I'm wrong! It's not a criticism, Annabel, for goodness' sake, but she was loud enough, wasn't she? Not like our quiet Nancy here.' Ginny chuckled amiably. 'I always did wonder if there was a chance Molly was so excitable because of all those extra *feelings* you must have had rushing around your body while you were carrying her. Not your fault, of course. But grief does take its toll on the system if you allow it. How far along your pregnancy were you when your poor father left this world? Six months? Seven?'

Nancy stared at her mother's hands, Annabel's spoon clamped like a holy object in rigid fingers. Her dessert had turned already, a milky white slick engulfing stewed hand-picked fruit. All that effort, mush.

'Nine,' said Annabel. She made a small noise in the back of her throat.

'There, see? A difficult time for you. Mourning your poor father, struggling to keep on top of a new baby, a toddler *and* a husband away at work every hour God sent. Had I given you that piano, even later on down the line, you'd have been reminded of that awful period, surely?' Ginny pushed her pudding bowl away from her, untouched. 'Sentimentality is no good. Better to keep moving forward and let the past alone. You'd never have kept it tuned anyway.'

The pie crust poking out of Annabel's bowl was suddenly an affront. Attentive crimping of pastry she'd kneaded and rolled thin as a pound coin for them all. *She bullies Mum*, Molly had declared from the bottom bunk one night. *And one day, Mum's going to have to deal with it. She's going to have to toughen up and tell her to just. Fuck. Off.*

That day wasn't today, Nancy didn't think. Annabel had shrunk, small movements only, as if one wrong action might undo her. Nancy took another spoonful of pie and ice cream and shovelled it into her mouth. She chewed, swallowed.

'I didn't realise Grandpa died so close to you having Molly. Sorry, Mum. That must have been so difficult.'

Ernest breathed too loudly and gave away his position. Ginny looked at him, then to Clarence, as if she too had just remembered they were also at the table. Annabel shook her head slightly, a warning for Nancy to not push her over the edge with one misplaced kindness.

'How is your pudding, Mr Robinson?' Annabel asked, her expression bright again.

Ernie's voice was calmer now, careful. 'Quite delicious, thank you, Annabel. The frangipane just gives it that . . . lift. A million miles more delicious than Beckitt's, which I like very much as you know.'

'That's kind,' said Annabel, composed once more. She topped up Ernest's wine glass. Ginny put a hand over hers. Clarence shifted beside Nancy. He bent down for something on the floor. 'More wine, Clarence?' asked Annabel, not realising the bottle in her hand was already empty. Nancy watched her closely.

'Not for me, thank you. I'm taking things steady today, I think.'

Ginny smiled brightly. 'Yes, what was this big party last night? You've got quite the cosy social quartet going.'

'We didn't stay,' said Annabel.

'Did you miss the commotion?' asked Ernie.

'Commotion?' asked Annabel.

Clarence laid the napkin he'd picked up from the floor back in Nancy's lap. She looked at him, smiling a thank you.

'Oh yes,' said Ernie. 'Between a guest and the young man marshalling the cars. Heated voices there for a second.'

'It's not a Whittacker's knees-up if there aren't heated voices,' smiled Clarence.

'What was it about?' asked Nancy. She had no interest. Could not care less. All she'd like to know was why Grandpa James's piano hadn't gone to Annabel. Who would've loved and cherished it, and not hacked it into a novelty bar. How Ginny could ever have thought that was OK. Or how it was Ginny could have *so* much fight in her, yet never fight for Annabel.

Clarence set his forearm across the table, his skin much browner than Nancy's sickly pallor. She pulled her arms back into herself.

'Freddie Blumfield took one of the ladies out for a *sit* in his sports car,' he said. 'Claimed someone had deliberately put sheep muck on his driver's seat, ruined his new trousers and upholstery. But, you know . . . decent guy like Freddie. If it's suspects he wants, they'd have to form an orderly queue.'

Nancy pushed a piece of apple around her bowl with her spoon. Clarence ran a thumb along the bottom edge of his lip, watching her.

'Heathens,' said Ginny.

'This Freddie chap,' said Ernie, 'didn't have anything to do with the ruckus near Kenning's smallholding, did he, Clarence?'

'I heard about the screaming,' said Clarence.

'Screaming?' said Nancy.

'Loud enough that two of the Kenning lads went looking. Screaming like banshees, they said.' Nancy looked at her mum. 'They were right to check, too. So many people just turn away nowadays, don't they?' Ernest shook his head forlornly. Annabel tapped Nancy's foot under the table. 'So few people look out for each other any more, I just don't understand it. And now there are all these other worries, youngsters on phones and the like. How do you keep an ear or eye out for all that; how do you deal with bullies now? If you can't catch hold of them?'

'There's only ever been one way to deal with bullies,' said Ginny. 'And that's whoever's supposedly being bullied standing on their own two feet and dealing with it themselves. No one ever bullied my son. He wouldn't put up with it.'

'I guess we're all different,' said Clarence.

'Surprisingly so,' piped Ginny. 'Even between siblings. Take my two, chalk and cheese. Much like my granddaughters. Nancy here would do *anything* when asked, no quibble, but her sister! Complete lack of discipline. No father, no discipline. At least Nancy got a taste of family structure before he left. You've never been unruly, have you, darling?'

'Molly wasn't that unruly,' Annabel said quietly.

'*Spirited*,' ventured Ernie diplomatically.

Nancy opened her mouth to say something, adrenalin beginning its familiar tingle through her body.

'Molly *was* unruly, Ernie,' said Clarence, 'if you don't mind me saying, Annabel.' He proceeded with caution. 'She was the only girl I ever saw scare Mrs Reeves's German pointer off so we could cross the canal lock and get down the towpath without having to go all the way around.'

'And how did she do that?' humoured Ginny.

'Barking,' said Clarence. As if the answer was obvious. 'She stood there and barked like a wild thing while the rest of us stood behind her, trying not to bolt. She barked and snarled until Reeves's dog thought twice and decided there were fiercer creatures on the towpath that day.'

They'd never heard this. It was a new piece of knowledge, a new piece of Molly. Annabel put her hand over her mouth. She was going to cry, any second now, but Clarence grinned, and it was as if it reached down into Annabel's stomach and pulled the laughter clear out of her.

'Oh my gosh,' she chortled into her hand. 'Barking? Blimey.'

'Sounds as though I got off lightly then,' chuckled Ernest, shifting in his seat. 'Could've been worse had it been your girl and not her dog chasing me up onto my shed roof.'

Annabel smiled behind her napkin. 'Goodness.'

Clarence swept a pastry crumb from his shirt. He spoke to Ginny then.

'Like I said, we're all different. Some of us are tougher than others. Not everyone's a fighter.'

'Agreed,' said Ernest, holding his glass aloft. 'Absolutely spot-on. My son, in fact, Matthew . . . he wasn't what you'd call a fighter. I don't think he'd have got across that canal lock, that's for sure. But he did have a good group of pals around him and they all stuck together. All for one, and all that. I think that's half the battle, isn't it? Surrounding yourself with good people, who'll stand by you and fight your corner when you need them.'

'And what does your gentle-hearted son do?' asked Ginny, already on the hunt for her next target. 'Is he local or too far for you to enjoy your Sunday lunches with?'

Ernest smoothed the edges of his moustache and then cradled his great hands around his pudding bowl.

'I'm afraid Matthew doesn't do anything any more.'

'Job-seeker, is he?'

'No,' said Ernest, tapping the tips of his thumbs together. 'We lost him. Just over two years ago. Quite unexpectedly. Just a routine operation, but, well, the anaesthetic didn't agree with him, unfortunately.' Annabel lifted her head, giving Ernest her full attention for the first time since he'd arrived. 'It happened not long before I bought next door. Which is a shame: he'd have liked the walk down to the pub on the canal, even past the unfriendly dogs. We enjoyed our pork scratchings and guest beers. But,' Ernie drummed his fingers lightly on the table, 'one day, when Ray's old enough, I shall introduce him to the true delights of . . .' he fanned his great hands through the air, 'craft brews and bar snacks.'

Annabel pushed the hair away from her cheek. 'I'm so sorry, Ernest. How old was he?'

Ernie's chin moved into his chest. 'Matthew? Forty. Which, I know, didn't make him a child. But . . .'

'But he's *your* child,' said Annabel.

There were depths so unfathomable, they were hard to peer into even from afar. Like the heartache of parents with lost children. Nancy wondered if there could be anything other than the treading of water for them, for every second onwards. She looked down, away from them both, at the napkin in her lap folded once over. She opened it out for something to do with her hands. Sitting on the white linen with no place at all being there was the inimitable dark form of a sycamore helicopter, wishbone-shaped and perfect.

'That he is,' said Ernest. 'And I'd have wished for a little longer with him had I known what was to happen. But it's true what they say, isn't it? Quality, not quantity.'

Nancy heard her mother's gentle agreement but didn't

look up. She kept her eyes on the tiny, perfect seed in her lap, felt her breathing shallow, thoughts colliding in her head. She swallowed and looked from her napkin to Clarence, but he was unreadable now, listening to Ernest speaking softly of his own unspent wishes.

Ginny went to use the bathroom during coffee. Something hadn't agreed with her. Perhaps it was the common ground that had unexpectedly opened out between Annabel and Ernie. Something upon which no one else in the room had more authority than the two of them. So Ginny had made her excuses and gone for a sit on the upstairs toilet, leaving Nancy and Annabel to tie up the conversations on Ernest's greenfly problem and Clarence's dubious experiences playing back-alley music clubs. Something had happened in the kitchen. Nancy felt it when they walked out into the hallway and the air there felt different. As if they were moving away from the scene of something unprecedented.

'Nancy, Annabel . . .' said Ernest, shuffling through the doorway after Clarence. He glanced upstairs on his way out. 'I haven't felt that much fear I'd put my elbows on the table since eating supper next to my headmaster at the boarding school gala.' Annabel smiled into her chest. 'If my table manners weren't too lacking, I'd very much like the chance to try it again sometime.'

Annabel smoothed the hem of her blouse. 'Thank you for coming, Ernest. And for being so gracious.' She'd only attempted the last-minute colcannon recipe she'd found on the iPad last night so that Ernie didn't feel compelled to share his own one day. Maybe he'd still get the chance.

Ernie pretended to tip his hat to her. 'Until the next time then.'

'Annabel?' came Ginny's muffled voice from upstairs.

Nancy smiled passively and patted her thighs. 'Probably run out of loo roll.'

'I'll go.' Annabel gave her last thanks and apologies of the lunch hour and headed upstairs.

Ernie winked at Nancy and touched Clarence softly on the elbow. 'I'll see you two kids again.' They watched him leave. Nancy had slipped Clarence's helicopter into the crumbling clay candle holder Annabel loved, where its safety was guaranteed. Wishes didn't come along all that often nowadays.

When Ernest had disappeared the other side of his hedgerow, Clarence set his hands in his jean pockets and turned back to Nancy, hovering on the *You Again?* doormat.

'So, we, er, covered death, favouritism, the great British weather and dry beef . . . all in two courses.' He rubbed his jaw and grinned. 'I feel like I got off lightly.'

Nancy felt a confused grin slide over her face. 'What do you mean?'

Clarence gave a sheepish smile and lolled his head like a boy.

'We didn't even touch alcoholism and mental health.'

His shoulders rolled forward, arms straight down into his pockets. Should she ask about Birdie? Were some things better off limits? There had been no more expansion on the heart attack talk, thank God. It seemed even Ginny knew where to draw the line sometimes. Surely alcoholism and mental health were somewhere the other side of that line too.

'Something to look forward to,' said Nancy.

Clarence smiled at his shoes. Annabel hadn't asked after Birdie either, perhaps in case Ginny sank her dentures too far into that conversation too.

'Would you tell your mum the beef was perfect. Like, amazing perfect.'

'I'll tell her.'

Clarence nodded. 'Thanks for having me. See you around, Nance.' He turned for the path.

'Clarence?' It was roughly twenty years too late and perhaps meant very little anyway, coming from someone like her who, unlike Mol, didn't know how to just bang out an arm and grab for all the answers, but, 'I hope your mum's feeling better soon. And . . . if there's anything we can do, just, you know . . . shout.'

Clarence looked up the street towards his empty house. He smiled lopsidedly, and with just that small trickery of the lips and eyes was a twelve-year-old boy again.

'It's been good seeing you, Nancy.'

'You too.' And against all expectation and reason, she realised it was true.

Chapter 20

Morning was still hours away when Nancy first awoke. The alertness was instant. She waited for the pieces to come back to her, familiar jagged edges of a dream that had kept shattering itself and re-forming down the last two years. She waited for the telltale patter of adrenalin running riot through her body, a heartbeat struggling to keep up. She listened for it all, but all was calm. Her dream had shapeshifted. She'd dreamt about the snow on the back fields. A pair of crows like two black eyes rolling about in it. Clarence on the furlong picking through the fallen helicopters, folding them like gifts inside napkins white as winter itself.

Nancy got onto her elbows, blinked at the moonlight pressing in on the curtains. She tried to place the time. Maybe two? Maybe earlier. Somewhere in the house a familiar riff pulsed through the dark. Nancy listened. John Lennon, gently but assuredly working his message . . . 'Whatever Gets You Thru the Night'.

Nancy sat up in bed and pinched her eyes. *Music.*

Dampened by carpet and floorboards. She planted her feet on the floor. Traipsed across the room. Picked her cardigan off the back of the door and pushed her arms into it. On the landing, the melody was clearer. Annabel's door stood open, her bed untouched. Unslept in. Across the hall, Mol's room the same.

Downstairs, Nancy kept bare feet to the hallway rug. Fig was snoring in the kitchen, still satisfied from her bellyful of leftover roast, unmoved by the ballad slipping now from beneath the living room door. Nancy touched the door handle and waited for a sound to tell her to leave it alone, go back to bed. But none came. She pushed inside.

Annabel sat on the lounge rug between the fire and the footstool, a stack of photo albums strewn about her like flotsam bobbing away from a capsized boat.

'Mum?'

The clock said almost 3 a.m. Nancy stepped closer, carefully, like those mothers who had to get their sleepwalking children safely back to bed without waking and startling them to death. Annabel listed like a ship then, eyes tired and distant. Nancy saw the Courvoisier bottle beside her, an old raffle ticket still stuck to its neck. It must've been gathering dust in the sideboard, for years probably. Annabel didn't drink cognac, she barely drank shandy. For what it was worth, Nancy pushed the corked cap back into the bottle neck. She set it down on the sideboard and switched on another lamp, hoping the light might chase back some of the worry. It had worked when she was a child, waiting for their dad to get home through the dark.

Annabel tucked her legs against her body like a teenager.

She was wearing socks with strawberries on them, red as her cheeks, cheeks that bore the telltale sheen of recent tears. One of her grips had come loose and was hanging by a few strands of auburn hair over her ear. Nancy fixed it back into place.

'Mum?' Annabel smiled absently skywards. The alcohol had softened the creases at her eyes, her cheeks puffy where she'd rubbed the tears from them. Nancy wiped her thumb over them. 'What's going on?'

Annabel was no drinker. Not given to the bursts of laughter or anger or confidence or tears that alcohol drew from a person. She'd warned them enough, that drinking was like giving someone else the key to your house and hoping nothing was disturbed or, worse, discovered in there before the key was returned.

Nancy sat herself down on the footstool until the record fell silent. Dull rotations of the needle heralding the end of the line.

'Shall we get you up to bed, Mum?' Annabel slumped forward and pushed both hands through her hair, shaking her head at a problem Nancy couldn't see.

'No. Not yet. I can't find it. I have to find it first.'

'Find what, Mum?'

Annabel was instantly bereft. 'The photo . . . you took when I was holding her and she was feeding the geese. The little Polaroid camera you had for your birthday. Just before it pecked her finger, do you remember?' Her speech was slow and rounded. Her shoulders started to shake about her, breaths snatched through the fissures left between tears and words.

'I remember it, Mum. I remember it. Don't worry, we'll

find it.' Nancy picked up two of the photo albums off the rug and shuffled into their place.

'I thought it was in this one,' said Annabel, clumsily delivering another album into Nancy's lap. 'But I can't find it. I think I've lost it.' There was a desperation about her, like a woman watching her house burn down, and Nancy was suddenly awake, alert, tasked with tackling the flames, saving what she could.

'It's OK, we'll find it. I promise.'

She turned the first album over, started at the front, where it was safe. There would be no final photographs at this end of any of the albums, no pencilled eyebrows or wigs or pronounced veins beneath pale, delicate skin. Annabel had made sure of it. She'd painstakingly pored through boxes of photographs before Molly's service, sticking and annotating, everything moving in perfect chronological sequence from when Molly was little to the last photos taken of her, so that whichever album was picked up by those who came back to the house, snapshots of the full spectrum of Molly's near twenty-seven vibrant years could be seen in full technicolour glory.

'How old was she?' The Polaroid camera had been for Nancy's seventh or eighth birthday maybe, Molly would've been four or five then. Nancy flipped through the first inserts, photos of Annabel looking like a child herself, holding one of them in the hospital swaddled like a grub in pink crochet. Had to be Nancy, Annabel's big loose waves and fuller cheeks giving away her youth. Uncle Julian had said how their mum had got skinny as a lathe after having Molly, though, and how his girlfriend back then had wanted to know her secret.

But Nancy knew, now. She'd been mourning Grandpa James. Their past afternoons sitting together on his piano stool. Just as she was about to venture into life with two children and, soon enough, an abandoned marriage.

Nancy leant in, while her mum wouldn't notice, and softly pressed a kiss to her cheek. She got back to flicking through the album pages, discoloured now, sticky cellophane curled at the corners. Page after page of Molly's milestones, sitting up chewing a slobbered finger, crawling down a garden after someone's tortoise. A nice one of Annabel beaming, holding Mol's hands above her head, steadying her as she walked; then Nancy standing with her toddler sister, holding a watering can together . . . sharing a sandwich . . . first haircuts together . . . Annabel splashing in a paddling pool beside them, Dad's hairy leg and Adidas pump just in frame. Nancy found herself sinking into them, looking, flipping, hovering, remembering.

A photograph showed a pretty tea set on a picnic blanket in the back garden, Nancy pouring, Molly's great chubby thigh crawling out of shot. Nancy laughed then. Her eyes moved to another picture of them both, years later, two little girls, feet turned out and wide grins in baggy swimsuits on a beach somewhere. And then a wonky Polaroid photo of Annabel watching Molly, carefully helping her concentrate on the seeds lying on her upturned palm. Nancy slipped it from its sleeve.

'Found it.'

Annabel lifted her head. For a second she seemed focused on the photograph, then her eyes glazed again. She clutched the photo to her face and sobbed into it, snatched wet breaths. The hairs stood on Nancy's neck.

'I don't know what to do, Nancy. I don't know what to do. I don't know how to be her mum any more.'

Annabel's body shuddered. Nancy hovered uselessly nearby. This was the job she'd shied from. She wasn't qualified for. To *look out for Mum*, to offer reassurance. But Annabel had just given shape to something. The thing Nancy hadn't been able to put her fingers around. Now it sat in her hands, solid and real, staring straight back up at her. She didn't know how to be Molly's sister any more.

'Do you think she thought I was a good mum, Nancy? Do you think she knew I tried my best?'

'Why would you even say that?' Nancy swallowed. Annabel began sobbing silently into her hand. Nancy teased the photograph from her mother's fingers, putting it safely on the footstool. Mol's tiny, perfect hand just peeped out from the sleeve of a red duffle coat. It suddenly hurt to look at it. 'She knew, Mum. Of course she did.' And the thought grounded her. 'What's started all this?'

Annabel was barely coherent. 'I should've tried harder. I didn't know what was happening. I mean, I knew it wasn't right. *I* wasn't right. I was just so tired all the time, much more tired than when you came along. But I had two children then, you see? So I thought, *Well, of course you're tired!* But I couldn't sleep. And your father kept saying, if I could just . . . pull myself together a little and . . . eat properly . . . it would pass. Because it was upsetting him too, I could see that. And I didn't *want* to upset him, Nancy, *honestly*. I didn't *mean* to drive him away from you girls. Your gran warned me I would if I wasn't careful. I'm so sorry.'

263

They'd never wanted for anything. Annabel had waded through the hardships of bringing up two girls alone without showing it to them. There had been times she was sick, bedridden with flu, but only between the responsibilities of getting them up and washed and dressed and off to school, and then later waiting to collect them again, making dinner, bathing them, a story before bed. She had picked and chosen the hours she could be ill, the hours she could take off, and they'd never been the hours that they'd needed her. She'd gone without. She'd gone to Ginny, when there was no more time to pay off a school trip, or there'd been a problem with her bank card in the supermarket and they'd had to leave their basket behind with the cashier. This was how their dad's support made its way from him to them, landing when it landed, sometimes getting lost along the way. Banks could be funny things, Annabel had told them. But she had never shown the signs of strain. Never made them feel less than anyone else.

Nancy looked at the album in her lap. All the years inside it, all the photos he wouldn't be in, all the time she'd spent waiting. For someone to come back who had never really been there with them in the first place. Molly had been sharp enough to give up on him before she was even out of primary school. But Nancy, she waited for him even now. That small part of herself that didn't want to know better still waited for their father to look back.

'You didn't drive anyone away, Mum. He left of his own accord.' Ginny was wrong.

'I should've done better for you, and for Molly, and who knows what might've been diff—'

'No,' said Nancy firmly. *Enough now.* 'It's just the brandy, Mum. It's playing tricks on you, that's all. Let's get you upstairs.'

Alcohol was like music. A spiteful friend. One who'd take you gently by the hand and lead you safely through a dense, desolate forest in the dead of night, only to walk you straight off a precipice the other side. Annabel fixed desperate ice-blue eyes on Nancy.

'I *loved* spending time with my father.'

'I know.' But Annabel didn't have a mother like they did.

Nancy put a hand on her mum's cheek, Annabel's skin hot and wet. She wiped Annabel's eyes and took her face in her hands.

'Do you know what I think, Mum?' For what it was worth. Annabel blinked at her, at best only half there. 'I think Mol must've got her fight from you, even if you don't know it.'

Annabel squinted through the haze. 'From me?'

All Molly had ever had in her arsenal was a cast-iron will and a mother who was there to ride or die with her, to the very end.

'She's the bravest girl I'll ever know, Mum. Where else did it come from? It was only ever the three of us, really. Wasn't it?'

'You think that *I* made her tough?'

'Well I know I didn't.' Nancy half laughed. 'You emboldened her, Mum. You gave her a happy life full of colour, where she was loved and safe and got to do all the things she wanted to do.' But Molly's fate was never in their hands. Not even Annabel could've kept her here longer. Loving a person didn't buy you sway. Even a quiet, fierce love like Annabel's.

'But what do I do now, Nancy? I need to be her mum still. I don't want to learn to live without her; I don't think I can.'

Nancy's throat tightened. What were they supposed to do now? Or in a week's time? Or next year? Or in ten?

'I don't know.' It was the only answer she had, and it wasn't enough. Annabel needed more. 'Maybe all we can do is . . . try and live like she's still here.'

The brandy hadn't been enough to knock Annabel completely off track. She'd insisted on doing most of the work, pulling herself up one stair at a time. Nancy had held on, though, just in case. Close enough to smell Annabel's skin, echoes of the day's cooking still in her hair, the washing powder on her clothes. She had eased the strawberry socks off over her mum's feet. Unbuttoned her blouse, fed a nightshirt over her head. She'd pulled Annabel's auburn waves free, untangled the worst from her thin gold necklace, tucked her in. When she pressed a kiss to her mum's head, she found that one of the feathers from her down pillows had settled itself in Annabel's hair. She set it down next to the bedside clock for Annabel to find in the morning, and watched her slip into a deep sleep before letting herself out, pulling the door to just enough that she would still hear her through the last of the night. Had Ginny ever done the same for her? Maybe she had.

Nancy turned off all the lights downstairs, reassured Fig and checked the doors were locked. The house felt suddenly vast. A wide-open space of unfamiliarity. She looked around for something, anything, to anchor her. Her eyes coasted to the clay candle holder trying to keep itself together on Annabel's kitchen shelf. When she went back upstairs, it was

Molly's room she gravitated to. Sitting on the windowsill a while, she watched the stars through the clouds over a silent street, taking in the closer shapes and shadows of Molly's dressing gown still hanging on her wardrobe door, the bracelets stacked on her trinket box, framed photos sitting on her dresser. In one of them, Molly was lying across the bar at the Jack, a full pint balanced on her forehead. In another, she was with her mates at Glasto, flowers in their hair. And in the last one, two gangly girls with straggled dark plaits had parked up their too-heavy BMXs at the trunk of a huge tree.

Nancy looked about her. It didn't feel like a museum any more, this place she'd avoided looking at. It was just Molly's room again. She glanced over at the bed and thought about lying down there too. Resting her head where Mol had rested. Looking at the ceiling she'd looked at. She could feel it, the part of her that wanted to drift away to where Molly had drifted, just for a little while, just so Mol hadn't gone there alone. But Molly had died. She had died. And Nancy was alive. And this was Molly's room and Molly's rules. Rules she'd been explicitly clear about.

There is to be no bloody moping. I've got cancer, not a sudden desire to watch life-affirming movies or read motivational quotes. Jesus Christ. And I'm not eating superfoods, hell no. Unless they're dipped in chocolate. Or peanut butter. Or both. I AM drinking on birthdays, and they don't just have to be mine. No visitors if they haven't bothered in the last year. And no, Gran is not exempt from that rule, Mum. She's always detested me anyway, like I give a crap, but now I'm on my way out, she extra doubly with a cherry on the top can't come over here and piss me off. Well,

267

she can try, but I won't be held responsible. It's about time someone told her to take her head out of her wrinkly old arse. And Dad? Well, if anyone can nail him down, I guess we'll play that one by ear. But this is where we're at, folks. This is just the way it is. It's the shits, but, y'know, shit happens. And on the upside, it's just about us now. It's always just been us! The Woods girls. Now, we just get to be less fucking polite about it.

Nancy thought of white sand. Warm waters lapping a foreign beach. That nameless place she'd tried to keep her sister young and healthy and glorious. But Annabel didn't know that place. And Nancy couldn't keep going there without her.

She opened her hand and looked at the perfect sycamore pod Clarence had slipped into her lap under the dinner table. She held it in front of her face and spun it between her thumb and finger, back and forth, this way and that. She undid the catch and pushed open Molly's bedroom window. A wash of cool air blew in. She whispered into it.

'If you can work any kind of magic up there, Mol, or wherever you are, now's a good time.'

She wasn't sure what it was she was wishing for, all she knew was that when she set the sycamore helicopter spinning into the darkness, it was for their mum. It was for Annabel.

Chapter 21

Nancy propped a note against the jug holding Ernest's chrysanthemums on the off chance Annabel made it off the bathroom floor before they got back. Efficient in all things, Annabel had decided somewhere around the 4 a.m. mark to conserve energy and sleep nearer the toilet for a couple of hours, foetal-positioned. Nancy had woken with a charge of energy rippling through her body. It was dizzying, this new sensation. She tried to put a name to it, the thing that Molly would call *pulling your head out of your own arse*. Purpose. It felt like purpose, a thing that Nancy should and could and would do now, because her mum needed her to.

When Annabel was ready to rejoin the land of the living, there was coffee in the pot, two ibuprofens on the side and a new batch of granola Nancy had managed to pull together from the oats and nuts lurking at the back of Annabel's baking cupboard. A hit of cinnamon and turmeric and the lot had gone into one of Annabel's Kilner jars. Nancy reread the note she'd left.

Trust me, just add milk x

PS Beth found keys, gone to fetch with Fig x

She pushed a handful of poop bags into the pocket of her hoodie. Her headphones were still in there from the last time she'd ventured out alone into a world of people she didn't want to speak to. She turned them over in her hand. Fig nudged her leg and whimpered at the dog lead waiting on the sideboard. Nancy clipped it to her collar.

'Come on then, ginge,' she yawned. 'Time to be useful.'

Outside was a perfect September morning. Hazy blues and yellows and, once they'd made it off Mistleton Road, just enough breeze to animate the last of the wheatfields still waiting for harvest. From the bottom of Whittacker's valley the crop took on the look of a pale golden wave, ribboning down the hillside in one fluid current. Fig lumbered over the millstream cutting through the first meadow and waited for Nancy to follow on. Once onto the incline, the dog blended into the crops. Nancy kept to the margin around the field's perimeter, the tip of Fig's tail or head sporadically popping up into view, ears flapping, eyes darting around for her human.

It was Fig who spotted the other dog first, way before Nancy noticed the girl walking down the far side of the wheatfield. Nancy slipped a hand into the neck of her hoodie before their paths inevitably crossed, fishing for the wire to her earphones. She pictured them still sitting on the dresser in the hall. The girl walked closer, sunshine warming through the plum tones of her hair. Nancy looked over the wheat for Fig and any dubious behaviour that might land them in trouble.

'Morning!' the girl called. She slowed and yelled back

270

over her shoulder for her dog. 'Skye, come on.' Playful barks came from somewhere they couldn't see. The sun mustered itself overhead, a sudden tide of soft light flowed across the hillsides like spilt nectar.

'Morning,' replied Nancy. 'Beautiful day.'

'Did you see that *amazeballs* sky half an hour ago? Totally worth getting up for.' She wasn't much younger than Nancy. Young enough for a tongue stud and *Goonies* T-shirt. She might've gone to school with Mol, or maybe not. Behind her heavy-framed glasses it was hard deciding if she looked familiar.

'Yeah, I saw it. It was really something,' said Nancy.

Mol had tried a similar purple tint in her hair once. Nancy had copied but thought it too adventurous, immediately returning to the salon for another full head of corrective brunette. She wished she'd persevered with it now, that she looked as fresh and luminous as this smiley girl shining in the morning sun with her plum hair and bright eyes.

'Can't beat this countryside, huh? What more could you ask than this every morning?'

Nancy followed her gaze across the valley and felt a shift. Her heart a screwed-up paper bag steadily uncrumpling, filling with air and soft colour and *room*. Room for something else.

'No,' she agreed. 'Some places are hard to beat.' And impossible to forget.

The girl grinned as if Nancy's was a foregone conclusion. Mistleton. It was just so achingly beautiful here. How had she turned her back on it so completely? How had she forgotten that a new day could start this way? Mornings had become efficiency. Runs and stats and BPMs. How to shave time.

271

How to save it. How to be faster, faster, faster. But she wanted more of this, mornings like this girl, carefree and marvelling at the wonders around her. And Nancy felt it then. She felt like she was *here*. Really here. All of her, her whole self. Like this girl with her dog, basking in the privilege of a new day. And it felt good just standing close to it, perhaps in the same way it felt good to some people to stand close to Freddie Blumfield's vintage car.

The sounds of two dogs working something out between them erupted from the crops.

'What kind of dog have you got in there?' asked Nancy.

'Blue merle Border Collie. Yours?'

Fig rolled out of the wheat onto the track in a plume of dust, scrambled to her feet and skittered back in there again.

'Um, red menace . . . some sort of Lab cross?'

'Crossed with?'

'A walrus, or a Zeppelin or something.' The girl laughed. Her smile dipped at the edges. Annabel's did something similar. The familiarity made Nancy glad she'd left the earphones. 'She's not mine. I don't usually walk her.'

'No, I think I'd have seen you. The dog, though . . . You're Molly's sister, aren't you?'

Nancy looked out across the landscape, golden light kissing the hillside. *Are*. Not *was*. A constant and infinite thing. 'I am.'

The girl nodded. 'I liked her very much. She was a lot of fun.'

'She was.' Nancy smiled into herself. 'She was a lot of everything.' She nodded towards the barking. 'Do you walk here every morning?'

The girl held her face to the sun and smiled. 'I'm always here.'

Nancy didn't do this. She didn't open herself up to new people: single file, that was her usual route, the most fuss-free orderly way forwards, she'd thought.

'Maybe I'll see you tomorrow then,' she said.

A grey Collie with mottled fur and one piercing blue eye shot out of the wheatfield and trotted towards them.

'Come on then, Skye. Well, it was nice to meet you. And your red part-Lab, part-walrus menace.' The girl grinned at Nancy. 'See you around!'

Nancy held her hand up in a quick wave. 'Yeah. See you around.'

The girl and her dog started off. *Never Say Die*, her T-shirt said.

'Never say die, Mol,' said Nancy quietly. She watched the girl walk up to the brow of Coleman's Hill, where the sun blazed fiercest across the top of the valley. Nancy watched them until the light swallowed them up. She looked out over all that lay before her, the way the haze fell across the land, how the sycamore stood like a breakwater against time itself, both changed and unchanged by the seasons it had lived through. When the girl and her dog were completely out of sight, Nancy realised, so was Fig.

'Fig?' She looked to the top end of the wheatfield and called again. She took a slow walk up there. But there was no unnatural movement in the crop, no red form to break the patterns the breeze put there. A bang crackled through the distance, and Nancy watched the birds scatter from the copse of trees ahead. She shouted louder this time. 'Fig? Come on now!'

Nothing. Twenty minutes passed while Nancy walked back down into the valley to retrace her steps, all the way up again to the spot Fig had played with the grey Collie. The first butterflies started to stir in her stomach. There was a time Molly had wandered off from her in the supermarket and Nancy, realising there was an empty spot beside her where they'd stood looking for banana tarantulas, had felt a sticky ball of panic in her stomach. The feeling of not being careful enough with something you'd been entrusted with. She picked up her pace up the hillside, calling and looking and heading in the general direction of Beth's farmhouse further up the valley, just past the livery yard and barn where the anniversary party had been. 'Fig? Fig, here, girl!' She told herself it was too early to panic. Once she reached the brow, she'd be able to see every part of the valley Fig could've possibly reached.

Back at the brow, she scanned everything below her again, right down to the sycamore three fields over. *Nothing.* Another bang fractured the air. Bird scarer? Or shotgun? *Do not panic.* Fig must be over the ridge. Had to be. But at the other side of the ridge, Nancy's heart sank. Nothing to see but the openness of fields Whittacker had already harvested. Two tractors worked a field apart, scratching the surface of the earth with the stubble rakes dragged behind them. Nancy shielded her eyes from the sun and felt a thin sweat there. She'd stalked back up the hillside too fast. Her body felt heavy. Strange. As if she were slowly setting like candle wax. She scanned from horizon to hedgerow and back again.

'Fig! Come on, girl!' *Please.*

Whittacker had shot dogs before now. For bothering his sheep, getting too close. Nancy hadn't seen any sheep up here, but what if Fig had got up by the farm?

'Fig?' She'd lost her. She'd really lost her. The long tentacles of panic reached forwards. How would she explain it to Annabel? That she'd walked Molly's dog straight out here where people were legally allowed to kill her on sight? The adrenalin had started gradually at first, like a tap turned on to a trickle, but she was filling up now, fast. The fight-or-flight chemicals doing things to her skin, moving the blood around too quickly, making her head throb. 'Fig! Come on! This way!' But the shouting made her more panicked, more breathless.

One of the tractors stopped rolling. The door swung open and the driver jumped down into the dust. He started walking across the earth. Come to tell her off for leaving the right of way, trampling the crop. She blinked into the sun as he threw his arm over his head.

'Nancy?'

Clarence pushed his sleeves up and covered the last metres between them.

'Hi.' She tried to control her breathing. 'I didn't see it was you.'

'Yeah, how about that morning sun? Don't usually get to see it much, but there were a few earlier shifts going so they let me switch. Makes things a bit easier when you're functioning at the same time as the rest of the world.'

Nancy nodded. She didn't have the energy to talk about the weather any more this morning.

'Have you seen Fig?' She twisted the lead in her hands.

275

'I've lost her, about half an hour ago now.' Her voice twisted too. 'I have to find her, I can't go home without her.'

'Hey, don't worry.' There was Clarence with his upturned hands again. The horse whisperer. 'Did you see which way she went?'

Nancy shook her head. The need to cry suddenly filled her like tar, black and viscous.

'What if Whittacker shoots her?' She swallowed. Saying *shoots* out loud made her want to throw up.

Clarence laughed and rocked back on his heels.

'Whittacker? He mostly only aims the TV remote these days. Beth, on the other hand . . .'

Nancy tried to catch her breath, but it seemed to stick just under her ribs, where the sickly feeling was growing.

'I was headed to Beth's. I'll go straight there.' Before she could reach for her guns.

'Yeah, well, you probably should. Some bright spark at the catering company left one of their bins open behind the barn Saturday night. Beth's had everything except Nessie rocking up there for a raid. Maybe you'll find Fig there too?'

Nancy tried to take in more air, but it was no good. She set her hands on her knees for a second, just until her lungs slowed. Clarence ducked his head for a better look at her, not a bit of effort to hide his concern.

'Hey, are you OK? Do you need to sit down?'

Her grandmother's elephantine slip of the tongue yesterday stood proudly between them. Nancy shook her head and straightened up, before Ginny's truth bomb could cause any more embarrassment. It was nothing to do with Clarence, or anyone.

'I'm absolutely fine.' There would be no more interruptions from her body, she would take her pills and her gentle exercise and eat properly and go to her appointment at bloody cardiac rehab this week and be healthy and reliable and there when Annabel needed her to be. 'I just need to find Fig. Before she does anything . . . we can't fix.' But it had already been too long, she could be miles away. Something re-tightened itself in Nancy's chest.

'I'm due a breakfast break. I'll come with you. Four eyes are better than two, right? How is she at crossing cattle grids?'

Nancy tried to get a handle on the tugging feeling moving through her body. She looked in the direction of the main farm, the cattle grids at the gates. How was Fig at tripping the light fantastic over metal bars?

'Depends what's in that bin, I suppose.'

Clarence wiped his hands on a rag and stuffed it into his back pocket. Hands that were meant for piano keys and guitar strings, and nearly signing autographs. He started walking along the grooves in the field, turning his body for Nancy to follow.

'You sure you're OK?'

Nancy nodded and followed him, concentrating on her feet, her breathing. Clarence walked steadily, but every step Nancy took asked for more oxygen than the air was giving her. At the cattle grid, she wanted to hold onto the fence post, just for a minute, but the thought of Clarence slowing down any more for her was too much. They'd reached the edge of the first barn before the faintness made its lunge.

'I need to stop a sec.' Was that wheezing her? *Shit*. She

needed air. She slouched against the corner of the barn, blackened weatherboards warm against her back.

'Nance?'

No, this was not happening. Not here. Anywhere but here. She closed her eyes while the palpitations tried to run away from her. *Stay calm.* It wasn't as bad as before, she didn't think, so that was something. She'd overdone it on the hill, that was all.

Clarence doubled back. 'Hey, hey . . . you said you were fine!'

'I *am* fine.' She kept her eyes closed. 'I just need a second. Or maybe a minute.' *Just a minute.* She held two fingers up. 'Two, max.' But it was suddenly there, an arm slipping behind her shoulder blades. 'What are you . . .' but her head lolled back of its own accord. She found herself looking up at the sky for a second, at all that blue above, while she tried catching that one big elusive lungful of air. It was a perfect cloudless sky, she noticed, but then the blue turned to other colours, the dark underside of a roof with rafters and thick timber trusses and strings of unlit light bulbs.

'Let's just sit you down here a second. Breathe, OK?' Clarence propped her against a stack of hay bales and crouched down in front of her, careful not to touch her again. 'Slow and steady, in through your nose . . . that's it, and back out . . .'

'Sorry,' she managed.

'What for?'

She tried counting it away like before, slow and steady, *one hundred . . . ninety-nine . . . ninety-eight . . .* 'I'm fine, honest.'

278

'You don't look fine. You're pretty pale. Should I call Annabel?' Nancy blinked at him. They'd been here before. Clarence trying his best, asking to call her mother.

'No. Thanks. Really.' She concentrated. *Ninety-one . . . ninety . . . eighty-nine . . .* Her breathing started to settle, she could feel it calming again, as soon as she'd stopped moving. 'Sorry,' she said again. 'Don't call her, she'll only worry.'

Annabel would still be sleeping it off, she thought, but Nancy wouldn't share this knowledge with Clarence, who'd seen enough of mothers undone by too much brandy.

Clarence was staring. He rubbed his forehead and looked Nancy over, indiscreetly searching for signs of something fixable.

'Help me out here, Nancy. What do you need?' He scratched his eyebrow with his thumb and frowned. He'd always looked serious. Clarence Ludlow had been a serious little boy. A serious teenager with his serious name. Molly must have mocked him mercilessly for it all.

'I just need to find Fig,' she tried in a straight voice, but the air was going again. 'I can't lose her, Clarence. I can't . . . lose her dog. Mum can't lose any more of . . .'

Her throat tightened, ready to swallow back any tears. She thought then that she might've just about got it trapped, caught by the tip of its wing before it could escape from her into the open – the crying she'd managed to contain all this time – so it wouldn't get away and undo her.

Clarence sat down on the bale beside her.

'We'll find Fig. But I think Annabel will be more concerned with knowing you're OK, Nance. Are you?'

Clarence was trying to be careful too. Always trying.

Nancy suddenly felt tired again, tired of holding all the dark parts inside out of the light, where they couldn't be looked at or poked. It was just so draining. This was why most people cried, to decompress, ease off some of the pressure inside. But it was unfair to inflict tears upon someone who'd only ever tried to be kind to you, never asking anything in return. An unfair game with unfair disadvantages.

Her voice almost cracked, but she held it steady.

'Annabel thinks I'm better than I am. A better person, I mean.' Today was supposed to be the first move in a new direction, helping, being there, but it felt like it was already slipping through her fingers. 'You know me, though, don't you, Clarence?' A no-show.

'Not really, no. You're a bit of a mystery actually, Nance.'

He knew her enough to give her a helicopter wish. She looked into her lap, thought of him watching her picking through the snow for them.

'I'm sorry I shouted at you. On the furlong.' He squinted for a second, kept his eyes on her while she felt her mouth wobble around the words she wanted to get out intact. 'I was ashamed at what you saw. I didn't go to her. And I didn't say goodbye. And now there's nowhere to go and say goodbye. Because she didn't want us crying over a headstone. So she hasn't got one. So there's nowhere to go and say *anything*.'

Clarence was motionless. Dust from the barn floor floated between them in the shard of sunlight that had followed them in through the doors.

'That's the way of it sometimes, Nance. Mol knew what she wanted.'

'She wanted me to be there. At the house. I threw away my last chance to be with her.' And Clarence had seen her do it.

Clarence sighed long and slow. Dust motes spun away from him through the blade of light touching his face.

'There's more than one way to be with someone, Nance.'

Nancy blinked at him. 'She's *gone*, Clarence. We've lost her. She's not . . . over the hills and far away somewhere with Fig.' There was something in her voice she didn't recognise, a hard inflection she didn't like. But Clarence was unaffected.

'Have you looked for her?'

'What?'

Clarence frowned at her. 'You're a smart girl, Nance. You always were the smartest. You know characters that big don't just poof into thin air. Atom bombs have smaller fallouts.'

Nancy blinked again. Her trail of thought, shut off like a kinked hose. 'Mol's gone, Clarence.'

'Maybe you're just not looking for her in the right places?' He picked up a spear of hay and moved it around in the dust on the floor. 'There are ways to find a person who feels lost to you, Nancy. It won't make sense to everyone, but it's always made sense to me.'

Nancy swallowed. 'What has?'

'My mum, half my life she's been lost. In the room, but not in the room. Talking to me, but not with me. Half of our time together has been like living on either side of a thick piece of glass. But when I was little, I found that I could, sort of, find my way back to her . . . in other ways.'

Nancy shifted herself. Waited for him to go on.

'I'd read her favourite poems, or learn her favourite songs, play them for her on her piano while she lay down

281

upstairs not wanting to speak to me that day. Crazy rituals, I guess. But she was always there, Nance. In those songs, and words . . . in my fingers when I play the notes or turn the pages. Wherever my mum is, wherever it is she goes off to in herself, that mysterious place I can't follow her into . . . she is always still there in those things that ground her in our life. Traces of her, waiting for me to find them.'

Crazy rituals. Like sending text messages into the void. Hoping they'd somehow make it to the other side. Knowing they'd never be answered.

'Life, the people in it . . . none of it comes as a neatly packaged, perfectly formed gift, Nance. Love is no different. Sometimes it comes in pieces. It's how you choose to pick them all up and hold on to them that makes the difference.'

Nancy watched the patterns Clarence scratched into the dust. Round and round in a figure of eight.

'I can't even find an overweight red-furred dog in an open field, Clarence.' How would she find her way back to Molly? She couldn't even talk about her properly. To Annabel. Or Clarence. Who'd loved her too.

'And?'

'And . . . it's like our life together . . . doesn't exist any more. Wiped from the map. And my mum . . . we've sort of lost our way. I thought everything was moving along OK for Annabel, but now I'm home . . .'

'Things look different up close? Don't they always?'

'It's not just that.' Nancy pushed her hair back through her hands. 'It's like . . . we were made up of coordinates, three sets, and now Mol's not here, we're never going to be able to find our way back to each other.'

Clarence was watching her, waiting for her to catch up, it felt. 'You'll find your way. Keep looking.'

Nancy shook her head to herself. 'Where, Clarence? That place just doesn't exist any more. And it hurts being reminded of it. It's safer not to look in the first place.'

'Safe? There's no such thing. Nancy, this is *life*. Welcome. It's joyous and painful and everything else in between, but it is never *safe*. I don't want *safe*.'

'You don't?' Clarence who'd lived a life of turmoil, one extreme to the next in ten breakneck seconds, Birdie behind the wheel of their runaway car.

'You've got to take your chances and keep going. Squeeze out every bit of colour along the way. Knowing how to fly . . . it's my mum's greatest gift.'

'Birdie knows how to fly?'

'I reckon,' smiled Clarence. 'When she's on a high, she knows to go as far up as she can. In the spaces between her tough days, she gets as much living done as she can shoehorn in. Honestly, it's exhausting, but . . . I *love* that she wastes not a single second of it. And if I wasted a second of *my* life, how could I look her in the eye?'

'Wow,' said Nancy. 'No wonder you were drawn to Mol. You're used to the colour.' Everyone else must look pretty dull next to the mainstay women in Clarence's world.

'People are colourful, Nance. Even if they don't know it.'

'*Some* people are colourful,' corrected Nancy. 'Most are just . . . disappointing.'

'Whoa, not all of us, surely?'

She didn't mean Clarence. Didn't know him enough either

283

way. You had to get up close to a person before they could really feel out of reach.

'It's just part of the human condition, Clarence.'

'Excellent. Crushing disappointment. Something to look forward to.'

'You might get lucky. I just don't think the odds are all that great, for any sort of relationship really. The more you love something, the more it hurts when it eventually, inevitably implodes.'

Clarence was shaking his head now. 'Nance, you're killing me here. Every song I ever wrote pretty much is based on the premise that . . . love will endure!'

He looked up at her as if he honestly had no clue what she was talking about. Nancy smiled at him, as if spelling out the obvious. Love, in all its manifestations, was going to hurt. Like the five-scoopers at Scorlucci's, the sharp, splitting brain freeze that would strike them down after the sweetness of the sugar hit. Love was pain, in thirty different flavours.

'I don't know why you would think like that, Nancy. It's so different to how . . .' To how Molly saw the world.

'Because you can't keep them, Clarence. No matter how much you love them.'

A woman's voice reached ahead through the barn doors.

'Barney? Is that you in there? Until everything's cleaned up, could you *please* keep these doors closed or it'll be like Noah's bloody ark again.'

Beth's voice was easy to place. Clarence looked across the gloom towards the yard outside. Beth's footsteps growing closer. Nancy tucked her hair behind her ears, tried to feel

284

casual in her own body again. Beth could sniff a drama at a hundred paces. Clarence held out his hand. Nancy took it, letting him pull her to her feet.

'Feeling OK?' he asked.

'Yeah. Thanks.' No more uphilling, though. Not yet.

Clarence smiled, but there was a new tension in his jaw.

'Oh, hi, Clarence. And . . . *Nancy*?'

Nancy intercepted Beth with a wide smile. 'Hey, you found the keys! I can't believe it. Are they in here, or . . .?'

Beth looked from Nancy to Clarence, Nancy stealing the chance to furtively rub at the tightness over her ribs. 'No, they're up at the house. I've got something else of yours up there too. I'm not sure you want it, though, it's covered in fox shit.'

Chapter 22

Clarence pulled up to a stop on his driveway. Fig sat up front with them in the van, swaddled in an old towel from Beth's stable block and stinking to high heaven, stationed between them like a chaperone, or a shamed teenager being driven home in silence. They'd found her up by the farmhouse, fraternising with one of the working dogs and smeared collar to shoulder in the foulest substance ever suffered by human nostrils. Clarence had tied her to one of the gates in the livery yard and hosed her off, lathering the worst of the fox poo with the Fairy Liquid Beth's husband had found. He had kept his head facing away over his shoulder throughout, trying not to heave, while Beth had stood next to Nancy grinning over a mug of honeyed tea.

Nancy bit a smile in the passenger seat, Fig happily panting towards Clarence. Clarence had got the worst shoulder, despite the hosing in Beth's yard. Twice he'd heaved towards his open window, both times smiling an apology at Nancy with watery blue eyes. Twice she'd laughed silently out of her own window. There'd hadn't been much conversation on the way back to the house, just an easy quiet, around the heaving.

She waited for him to shut off the engine, casually stealing a look at Birdie's home, the neat little porchway bleached white where the ivy didn't touch, the storm lantern by the door. Just through the side window, a glimpse of Birdie's hallway, a little of the living room beyond, just an edge of a piano against the far wall. She unclicked her belt.

Clarence cleared his throat quietly. 'So, can I ask you something?'

Nancy's hand hovered at the belt buckle. She looked around Fig to Clarence in the driver's seat.

'Sure.'

'This thing, your heart . . .'

'That was just my gran, exaggerating.'

'Your gran didn't make you nearly pass out up by the yard though, did she? What happened up there?'

'It's no big deal. I just felt a little . . . buzzy.' But the look on Clarence's face said it wasn't going to be enough, certainly not after his efforts with the fox poo. Nancy smiled, shrugged, tried to keep it small, contained. 'The muscle, sometimes it backfires or something. Like a car. It's temporary, I just need to give it chance to settle down again. Like a swollen ankle.'

'Swollen ankle? Should you be hiking up Saxon's Hill with a swollen ankle?'

'Probably not. I'd have been fine if Fig hadn't stressed me out. The adrenalin doesn't agree with me, apparently. That's all. Sorry about the drama. And the smell.' She grimaced. 'Fig owes you one, big time, for letting her in your truck.'

He'd insisted on driving them home, a quick drop-off then

back to work. Nancy had said how happy she was to walk but was quietly relieved when Clarence hadn't made her.

'Are you sure you don't want me to drop you outside yours?'

'No, really, there's no need.' She clambered out of the van, Fig following, leaving the towel behind for Clarence. She slammed the door shut then held onto the window ledge. 'Shall I take that, get it washed and back to Beth?'

'No, it's OK. I'll sort it.'

'OK. Well, thanks for the ride.'

'Yeah. Hey, Nance?' She slowed on the driveway. 'Do they still let dogs in the Jack?'

Nancy frowned and looked down at Fig. 'Not ones like this, I'll bet. Why?'

'I was thinking . . . she might want to take me sometime. See if the beer is any cooler these days. Maybe buy me one to say thanks for the shower?'

'Fig?'

'You could always . . . tag along?'

Clarence moved his arm from where it had been resting over the middle seat. He rolled his shoulders forwards, waiting for Nancy's answer, which had already stretched past the point of awkward. Hadn't they covered this already? Up on Beth's hay bales? The inevitability of the human condition? The crash that would always come after the climb, sooner or later. The Icarus paradox.

'It's just a warm beer, Nance.'

Her heart began a gentle thumping, but there was a difference between panicking for lost dogs and more frightening things, like drinks. She thought of Annabel then, making herself go to all those hobby clubs with people, real people, when she had always been more suited to staying home in her own company.

It fell out of her mouth. Before she could change her mind. 'Sure.'

'Tomorrow?' asked Clarence. He looked surprised. 'Eight OK?'

'Yep . . . eight works.'

She saw a smile then, just at the corner of his mouth.

'See you at eight then. I'll meet you there.'

Nancy left him on the driveway and walked the pavement to the sounds of Clarence pulling onto Mountford Road, driving back to work. The birds yabbered above them in the damson trees as Fig walked underneath, a mail van pulled up at the postbox at the top of the road, the thrum of a lawnmower bounced between the buildings. Normal things on a normal day. But this was not normal. She walked the last few yards, past Ernie's front garden with its massive horse chestnut tree, to her mum's house, wondering what a normal day might look like to Clarence, how different it was now that he was home so much, and not living the dream. How quickly *normal* had shifted for him, how long it would take to return once Birdie was home again.

Fig trotted through the house, glugged from her bowl and settled herself straight into her bed, already spent for the day. Nancy took in the sheer cheek of her. She pulled her phone from her pocket to send Beth a quick thank-you text for saving the day, but found herself obeying old instincts instead.

This dog has shaved years off me today.

Fig wagged her tail for no particular reason. Nancy gave her a soft fuss behind the ear.

She misses you. Clarence and Beth miss you. We all miss you xx

She hit send and sank the phone back into her pocket. She noticed the ibuprofen slip on the kitchen table and picked the foil off the blister pack where two pills had been popped free. The granola was still there, untouched. Outside, far enough down the garden that Ernest wouldn't see her past the fruit trees, Annabel sat in the swing seat facing the meadows. Her head moved to follow a flock of something over the millstream. Nancy hooked Fig's lead on the back of the door to the downstairs loo. One of Mol's stickers came away from the map, flittering to the floor. She picked it up. There were no obvious signs to show where it had come from, which of Mol's suggestions it had pinpointed. She examined the turquoise sticky dot on her finger, made a mental note to move the map, before any more of the stickers could be knocked off. She tried to pick somewhere to put the coloured dot. Life sure would be simpler if there was a stickered path to show the way. To map the course.

She left, taking the sticky dot with her for now, for safe keeping, and pushed through the back doors into the garden. The shadow of last night was still at Annabel's shoulder. Only Molly would be able to show Annabel how to still be her mother. Only Mol had that power.

'Mum?'

Annabel was wrapped in a chunky cardigan, tufted in places so that from behind she looked like a misshapen conker fallen onto the swing chair. Nancy sat down beside her, the two of them motionless on a chair made for movement.

'Hi, love.' Annabel smiled but didn't look up.

'How's the head?'

'Feeling sorry for itself.' She smiled again, wrapping her cardigan tightly around herself. 'I can't think how poor Birdie gets on.'

Nancy studied their mum's profile as she watched the meadow. The pale blue of her eyes. Her tiredness.

'If I'd have known there was an old bottle of Courvoisier in the sideboard, I'd have glugged it before Gran arrived yesterday. Could've saved you half a headache.'

'Sorry, Nance. I don't know what came over me last night. That's not the norm, I don't want you to think that's what I do here all week, when you're not here, I don't even like alcohol. It had just . . . been a bit of a day.'

'Mum. You don't need to say anything. I know. We all need a blowout from time to time.' Picking up a few bottles a week on the way home from work had become standard practice. The relief Nancy felt was no small thing, that while here she'd been able to go without. That it hadn't become another part of her that she couldn't completely get a hold of. 'Can I get you something to eat? You'll feel better.'

'I'm supposed to be looking after you,' said Annabel.

'You are. How about some granola? Or a poached egg?' Annabel put a hand over her stomach. 'OK, no eggs. Got it.'

'Sorry, love. I'll be better in a few hours.'

'Well . . . you've got until tomorrow.'

Annabel smiled wearily. 'To do what, sweetheart?'

291

Nancy tried for a stern expression. 'To straighten yourself out, young lady.'

Annabel almost laughed and returned her gaze to the fields. 'I think it might take longer than that, kiddo.' She looked like she might cry again, or go back inside and crack on with the brandy.

'Look, Mum . . . today has been really weird already and this is my first go at a motivational speech that doesn't involve brand awareness and audience saturation, so just . . . bear with.' Nancy reached over and took hold of her mum's hand. Annabel's fingers closed tightly around hers. 'First, we need you to get over your stinking hangover. So you've got today to lounge around in your pyjamas and this strange cardi you've got going on. The whole day to feel sorry for yourself for overdoing it last night, feel sorry for *me*, eat my super-granola and binge-watch some crap with me on Netflix. But tomorrow . . .' Annabel's lip wobbled. Nancy gave her hand another squeeze. 'If you don't mind missing whatever group it is you've got going on with the WI or gardener's guild, I thought we could go and do something together?'

'You and me? Again?'

'Yeah. But not to the pottery barn, somewhere just the two of us. On our own. I thought maybe we could go and visit the estuary. See how we feel about . . . scattering some of Mol's ashes there. Eventually.'

She couldn't help the caveat. She wasn't ready, not yet. But Annabel needed to be Molly's mum, and this was something only a mother could do, decide if the scenery was beautiful enough, worthy enough for her daughter.

'OK, Nance.'

Nancy exhaled deeply. 'I'll have to be back by six, though. I need to shower, and find something to wear, and maybe down the rest of your brandy before I change my mind and cancel.'

'Cancel what?'

She wasn't really sure. 'I think . . . a *date*.' She'd allow herself one beer. Then cruise back to fruit juices.

'With Clarence?' Annabel spasmed to life, a yip jumping from her throat. 'Ah, Nancy! That's *wonderful*! Oh, that boy.'

Oh God. Nancy might need the brandy now. 'Don't get too excited, Mum. It's just . . . a warm beer.'

But she could already feel the sticky film of anticipation along her lip, the same stickiness she'd feel before facing down a delegation of clients when the budget had gone to shit. A nervous, hopeful, resigned kind of trepidation she liked to run out of her system with 10K around Chortley Park.

'She was right,' said Annabel, smiling towards the meadows.

'Who was?'

'Your sister. She said she knew you both better than you know yourselves. That it might take you a while, but . . .' Nancy thumbed Molly's turquoise sticker as Annabel hypothesised about forces Nancy didn't believe in. '... some things are just . . . mapped.'

Chapter 23

The exercise bikes at Garfield's were old and peeling, spongy grab handles flaking away in chunks so that polished gym bunnies like Nancy and Haima could feel aligned with their inner Rocky Balboas, working out rough-tough style, honest exercise minus the glitz, or so the theory went. Nancy knew the mood-boosting benefits of spinning. Biking was the perfect low-impact cardiovascular exercise, she had assured her mum at the cycle hire shop. But Garfield's, for all its mood boosting, had absolutely nothing on the ride they were enjoying down to the estuary this morning.

'Isn't this *beautiful*?' Annabel called ahead. Her bike wheels whirred reassuringly behind Nancy's. The estuary path was flanked by a rising wall of pine, green shadows arching around the sweep of the cycle lane like outstretched wings. To the left of them, the ocean reached a long silvery finger into the land, beckoning them towards the coastline they'd spent bygone days along, bucketing crabs, drawing their names in sand and, later, sitting around beach fires with other teenagers and beer bottles and stories.

Nancy pedalled on, inhaled a great lungful of cool coastal air, felt it fill her up. You didn't get this at Garfield's, how had she not realised?

'It's so beautiful, Mum. I'd forgotten!'

Today had been for Annabel, but the endorphins flowed through Nancy now like warm honey. *How* had she forgotten this place? This feeling. They used to come here every weekend through summer, Annabel following them on foot with the buckets and bacon rind as they bombed up and down the cycle path to the water.

Nancy glanced back over her shoulder, Annabel swaying with her body to the movement of her pedalling, the breeze flicking her curls back over her shoulders. It turned out Mol must've inherited her cast-iron hangover resilience straight from their mum, who'd bounced out of bed this morning like a spring lamb. Her enthusiasm might've wobbled Nancy, but then they'd clipped their helmets on and taken the sweep out past the last of the dunes, and all hesitancy had thinned away. Annabel hadn't ever said where she thought they should scatter Molly's ashes, had never pushed for it to be dealt with. They hadn't brought them today: this was a recce, after all, nothing more . . . But for the first time, Nancy found herself trying to unpick her own matted logic. She'd wanted to keep Molly safe. But a tub in their mum's wardrobe, that wasn't where she should be. No part of her should be in there. *Everywhere and nowhere*. Had Mol really needed to say, *But not next to Mum's weird cardigans*?

'How far are we going?' called Annabel.

The sun picked out the inlet, still at least two miles away. 'All the way, Mum. Just keep pedalling!'

'What?'

'Keep pedalling!'

They would go all the way to Mol's best crabbing spot and back again.

The morning rolled over and stretched itself into an afternoon spent picking through the olives and breads and cheeses Nancy had packed into a small picnic, and the many stories they could remember of their days together on the sands. It had felt critical, yesterday, to figure out a way to carefully remind Annabel what the signature of Mol's life had been. The mischief and melodrama and fun of her. The absolute absence of unhappiness. But today, it had felt less of an effort, more an easy remembrance, an old choreography finding itself again, back into your fingers and muscles and feet. Like riding a bike.

They'd spent a slow, easy afternoon together, watching the water follow its own rhythm, in and out of the land, the push-pull of inevitability, back and forth, day and night, sunshine and snow. They'd sat and snacked and watched and reminded each other how much Molly had loved her life. Loved her people. And she had been loved back, and there wasn't anything, *anything*, that could ever undo these truths. Annabel would always be her mum. Nancy would always be her sister. Just as surely as the tide would always, eventually, come back in.

But beautiful as it was, the estuary did not feel like the place to give Molly's ashes back to the land. Even with the promise of coastal breezes and brackish currents to carry her far and wide, the feeling had quietly grown through the afternoon. Nancy didn't want to leave her here. She looked out at the sunlight dancing on the water, at all this peacefulness, and willed herself to be more open to it. She couldn't explain why exactly, but it just didn't feel . . .

'Nance?'

'Hmm?'

'I absolutely love it here. But . . . I'm not sure why . . . I don't think this is the right place for her. It's *completely* stunning, but it just doesn't feel . . .'

'I know, Mum.' The relief was almost overwhelming. 'We'll find the place.'

It was mid afternoon before Nancy watched her mum clamber back onto her bike and push off again. Annabel led the way this time, back to the estuary path, concentrating on her resurrected balance. At some point during the day, Nancy had found hers too. A new rhythm with Annabel, the equal sharing of one load.

'Are you eating before you go out later? Or do you think you'll have a meal with Clarence?' called Annabel over her shoulder.

Nancy's stomach rolled over. They'd be back at the hire shop soon. Quick handover, drive home. Snack if she could stomach one.

'It's just the Jack, Mum. We're not having three courses of bar snacks.'

Nancy's front wheel hit a dink in the path; she wobbled violently then righted herself. Her heart pounded. She had nothing to wear, everything she'd brought was plain. Wearing Mol's things, no. Not for a drink. With Clarence. A drink with Clarence Ludlow in the Jack.

The visitor centre came into view through the trees. A series of large timber-clad huts made up the educational workshops, cycle hire and café serving light bites and coffees against an eclectic backdrop of English Heritage giftware and beady-eyed taxidermy. Annabel rang her bicycle bell.

'We've made it back in one piece!' she called triumphantly. 'Could we just pull in here for five, Nance? I could do with popping to the ladies'.'

They pushed past the dusty disabled parking bays and dismounted beside the tour bus parked alongside the visitor centre entrance.

'I'll wait with the bikes.'

Annabel nodded and disappeared through the automatic doors. Nancy watched the glass slide open for her, stickered with window transfers of winged bugs. Maybe damselflies? They used to chase them over the fields, petrol-blue toothpicks always too fast for any of them. The doors closed again and Nancy got a look at the rest of the graphics stuck to the glass. Egg . . . Hatching egg . . . Nymph . . . The life cycle of a mayfly. *Short and Sweet!* shouted the caption. She idled between the bikes and read the infographic. Twenty-four hours. Was that all they got? Twenty-four hours to pack it all in? She thought about all the time she'd wasted waiting for the wrong things, the wrong people. Mistakes not afforded to other creatures that had no time for dithering. Or regret.

The doors slid open again and *Short* and *Sweet* parted for Annabel.

'All set?' asked Nancy.

Annabel nodded. 'My rear's aching like nobody's business.' She dropped to a whisper. 'I just used the *grab rail* to get back off the loo. Now my ruddy shoelace needs tying. Can we move over to those picnic tables so I don't have to bend so far?'

'You should've tied it while you were on the loo,' smiled Nancy.

They crossed the grass, propping both bikes against the first bench. Annabel sat carefully on a bottom not used to bicycles. 'Here, let me do it.' Nancy knelt and started tying her mum's bootlace. 'You've tied mine enough.'

A fleck of white fluttered past her fingers, snagging in the grass just in front of Annabel's boot. Nancy's hands slowed. Annabel reached down for the small, perfect feather before the breeze could steal it again.

'Better take it home . . . just in case.'

Nancy finished her double knot. 'You never know, right?'

Annabel smiled down at herself. 'It's silly.'

'It's not silly,' said Nancy, standing.

'The things we do, hey?'

Nancy hung her helmet over the handlebars of her bike. 'Ready?'

'Yep.'

They pushed the bikes towards the hire station, a timber chalet the other side of the car park they needed to catch before closing. Nancy craned her head. They couldn't see the chalet yet, the car park had filled with two large coaches, blocking the view.

'Nance?'

'Yeah?'

'I've had a really lovely time with you today. Going to the waterfront. I haven't been down there for so long. It was . . . wonderful.'

'Better than crochet club?' smiled Nancy, relieved that it had been, surely.

Annabel pulled a stilted smile. She walked quietly for a while.

'Nancy? I wanted to speak to you about something actually.' Her smile fell lopsidedly. 'I was thinking about it all day yesterday actually. I don't want there to be any . . . silly untruths between us.'

Nancy felt herself slow, feet hesitant, a trip hazard ahead. She'd thought about it down by the water today, about telling Annabel what the doctors had really said, explaining why Takotsubo was different to a minor heart attack, better, really. If you were being objective about it. More fixable. Less dramatic. Sort of. But it would've spoiled the day, knowing this thing in her daughter's chest wasn't just down to bad luck or lifestyle or busyness, but something deeper-rooted. Annabel didn't need to know, what was the point when the outcome was the same anyway?

'Untruths?' she asked gingerly. Could Annabel have seen the papers in Nancy's case? No. Annabel wouldn't pry, no way. The iPad, then? But Nancy had been careful, hadn't she? When she'd used it to read up on her cardiomyopathy, she'd always been careful to scrub the history.

'I should've said something the other night. When the brandy had taken over,' laughed Annabel nervously.

Nancy braced herself. It was going to be even harder hearing her mum talk about it now, while she was sober.

'About what?' She kept her eyes on the path.

'No, it's nothing *terrible*. Not really,' reassured Annabel. 'It's just . . . I haven't been going to crochet club, Nance. Or any club.'

Nancy frowned. 'I don't follow.'

'Don't be cross. I just . . . I didn't want you ever to feel you had to come home and keep tabs on me, or worry about what I was doing or *not* doing with myself. You know? I thought it would be best if you just thought I had one or two pastimes. That's all.'

Nancy watched her bike wheel rolling slowly over the path. She ran through them all. Flower-arranging. Cake and conversation mornings at the care home. Basket-weaving. Artisanal bread club. Gardeners' meets. WI. Everything Annabel had phoned up and chatted animatedly about. For almost *two years*.

'Nancy, say something.'

Nancy's wheel wobbled before she righted it again. 'But . . . you're always at them?' She'd never bothered to dig deeper, though, ask questions, learn more. 'All the time I've been home, you . . .' Annabel had never brought a single flower arrangement back. No cakes or crochet. All those hours she'd spent away from the house. Away from Nancy. 'Where have you *been*?'

'Nowhere really. Everywhere,' Annabel sputtered. 'Around.'

'Around? You've been *out* for nearly two years, Mum! Every time I called, you'd have to call back?'

'The answer machine has been a handy accomplice, Nance.'

301

'But I've been home nearly a fortnight. Where have you been going? Why have you *still* been going?'

Annabel winced. 'I didn't want to leave you home alone, but I know you like your space. How stifled you felt being back here. You were so quick to get out into the world, find your own home, be your own person, be independent from everything else. I could see how much you wanted to stay in your apartment when I picked you up from the hospital, it was plain as your nose, love. You looked *panic-stricken* at the prospect of coming home with me. I didn't want to make it . . . worse. So I thought I'd give you a few hours each day to yourself, take myself off to a few places to sit with my book, and a flask and sandwich.'

Nancy put her hand on Annabel's handlebars, bringing them both to a wobbled halt.

'Like where?' This was not OK. Why exactly, Nancy couldn't put her finger on, and then it hit her, like a shoe flung from a tree. Her mum had been hiding. From *her*.

Annabel was watching her. Eyes worried and uncertain. A look passed over her face as if she'd been caught doing something unforgivable.

'Car parks. Mainly. Until last Tuesday. It's surprising how many people you know in a car park, I found myself having to move further afield. I'd been ending up towards the woods over by Cranton, but then last Tuesday a plain-clothed police officer came over to the car and tapped my window.'

'Plain-clothes police?'

'A *sting*. He said they'd been watching me for some time and was I aware my number plate had been reported as a *repeat visitor*. Did I know I'd parked in a *hotspot*. It was the way he said *frequenting*, as if I knew exactly what he was going to say next. Nancy, it was awful. He really startled me when he tapped the window. I dropped my pickled onion. It rolled somewhere under my driver's seat and I can't ruddy get at it. Now the truck smells of vinegar.'

'Hotspot for what, Mum?' It was as if her mum had been leading a double life. Annabel checked about them and mouthed something. Nancy squinted. Annabel mouthed it again, slowly.

'Bloody *dogging*?' exclaimed Nancy.

Annabel slunk into her shoulders. A rabble of schoolchildren trailed like ants from the gift shop towards the parked buses.

'Shh! Well, yes. But I wasn't there for *that*, Nancy, ruddy heck.'

Nancy imagined the scene, her mother parked up in remote areas of natural interest. The sort of *natural interest* other people there, strange men, might've been taking in her, eating her pickled onions alone, oblivious.

She shook her head to herself, blinked at the ground. 'Oh my God. I'm sorry, Mum.'

Annabel smiled nervously. 'Whatever for?'

'For chasing you out.' For making her think she couldn't tell her own kid when she was having a rough day, leaving Nancy to catch the tail end of it instead, sitting on the lounge floor with a brandy bottle. She was suddenly sorry for lots of things. For telling Annabel she shouldn't sleep in Mol's bed. Giving her a heart condition to worry over and not even being completely honest about that either. 'I love you, Mum. I worry about you, but I don't even worry in the right places, about the right things.' When Molly would know instinctively.

'Well I hope you aren't worrying that I'm cruising beauty spots to satisfy my needs? Because trust me, Nance, you needn't.'

'No.' A hard lump was forming in her throat. 'I worry that . . . you're *alone*.'

Annabel searched for the right words. 'I like being alone. I'd always rather be with you girls. But otherwise, I'm OK by myself. I think people think you have to have a plan, a strategy for companionship, but believe me when I say this, Nance, I like my own company. Some folks throw themselves into busyness or work or action of some kind, but we're all different. You like being at work. But I like being home. I like having your sister's things around me. *Your* things around me. Even Fig around me! I'm OK, Nance. Really, I am. Apart from being saddle sore. I'm OK. And I want you to know that. I want you to visit because you *want* to. Not because you think you need to. I don't ever want to take away your breathing space, Nancy. There's no darker force than an overbearing parent, trust me. I never wanted to be that to you girls.'

'You think you're overbearing?'

'Well, I hope not. But these things come about, don't they? Passed down. And it isn't what I think that matters anyway. It's what *you* think. I never wanted you to feel I was sticking my oar in. Molly was different . . . boy, did she love attention. *Thrived* in a crowd. Even when it was just a crowd of one. But you, Nance . . . I think you're still finding your way.'

Annabel put her hand over Nancy's. Nancy's brain hurt.

304

She took in a great juddery breath like the ones children took after crying.

'No more car parks, Mum. Because actually there are darker forces than overbearing mothers . . . like strangers winking at you from behind the trees up Cranton Woods.'

Annabel grinned at her handlebars. She held up a three-fingered salute.

'Brownie promise.' Her eyes were shockingly blue when threatening tears. 'No more car parks. Or secrets.' Nancy bit her lip. 'We're going to be OK, Nance.' Annabel gave her another smile. 'And even when I'm moaning about my tender parts later, I just want you to know . . . today's been one of my absolute *favourite* days.'

She pushed Nancy's hair aside and tucked it behind her ears.

'Shall we ride the last bit? Before I start acting my age again?' Nancy nodded. 'Come on then, kiddo. Cock a leg.'

Nancy got back on her bike. 'Cock a leg? Where'd you pick that up?'

'Not sure, might've heard it up Cranton Woods car park.'

Nancy shook her head. 'Do *not* need to know.'

'It's not all bad,' said Annabel, trying to catch her pedals. 'The officer who knocked my window was lovely, he had one of those fashionable moustaches you see all the time nowadays on young men who like to wear tight trousers. You know the ones.'

'You're a moustache connoisseur now then, Mum? Ernie's got a lovely moustache, don't you think?'

'Just concentrate on the path.'

The path took them towards the school kids, milling

around the bus doors in their blazers and untucked shirts. A shoal of young teenagers suddenly dispersed like fish around a predator.

'Er, don't get it on me!' squealed one girl. 'I hate milkshake.' Other girls were laughing now too, pointing at the boy looking down at the pink mess dripping from his trousers.

'Robinson, you look *shaken* . . . get it?'

'Who was that?' barked the only teacher. 'Ray? How did that happen?'

Annabel braked too hard and pattered along on her tiptoes to save her balance. She turned her head fast enough that her helmet slipped back, sitting wonkily on her head.

'Did you see that?' she asked Nancy. 'That's Ernest's grandson, did you see that boy blow milkshake from his straw?' Nancy looked past her mum's shocked expression. Ray was doing his best with the tissues his teacher handed him.

'I didn't see.'

'That boy there. With the white hair. I know that boy, I've seen him up and down our street,' said Annabel.

'Yeah. He lives on the corner of Spring Lane. With the double garage and private number plates.'

'How do you know?'

Ray had told her. On their walk back from the sycamore. 'I think Ray's had some trouble making friends.'

'Hey, you there!' Annabel called across the car park. Damsons . . . milkshakes . . . nothing brought out her protective streak like a launched missile and a gang of sniggering youths.

'Mum, don't.'

'What do you mean?'

'You might make it worse.'

'I saw him do it! If I go over there now and tell their teacher, at least they'll know Ray hasn't snitched.'

Nancy felt a familiar cowardice slide over her. 'You might just make the blond kid sneakier, more careful about who's watching next time.' Mean kids were all the same.

'What do you suggest, then? We can't do nothing.'

'I don't know.'

Nancy looked at Ray dabbing pink milk from his trousers, moving the mess around into a larger blob of disaster. There wasn't another kid in sight trying to give him a hand. No one giving the blond boy any grief, or telling the giggling girls to shut up. No fearless sibling like Mol to jump in and avenge him. Ray looked up at Nancy then, a moment of recognition before turning away, sinking back into his predicament.

'One of us should probably speak to Ernest,' said Annabel.

Nancy remembered the feeling of worry she'd had for Mol, getting up the sycamore in time and away from Freddie. How useless she'd been then too. 'Yeah, one of us probably should.'

Chapter 24

'Leeches have thirty-two brains.'

It was not the first interesting wildlife fact Ray had shared since Annabel had gone next door, sending Ray straight back around here for a nibble on anything he liked the look of in the fridge. Female anacondas outsized their male counterparts by almost double the footage, said Ray, outgunning the opposite sex more than any other animal species on earth. Nancy wondered what Ray would make of her grandmother, what his scientific appraisal might be. How he'd fare getting too close to someone like Ginny, with her sharp teeth and vice-like grip.

'And they have ten eyes. But they can't see very well.'

Nancy threw the ball again for Fig. They were taking it in turns.

'What did you say your friend's name was again, Ray? With the blond hair?'

'Oliver. But I don't think he's my friend now.'

'That might be a good thing.' They were sitting in Annabel's rusty garden chairs. Swinging and creaking, watching the birds over the meadows, Ray still in his school blazer and replacement school sports shorts, Nancy still wearing what she'd cycled to the estuary in. She needed a shower. But Ray needed someone to talk leeches with first. 'Who wants to be friends with someone who has thirty-one and a half fewer brains than a leech anyway, right?'

Fig trotted the ball back to Ray's lap. He lobbed it again. Scooped another spoonful of leftover tart and ice cream.

'Is that what your mum is talking to my grandpa about?' he asked, shovelling the spoon into his mouth. 'Grandpa doesn't normally let me eat ice cream before dinner.'

Nancy looked over the hedgerow to the back of Ernest's house.

'Maybe.' Annabel had kept watch for them from the lounge window. Ernest had given Ray a ride home from school, saving him any more bus time with Oliver and his milkshake. 'They might just be talking about your grandpa's allotment. Mum's always loved the idea of an allotment.'

'You can come see it one day, if you like.'

Nancy glanced sideways at him, Ray scratching his nose with his spoon handle. She smiled at her lap.

'Thanks, Ray. I might.'

'My grandpa is brilliant at growing fruit and vegetables. Your mum can come too. I'll ask my grandpa. He doesn't let everyone in there, but if I take the rest of her pie back for him to eat, he will definitely say she's allowed.'

'That good, huh? Well my mum's pretty brilliant at making great pies with fruit and vegetables. You should try her cheese and leek tarts.' Nancy kissed her fingers, chef-style.

'My grandpa says he really *digs* leeks. Get it?'

Nancy laughed. She tapped her lips with her own spoon, thinking, then set it down with her bowl in the grass.

'You've got to tell your grandpa what's going on, Ray. I know it's hard. But nothing changes until you talk about the things that are worrying you.'

'Like what?'

'Like . . . maybe making some nicer friends?'

'I do have nicer friends.'

'At school?'

Ray nodded. 'And on my road. But I like staying at Grandpa's. If I tell him I don't have any friends here, then he will say I should go back to my house after school instead. On the other bus. But I like coming here when my mum's working. Or I have to go next door to Mrs Ogilvy's house and wait for Mum to finish.'

'And you don't like going to Mrs Ogilvy's house?'

Ray shrugged. 'It's OK. But when she makes tomato chutney, the house smells funny, and she doesn't like me playing outside with my friends and our bikes and footballs because the road is too fast and she says I might get boshed by a car. But I wouldn't. I'm not a baby like the other kids she looks after.'

Ray wasn't alone in the world then. Not chronically unhappy, not friendless. Just stuck with one kid giving him a hard time this side of town.

'So apart from Oliver being a bit of a sh—' She stopped herself. 'A *toad* . . . you like it here?'

'Yep. I like playing in the street. And my grandpa's toasted cheese sandwiches. And especially climbing the massive tree with all the names dug into the trunk. We haven't got a tree like that by us.'

From ground level, you couldn't see all the initials scored crudely into the sycamore bark. It was a primitive leaderboard on which everyone had wanted to stamp their name the highest. You had to go high for the initials, but not everyone had the stomach for heights.

'You're a decent climber then, Ray. Did you see an *NW* up there? You probably didn't. Sort of penned on the bark, not dug in?' He shook his head. No surprise. Not everyone was dedicated enough to hang on tight and actually *carve* their initials into that tree trunk. Marker pen was the next best thing for more cautious kids, kids like Nancy. Marker pen didn't last decades, though, not unless it was perfectly preserved on a bedroom wall somewhere.

'No. I only saw the ones scratched in.'

Nancy nodded. 'You must've climbed pretty high to see those. Be careful up there. Gravity is not always your friend, remember?'

Ray's chewing slowed. 'You won't tell my grandpa, will you?'

'You can't ask me things like that, Ray. I'm an adult. When you grow up, there are rules about being sensible and speaking to other adults and all that kinda stuff.'

'But you're my friend.'

Nancy stilled. As if trying not to frighten a bird from the garden. Ray's big dark eyes fixed on her like buttons. He shrugged and puffed the hair from his eyes. 'You talk to me like you're my friend now. Not like the first day when you had loo roll in your nostril and you were *quite* moody. My

311

grandpa says I have to be more careful about who I should be friends with and not chase the wrong balloon.'

'The wrong balloon?'

'Grandpa said sometimes we can be so frightened of not having something that we run after the wrong thing instead of having a proper look around ourselves for it. He said my dad did it when he was little. Dad thought his yellow balloon was blowing away and ran after it and nearly got lost, but my granny had it all along. He was chasing the wrong balloon.'

'Right.'

'Grandpa said sometimes people can be the wrong balloon and I should think about it more carefully, so I've been thinking about it more carefully and now I think you're nicer than before. And you gave me quite a big slice of this pie. And you didn't tell me off when I nearly fell on you under the massive tree even though that was actually more your fault anyway so . . .' He stopped for breath and went in for another spoonful of pie.

Nancy stared at him, then cast her eyes across the meadows. It was a lot to take in, being the right balloon.

'So . . .' she found herself smiling, 'we're friends?'

Ray chomped at her. He had an ice-cream moustache. 'Yes please.'

Freddie Blumfield would've had a field day with a boy like Ray. Nancy felt something vicious stir inside her. She'd been a pretty useless big sister for Mol when it came to push and shove with other kids. Mol had always had it covered, maybe she knew she had to. But for Ray, Nancy could see herself throwing a shoe or two in this Oliver kid's direction.

'Fig's licking your bowl,' said Ray.

Nancy swished her hand. 'Hey, get out of there. Oh, *Fig*.' She fished Fig's ice-creamy ball from her own bowl and lobbed it back down the garden.

'So, now we're friends,' said Ray, 'you won't tell my grandpa I climb the massive tree on my own?'

Fig ambled back up the lawn towards them. Nancy wondered if she was being hustled.

'Deal. But with conditions. Number one, it's *the sycamore*. And the track it's on is known around here as *the furlong*. You've got to know this stuff if you're going to be hanging around here with the local kids.'

Ray stopped chewing, as if Nancy was finally offering a fair trade of information in return for the nugget about leech brains.

'What's number two?'

Nancy thought on it. 'This is the big one, Ray. Promise you won't climb any higher than the heart cut into the trunk? Not until you're at least . . . twenty-five.' He'd be unlucky to fall from the heart and get worse than a broken arm, and there were tougher things a kid had to get over than a broken arm.

'The heart that's been all scratched out?'

'Yeah. It gets pretty gnarly up there once you're above the heart.' Lucy Hemmings had scratched her heart out the same day it had been scratched in. Hearts got broken all the time, in all sorts of ways. They just weren't always cut into tree trunks, and sometimes straight back out of them again, for everyone to see.

Clarence pressed his way back into Nancy's thoughts. If she was honest about it, he'd pressed his way in more than

313

once since dropping her and Fig home yesterday. He was like something deeply hidden showing itself again, something precious lost on a beach, working its way to the surface.

Ray held out a hand. 'I promise. Only as high as the heart.' Nancy shook his hand. Fig arrived, dropping her ball for Ray this time. 'Your phone's ringing inside.'

'Oh. Thanks, Ray. Back in a sec. I'll take your bowl, before Fig snouts that one too.' Nancy gathered their dishes and jogged into the house, setting them down on her way through the kitchen. She snatched up the receiver and caught sight of the hall clock. Less than two hours to get showered, do something decent with her hair, walk to the Jack.

'Hello?'

'Nancy? Honey pie, is that you?'

'Dad?'

'Hey! How's my baby? What's been goin' on, I thought you might've called your old pa! How's everything settling down, back to normal yet, baby?'

His voice was like a small stone, hitting just the right part of the head to create an impact bigger than itself.

'Dad? Hi, how are you? I thought . . . Mum said you were going to call *me*? Sorry, I . . .' Nancy's reflection frowned back from the dresser mirror.

'That's OK, baby, that's OK! Your mum's been keeping me informed, told me everything, and I've gotta say, Nance, she had me scared there for a while, but you're on the mend so that's all we can ask for and a huge relief for all. Huge. She says you're recuperating there for a little while, and then what? When are they expecting you back at the grindstone? You're just like your old man, honey, can't keep away.'

'Um, they're not expecting me, actually. They, er . . . they just want me to take it easy, slow and steady, you know.' She was still frowning. She turned her back to the mirror.

'I'm coming to see you, baby!'

'You are? *Great*.'

'Of course I am! Don't sound so surprised. You're my girl, I've been worried, Nance. I'm coming to see you, we're going to have something to eat, spend some time together and you can tell me all about this great job you've been working on. I got your emails, a Christmas ad, that's great, honey. My little girl, a broadcaster!'

'Great,' parroted Nancy. 'When are you thinking? I'm not sure when I'll be back at the apartment . . . or did you mean you might come to Mum's sometime?' He might come. She'd always driven to meet him, a restaurant or café somewhere. But he might come here this time. The hope floated balloon-like through her thoughts.

'Of course to Mum's, that's where you are, isn't it? I'm coming now! I've already left, I'm about an hour and a half away.'

'*Now?*'

'I know it's short notice, honey, but your mother said last week that you aren't making plans and it's already been too long. Hey, I've given you nearly three weeks to get your strength up! Isn't that long enough? Why should your mum get you to herself?'

The hallway clock was heading for 6.30. Nancy listened to Ray playing in the back garden with Fig's ball. Throwing and catching, Fig bounding back every time, always coming back for more. Familiar patterns. The same old anticipation and fleeting reward. Him throwing the curveballs. Nancy always running after them.

She shook her head to clear it. 'Dad, I'd love to have dinner with you tonight, but . . .' She'd never, *ever* turned him down. Never rain-checked. 'I wish you'd called sooner. Mum's right, I haven't made many plans, but it's just that tonight, I'm actually meeting a friend and—'

'Can't you rearrange, baby? To see your old pa? I've missed you so much, honey. It'd be really great to see you. Listen, I've got to go, I'm parked up in one of the drive-thru bays and some prat's waving at me to move. Can you believe I've had to park up for a coffee? Look, how about you get yourself ready for meeting your friend and see how you feel when I get there, huh? We'll figure something out. I don't mind her tagging along. I'm buying though, remember! And ask your mother to put the dog away, it ruined my best suit trousers last time I was at the house. Love you, honey, gotta go, see you soon.'

She pictured him sitting in a bay at McDonald's, drumming his fingers impatiently on the wheel of his sporty two-seater.

'OK,' she replied, but he'd already clicked off.

Nancy set the phone down as Annabel blustered in through the front door, stamping her baked bean gardening shoes on the doormat.

'Is he OK? Did you feed him? I've told Ernest to get the trousers straight into the wash before everywhere smells of curdled milk.'

Nancy took her hand off the receiver.

'Yeah, we had the last of Sunday's pie.'

She needed to call Clarence. Put him back an hour. Or something.

'OK, good.' Annabel's face was tight, her mouth firm and preoccupied.

'What did Ernie say?'

Her mouth wobbled then, just the slightest dissent before regaining control.

'I'll never know why some people are just so . . . hard-hearted. They teased him, you know. When his father passed away. Ernie's worried the other boys see him as an easy target. Someone they can be mean to because his dad can't go around and knock on their parents' doors. He thinks Ray will have to try and stand up to them. But I tried to tell him, not everyone is built that way, built like our Mol . . . frightened of nothing and no one.' Annabel pinched the bridge of her nose and breathed steadily.

'Mum, don't get upset. Ray's OK. I've spoken to him, I'm sure they're just being kids.' Clarence had been tormented in high school by boys who thought it was hilarious that some mums drank instead of taking their medicine. 'Maybe Ernie could go and speak to the other boy's parents? Nip it in the bud or something?' But the sinking feeling was still there.

Annabel snatched the scarf from her shoulders. 'Ray's made him promise not to. Ernest doesn't know what to do for the best, and he doesn't want to worry his daughter-in-law: what if she decides to keep Ray from coming back here after school? Ernest adores having him.' She stalked silently through to the kitchen, the frustration in her footsteps dampened by the squeak of rubber shoes. She stabbed the button on the kettle with her thumb. 'Well, he'd better watch his step.'

'Ray?'

'No, of course not Ray! That Oliver weasel. Because we're on to him.'

Nancy's eyes widened. 'Oh. Good . . . Who's we?'

'Ernest and me. We're going to put our heads together.'

Fig barked out the back. Ray responded with a flurry of friendly instruction. *That's it, girl. Now sit. Stay . . . staaay . . .*

Annabel watched him out there playing with Molly's dog, then sniffed authoritatively and fished a cup from the cupboard.

'Who was on the phone?'

Nancy passed the milk. 'Dad.'

Annabel pivoted. 'Richard, really? That's great! I'm so glad you've spoken to him.'

'Yep. You might get to too. He's visiting. Tonight.'

'*Here?*'

'He's on his way.'

'Now?' Annabel baulked.

Nancy held up her hands. The inner workings of her dad's life were more a mystery now than they'd ever been. 'He wants to go for dinner somewhere.'

'But we've eaten early, you're seeing Clarence.'

'I would've told him if he'd given me a chance.' She'd spent days in a hospital bed waiting for him to call. As soon as Annabel had jogged along the ward corridor, pale and panicked, Nancy knew he knew too. That he could've called at any second, rung the ward with a message. Now a part of her wished she hadn't picked up the phone.

Annabel lifted a tea towel and folded it into neat quarters.

'I expect Clarence will be coming straight from the hospital. He might not have his phone turned on in there, if you're going to call and cancel,' she warned.

Clarence would understand. Nancy felt a pang of guilt. She should be glad her dad was fit and well enough to just jump on a motorway and head over. Clarence would prefer it, a healthy erratic parent to an unhealthy one. Although Mol said she'd prefer a manic mother with a rum habit to a flight-risk father with a foot fetish any day. It hadn't mattered that it wasn't really a *foot fetish* in action Nancy had stumbled upon in their dad's factory office, but an act of tenderness, affection, maybe even love. *Even fucking worse*, Mol had said. Preferring another woman's feet was one thing. Preferring her heart or mind was something else entirely. As it was, none of Hazel's anatomy had been enough to keep their father's attention for long.

'I don't have his number,' said Nancy. 'I'll nip over to the house, explain.'

'And if he doesn't go home first?'

'I'll have to leave a message at the Jack. Ask if we can do it some other time.' It wasn't every day her father came home.

319

Chapter 25

Nancy gave the T-shirt another once-over in the mirror on her mum's bedroom dresser. She'd get away with it. It was casual, but not too casual with a sweep of mascara and just enough blush to bring a bit of something to her cheeks. Dads liked their daughters to look healthy and happy. She swept back the hair around her eyes and checked that the droplet earrings Annabel had lent her were both hanging securely. She hadn't noticed it until now, but all the walks with Fig had shaken off the dishwater pallor she'd left the hospital with. She'd barely recognised the husk looking back at her from the truck wing mirror that first ride home from the hospital car park. She hadn't recognised herself for a long time. When she got back to the city, she'd make an effort to run more around Chortley Park and less on the treadmills at Garfield's. Give the sun a fighting chance to keep up its good work on her skin.

Annabel's bedside clock called almost 7.30. A familiar feeling of nervy anticipation moved through her. He'd be here any minute. Richard Woods wasn't exactly regular as clockwork, but once he eventually set a time, he usually stuck to it. Something noisy pulled up on the road out front. It didn't sound like her dad's two-seater, but by the time she'd crossed the landing to take a quick look through the front bedroom window, the door knocker had rattled and Fig erupted into life downstairs. Nancy stole a quick glance further up the street, Clarence's driveway still empty. If she didn't catch him in the next half-hour, it would have to be a grovelling apology left behind the bar for him.

Down in the hallway, her dad was giving her mum a friendly peck on the cheek. Nancy hovered at the top of the stairs while he stomped his loafers on the doormat more times than was necessary. He sank his hands into his pockets.

'How's she doing, Annie?' Voice warm and steady. They'd waited up here to watch him walk in through that door more times than Nancy could count, to hear the same easy, even voice, even after Hazel had come to collect him and his carful of black bags. The beautiful shoes had been replaced with weekend pumps, so ordinary. Nancy had hated her then. For those boring pumps. It was easier to understand when you'd been swapped for something dazzling.

'Hey, here she is! How're we doing, honey?' He beamed upstairs at Nancy. His hair was greyer now, but he looked good for it, and the coastal sunshine had given him a gently weathered look.

Nancy scooped her jacket from the handrail on her way downstairs.

'Hi, Dad.'

'Hey, you look great! Annie, doesn't she look great? Are

321

you sure those doctors know what they're talking about? You look beautiful as ever, honey, fit as a fiddle!'

He pulled her into a firm bear hug. Nancy took in a deep breath of him, patted his back, permission to release her.

'I feel good, Dad. Absolutely fine.'

He planted a kiss on her head and fixed her with the warm blue eyes that had brought him a steady stream of Hazels over the years.

'That's great, honey. I knew you'd get a handle on this. So what's the status quo? When are you back to the Batcave? And what about this campaign? Who's it for, one of the big supermarkets? Or can't you say?'

'Richard, give her a chance. There's no rush. You can get up to speed over a nice drink.' But this was how he was, always on the hop, always moving, always talking.

Fig ramped up the barking from the kitchen. Annabel gestured towards the racket. 'Are you staying for a cup of tea first or getting straight off?' He checked his watch. If they had tea, Nancy would have time to nip up and pop a note through Clarence's letter box. A note and a phone call to the pub would be better than one or the other.

'No thanks, Annie,' interjected her dad. 'I'm taking my little girl out for dinner, as promised. I thought we could try the bistro on the square, I just drove past there on my way in and they didn't look too busy.' He gritted his teeth. 'I do have to be away for nine thirty though, I'm afraid, honey. We might have to get you a dessert in a doggy bag, or, *hey*! We could grab you one of those ice creams you used to love so much from the little old Italian guy's, if they're open? We'll bring something back for you too, Annie!' he beamed. The

322

front door hadn't even closed yet and already an escape route was taking shape.

Annabel glanced at Nancy, who pretended not to notice.

'The bistro's fine, Dad,' she smiled. He stepped back onto the *You Again?* doormat.

'Shall we make tracks then, baby?'

'Richard, is that yours?' Annabel nodded at the minivan parked on the pavement. It was bigger and older than Clarence's truck, which Nancy could see still wasn't back on Birdie's drive. Beth said Clarence liked to stay on the ward until after his mother had finished eating her evening meal. But Birdie didn't always want to eat.

'God, no!' said Nancy's dad. 'I've borrowed it from a friend. I'm picking up a stack of teak decking later from a fella in Worcester. Great little bargain. Prompt collection, though, the listing said. When I called to arrange, he sounded like he was just realising how much more he could've got for it. I could use the synthetic imitation stuff, but you can't beat the real deal, so it needs collecting before he relists it for more cash.'

'And you're collecting this teak decking . . . tonight?' asked Annabel.

'He's only an hour further up the M5 from here, so it made sense to fetch it while I was coming to see my baby girl.' He jangled the keys in his pocket. Annabel twisted the ring on her finger and looked at Nancy again.

'Lucky,' smiled Nancy. There was a dull headache starting in her right temple.

Her dad smiled like a child. 'What is, sugar plum?'

'Worcester,' she said. 'Teak planks.' Mol had never been

323

as fussed when he'd come to take them out for the day. She'd stopped waiting at the top of the stairs as soon as he had stopped turning up on birthdays. But not Nancy. Nancy had waited. And waited. 'Lucky you found such a bargain all the way down here by Mum's.'

Her dad shrugged, a boyish gesture in a sixty-year-old man.

'Lady Luck strikes where she strikes, Nance.' But she'd never been known to strike in Mistleton.

She was supposed to be setting off for the Jack soon. Taking a nice walk along the canal, sitting down in a pub they'd spent their late teens and early twenties in, with an old school friend who'd played in their house, looked after Mol at parties in the woods, fended off Gran at Sunday lunch last weekend. A schoolfriend her dad wouldn't even remember the name of, and Nancy was about to blow him off for a couple of hours stolen from an eBay collection.

'Actually, Dad, I'm not all that hungry. You go for food and your *real deal* wood and I'll see you when it's more convenient . . . for you or for me or . . . Mr eBay or whoever.'

'Nancy?' said Annabel softly.

Her dad showed his palms. 'Hey, of course it's convenient, baby! I'm here! What do you mean, you're not hungry?' Nancy looked at the keys in his hand, where he always kept them, ready.

'Mum and I ate already, Dad. That's what people do in the absence of plans, they eat at dinner time. You didn't call until an hour or so ago and we'd already eaten. You should've said when you won your eBay bid that you only had a couple of hours and we'd have better accommodated you. Mum could've eaten alone and I could've sat on the top step waiting for you to *actually* turn up.'

He was smiling when he glanced at Annabel, as if she might have the solution to this new puzzle, the twisting of his poker-straight daughter. 'Honey, why are you acting this way, is there something wrong?'

She'd followed the wrong balloon. For thirty-two years. And only Molly had had the sense to see it.

'Nope. Not a thing.' She picked up her phone and purse. 'Enjoy your new boat decking. I hope it doesn't disappoint you, Dad.' Sometimes you had to look at a thing in the flesh, take a long, hard look at it, before you could see what its limitations were. What its limitations would always be. And stop waiting for it to be something else.

'Nancy?' her dad said indignantly.

'An apple is an apple, Dad. And that's OK. I love apples. I love you. But you will never be anything like a pear.' And she'd only just realised it.

He blinked at Annabel, who seemed to have found something of deep interest in the pattern of the tiled floor.

'Annie, does she need the doct—' Nancy planted a kiss on his cheek and stepped out through the front door before he could finish speaking.

'A friend is waiting for me, I'm going to meet them like I said I would. I'll call you when I'm back at work, Dad. We can have lunch or dinner or something. You can choose. Just try and give me some notice next time. Mum, I'll see you in a few hours. If it turns into a late one . . .' and something inside her fluttered at the possibility, 'I'll call.'

Chapter 26

Hanging baskets dripped from the red-brick walls of the Jackdaw Inn in bursts of autumnal colour. The names of Ronnie and Ivy Spink, who'd once sold them penny chews over the counter when they were girls and later gave them each a job waitressing Sunday lunches, still sat on the plaque in the front vestibule of the old pub. The Spinks must be clocking up their third or maybe even fourth decade running the Jack, Nancy thought, as she passed beneath their names and pushed through the heavy door into what would've been her local too, had she stayed.

The pub door closed sluggishly behind her. *Ronnie and Ivy Spink*. Thirty years or more in the same place. *Settled*. Two trees grown together from the same patch of earth. It could happen.

Nancy stepped into the pub lounge, ale and smoke ingrained in its fabric, rich polished wood and stained-glass booths partitioned like the stables in Beth's livery yard, separating clusters of drinkers from each other. Clarence wasn't sitting in any of them. She scanned the bar, again, then the inglenook. A familiar lone character sat next to the dead fireplace, as if waiting to harness the warmth he knew would come eventually. Nancy gave the huddled form a fleeting smile. Dodgy Roger was part of the Jack's fixtures and fittings, hunkered inside his chunky roll-neck, white hair like thistledown poking in every direction. He looked up at Nancy from his empty pint glass and backgammon game, pipe hanging redundantly from his mouth. She gave him another smile and headed for the bar. Clarence definitely didn't seem to be here yet. There was an urge to check the time on her phone, but she knew she'd walked into the pub at exactly one minute to. On time, but not too eager. She idled next to one of the bar stools, deciding to stand, then gave the few pockets of people seated in the lounge booths another glance in case Clarence was among them. He could be in the loo, but his truck hadn't been in the car park. She caught herself wondering, would he leave it here overnight? If they decided to walk home later along the canal.

A warm voice rose from behind the bar.

'Hello, stranger!' Ivy Spink pressed her hand onto her knee and pushed herself upwards. Ivy's was a friendly, round face, with make-up sturdy enough for a long shift behind the bar. 'How are you, lovey? I haven't seen you since . . .' Nancy watched the recollection of Molly's wake slide over her, Ronnie's dash back to the pub for emergency supplies when the guests had kept piling into the house, all their borrowed glasses.

'Hi, Ivy. Keeping the salt and vinegar restocked down there, I see.'

'It's the kids, always in here for crisps and chews.'

Nancy smiled. 'You're looking well, how's Ronnie?'

'Same as ever!' said Ivy, opening another box of crisps, forcing the Sellotape seal with the handle of a teaspoon. 'Still a pain in my neck. Can't grumble, though. I heard you were visiting your mother. I see her occasionally, usually the butcher's, I don't think she's ever been in here other than that New Year your sister dragged her out and bullied her into sampling Ronnie's snowball flambé.'

'I did hear something about that.'

'I made Molly stand next to her, you know, like a bookend, in case your mother fell off her stool.'

Nancy's eyes drifted over to the back of the bar, photos of the decades, Christmas Eves and New Years and jubilees past, familiar faces making merry mischief. One familiar face in particular was everywhere. And always about her, chaos. Happy chaos.

'She was a pain in my neck too, you know,' said Ivy, acknowledging the same girl in the photos. 'But a pain I'll never not miss. We raise a glass to her, you know. Every Christmas.'

Nancy nodded. In the lounge the other side of the bar, she could pick out a small cluster of musicians making themselves comfortable in the corner the bands usually played. Clarence wasn't there either. Nancy found the photo behind the bar again, of Clarence and Mol together in the band corner, Clarence patiently drinking a beer while Mol pretended to be lead guitarist for him, guitar thrashing skyward, hair flicked wildly around her head. She squinted at the photo.

'Is that *me*? In the background, waitressing?'

Ivy checked over her shoulder. 'Sure is. Don't you remember that night? That sister of yours almost broke my jukebox swinging that thing around.' She rolled her eyes, leant in over the bar. 'But she also drummed up more tips for you girls waiting tables that night than you knew what to do with. Good job, with you saving to go off to university.'

Nancy studied the photo, the only one, she thought, with the three of them together. 'I remember. She broke Clarence's guitar.' That was where the tips pot had ended up, in Clarence's guitar repair fund. They hadn't all been on board, but Nancy had talked them round. It would've been criminal for Clarence not to play. Plus, Clarence meant Molly, and Molly brought in the tips.

Ivy patted the bar. 'Good job he got it mended. So, what can I get you, lovey?'

It was five past. Nancy chewed her lip. Should she wait or order for them both? She glanced to the car park again. Dodgy Roger stared back from the inglenook.

'I'll just have a, um . . .' What should she have? 'Orange juice, please.' She was going to be a real thrill when Clarence got here. A teetotal treat.

'Don't mind him,' said Ivy quietly, nodding towards the inglenook. 'Poor old Rodge has been on the slow slip for some time now.' She nipped the top off a bottle of Britvic then tapped the bottle opener to her temple. 'He's got a touch of *the dementia*, forgets he knows half the people he's talking to, the love. Hasn't forgotten his way along the canal path to that spot by my fireplace yet, mind.'

Nancy held out a note. She sipped her drink while Ivy rang it through the till.

'Here's your change, lovey. I'll leave you in peace. The snacks won't get themselves up from the cellar,' she huffed, disappearing though the far door.

Nancy checked her earrings and sipped her drink again. She pushed her jacket sleeves up her forearms, then decided against it and smoothed them back down. She had another sip and tucked her hair behind her ear, rechecking the earrings she might've disturbed. *Not quite ten past.* This time her phone went onto the bar, clock side up. She sipped again, draining the glass already. When Ivy came back, Nancy ordered a taller drink, lime and soda. Twenty past came around and her bladder made its first protest. Another car rumbled into the car park. Still no Clarence.

A quick tap on her phone screen and 20:21 stared back at her. Anything past fifteen minutes was significant, wasn't it? Flat tyre territory? A call ahead? He could've got her number off Beth, or Annabel. Or called the pub with a message like Nancy was going to. Did it count that he probably thought Fig was here, keeping her company? That *was* technically the plan. But given Fig's track record of misbehaviour, chasing old men onto roofs, rolling in poo and the like, Nancy had decided to leave her. And now she was sitting here like a complete loner, clock-watching, instead of dog-watching at least. She gulped the last of her lime and soda and turned her phone face-down. A hot feeling sat on her neck. Maybe he wasn't coming.

'Not saying hello, then?'

Dodgy Roger tapped his dead pipe against the inside of the fire grate and opened a leather pouch of tobacco onto his table. 'Where have you been, trouble?' Nancy looked over her shoulder down the bar to see who he was talking to. 'Don't think I've forgotten.' He tapped his pipe like a gavel onto a shiny red backgammon chip. 'Seven games, fiver a game, by my reckoning you still owe me thirty-five pounds and a rematch.'

Nancy smiled apologetically. 'Sorry, Roger, but I think—'

'Roger?' He whooped at the ceiling, flashing neat dentures mismatched to the rest of him. 'Well who washed your mouth out with soap suds? What happened to Dodgy Rodge? Where have you been anyway, lady? There's something different about you.' Nancy tried to make sense of him. 'Brunette now, then? How long until you're a redhead again? I didn't mind the red, truth be told, better than the other thing you did.' He waggled a wrinkly finger towards his own head and then Nancy's. 'Never was a fan of the time you clippered the lot off. Bald as an egg and still bold as brass. In the winter too, crazy girl. What young lady in their right mind gets rid of all their hair only to have to wear a woolly hat when they're inside the pub? No, I didn't much like your bald image, didn't suit you. Made you look . . . sickly.'

Molly had worn the wigs at first. And pencilled in eyebrows in matching shades. And then she'd stopped. As if she'd decided there were better ways to spend the extra minutes. Like being here, tormenting Dodgy Roger over his backgammon board.

'I, er . . .' Nancy looked for help then from Ivy, polishing pint glasses. Ivy shrugged a shoulder as if she knew the trick Dodgy Roger's eyes were playing on his ailing mind. People had said they'd looked alike, as siblings often did to outsiders, but the differences had always been easier to see,

Nancy thought. She gave the car park one last futile look through the window. Clarence wasn't coming.

Dodgy Roger moved his leg, pushing the barstool opposite his own out from the table in invitation.

'Are you going to pay your debts or what, trouble? And you promised me a rematch.'

Nancy looked at Ivy again, pretending not to listen. There was no point going back to the house. She didn't want to go back yet either. Her dad would still be killing time there for the next hour at least. Dodgy Roger tapped his backgammon chip again. She could get cashback off Ivy and just pay him now, clear Mol's debt. Or . . .

'Thirty-five?'

'And a rematch,' replied Dodgy Roger. 'And no cheating this time.' He started stacking the playing chips in his wrinkled hands. Nancy migrated from the bar to the stool he had pushed out for her.

'Double or quits?'

'Get yourself a drink before you sit down. And another beer with a Scotch chaser for me, Ivy. Molly here's buying.'

Nancy nodded to herself and drifted back to the bar.

'Just the beer and Scotch?' asked Ivy. She gave Nancy's hand a quick and gentle pat.

There would be no warm beer for Clarence. 'And a glass of red, please, Ivy. Whatever you've already got open back there. Large.'

Nancy was on to her second glass before she felt the first rumblings of annoyance. The flat tyre theory had run out of road about half an hour ago. Clarence hadn't turned up and he hadn't left a message. Birdie was taking her time over her meal tonight then. It had taken him nearly an hour just to get her out of the river the day she had thrown Clarence's tin of home-made fishing flies into the shallows. An hour of trying to talk her out of the water, the whole time Birdie dipping her long, skinny arms in and out of the wet like a shivering heron, trying to undo her mistake. Nancy wanted to be more understanding, but an old disappointment had re-formed itself, the waiting around, expectant looks through windows, for someone who just wasn't guaranteed to turn up. She'd exchanged one wait for another, her father back at the house for Clarence here instead.

The folky two-piece had set up at the back of the lounge, violin and guitar thrumming lazily through the pub. Nancy felt faintly buzzy, just around the edges. She liked it. She'd missed it. Dodgy Roger yabbered on, thrashing her at backgammon, while Nancy felt herself lean into the woolly feeling in her head, settling back into the music like a warm cushion.

Later, when she admitted defeat and pushed a few notes across the table, Roger put his hand over hers, tucking the cash beneath her fingers. The unexpected warmth of his skin on hers sobered her.

'How about you keep it, trouble?'

'But I lost.' She was sober enough to know that much.

'You look like you've lost enough for one day. Whatever's making you blue, I'm not adding to it.'

'I'm not blue,' Nancy guffawed. 'I'm just . . . horrific at backgammon, Rodge.' She let the last of her wine slip down her throat.

The old man eyed her steadily from beneath his cap, face

as wrinkled and cragged as parched earth. He was *so* old. So much older than so many people would ever get to be.

His eyes narrowed. 'Can't shut you up normally, not for love nor money. You haven't even told me where you've been hiding all this time.' Nancy sloshed the last of the bottle into her wine glass. 'Off on your travels, was it?'

'Yep,' agreed Nancy. Time for home. Maybe a little nightcap, Annabel's dusty cognac.

'So you talked her into it then?'

'What?'

'Those crazy English places with the hare-brained attractions you wanted to go visiting with your sister . . . the one with the stick up her behind . . . instead of the posh places overseas she had in mind? You got her there in the end then?'

Chapter 27

A slick of moonlight sat on the surface of the canal. It moved more than Nancy thought it probably should. Canals were still creatures, but the light swayed and the nausea in her swayed with it. She pushed herself back from the bridge stones.

'You are drunk,' she told herself wisely. But not so drunk she was about to risk staggering home along a path next to a ribbon of black water. If Clarence had materialised, they might've walked the canal towpath together, safe and sound. It was a narrow path, perhaps their shoulders would've brushed. But Clarence hadn't come.

Nancy saluted the moonlight. 'Message received, Captain Ludlow!'

Her feet began their inevitable shuffle back towards the Jack's empty beer garden, the September air sweet and balmy. There was a chance she just might throw up. She made it to the car park, weighing up this very possibility, then the road, then the lane. The moonlight leading her back to familiar hedgerows and pavements and street lights again.

When she rounded Mountford Road, her feet stopped. Clarence's truck sat on his mother's driveway. A punchline. Her legs felt suddenly jelly-like, but she let them carry her to the front of Birdie's house, everything dark except for the downstairs window. She reached the front step before stopping to wonder what she was actually doing there. Something turned and twisted in her stomach, pushing her on, pulling her back.

Clarence sat at the piano by lamplight, his back to the hallway and porch window. He lifted a beer bottle from the top of the piano, tilted his head, drank, reached an arm to the floor, sinuous and stark against the rolled cuffs of his shirt. He set the bottle down next to the leg of his piano stool. Nancy totally got it. He had thought it over, her pessimistic wisdom, her many questionable decisions, her defective body. Why bother? *Why indeed.*

His hands moved from view towards the ivory keys. Nancy waited for the first melody to find its way through those fingertips, through the hands and wrists and arms that had briefly carried her into the barn. She waited for the notes to come, from hidden hammers touching hidden strings, gifting the music out into the air between them. But Clarence didn't play. Birdie's home was soundless.

She thought to knock, to remind him of their plans, *his* plans – he'd suggested the drink in the first place. But her hands didn't move from her sides. Her feet wouldn't move either. She hovered there this way for a minute until finally she turned for home and walked away, blanking out the mysteries of what her feet and other more complicated parts of her anatomy might want.

She didn't make the other side of the road before the rolls of nausea moved back in, a tide of inevitability. Outside Annabel's, the tatty white transit her dad had arrived in earlier sat parked in the same spot. Nancy tried making sense of it, here, still. A UFO on Normal Street.

She patted the van on her way past. 'Couldn't he get you started?'

Halfway down the garden path, she felt herself list onto Annabel's dahlias before she could right herself to the horizon, her left side almost going out from under her.

'Oops, steady,' she warned, trying for a level voice at least. She fumbled her key into the lock, the hole shrinking away from her each time she got close. 'Yes, doormat, it's me. *Again*.'

Inside, the rich aroma of filter coffee turbo-charged Nancy's queasiness. Annabel had rolled out the big guns for her dad then, something Colombian and freshly ground, him the guest now in the boneyard of his former life. Fig skittered along the hallway from the kitchen, tail wagging like a bullwhip.

'Hello, monster dog.' She cracked Nancy one across the knees. 'Ow!' The volume of her own voice startled her. 'You should be thanking me, I saved you from getting stood up tonight too!' She whispered then. 'Shh! Listen, Fig . . .' she heard the drawl in her own voice, 'there is a *teeny* chance I'm about to puke, so I'm going straight upstairs to beddy-byes before I get told off . . . wanna come? Yes you do, you want to snooze on my bed, don't you?' She'd got a hand on the newel post when the lounge door opened.

'Sweetheart?'

'Yep?'

Annabel looked odd, startled, as if she'd disturbed an intruder. 'Everything OK?'

'Yep.' Nancy held on tight to the banister in case she started swaying with the motion of the house. 'Goodnight then, Mum.'

'Nancy?' pressed Annabel. 'Come and say goodnight to your dad first? He's hung on for you to get home.' She pulled the lounge door closed behind her and moved further into the hallway. 'He's worried he's upset you.'

Nancy snorted at the ceiling. 'It's only taken him twenty-odd years!'

Only Molly had ever blamed him. Nancy had always looked for the failings closer to home, her own failings . . . Ginny's failings . . . Only Molly had ever pointed the cross hairs firmly beyond the garden fence.

'He's leaving soon, Nancy, he's waited all this time. Just give him a few minutes, please?'

Waited. He didn't know what it was to wait for anything. Everything reachable, instant, fleeting. Nippy cars. Flighty women. Nancy pinched her eyes. She was just so bloody tired.

'You're always so forgiving, Mum. We don't deserve it.'

Annabel stared at her. Nancy let go of the newel post, but the ground moved out from under her. She staggered sideways across the hallway towards the dresser, which would've been completely survivable had Fig not been in the way. The ground rushed up and thudded into her back, knocking the breath from her.

Her dad appeared upside-down in the lounge doorway. 'What the hell, Nancy?'

Nancy groaned, then giggled, both parents' expressions hilarious.

'I blame the octopus,' she chuckled. 'Hope it doesn't climb out of its pot again and try and *kill* me.'

'What's she saying, Annie? She's not making any sense!'

'Nancy? Good God, have you been drinking?'

Her dad bent down to help Annabel's efforts. Nancy felt him get her other arm, scooping her off the floor like a wet insect. *Poor mayflies*, she thought. *Twenty-four poxy hours.*

'Seriously, Annie?' snapped her dad. 'You have to ask? Can't you smell it? She's hammered.'

'Bingo, Daddio,' said Nancy from the tiles. She touched her nose like they were all in on the same game of charades. They *were* all playing charades, she suspected, just not necessarily the same game.

'Please say you have not been drinking?' Annabel pleaded.

'Sorry, Mum. But I met a tall, dark, handsome stranger at the Jack who swept me off my feet and we've been buying each other drinks and bar snacks all night. Did you know Mojos are *five pence each now*? Bloody inflation. On *penny* chews! We ate them all. And a *lot* of pork scratchings. I did get one with a bristle on it, though.' Too far. Her stomach rolled. She put a hand over her mouth, just in case.

'Richard?' said Annabel desperately.

'Great, Nancy,' said her dad, who was doing most of the heavy lifting into the lounge.

They set her down on the sofa, Annabel pulling off

Nancy's shoes while her dad shut Fig out of the lounge. He started jangling his keys then, pacing to and fro in front of the mantelpiece and Ginny's beady-eyed Staffordshire dogs. It was making Nancy seasick.

'Relax, Dad. He wasn't nearly as handsome as you,' she said angelically. 'He wasn't even tall, or dark-haired. White-haired, actually, but might've been dark once, who knows? He's so lovely . . . a lovely man . . . His fingernails were a bit grim though, he uses them to scrape out his pipe dregs, but . . .' They were both staring down at her on the sofa. '. . . he's a one-woman guy so he's got that going for him!' Rodge had told her all about his wife, about love that outlived people and soulmates and . . . other bullshit like that. Nancy rubbed a sluggish hand over her face and giggled.

'She's not supposed to drink, Richard,' said Annabel frantically. 'She's on beta blockers. Nancy, why have you done this? Your medication . . . your rehab plan, Nancy, your poor body, what are you *thinking*?'

Nancy broke into giggles on the sofa. It was so ridiculous! Of all the farcical conditions you could give yourself, how the doctors had described her *poor body* while she'd made Annabel wait outside in the corridor.

'It's just an octopus in there, Mum. I'll have my medicine tomorrow and it will go back in its pot and the pot will go back to normal shape again. I will go back to my apartment and my nice rug and everything will be tickety-boo.'

'What the hell is she talking about, Annie, *octopus*? Nancy, you've only been gone a few hours! You're supposed to be smarter than this, not getting wasted with strange men, worrying your mother, worrying the both of us!'

'Worry? Oh don't *worry*, Dad . . . the last thing we want is to ruin your worry-free existence. Leave the tough stuff to us girls. You concentrate on your *toe jobs* and . . . eBay bargains.

'Nancy,' stammered Annabel.

'Some arsehole's spiked her drink, Annie!'

'Nancy?'

'It's all right, Mum. We know all about it, don't we? Getting on with things. That's what we do. I just needed a little blowout, like you did. No drink has spiked my arsehole, I promise.'

A hand arrived on her forehead, feeling for a temperature, or something more deeply ingrained perhaps. Annabel cleared her throat and spoke calmly.

'You can't mess around with this, Nancy. You've had a heart attack.'

Nancy pulled her mum's hand from her head. She squeezed it before pushing it away.

'*Well* . . . It wasn't *exactly* a heart attack. *Surprise!*' She tried to smile, but the nausea was building in waves, churning things up from the bottom.

Her dad's keys stopped jangling. 'Not exactly? Not exactly a *heart attack*? You can't lie about things like that. Jesus, Nancy.'

'And what *can* you lie about, Dad? Everything else? Where is the line?'

'Richard, let's get her to bed. We can talk in the morning, sweetheart . . . about whatever you want to.'

'And I didn't *lie*. I said *heart attack* because that's what they said, at first. And because it was a *hell* of a lot easier to say *afterwards*.' She laughed again. 'Zack-o-turbo,' she tried.

More giggling. 'Sack-o-sumo . . . no, that's not right. Taco-zoomo? Sorry, Mum, and Dad . . . I don't even know why I'm laughing! An octopus pot! What even is that?' She sniggered. 'No, you're right, it isn't very funny actually, literally having an out-of-shape heart . . . and even less funny that it feels like there might actually be an octopus inside it sometimes, trying to bump me off!' She snorted and made a throttling gesture at her neck. She was crying now, with laughter. It felt ace.

The laughter died in her throat. 'I bet Ray knows a thing or two about octopuses,' she mumbled. She felt the tears suddenly there, waiting to rush her. 'And mayflies.'

'That's it,' erupted Richard. 'Who the fuck is *Ray*? Is this the joker you've been drinking with? Did that bastard spike your drink?'

Annabel's voice rose. 'Richard, *please*! Let her speak. She never speaks! Don't you know that?'

'But she's not talking any sense, Annie! *We* should be speaking, to a goddam doctor! Right now!'

Nancy pulled herself up again to a seated position. She put her head between her legs for a little minute.

'A doctor? You're a bit late for that, aren't you, Dad?' She looked up at him. The movement made her shaky, like climbing too high up the sycamore and not being able to go back. She should stop now, but she couldn't. Decades of stretching and bending for him, Molly knowing all along how stupid she was, how suckered, all snapping back into place like a bow string.

'Why didn't you call the doctor when Mum needed you to, Dad? When she was heartbroken for Grandpa James and had a new baby to look after *and* a toddler and with Gran being a total bitch to her? Why didn't you *talk to a doctor* then? Too busy doing *overtime*?'

Something moved through her like a warning. Not tears, rage.

'Richard, she needs to calm down, not get more worked up. Nancy, let Dad help you up to bed.'

He tried doing as he was told, but Nancy batted his hand away. Her voice climbed. 'I'm not worked up, Mum. I just get it now. I need to stop chasing the wrong balloons! I need to be less of an idiot and . . . more like my sister, who was *really fucking smart* . . . and right about things . . . and people. She was right about everything! She was right about the fucking *cheese*-rolling festival. We should've just fucking well gone!'

Nancy's head swam. By some gymnastical feat realised only by the superhuman or extremely drunk, she managed to rise from the sofa, navigate the coffee table and reach the fireplace all in one fluid movement. They'd hide things inside the Staffordshire dogs when they were little. Small things, like their favourite Christmas chocolates, bubblegum, anything slight enough to fit through the holes in the bases of the china figures. Her drunken brain, woefully less gymnastic than her drunken body, realised too late that the hidey-hole in the bottom of one of the Staffordshire dogs was not going to contain *all* of the vomit.

'For Christ's sake, Nancy!' boomed her dad. He faded away, though, as invariably he did. The last thing that made it through the haze, sharp and clear as splintered glass, was Molly's voice. *Wow, Nance. Just . . . wow.*

Chapter 28

The panic is there. Nancy's aware of it, but it's dull. A pressure once-removed. A gale outside a window. She's here. Fireworks fracture the dark. The car is fast, but it's doing what she tells it this time. Her foot presses further down on the pedal, the snow doesn't seem to matter, no drag, no skid. Like driving on dry clay. The sycamore is dressed in white, she hasn't seen it before, how high it hulks against the darkness with the snow to pick out its towering silhouette, but this time she doesn't have to watch for ice and boulders, doesn't have to keep her eyes on the road, she's getting there just fine. She's going to get there.

She drives down the furlong and looks all the way to the top of the sycamore. Ray is up there. He's sitting at its highest branch. She's knows it is Ray, tiny as he is. She feels the worry then, it tells her to pull over, remind him to be careful. *No higher than the heart, Ray*, she will say. And *Put on your coat. It's snowing.*

Clarence is waiting. Fireworks crackle soundlessly in the

distance and Nancy's already out of the car. She wants to ask him, *Why do you have feathers in your hair, Clarence?* But they are falling everywhere, like snow. White feathers falling to earth. Clarence doesn't speak. When Nancy looks to their feet, the feathers are like carpet between them. They line the track all the way across the meadows, a white ribbon. She could stay, but there's something waiting for her there, at the end of the furlong. At the end of their street. At the top of their stairs. She runs to it.

Molly is on her bed, cross-legged. Her hair falls over her shoulders, she looks up from painting her nails, purple glitter catching the light. *Hey, Nance.* As if she's been here all along. *Where have you been, Mol?* Nancy wants to say, but if she speaks, if she touches it, it will pop on her fingertips. Molly smiles. It reaches her green eyes. Her cheeks are pink, flushed with warmth, her body lithe, moving as she commands it. She is defined, luminous, she is Molly.

I knew you'd come, she says.

Nancy opened her eyes. She managed two narrow slits before feeling the tears slide over her nose. She closed her eyes again, turned her face into the cushions, wiping the wet off herself. Her body felt as if it was the other side of something. Made of lead. She imagined a mass with its own gravity shifting inside her, turning in on itself, sinking through its own middle. She wanted to sink with it. All the way back to Molly, but the birdsong was telling her, it's too late. Her dream already slipping back under the surface, sinking back to the bottom for her to find again another time. Loss was a creature that returned, to chew again and again on its mangled prize. But

Nancy wanted to welcome it back in this time, this time it gave a gift first, before stealing her away again. For a few precious moments, it gave her Molly.

The clattering and squeaking of a bin lorry further up the street chipped into her consciousness. Men's voices out there, level with her window. She was on the sofa. Alone, if you didn't count the mass of ginger fur pinning her lower body.

'Fig, off . . .' Fig yawned and slid reluctantly to the floor. Nancy put a hand over her eyes. Her head felt like a bucket of smashed glass. *Shit.* It started to come back to her. She rolled onto her side and felt a deep ache in her legs, long bruise along her backside and a chronic case of pins and needles pummelling her right buttock. The pins and needles started and stopped. And again. A uniform rhythm of buzzing continuing against her backside. She got a hand into her jeans pocket and fished out the vibrating phone.

'Hello?'

'Heavy night, doll?'

'Haima?'

'Yes, Haima. Who else would be ringing to check you haven't choked on your own upchuck? Jesus, answer your phone!'

A solitary Staffordshire dog looked down from the mantelpiece. Annabel's hearthrug had gone too. 'How did you know I was sick?'

'You called? I was up to my eyeballs digging through non-disclosures for this morning's meeting and you ring, rambling about an *octopus* bursting out of your chest *Alien*-style, like I needed that conversation in an empty office.

Aren't you supposed to be off the drink? Not dangling over canal bridges half cut while you try and pitch yourself, *so* badly, for work that's not earmarked for you? And now you've got me chasing you on my way back into the office because *stupidly* I woke up in the middle of the night and convinced myself that, apart from this meeting falling apart today, my friend might actually have fallen in a canal last night because she *didn't* call me when she got home like she promised.'

Haima's voice hurt Nancy's head. 'Sorry.' She had an inkling she'd be saying that more than once today. 'I can't even remember calling.' The bits she could remember were not good. She sank back into the sofa and pulled a cushion over her head, sandwiching the phone against her ear.

'Well, you're alive, doll. That's half of the day's headaches sorted.'

'What's going on at work?' groaned Nancy.

'I already told you. Look, I'm nearly at the office so I'll cut to the chase. Again. This bug, I'm losing serious manpower. No one's even looked at the decoy campaign yet and—'

'I could do it.' Nancy was suddenly alert, ish. 'Just a couple of days a week? From home?'

'I'll think about it.'

'OK. Thanks.' Fig investigated the tea tray left on the footstool. Then the bucket on the floor. 'Thanks for checking in on me too.'

'No problem. I've gotta run. Stay off the canals.'

'Yeah.'

The universe, no, *Haima*, had gifted her a grappling hook.

Something to throw in the direction of Nancy's real life, pull herself back there with. She pushed the cushion back off her head and pulled the tray closer. Two paracetamol and a small jug of milk sat beside a bowl of her own hangover granola. Annabel had left a note too.

Keep pedalling xxx

Nancy necked the paracetamol and rose steadily to her feet. In the kitchen, she leant against the patio door, assessing the landscape, what the day might hold besides an apocalyptic headache. She rubbed at her chest, nothing felt off. Annabel was at the end of the garden, morning curls floating like spun sugar about her head while she listened intently to what Ernest was saying over the fence. Nancy left them to it and filled the kettle. She picked a cup from the drainer and noticed a stack of papers poking from behind the microwave, lime-green felt tip angrily encircling a small subheading. *Takotsubo cardiomyopathy.* She read it again, instantly sobered. She held up the printouts, eyes racing over the parts Annabel had highlighted. *Heart muscle suddenly weakened . . . Japanese octopus trap . . . left ventricle enlarged . . . distress trigger . . . bereavement.* Bereavement wasn't circled. It stood out all by itself.

The patio door slid open behind her. 'Hi.' Annabel waited at the door.

'Hi.'

Annabel looked at the papers in Nancy's hand and offered a weak smile.

'You were almost right. It was such a strange word you were trying to say. I only had to try a few times with the iPad and, well . . . Google's clever, isn't it?' She moved tentatively into the kitchen. 'Why didn't you say, Nance?'

'Because . . . you didn't need it. And it makes no odds.'

Annabel blinked rapidly. She looked tired. Nancy glanced away. Hangovers always made you more emotional, she refused to be undone now by a heavy session and a bad head.

'I've read everything on Google, over and over, and . . . do you know what else they call it? This Takotsubo condition?' Nancy swallowed and concentrated on the fruit trees down the garden. The promise of Whittacker's meadows beyond the fence. 'Nancy, please look at me.'

Broken heart syndrome, the consultant had called it. The damage to the heart muscle could be treated, but there was no cure for the condition itself. Other than maybe a time machine. He'd tried the hard sell on psychological therapy. But sitting in a circle *sharing* over tea and plain biscuits didn't really jump out and grab much. The cardio rehab group had been enough of a stretch.

'I know what they call it. You don't need to say it, Mum.' It sounded so flimsy out loud. So completely weak and wishy-washy. An affront to Molly's herculean efforts to get better. 'Everything will be back to normal soon. Haima's letting me do a little work.'

Annabel put both hands over her eyes and stood there, deep-breathing. This was new. Nancy swallowed and waited for her to say something.

Annabel braced her hands on the back of a kitchen chair and stared at her. 'If you think you can just keep on pressing forward until you feel *normal* again, Nancy, I can tell you now that this is going to come back and bite you hard. Do you know why? Nancy, *look* at me.'

Nancy scratched her nose and did as she was told. 'Why?' she tried brightly, but her voice wobbled.

'Because it will never feel normal that she died, Nancy. And nor should it.'

A sickly heat moved through her body. Annabel was right. It would never be normal. *They* would never be normal again. It would never be any less appalling. That Molly had gotten sick, instead of all the wicked people in the world who had better chromosomes, better *luck* . . . or that she'd never fall in love, or out of love, or have children or more dogs or tattoos . . . she'd never see a morning over the meadows again, or laugh, or cry, or hear music and be moved by it, be touched, or felt, or held, or dye her hair blue . . . she wouldn't even get a mayfly's worth. It was all gone.

Nancy pivoted just in time. Annabel skipped over to the sink with her, caught her hair, scooping it back with a deftness that came from years of looking after others.

'It's OK, sweetheart. Is that the last of it?' She rubbed Nancy's back until her body stopped spasming. Nancy wanted to cry into the sink but yanked the tap on instead, rinsing everything away before her mum had to look at it.

'I need to shower. I know you want to talk, but can we do it later?'

'Sure. Later. Whenever you're ready. And then maybe one of us could call your dad?'

Nancy leant back against the counter. Her dad. *Shit.* 'Doubt he'll want me to call for a while.'

Annabel passed her a handful of kitchen towel. 'He stayed with you until sun-up. So you had, and I quote, *someone to keep your airways clear*. He said it was his turn for a sleepless night.'

'Dad stayed? Here?'

Annabel nodded. 'In the armchair next to the sofa. I was just explaining to Ernest, in case he thought we were being burgled or something. I mean, that van outside all night . . .' They fell into a silence.

'Was Dad OK? When he left?'

Annabel tucked the hair behind Nancy's ear and grimaced at it.

'He was OK. He said you have a mouth like your sister's. But that he probably had it coming. He also said it isn't easy standing up to your own parents, even when we're adults ourselves.' Annabel smiled lopsidedly. 'He knows he's not perfect, Nance. None of us get it all right. Most of us are just treading water. Swans up top. Frantic kicking beneath the waterline.' She dabbed Nancy's hair with the kitchen towel.

'I'm going to go and shampoo that.' Nancy walked for the hallway.

'Nance, just before you go up . . .' Nancy hung back in the kitchen doorway. 'Last night . . . Clarence . . .'

She held her hand up. 'Mum, can we talk about it later?' She did not have the energy to get into being stood up for an evening at a piano. 'We didn't even meet, and I'm glad, we don't have anything in common and—'

'Birdie died last night.'

The air felt suddenly thick in Nancy's ears. Reality changing state. She stepped back into the kitchen. 'When?'

'Just as Clarence was leaving the hospital, Ernest said.'

'He was with her?'

'Yes. Thankfully. For them both.' Nancy pictured him there, at Birdie's piano. Soundless. Annabel touched a hand to her shoulder. 'Hopefully that will bring him some small comfort. I know how hard it's been for you, Nance, not having the same chance.'

Chapter 29

'Has she grounded you? You've been dragging that poor dog up and down for the last twenty minutes, anyone would think you're not allowed further than the postbox after misbehaving yourself on the old pop last night.' Ernie's moustache moved like walrus whiskers as he chortled. Something shiny brown clung to his bristles. Nancy pushed the sunglasses back up her nose. Annabel had thrust them at her along with the dog lead and a prescription for fresh air.

'Something like that.' She leant back against Ernie's fence while Fig weighed which way they would walk next, back up Mountford Road or back down it.

Ernie folded his arms and perched over his fence so they were shoulder to shoulder now, the brim of his panama hat almost touching Nancy's head. He studied Clarence's house, speaking as if they were sharing a secret.

'Radical idea, but you could always just go on up there and knock.'

Nancy sighed. The fresh air wasn't working. 'I know.

It's not that simple, though.' She'd been so selfish. So short-sighted. She had been going to ask properly about Birdie, but Birdie was such a big subject, there hadn't been a big enough run-up to it. So it had been left alone, and now it had been left too late.

'I know,' conceded Ernie. 'It's a minefield. Should you? Shouldn't you? Do you go in person or send a card? Do they want comfort? Or solitude? Is there any point in any of it anyway, when there's nothing in the world you can say or do to make it any different?'

'Exactly.'

He pulled a handkerchief from his shirt pocket and addressed his moustache. 'We human beings are complicated things, are we not?' Clarence's downstairs light was still on. On one of the brightest, sunshiniest mornings of the year. *Summer's swan song*, Annabel had said after nudging Nancy out into it.

'I suppose we are.'

'And all too often so easily spooked,' he said softly. 'The morning I moved into this place and saw all those cars parked along the road and all those people in your garden, laughing . . . and crying . . . well, we'd not long lost Ray's dad, so I knew. I knew what your mother must be feeling and I just wanted to offer her my best wishes, but I was so worried I'd make things worse for her. Say the wrong thing or knock at the wrong time. But now, I wished I'd knocked. Because there wasn't a person who came by the house after we lost Matthew, or his mother, who ever made me feel worse. They brought comfort, sometimes by saying nothing at all, just by . . . knocking on the door. That's the power people don't always realise they have, to just turn up and knock. Letting you know they're *there*, when you're ready to open the curtains again.'

Clarence hadn't drawn any of his curtains. Had he sat there all night at Birdie's piano, the universe indifferently spinning on around their home? Was he still sitting there now?

Ernie nudged her gently with his big shoulder. 'What's the frightening part?'

Nancy felt her shoulders drop. What *was* the frightening part? 'Not everyone is like you, Ernie.'

'No?' he asked innocently.

Nancy smiled. 'You do remember meeting my grandmother?'

'I certainly do. Your point?'

'Not everyone shines a light. And not everyone wants to be shone on, either.' It was the thought that had pushed her past Clarence's house four times this morning already, that he was better off being left alone. Better off waiting for someone else to knock.

'Oh, I don't know,' shrugged Ernie. 'I found your grandmother shines a light of sorts. More like a flame-thrower but . . .' Nancy smiled. Ernie took his cue and snorted softly over his moustache. The sound rose like warm air over them and disappeared into the endless blue above. 'You are not like your grandmother, young lady. You're you. And if you're worrying if that's going to be enough then, well, you're worrying about the wrong thing. And I'm not saying I have all the answers or that young Clarence wants to be, as you put it, *shone on* . . . but maybe all you should be worrying about just now is making sure that lad up there hears you knock.'

Nancy looked up the street. She chewed the inside of her cheek until it stung. People had come and gone all New Year's Day to their house. Hungover. Driven by friends through the snow and ice. Ashen with disbelief. But they'd come, posting cards, offering doorstep condolences. Nancy had fielded them so Annabel could sit in the garden alone, frozen. And then their dad had arrived, and he'd fielded the condolences so Nancy could hide too, organising, writing lists, making online enquiries because everywhere was shut. New Year's Day! She'd thrown herself into car repairs and orders of service and flowers and songs and biodegradable eco-friendly sustainable caskets because Molly had been a vegan once for about four hours so it seemed only right to think about carbon footprints. It had been a busy, busy day, the Day After. People had come, and they'd pushed the hours on. But it was all quiet along Mountford Road today. No one had pulled up outside Clarence's house all morning bar Betty Hollins with some of the church ladies, and they hadn't made it past the porch, Annabel said.

'Hi, Fig.' Ray appeared on Ernie's garden path, a plated sandwich in his hands. Fig jumped at the fence, sniffing the air.

'You managed it then, lad?'

'I burnt the bacon a bit, Grandpa. The kitchen's quite smoky. I prefer crispy, though.'

'Crispy's perfect. And you've turned off the gas?'

Ray nodded. 'Gas off.'

'You let him fry bacon?' asked Nancy.

'Certainly. Makes a mean bacon sandwich, don't you, Ray? Camping rule numero two, second only to pitching your tent on the flat . . . cooking up a winning bacon butty for breakfast. Oh heck, Ray, you haven't?' Ray stopped chomping the first half of his two bacon sandwiches. Ernie straightened up, pushing his hat up his forehead. 'I thought you were doing me another?'

Ray looked at the plate. 'I have, Grandpa. Here.'

'You've put ketchup on it! Ray, rule numero three, brown sauce. It's only *ever* brown on a bacon sandwich.' Ray looked at his work, unconvinced.

'I'm with you, Ray,' said Nancy. 'Red all the way. Or none at all.'

'See, Grandpa. Nancy knows. Fig can—'

'Don't you dare give that dog my bacon, young Ray. She chased me onto my shed roof, lest we forget.'

Ray did something then Nancy hadn't seen before. He giggled. Ketchup-faced, eyes scrunched.

'Yeah, she did, Grandpa.' He grinned and held his plate over the fence. 'Do you like it crispy, Nancy?'

The thought of a greasy sandwich made her feel sick again. But she thought of Pete in the apartment next door, trying to share his lettuce leaves. Not asking again.

'I do, actually, Ray. Just half, though, thanks.' She bit in, purging all thoughts of young boys' hand hygiene. 'It's good.' She chewed. 'Ernie, you don't know what you're missing.'

'Can Fig stay and play for a while, Grandpa?'

'I suppose it'll save her being dragged on another circuit past number five.'

Nancy glanced at Clarence's house again. Ernie held his hand out for Fig's lead.

'No cowboys and Indians,' said Nancy, slipping Fig the

rest of her sandwich. She didn't ask why Ray wasn't at school this morning, she didn't really need to.

'Agreed,' said Ernie. He nodded up the road. 'See you shortly then.'

Nancy swatted the crumbs off her vest, checked her lip for ketchup and started walking. *Just knock. He doesn't have to answer. He can ignore it. And if he doesn't ignore it . . .* Her feet slowed. If Clarence did answer, what would she say? She hadn't been on this side of the chasm before. The painless side. There were people she'd cut off completely for not getting in touch in the weeks after the news about Molly had filtered out. For not knocking on Annabel's door. She'd been surgical, who to let in, who to shut out. If they didn't call, they were done. But now she was walking up Clarence's drive, it wasn't as clean-cut.

Someone had left a pie box on Birdie's porch. Fruit. Still warm enough to smell. The Betty Hollinses of the world were up baking fresh pies to go before 9 a.m. on a midweek morning. Here Nancy was, hungover and empty-handed. She blinked at the doorbell, then pressed it quick. An ant crawled across the pie box. Then another. Then two more. She tapped the box. *Shoo.* Did the doorbell ring? She hadn't heard it, but she hadn't been concentrating. Should she knock too? She didn't want to beat the door down. And what if he was in bed? She'd knock. Just once, then she'd leave him in peace.

Another ant trailed across the box lid. 'Off,' she whispered, swatting it away. She picked up the box, held it on her left hand and moved to knock the door with her right, but when she swung, the door wasn't there. Her weight shifted unexpectedly. Clarence stood in the open doorway as the fruit pie overbalanced from her hand. It wobbled off her palm and hit the deck, upended.

For a second, she stared down at it, then slunk to the ground, pushing cracked pie crust back together, a purple disaster in her hands.

'I'll fix it and bring it back,' she said optimistically.

Clarence hunkered back out of the doorway, his toes just out of reach of the sunlight on the floor, as if this beautiful summer morning did not also belong to him. Nancy watched his body retreat. He stood, waiting. She stopped her efforts with Betty's pie and stood too. Clarence's stillness was overwhelming, and it stilled Nancy too.

'I, er . . .' The words evaporated from her head. Clarence's eyes were tired and unreadable. Had he been crying? Or could he control his tears the same way Nancy could now?

The longer Clarence waited for her to speak, the more void-like Nancy's brain became. She wished she was an ant and could disappear between the cracks of the path. She should know what to say, but she didn't. There was nothing. Finally, her mouth kicked into autopilot.

'Ernie spoke to my mum. He said he'd seen you last night and . . . I'm so sorry, Clarence.'

Clarence nodded, rubbed a hand over his mouth. 'Yeah.' Nancy looked at her feet. 'In a better place now, that's what they say, isn't it, Nance?'

'Yeah,' swallowed Nancy. 'It's what people say.'

She understood his need to know for sure. But she was still undecided on all of that. She'd never pictured Molly in Heaven, or even what Heaven might look like. What it might be for Molly. The best she had come up with was a construct, a fantasy, an island paradise to plonk her on for safe keeping. Without this, it had felt utterly hopeless, to think of her in a peaceful, painless place. Impossible to think of Molly outside of the last months. The tests. The medicines. The sickness and nosebleeds and infections. The fading hope. But that wasn't all there was, it could *not* be all there was. She saw that now. Molly deserved to be more than that. To not be kept in that place. In either of those places. She belonged here. In the life she had lived. In Mistleton.

Clarence looked past her towards the road they'd all played on as children, his thoughts trailing away somewhere. Nancy watched them move over his face, until he came back again.

'Yesterday . . .' He hesitated. 'I meant to call you from the hospital.'

'Oh, it's OK. Of course it is.' She'd been getting drunk in the Jack while Clarence had spent the last moments of Birdie's life comforting her. Being with her. Like good people, braver people, did. Nancy imagined him holding his mum's hand. The picture fixing itself to her brain. She spoke, just to get rid of it.

'Have you had anything to eat yet today? I could, I don't know, make you a coffee and some toast or . . . go grab you something and just drop it by the door?' Ernie was watching from his garden bench. 'Bacon sandwich?' she babbled.

'Thanks, Nancy.' Clarence moved back into the doorway and put his hand on its edge. 'For stopping by.'

'Sure. Of course.' She clutched the pie box and instinctively stepped backwards. The door closed softly between them.

* * *

360

Ernie slapped his newspaper on his bench and strolled to the fence. 'How is the lad?' Nancy exhaled deeply. Clarence was in pain. There was just so much pain involved in loving a person, it was inhumane. Ernie patted her elbow. 'It'll take time.'

Nancy straightened her shoulders. She pushed her sunglasses back up her nose with sticky fingers. 'I know. Do you mind if I leave Fig while I run this home?' Ernie sized up the mess on her hands, the crumpled box.

'Best not to ask?'

'Yep.'

'Come and get her when you're ready. Ray'll want to make her a bacon sandwich, I expect. When he's finished scratching her belly.'

'Thanks, Ernie. You're a good neighbour.' There was no saying how Annabel would've been if Ernie had knocked the day he moved in. How he'd have felt when the door closed again. Nancy reached Annabel's gate. 'Ernie?' she called back.

'Yes, flower?'

'It's brown.'

'What is?'

'My mum's favourite. If you ever have another bacon sandwich surplus . . .'

Chapter 30

'Mum?' Nancy shut the front door with her bottom and zipped through the hall into the kitchen, throwing the pie box down on the counter next to the papers Annabel had printed. She picked them up and shoved them back behind the microwave. *One problem at a time.* She heard the lounge door and yelled in that direction. 'Mum? You know you said to us when we each hit eighteen that we had one No-Questions-Asked-Mum-Will-Fix-It token to use if we did something really stupid and needed your help? And I never cashed mine in?' Molly's cash-in had been a two-hundred-mile round trip to pick her up from a dairy farm in Cumbria after an illegal rave once the police had arrived and Mol's ride had scarpered without her. Annabel appeared in the kitchen doorway. Nancy pointed a sticky purple finger at Clarence's pie. 'I'm cashing it in now, can you fix this? Pronto? I know we've got the apples, but it's got bloody berries in it too and Betty Hollins is bound to go back for her china plate so I

362

have to fix her pie for Clarence.' The plate, miraculously, had survived the fall.

An unexpected voice rumbled over Annabel's shoulder.

'Nancy Fancy-Pants, how are we doing?' Uncle Julian's face shone with all the warmth of a fun absentee uncle. His chin sank into his neck as he grinned. 'You look like you've been shot! Not even . . . nine thirty a.m. and you've been out tearing up the neighbourhood?'

Nancy blinked at the mess she'd got on her top, then back to him. 'Uncle Jules? You're here?' His hairline had receded further over his head since the funeral, but he was still persevering with the middle-aged-surfer back-and-sides thing.

'Come to see with his own eyes that his niece is all right,' followed another voice down the hallway. Ginny's walking stick thumped along the tiles. She ushered Annabel through the kitchen doorway.

'Hello, Gran. Another visit, so soon?'

Annabel twisted her earring and looked vacantly through the French doors. Ginny pointed a finger over her walking stick to Nancy's stained vest.

'Well you've more colour about you today. In your cheeks . . . on your clothes. Go on upstairs and change while your mother makes us a cup of tea. Then you can tell us how you've come to have only one hearth spaniel sitting on your mantel, Annabel.'

Annabel turned for the kettle before Nancy could look an apology at her for the Staffordshire dog. Uncle Julian rolled his eyes over Ginny's shoulder as if she were a burden equally shared between them. She wasn't.

'I'll be two minutes, Mum.' Nancy gave both surprise visitors a peck on the cheek as she passed them.

* * *

Julian was flipping through the LPs in the lounge when Nancy got back downstairs.

'Shall we take the tea out in the garden, Uncle Jules?' she chirped. 'It's such a lovely morning.'

'You made me jump!'

She gave him an innocent smile. 'Come on then.' Before he swiped that Bob Seger album he was holding.

In the kitchen, Annabel remained eyes-down, focused on the things she was setting onto the tea tray. Nancy sank her hands into her pockets. Four adults, one room, no one talking.

'Nice of you to come and visit with Gran, Uncle Jules.'

Julian picked up one of the biscuits Annabel had laid out. He chomped it down in two takes. 'Sure thing. Just checking in on my little sister, and you too, Nance. You both look great.' He took another biscuit before Annabel moved them to the tray. Gran had made him drive her over here for something. Nancy could smell it. A deliberate act, like leaving a glove behind, to achieve something she couldn't quite put her finger on. But she knew to look out for it now.

'Cool,' she said. She opened the doors onto the garden. 'Ready?' Annabel gave her a bright smile and nodded before it dissolved again.

'Mind your step, my darling,' warned Ginny, manoeuvring herself outside. She thumped her stick against the only cracked paving stone. 'We don't want *broken neck* added to our health worries, do we?'

'I've been meaning to get that replaced,' said Annabel, carrying out the tray.

'Mum's treated herself to a new bistro set,' said Nancy. 'We only put it up last weekend, didn't we, Mum? I talked her into it. The weather's been so nice, and having breakfast outside is always a good start to the day.' And there was more chance of Annabel inviting someone round, Ernie perhaps, if there was somewhere comfortable they could both sit, maybe watch the sky changing over the back meadows.

'Oh yes,' observed Ginny. 'Like the lovely metal bistro sets they have at Hollyfields, but plastic.'

Nancy had made the argument for a more expensive set when they'd looked online. Annabel had made a stronger counter-argument for not paying too much for anything fated to Fig's habitual chewing habit.

'Shall I pour?' asked Annabel.

'I'll do it, Mum. You sit down.'

'Stir it first, Annab—' Ginny switched focus to something Ernie's side of the fence. Ray stared back, hair in his eyes. He was holding something, the other end draped around his neck. He clicked it with his thumb before calling over.

'Nancy, I just hid some bacon for Fig and made her wait and she sniffed it out all the way upstairs in Grandpa's sock drawer and it only took her 19.86 seconds to find it.' He waved the stopwatch.

'That's 5.12 seconds shaved off her first run, isn't it, Ray?' called Ernest, plodding down his garden, hat, head and shoulders bobbing above the fence line.

'Good Lord,' said Ginny under her breath. She patted the arms of her chair with long, slender hands. The polish on one of her fingers had chipped. Nancy scanned the rest, analysing that one imperfect nail. A glitch in the matrix.

'Mol's Fig?' asked Uncle Julian. 'Rifling the neighbours' houses now, is she? In under twenty seconds!' Nancy smiled with him. *Almost as efficiently as you*, she thought.

'She'll move even faster for sausage,' Nancy called over the fence. Ernie waved over. Annabel gave him a quick nod back.

'Who's the big guy?' asked Julian quietly. Annabel thrust a cup and saucer towards him.

'That's Ernie,' said Nancy. 'Ray's grandad.'

'Morning,' waved Julian. 'Beautiful day!' Uncle Julian liked people. Anyone really. Women especially, so much so he'd never successfully landed on any one woman for long before trying the next. It all just seemed to wash over him, Ginny always helping the criticism to flow, why this fiancée wasn't right for her boy, why that one wasn't either. Ginny always somewhere near the wheel.

'It's a belter, sir!' replied Ernie.

'Don't encourage them, Julian,' muttered Ginny, looking into her lap, pretending not to speak at all. 'Can't they see we're having a family gathering? Annabel, shoo him off.'

Nancy watched her grandmother carefully. Ray had told her that a piranha could smell a drop of blood in two hundred litres of water. And then come looking for something to bite into. Was this why Annabel had never asked anyone else to be part of her world? Why there had never been another man in her life? When there were good men out there, men like Ernie? Was she just being careful, to keep the teeth away?

'Sugar?' asked Annabel. She spooned a heap into all four cups anyway.

'If you aren't careful, Annabel, he'll be around here all the time. You need a couple of quick-growing trees, privet perhaps, along that side boundary. Before he gets the wrong idea.'

Nancy looked at Julian. Conveniently interested in the biscuit between his fingers. She felt a prickle of adrenalin along her collarbone. Ginny was unreadable. Unmoved. Unaffected. Nancy remembered the look on her dad's face last night. She'd hurt him. He'd made some questionable decisions as a parent, but he wasn't cruel. He'd never meant to be hurtful; he'd meant to be selfish. It wasn't an excuse, but it wasn't meaningless either.

Ernie was still smiling over the fence. Julian, still munching, watching the fields. Annabel still stirring the teapot. What would Annabel have given for a selfish parent? Ginny folded her ladylike hands innocuously in her lap. Hands it was unimaginable to think of stroking a face or playing a joyous melody.

'Ernie?' His name left Nancy's mouth and expanded like contraband bubblegum, chewy and full and delicious. 'Would you like to join us?'

Annabel stopped stirring and stared at Nancy beside her.

'And leave this pair to their own devices? I'll have no bacon *or* sausages left!'

'Good luck with the sock drawer too!' said Julian, jovially closing down Ernie's invitation.

Ernie touched the brim of his hat. 'That too.' He winked at Nancy. 'Cheerio.'

'Thank heavens for that,' said Ginny.

Nancy shifted herself. 'Ernie's nice, Gran.'

'I'm sure he is.'

'Friendly chap,' agreed Julian, ever the toothless diplomat. He reminded Nancy of herself.

Ginny craned her neck toward Nancy then. 'But your mother doesn't want every single man in the vicinity hanging around trying their luck, does she?'

Nancy pressed her teeth together and smiled. 'Blimey, Mum, how many men have you had round here? What does Gran know that we don't?'

Annabel's cheek tensed. Uncle Julian chortled. Ginny did not. And neither did Nancy.

Ginny elongated her neck. 'As I said, my darling, nice as I am sure that gentleman is, your mother doesn't want to go giving any wrong ideas.'

'Maybe Mum's giving him the right idea.'

She felt the fight grow in her. She was. She was going to tell Ginny, right here, today. Right now. To leave their mother alone.

Ginny locked eyes on Nancy, just for a second, before looking at Annabel instead. Nancy opened her mouth to cut her off at the pass before she fired her next shot anywhere near Annabel, but Annabel put her hand over Nancy's under the table and held on. This was how she would tell them to quieten down when they were little, in a church pew or at Gran's dining table. A gentle hand and a gentle request. *No more.*

Nancy clenched her jaw, turned her palm upwards and held onto her mum's under the table. She breathed slowly and looked out over the meadows, the grasses barely moving in the breeze. They were both here, it was a beautiful morning, and Grandma Ginny and Uncle Julian would be gone again soon. And then Annabel would find the right berries and they would both fix Clarence's pie and see where the rest of the day took them. Peace. That was what her mum wanted. *Peace*.

Ginny lifted her cup from its saucer and sipped. Nancy hoped it was still hot enough to burn her tongue.

'Ah, *there's* the other one!' said Uncle Julian, with either impeccable timing or astounding obliviousness. He pointed another half-chewed Hobnob towards the china dog balanced on the utility windowsill.

Ginny held onto the table. 'Why on earth is it outside?'

'It's drying. I gave it a good clean this morning,' explained Annabel.

'They're a pair, Annabel. They're not worth anything apart. Or broken. I hope you didn't use anything caustic on it?'

Caustic. Now there was a word.

'No,' said Annabel calmly. 'Just Fairy Liquid, and the hose.'

'The hose? The *garden* hose? I passed those figurines on to you when I moved into Hollyfields. They were very dear to me. I was rather expecting they'd be treated respectfully in your care.'

'Mum treats everything in her care with respect. And tenderness. And warmth.'

Annabel's hand was back under the table. Not squeezing, just . . . holding. Holding Nancy's hand. Or maybe just asking for someone to hold hers.

'You never liked the mantel dogs, Mum,' said Annabel, unexpectedly. She kept her eyes on the distance. Whittacker's meadows, the trees along the horizon, wisps of cloud in a perfectly blue sky. 'And neither did I.'

'Of course I did,' snapped Ginny. Her eyes glowered, at Uncle Julian first, then to Nancy, searching for her ally. 'And what you do and do not like is your own business, Annabel, who am I to say? I thought you did like them or I wouldn't have gifted them to you at all.'

Beneath the table, Annabel's thumb ran a small circle over the back of Nancy's hand. Round and round. Then it stopped.

'I liked his piano. You knew I did, but you gave me the china dogs that had sat on it instead.'

Ginny laid her hand flat on the table and leant in. 'Your brother was the only one who'd ever taken so much as a lesson on that piano. You never would've dedicated yourself to learning.'

'Well, I gave it a *small* go,' said Julian from the sidelines. 'But I was no whizz. Sausage-fingered,' he said, wiggling a hand for Nancy.

'Of course I was going to give it to Julian, Annabel. You should've said if you were offended, but you didn't. You never do say though, do you?'

'But you didn't give it Julian, Mum. You gave it to his girlfriend. Whose name you can't even remember.'

'They were living together, Annabel.'

Nancy waited for the wheels to fall off her mum's sudden

runaway rebellion, but Annabel remained steady, rolling straight ahead in a set and certain line.

'No they weren't. Julian slept there when he felt like it. And then they broke up and Dad's piano was lost for ever. I loved it and you gave it to a stranger.'

'Rubbish,' spat Ginny. 'I'm sorry you're having to listen to this, Nancy, but I shan't have it. Annabel, your memory is somewhat unreliable. You could not play that piano, Julian had had lessons. Of *course* I offered it to him and his partner, it made sense; I wasn't to know they'd separate, or that you *loved* it as much as you say. You never showed any promise.'

'I was never allowed. Dad let me play, the melodies you didn't like to hear. So we only played when you went out. That was our time.'

Nancy held her breath.

'I'm not a mind-reader, Annabel. I can't guess what you all got up to when I went out, I can't guess what you're thinking either. Goodness knows there have been times we could've all benefited from being able to read what was going through your mind. Richard said as much before you separated! You can be very difficult, Annabel. I'm sorry, but you can.'

Annabel's hand left Nancy's. Her neck flushed red and blotchy.

'Don't do that,' said Nancy firmly.

Ginny turned cold blue eyes on her, but Nancy didn't shrink away like she had in the past. She didn't even blink, and she'd sit here all day not blinking like that ugly china dog if she had to.

Julian tried clearing his throat. Perhaps of all the biscuit crumbs. 'Why don't we go inside and see about getting these fireside figurines back together, spick and span?'

'Oh do be quiet, Julian,' snapped Ginny.

Annabel put her elbow on the table and set her forehead in her hand. Nancy touched her shoulder, ducking to see her face better.

'Mum?' Annabel rolled her head to one side and smiled at her. Nancy felt her throat close and her heart patter. 'Are you OK, Mum?'

Annabel leant forward and kissed her on the forehead. 'Want to come walk Fig with me?'

Nancy blinked at her. 'What?'

'Just you and me and all that countryside?'

'Now?' Nancy swallowed.

'Then we'll see what we can do for Betty's boshed berry pie.'

Annabel was smiling, as if she were suddenly untouchable. Nancy found herself smiling back. 'Sure.'

'Come on then, kiddo. Ray?' Annabel hollered towards the fence. 'Bring Fig around to the front for me, please.'

'OK, Mrs Woods,' came Ray's voice from over the boundary.

Annabel rose from her chair. Nancy followed suit, getting to her feet too. It felt like being back at high school and having a very cool friend to stand behind. It felt like standing behind Molly.

'Annabel. Where are you going? We're having tea!' demanded Ginny.

Annabel walked on, unlatching the side gate. 'For a very, very long walk. Stay as long as you like. But before you do go,

Mum, Ernest is my friend. And he is welcome here until *I* say he's not.' Nancy looked from her mum to her grandmother. *Holy shit.* 'And Julian?'

Uncle Jules looked like a boy about to have his bottom smacked. 'Yes, sis?'

'If you're going to help yourself to my records again on your way out, do me favour and just take them all. I'm tired of looking for things I love in the places they should be and finding they're nowhere to be seen.'

Julian gave a sheepish nod and Annabel was gone.

Ginny got to her feet and rounded the table. 'Nancy, darling . . .'

'Sit down, Mum,' breathed Julian.

'I will not,' she snapped. 'Nancy, what on earth is wrong with her? Is it her hormones?' But it was pointless. Grandma Ginny would never see it now. She'd been right all her life.

'Nancy, where are you going? Stay here with us. Wait until she's calmed down, don't *pander* to her.' Do this, do that. Tiptoe back to your father's office and fetch my glove.

Nancy tucked her hair behind her ears. *Fuck off, Gran.* It was there, on her tongue. Ready. But instead she said, 'No, Gran. I'm going for a walk, with my mum.'

'Walk? Where?'

Nancy shrugged. 'Wherever she wants to go. For as long as she wants me there. Maybe it's time you tried walking beside her too?'

Chapter 31

'Mum? Wait up.' Annabel was already past the postbox at the neck of Mountford Road, Fig excitedly trotting beside her. Annabel slowed but didn't stop. Nancy broke into a light jog to cover the last hundred yards between them. 'Hey, Speedy Gonzales . . . where are we going?' Annabel smiled over her shoulder and veered off the pavement for the footpath cutting behind their houses into Whittacker's meadows. Nancy caught up as Annabel unclipped Fig and made a steady leap over the first crossing of the stream. Fig followed her over the water, Nancy followed Fig. 'Mum! Where's the fire?' Annabel clambered over another grassy knoll. 'Mum!' Annabel stopped then and turned, setting both hands on her hips. Her chest heaved with fast breaths. 'You just pulled *a Molly*,' beamed Nancy. 'On *Gran*.' The rules had just flapped right out of the window. 'Are you OK?'

Annabel took in a long breath through her nose and released it slowly. 'I am absolutely fine. Your gran and I . . .' But the words evaded her.

'I know,' said Nancy. Mothers and daughters were tricky things to distil into something so simple as words.

Annabel watched Fig, shuffling away through the grasses towards the rise. 'She prefers it up there.'

'She does. She'll be on the ridge in no time if you don't watch her. It's the foxes, I think. She can smell them all over Saxon's Hill.'

Annabel blinked against the sun. Her eyes shone blue enough to make the sky back down. She held her face to it and closed her eyelids. 'What are we doing, hey, Nance?'

It sounded like a trick. Nancy hesitated. 'I don't know.'

'All this time we waste, not saying what we want to.' Nancy had a million words, all tucked away like coins lost down the back of a sofa, steadily devaluing over time. 'Last night . . . you said things to your father I haven't managed to in twenty-two years.' The full extent of which hadn't completely come back to Nancy yet. 'Things I've wanted to say to him, rightly or wrongly, but could never make come out. Every time I thought I might summon up the words, I seemed to always swallow them back again, pushing them all down inside, hoping they might all just . . . go away.'

'I'm sorry, Mum.'

'For what? Your dad and I spoke properly last night, for the first time since you were a little girl . . . and I wasn't much older than you now. A lifetime ago.' Annabel blinked and lost the first tears. 'We talked about you, Nance. Us . . . and Molly. And it was so good to talk about her. And it was so good to talk about *you*, with someone who loves you both so much too. And when your dad told me to get some sleep, I went up to bed and lay there thinking over and again – *how* did I make two such beautiful daughters, so tough and headstrong and ready to face their hurdles head-on? How did *I* manage that, Nance? When I've been frightened my whole life?' She wiped her cheek and looked over the meadows again.

Nancy tasted old lies in her mouth, and the truth trying to push its way past them. Her throat narrowed, but she would not cry. She would not ask for her mother's sympathy.

'We aren't the same, Mum. Molly was the brave one.' It was a fact that would never become any less colossal, and an apology that would never be colossal enough.

'Of course you are, Nancy. You're braver than me! I know how much you love your dad. I know you waited for him to come back to us for even longer than I did. And I know it's harder to tell the ones we love most what it is that frightens us and makes us feel the way we do, when it might risk pushing them further away. I thought about it again and again last night, Nance. If you could be straight with your dad who you love and want in your life, what excuse do I have for not being able to stand up to someone who I don't even . . .'

Nancy watched her trying to find the right words. The right feelings. She swallowed. 'You don't want Gran in your life?' *You don't love her?*

A look of bewilderment moved over Annabel's features. Nancy hadn't meant it to come out like it had, but she hadn't allowed herself to think it before, that even Annabel might have her limits on how much disappointment she could put up with, and what those limits might look like, what they might mean if she knew the things Clarence had seen just over there on the furlong, as the snow had fallen and the New Year fireworks had lit up the world.

Annabel shook her head gently. 'I do. But . . .' She twisted the dog lead in her hand. 'She doesn't make it easy.'

'I know,' said Nancy softly. 'I'm sorry, Mum.'

'Will you stop apologising? You have nothing in the world to be sorry for.' Annabel's face was so open and earnest. So completely certain. 'Except maybe that poor dog figurine. You should probably be sorry for that.'

But Nancy felt a caution blowing in. Annabel was walking too close to the furlong. The sycamore and its secrets.

'I need to tell you something, Mum.'

A bang crackled through the distance. Annabel jolted. Birds flew from the trees in the distance, crows cawed in protest, all eyes suddenly towards the ridge along the horizon. Annabel laughed and wiped the last wet from her cheek.

'Ruddy heck. Probably your gran firing up her broomstick?' She smiled. 'That'll scare the crows.' But another loud bang rumbled through the valley. Then a third. Annabel focused on the ridge and stopped smiling. 'Do you see Fig?'

Nancy shielded her eyes from the sun. Movement. Startled by the noise too. 'When did they move the sheep this side of the ridge?'

'Fig!' bellowed Annabel. 'Can you see her? My glasses are at home, I can't see her. Molly said she wouldn't hurt them, but . . .' But that wouldn't stop her scaring them half to death. 'Is she up there?' But Nancy couldn't see either. And then, more movement. Clusters of the flock, moving, dispersing, coming together again like starlings.

'She's in there with them.' Nancy broke across the grass and ran for the next shallow stream crossing. She misjudged it, stumbling onto the grassy bank chased by the sounds of Annabel through the water after her.

'Nancy, slow down!' But Annabel's voice was taut and Nancy couldn't stop. They weren't scaring the birds today. 'Nancy, wait!'

But she couldn't. There was no snow to slow her. No darkness. She ran like she'd trained herself to on Garfield's treadmills, and circuit after circuit around Chortley Park, faster, shorter, pricking away the seconds like daisy petals. She ran like Molly needed her to.

Voices rose over the hillside. Angry and urgent. A Land Rover sat in the gateway at the top of the field. Nancy couldn't see anyone, but she shouted for them anyway.

'That's my dog! I'm coming! I'll put her on the lead!' but she still couldn't see Fig, just the panicked white forms of Whittacker's sheep. She stumbled out of the meadow onto the track halfway up the furlong, Annabel trailing behind now. The sycamore sat behind her too, at the bottom of the dip, she could be there in seconds but she had to run uphill, not down. Her brain slowed but her legs pushed on, taking her up the furlong, and then Fig's fox-red form shot out through the hedgerow onto the track ahead.

'You stupid dog!' shouted Nancy, panic and exhaustion clawing each other's eyes out inside her body.

Fig looked at her unaffected, tongue hanging out of her mouth, pleased with herself. The relief flooded through Nancy with the lactic acid, hot intoxication. She felt the tremble when she opened her mouth to call again, but there was other shouting, from the figures at the top of the furlong, and from Annabel behind. Fig ignored them all and turned back for the sheep field.

'Fig!'

Fig trotted, started to run . . . then she stumbled, skidded down hard into the dirt, before the last lament of Whittacker's shotgun reached through the air.

Chapter 32

A polystyrene cup of chilled water arrived before Nancy's nose. 'Drink this.'

Beth had heard the shots. She'd left her horse with her father, confiscated the last of his cartridges and made him help lift Fig into the back of his Land Rover with one of his grandsons. Whittacker had scratched his sweaty head, half angry and half sorry, asking repeatedly where all the blood was, while Nancy and Annabel had sat in silent shock in the back seat.

There's no blood, Dad, because you didn't bloody hit her, Beth had shouted at him. *You can't shoot any more! And you* definitely *can't shoot once they're out of our fields. The furlong cuts a public footpath through there, Dad, you know that!*

Nancy drank all of the cold water. Two little girls sat on the bench opposite, nurturing a cardboard box with a tortoise inside. The youngest coaxed it to eat a dandelion, the older girl kept looking over as if Nancy were a strangely afflicted creature waiting to be seen by the vet too. Nancy watched Beth talking to the receptionist, who kept blinking and nodding at everything she said.

'Thanks, Helen, bill the yard account,' she heard. Beth swished her honey-blonde ponytail, patted the counter and came back to the seats. 'They'll call, Nance, if you want to go home? You still look spacey, why don't you go? Andy will phone when he's finished taking a look at her. I have to get going soon, find a new lock for the gun cabinet before that silly old sod shoots himself in the foot, but I promise Fig will be looked after.'

Nancy nodded. She did feel spacey. Like the adrenalin could flow again any second and wash her away.

'She shouldn't have been in there with your sheep, Beth. She would've gone back in there with them.' Whittacker was within his rights. They shouldn't have let her run so far.

'Yes, well,' sighed Beth. There had been hushed talk in the car park, father and daughter discussing police warnings. 'She's Mol's dog, Nance. She was never going to stick to rules or boundaries, was she?'

Annabel re-emerged from the bathroom. She'd been crying in there, eyes puffed pink with it. Beth touched her elbow. 'I've got to go, but I swear, Andy's the best in the business. He fixes the unfixable, Annabel.'

Annabel tried not to cry. 'Will the sheep be all right?'

'They're used to our dogs, and they're not in lamb. So I think they'll be fine . . . if my dad doesn't take any more potshots. It's the foxes, they drive him insane. He must've thought he'd spotted a whopper when Fig thundered into view. I know it doesn't help her now, but falling into that

381

badger sett might've saved her from Elmer Fudd today. Even a fractured pelvis is better than a gunshot, not that he'd have hit her anyway, the silly bugger. But maybe someone was looking out for her, just in case he got lucky with his aim.' Beth pecked Annabel on the cheek and squeezed Nancy softly on the shoulder. 'Let me know, won't you?'

Annabel nodded and watched her leave, resuming her slow wandering of the linoleum floor. They'd done this before, Nancy and her mum, circuiting and sitting in waiting rooms furnished with information pamphlets and wipeable surfaces.

'Mrs Woods?'

'Yes?' They both stood for the vet waiting in the far doorway. The tortoise girls watched intently until their mum touched them lightly on the knees.

'We've made her comfortable, would you like to come through and we can have a chat?' He was wearing burgundy scrubs. To mask all the blood in his line of work, no doubt. But Nancy had been just as confused as Whittacker: no blood, just Fig thrashing on the ground, yelping in sickeningly high pitch for someone to help her.

Her throat was too tight to speak.

'All right,' said Annabel, but her face said it too. Another piece of Molly was slipping through their fingers. Another noisy, chaotic part falling silent. Then what would there be?

Fig had been sedated so the damage could be looked at, but they'd already seen it on the furlong, the way her leg wouldn't hang right, bent up like a buckled bicycle wheel it was clear would never roll again. *I swear, she's just like a person, Nance*, Molly had said in the garden, wisps of breath pluming through icy December air. *She knows when I'm feeling rough, she sleeps on my legs, just letting me know she's there.* But dogs were not people, even a dog belonging to Molly. They were dogs. And vets didn't allow living things to be kept alive in suffering. They didn't keep on trying while hope faded and hearts broke. Only doctors did that.

'Nancy?' said Annabel, waiting at the corridor.

'Coming.'

The elder of the tortoise girls turned to her younger sister holding the box on her lap. Nancy watched as she tucked the hair behind the smaller girl's ear. And it started. A fist tightening inside her. The familiar bump bump bump of a heart backfiring while the creature that had made its home in there woke up again, wrapping and twisting and tightening itself until the blood whooshed around Nancy's body too quickly. Her trainers squeaked across the lino, but the sound was losing to the thrum of blood pulsing in her ears. She tried counting backwards while the vet led them through into a second room, *one hundred . . . ninety-nine . . . ninety-eight . . .* but it just felt as if she were bracing for impact.

In the centre of a well-lit room, Fig's ginger mass didn't look so formidable. Annabel followed the vet to his computer, listening carefully, processing every word so she could arm herself with information to do battle with later. This was her role. But Nancy's feet took her to Fig.

The tube poking down Fig's throat made her stall. Stupid really, to be melodramatic about a tube after seeing the same dog swallow a banana whole, skin and all. *Stupid.*

'Hey, crazy girl,' she whispered. She pushed her fingers through all that thick red fur. 'Just letting you know I'm here.' But Fig was too still. Too manageable. Too not Fig. 'I'm sorry, Fig.' But the octopus had already crawled out from its pot, reminding Nancy again, in case she'd ever forget, that she couldn't control any of it. It surged up through her middle until her shoulders curled forwards with the pull of it. She laid her head on Fig's neck. It all rushed in while her mum and the vet's voices slipped away. The first wretched sobs finally finding their escape. And out they came.

'Nancy?' A hand arrived on her back, but she couldn't move. She couldn't breathe. There was no air.

'I'll give you a minute before we take her into surgery,' said the vet. Strings Beth had pulled for them. The door clicked to behind him.

'Nancy, don't cry,' but Annabel was already undone again.

Nancy pushed her face deeper into Fig's fur, away from the sounds of her mum's soft weeping, and sobbed. The fur stuck to her face, dampening some of the ugly noises rising up in her.

'Oh Nancy. Just breathe, sweetheart. Just breathe.' Annabel pressed her head against Nancy's back and held her, Nancy kept hold of Fig, the slow, steady beat of her heart, all that soft warmth. 'We'll be OK. We'll be OK, love,' tried Annabel.

'No we won't,' cried Nancy. She couldn't stop herself, it had waited too long, too strong now to be held back, crashing through the levee she had painstakingly built.

'We will, love. They'll mend her, we have to stay positive.' Annabel repositioned the side of her face against Nancy's body, still holding on. 'Sweetheart?' Her voice hardened. She moved her head to Nancy's shoulder blade, pressed it there. 'Your heart's beating awfully fast, are you all right?' It was happening. Nancy could feel it in her ears and her chest and behind her eyes. Same drill as before, in her apartment. Annabel's voice was high. '*Please*, love, try to calm down. I'll get someone . . . I'll get the vet.'

'No,' Nancy tried, but the pressure found its way out like a geyser, thundering from her, blocking the escape for anything else. She felt her mother move, then her shirt lifting up off her back, above her bra, and . . . 'Mum? What are you *doing*?' The coldness hopscotched to a new spot over her ribs. Then another. Annabel listened carefully, the prongs of a stethoscope poking from her curls.

'It's too fast.'

'Mum, stop it! What are you doing?'

Annabel turned Nancy around with force, holding her by the shoulders. 'Deep breaths, right now, Nancy, in through your nose, out through your mouth. It'll slow you down, come on, in through the nose . . .'

Nancy pulled free, yanking her shirt back down. 'What are you doing, Mum? Where did you even get that?'

The stethoscope dangled redundantly from Annabel's ears. She pointed to the vet's desk, face flushed, eyes wild.

'And I'm trying to hear if my daughter's heart is about to give up, right here in front of me. That's what!'

'Well you shouldn't!'

Annabel recoiled. 'Why shouldn't I? I'm your *mum*.'

'I don't want you to do that any more. Trying to look after me.'

'Nancy?'

'You always see the good in people, Mum. And you put up with their shit all the time. *My* shit. But where was I?' She

385

snatched a breath. 'When you needed looking after, where was I, Mum?'

The door rattled open. A young veterinary nurse stood in the doorway. She glanced from Nancy to Annabel and ducked straight back out again.

Annabel put her hand on the trolley next to Fig. Waiting for the wave to hit. Nancy looked at her feet. Breathed past the pinching between her shoulder blades. She dared it. Let it come. Let it hurt.

'Nancy?'

But the quickening in Nancy's body hit a point and held there. She felt it beginning to fade again, to somewhere around the periphery, so that only one thing remained that she could fix herself on. Annabel had waited enough. She'd waited years for her husband to finally stop coming home late from the office and admit he wouldn't be coming home at all any more. She'd waited fifty-seven years to tell her own mother that she could be friends with whoever she wanted. She'd waited months, weeks, days, hours, seconds in recovery rooms and hospital corridors for the doctors to deliver Molly's miracle. She'd gone to church and waited there too, for God to deliver the same. And she'd waited beside Molly's bed into the early hours of a New Year's Day for Nancy to arrive through the snowfall before it was too late. Annabel had waited enough. Nancy would not make her wait another heartbeat for her.

'I didn't crash. The car was fine. I could've got home in time, but I didn't. I didn't want to.'

Another shudder, deep inside her chest. She waited for the adrenalin to do its worst, to send the blood too fast around her body, to narrow her arteries again and remind her heart there were things that would always be outside of her control.

Annabel reached a hand and set it against Nancy's cheek. 'I saw the car. The front, the lights were all broken.'

Nancy shook her head. Her mum was wrong. Annabel wiped the tears from her cheek.

'What I did that night makes no sense to me, Mum. You don't do that to the people you love. You don't abandon them. But this . . .' She set her mum's hand over her heart. The thudding inside. 'This *does* make sense to me. And it's OK. Because this tells me that I did love her, so much, because it hurts now, *so much*.'

'You didn't abandon her.'

A pain flared in Nancy's chest again, but it was hard to tell what sort of pain it was. The sort that came and went, or the sort that stayed for ever. She straightened her body anyway and looked into her mum's eyes so there was no misunderstanding. No more waiting for people to be better than they were.

'I ignored your calls, Mum, because I knew what you were going to say.' She put her hand over Annabel's and held it still over her defective organ, that spot where all the trouble was. 'I promised Mol I'd be there, *a hand to hold onto*,' she said. 'But I couldn't.'

Annabel stared at the back of Nancy's hand. Nancy watched the truth sinking into her mum's brain, cells and synapses all working together to deliver the message straight to where it would wound the most.

'She never felt abandoned by you, Nancy. Not *ever*. Do

you think that's the measure of your relationship? What happened in those minutes? Minutes in a lifetime?'

'They were her *last* minutes. I promised her I'd be there.'

'And you were. Do you honestly think she needed to feel your hand in hers to feel you with her? Can't you feel her still, without seeing her?'

Annabel moved her hand a little, listening with her fingers. Nancy breathed steadily until Annabel felt what she needed. She looked at Nancy again.

'We're more than flesh and bones, kiddo. So much more. All this . . .' she looked down at herself, patting her elbows then her middle, then her thighs softly, 'like she said, they're just the cars we travel in.'

There was a thing about mothers. They had all the answers when you were growing up, and then you got to a point where you realised, no, they didn't. They were just a few miles further down the road than you. They'd passed a few more milestones, seen a wider spectrum of views, knew where some of the potholes were. Not all, but some. They didn't have all the answers, but if you were ever headed out on a journey that was going to shake the wheels out from under you, mothers – *some mothers* – made for exceptional drivers.

Nancy closed the gap between them, wrapped her arms around her mum and held on. Her own body felt tight and uncomfortable, a trap for her to fall into, but if she was going to drop down dead now, or at any point before cardio club could straighten her out, there were things to get said first.

'I love you, Mum.'

'And I love you. Even though you whiff of dog a bit.' Nancy looked at Fig lying there. How were they going to survive another hit if the vet couldn't do what they needed him to do? 'I will always love you, Nancy,' whispered Annabel. 'There is nothing you could do to change that. It's kinda a for-ever deal.'

'OK.'

'But we've got to start laughing again. While we've still got all this breath in us. Or what's the point? Her not being here now can't be the biggest thing. The biggest thing is that she *was*. She *was* here. And we can't just have laughter in the part of our life Mol was here to boss us into it. Can't we come up with some ourselves? Isn't that a good way to honour her?'

'Bossing people around? Probably.' Nancy smiled into her mother's auburn curls. The heaviness pulled at her, but she didn't give it the attention it demanded. Annabel rubbed her gently on the back, soothing the storm with light fingers.

'We have to learn to be brave, Nance,' she said over Nancy's shoulder.

Nancy closed her eyes. The vet would come back soon and they would have to behave like normal people. But until then, she would do as her mother asked.

'Mum?' she asked after a while.

'Yes, sweetheart?'

Annabel had told her already, more than once Nancy had heard her say it, but she'd shut it out. Shut it down. Turned her back on it.

'It was peaceful for her, wasn't it?'

'Yes. It was very peaceful.'

'Her pain—'

Annabel cut her off with a whisper. 'She was comfortable. We were prepared.'

She repositioned her head over Nancy's shoulder. 'She'd had enough, Nance. It was time. So no more punishing yourself for not being there to hold her hand. I forbid it.'

But that wasn't the promise Nancy had made. The last thing Molly had wanted hadn't even been for herself.

'Mol didn't ask me to be there to hold *her* hand, Mum. She asked me to hold yours.'

Chapter 33

There was no separating Mrs Dutard from her cloche hats. Nancy gave the arrangement of peacock feathers beside Mrs Dutard's right ear another admiring glance and repositioned her aching bottom on the hard wooden pew of St Bart's church.

'OK?' whispered Annabel, fidgeting beside her. Nancy nodded. 'Phone turned off?'

'Yep.'

'Thank goodness. Or Haima will be ringing all through the service, too.'

There had been a small change in the plan since Fig's accident. It wasn't fair to skip out on Annabel and go back to the city, leaving her to deal with all the trauma, and Nancy hadn't wanted to. Now that Fig's basket wasn't there any more, Annabel had used the extra room in the kitchen to fold out the other leaf of the table, turning it over into a decent workspace with garden views and a ready supply of coffee and home-made croissants for Nancy. For the last fortnight, despite the inevitable non-stop phone calls and emails from Haima, Nancy had headed up a solid start at the decoy project for Deep Dish's Christmas campaign.

'These pews don't get any easier on the rear end, do they?' Annabel passed the order of service back to Nancy for another look before the service began, at the picture Clarence had chosen for the front. 'She was lucky in many ways,' said Annabel, nodding at the booklet. 'I dreamt of being able to play like Birdie, I used to open my windows when I heard her. I'll miss her beautiful music.'

Nancy looked at the photo of Birdie Ludlow again. Young, beautiful, cross-legged on a piano stool gazing at the dark-haired child in her arms. Nancy had counted eighteen people in the congregation, including the three of them, the vicar, Betty Hollins, Mrs Dutard and Dodgy Roger over there next to the baptismal font. But only two people mattered anyway, and they'd be here soon enough. In Birdie's tiny, complicated universe, all roads led back to Clarence, and he loved her. Birdie Ludlow was loved. Amen.

Ernie whispered across Annabel. 'I've brought a few notes for the collection, but I used my last envelope for Ray's school trip money to the arboretum. Will it matter, do you think? If I just pop it in the box?' Annabel reassuringly patted his forearm.

Clarence had suggested donations in place of flowers, to one of the charities that had helped Birdie over the years, but Annabel had insisted on picking flowers for her too. Ernie had donated hydrangea blooms and some of Ray's sunflower heads from their side of the fence, and Annabel had tied them in with the roses and dahlias she'd cut from her side. She'd come back to the churchyard later and lay them for Birdie then, when the congregation had all gone home and Clarence would be back at the house, processing the day's events, most likely alone.

Nancy glanced over her shoulder at the heavy chapel doors again. A shaft of morning light broke through the stained glass above. She scanned the faces she could see in the rows behind them, then the backs of the heads of those seated in the rows ahead. If she had a helicopter wish to spin now, she'd wish that just one of these people sitting here this morning would bring Clarence some small comfort today.

The chapel doors opened. The organist nodded at the verger, and Birdie's last music began.

When the service finished, Ernie folded his money and fed it into the box in the vestibule. They each walked past Clarence, offering their condolences. The men shook hands or patted Clarence's shoulder, the women mostly offered a kiss, or an affectionate touch of the cheek. Nancy managed yet another well-worn *I'm sorry, Clarence* before everyone followed instructions and made their way back to the house for light refreshment. Birdie was to be laid to rest in the churchyard with family only, and family only meant only Clarence.

Nancy sat in the back of Ernie's Volvo while he and Annabel spoke quietly and solemnly in the front, all the way back to the house.

'It was always just the two of them,' Annabel explained. 'There never really was anyone else.'

Ernie adjusted his tie, checked the rear-view, watched the

road. 'Perhaps it's as it should be then, that he does this last thing for his mother, without any interference.'

Nancy didn't want to interfere, not in any way, but the image she had of Clarence standing alone in the churchyard with the vicar sowed a deep unease in her for the rest of the ride home. She hadn't been able to think of anything else, not even when Betty Hollins had ushered them all in through Birdie's porch as if she were family, or when Annabel had introduced her to the two WI ladies helping Clarence with the tea and coffee provisions, pottering around Birdie's kitchen hunting for teaspoons. Clarence had arrived at the house half an hour ago now, and Nancy still hadn't thought of anything to say to him.

Molly would know. The urge to pull out a phone and text her sent Nancy's hand into her bag, just for a reassuring touch. But she left it there. Messages were for sending to those who weren't around already, and Molly had been making her presence felt all day. She'd been there in the church during Birdie's service, in the mischievous glug of whisky Dodgy Roger had slipped into his coffee just now across the lounge, and in the jasmine that had brushed Clarence's shoulder on his way into the churchyard.

Nancy's eyes sloped back to Clarence. She closed her bag, weighed her next move. Molly would just go on over there and grab him and hang onto him. Nancy could almost feel her elbowing her on. She had found herself these last two weeks opening herself to these influences. Sometimes it felt as though Mol's wisdom could be reached for and touched, like stretching an arm and picking a pear from one of Annabel's trees. Other times, Mol was quieter, and Nancy had to find her own way again. Molly didn't have a lot to offer on advertising campaigns, apparently. The thought had crossed Nancy's mind that maybe work was just too good at drowning out other noise, so she'd started taking longer lunches in the garden with Annabel without her phone, tea breaks, walks over the meadows, so there was always room for Molly to shout up if she wanted to. Sometimes Annabel walked with her up to the sycamore. Sometimes Nancy walked alone. When she thought of Fig up on the furlong, a pang of sadness flushed through her heart.

'OK, love?' asked Annabel, slipping another cup and saucer into Nancy's hand.

'Yes thanks, Mum.'

Across the living room, Clarence's shoulder was getting another paternal squeeze. Nancy watched the other man's hand on Clarence's arm. She thought about her own hand finding its way that close to Clarence again. Close enough to share a helicopter seed. Clarence glanced up. Nancy smiled, but he'd already looked away again. He would be going back to his own life soon, she supposed. Now that Birdie was gone, what else was there here for him?

The rest of Birdie's wake had followed the same steady pattern of intimate gatherings. Eventually someone helpful collected up the used serviettes, someone else washed up the cups and small sandwich plates, the afternoon drew to a gentle close. The last cars left Birdie's driveway and Clarence was alone again.

For the rest of the afternoon, Annabel continued her new foray into the heady world of eBay selling. A package had arrived for her by post in the week, a collection of LPs

Uncle Jules had returned, some of which Annabel realised she'd never liked all that much to begin with. But that hadn't stopped her flipping through them a few times, each time catching a smile to herself that Nancy had started to look out for. Annabel had got Nancy to pump her dad for the whole gamut of buying and selling tips lately. No one had picked up the Staffordshire dogs yet, but Annabel had gulped her first stiff Irish coffee in years after an exciting bidding frenzy on a Cat Stevens LP Uncle Jules hadn't yet been able to pull back out of his sleeve and reinstate to his sister's collection. While Annabel had perfected her item descriptions and bid-sniping, Nancy had worked through a few office emails, anything to help draw the day to an end, if only for Clarence's sake.

She'd been lying awake in bed for over an hour now. The hot bath had helped her body but not her brain, which felt now like a penny spinning around a jar. Since that last hiccup in the vet's, when the worry had ballooned again and her heart had felt like a tyre about to explode once and for all until Annabel had carefully settled it down again, Nancy had been more careful about this body of hers. More mindful of her role in getting better. Of listening to the therapists in cardiac rehab group, taking things steadier so the stress didn't get a chance to knock over all the other dominoes again; opening herself up to better relaxation techniques, better exercise, *talking*, and even reacquainting herself with her long-lost friend . . . music. Not the pretend kind, not silent headphones wedged into her ears to drown out the noise of the world, but real music. Familiar melodies and words. The soundtrack of a life she was lucky to live, for all its high and low notes.

But even music wasn't helping now. Three chapters of an

atrocious book off Mol's shelf and a mug of hot chocolate hadn't invited sleep in either. Clarence was still there every time she shut her eyes, standing alone in the churchyard, neat as a pin in his black suit.

It was no good. Nancy threw the covers back. She pulled on a cardigan over her nightie. She'd try the last of the hot chocolate in the pan. Annabel's soft snores followed her downstairs, otherwise the house was silent. In the kitchen, the habit of looking for Fig in her usual spot by the Aga was automatic. Nancy reheated the pan, poured what was left into her mug. The evening had been balmy, the sky a warm, hazy ink. She turned the kitchen lights off so she could look at the night properly. They would camp out in the garden on nights like this, when the darkness never fully came until just before the dawn. She slipped into Molly's pink wellies, turned the key in the back door and quietly let herself out into the garden. She sipped her hot chocolate and walked to the end of the lawn, balancing her elbows on the fence overlooking the world beyond Annabel's boundary. The air felt sweet and cool. She took in another great lungful of it and picked out the line of the millstream, how it reflected the moonlight like molten metal spilt across the meadow. Her eyes followed the waterline, appearing and disappearing behind the grasses until another shadow broke her view.

She blinked hard, letting her eyes make the necessary adjustments. The shadow moved, maybe a hundred yards from Annabel's fence, too tall for a fox. Nancy became motionless while the silhouette became less mistakable. Man-sized, crouching. A quick scraping noise broke the silence, sending a tiny shot of adrenalin through her heart.

The match flame flickered to life after the sound had already died. Clarence's features burst into fragments of orange light. He lit his cigarette, shook out the match, his face lost again to the shadows. Nancy watched from the fence as his silhouette straightened. The adrenalin had left something behind in her, not fight-or-flight exactly, but enough to . . . encourage. She set her mug down in the grass, stepped beneath the last pear tree, pulled herself up by its branches while she got her foot onto the low fence. The branches were thicker now, sturdier than they had been the last time she'd done this. She reached her other welly to the fence and rebalanced. After this, it was just one tiny leap of faith, a few feet, onto the grass the other side.

She hit the damp ground with more of a thud than she remembered. The grass was wet under her hands, but nothing hurt. The orange dot glowing at the end of Clarence's cigarette swung this side of him. He'd heard her. She trod carefully, fully aware that even Mol's clumpy Glasto wellies weren't going to save her ankles if she misstepped over the tufts and dinks. But she didn't trip. She didn't stumble. She walked a near-straight line through the late-September twilight to Clarence at the edge of the millstream, where the darkness was thickest closer to the earth. A little plume of smoke rose above him, up to the paler night sky.

'Hey.' Her voice sounded small and quiet. A moth in the dark.

'Hey,' replied Clarence.

'I couldn't sleep.'

Clarence didn't say anything at first. He pulled on his cigarette and looked upward before exhaling again. 'We don't have all this over the garden fences our side of the street.'

'No, I know.'

'It's a good view,' he said. 'Lot of moonlight.'

'I know.' He held out his cigarette. 'No thanks. I don't, er . . .'

'I know,' said Clarence. 'Neither do I.'

Nancy stood beside him and looked up too, so they were both facing the same stretch of infinity. They gazed into the universe for a while, until the first chill of the air made the hairs on her arms rise to attention. It felt like one of them might leave soon, another door closing between them.

'I'm sorry you lost your mum, Clarence. I wish I had something more comforting to say, but . . . I don't.'

Clarence kept his face to the sky. 'She was an enigma, huh, Nance?'

Nancy smiled at the darkness. 'Oh yeah.'

'Feels strange. Like she's somewhere else for a while. I guess that changes.' But it didn't sound like a question. Maybe he realised Nancy didn't have the answer anyway. 'I think I can feel her. It's like she's in the fabric of the universe or something. Like she hasn't really gone anywhere. Not yet, anyway. Was it like that at first with Mol?'

Molly's name was like a shooting star through the dark. The glowing tip of Clarence's cigarette moved towards his lips again. Nancy turned back to the infinite inky blue above them. The reliable moon.

'I'm still working all that out.' She rubbed the chill from her arms. 'St Bartholemew's looked beautiful today, Clarence. It will be nice to go there when you want to leave flowers for her.' There would always be somewhere for Birdie now.

He pulled on his cigarette. 'She thought flowers should be

growing wild, not picked in their prime.' One of the cards that had arrived at their house had said, *When God comes to pick flowers from his garden to take back into Heaven, he picks the most vibrant.* Annabel had appreciated the sentiment, but Nancy was with Birdie on that one. God should stick to yanking weeds.

'What did she like? Instead?'

'Rum. The parishioners won't approve if I start leaving her hip flasks down there, though.' His voice had softened. He sounded like he was smiling to himself. Nancy wondered what the shape of his mouth would look like, how it would feel if she could touch it with her fingers.

She wrapped herself into her cardigan. 'Guess not. You're going to have to figure out a way of dragging that piano down there then, huh?'

Clarence laughed at the sky. 'Yeah, she'd like *that*.'

A smile escaped Nancy too. It was the wrong time on the wrong day at the wrong corner of the universe, but she wanted to see Clarence smile so much it ached.

'There's no rush, Clarence. To do anything. You'll figure it out. We haven't even scattered Mol's ashes yet.'

Clarence shifted in the moonlight. Just enough light reaching the edges of his face to pick out the frown over his eyes.

'Do you have anywhere in mind? Like someplace special?'

'Not yet. But we will.' She believed now. That Mol would somehow help them figure it out. When the time was right.

'You'll know it when you feel it, Nancy.'

A breeze chased over the grasses, sending a shiver over the backs of her legs, all the way up her spine. The landing light of their house glowed back through the branches of Annabel's fruit trees. It was time to go. She tried to say *goodnight*, but nothing came. She pictured the colour of Clarence's skin when he'd sat in front of them in church today, his neck and the back of his ear. She thought about his immaculate white shirt collar. His tensed jaw, arms stiff by his sides, and hands all day with nothing to hold onto. She felt her pulse quicken. Clarence's hand, so close to her own. She kept her face to all that sky above them, and reached out her arm. Her little finger found his through the dark, then the others too. His hand moved, letting her in. He fed his fingers through hers. Nancy held her breath and Clarence Ludlow's hand and stared dead ahead at the night sky, waiting for the first thing to give her up, her lungs or Clarence's fingertips. But Clarence didn't let go.

Nancy concentrated on his breathing, suddenly all she could think of. Air passing in and out of his lips and body, air she could take into herself and hold onto. She heard herself swallow. Her own breathing. Clarence moved his body closer to hers. And then he was there, too close to her for the moonlight to find him. Featureless. His hand found its way to her waist. Then the hand she'd been holding broke free of hers. Clarence placed it gently at the side of her neck and then pressed his lips over Nancy's. He kissed her softly, the urgency building. Her body leant into his, a series of involuntary instincts all coordinating, her mouth opening for his, hands finding their place to hold on, feet in wellington boots reaching onto tiptoes for more.

Clarence kissed Nancy in the moonlight. When he stopped, he let his hands fall from her face, to find his way back to her fingertips. A cobweb connection between them. In this new silence, there was a crushing sense of something concluded, the feeling that something one-off had already reached its crescendo before its inevitable end, like the mayflies and their brutally short-but-sweet lifecycles. And then he found her in the dark again, pressed his mouth to hers, and it was as if Nancy felt herself touch the surface of water, and take second flight.

Chapter 34

'What's the matter, a million miles off or . . .?' But Haima was concentrating. Frowning towards Nancy's laptop. Nancy glanced about them at the other bistro tables scattered outside the park café, mothers and prams, office workers grabbing a bite in the leafy respite of Chortley Park before whipping back to their desks. No young women in trainers and earphones, trying to push their personal bests down to eleven unattainable minutes, though, not any more. Nancy looked down at her running shoes. She'd walked here from the hospital, her fourth weekly outpatient appointment done, to the promise of an informal work meeting with Haima ahead of her, and not at any point had she felt the need to get above a gentle stroll.

Haima shut the laptop and chewed her lip. Nancy pushed the sleeves of her hoodie back up her arms. 'Haima, c'mon. You haven't said a word for the entire pitch. If it needs reworking, it's no big deal, I can—'

'It doesn't need reworking, Nance. *We do. Shit.*'

Haima had asked to run through Nancy's ideas before she headed back to Mistleton. Now Nancy was thinking there might be more to it. She sat patiently with her ice cream while Haima fished her cigarettes from her bag. She'd graduated from vaping then, not a great advert for the stress levels at work. 'You look worried, why? It's only the backup concept.'

'And it's stronger than the *actual* campaign. We can't send them a great white shark and call it the *red herring*, Nance.' Haima considered her cigarettes, then lobbed them back into the bag. She leant across the table. 'When are you coming back? It's been six weeks since your heart octopus attack thingy, right? You said you didn't want to be away this long, so how about it? Back to normal? Monday morning, eight o'clock sharp? I mean, you're looking *great*, Nance. Different. I can't even put my finger on it, but—'

'Actually . . . I wanted to speak to you about that. My therapist has suggested . . . a more tapered return.'

Haima was fully up to speed on the sessions Nancy had been attending at the city hospital, how well her rehabilitation was going, how seamlessly they could make it fit into a working week, just as soon as Nancy's working week was defibrillated and back to a steady rhythm once more.

Haima looked at her, deadpan. 'Your therapist's suggestion?'

Nancy scooped from her tub of gelato and let it dissolve on her tongue. Not as good as Mr Scorlucci's rum 'n' raisin, but Clarence had tasked her with finding some solid city competition before he played his first solo side gig at the Crypt Rooms in the Blues Quarter next month. She thought of Clarence, sitting on his porch with a beer, strumming his guitar as softly as the night closed in around them. How she had found surprisingly little of the city to beat Mistleton yet. She tasted the last of the flavour on her lips. 'Uh-huh. He was thinking, maybe about me dropping to a four-day week . . . three in the office, one remote, and a long weekend to recuperate. Then building up from there in the new year maybe.' Or maybe not. She didn't know yet what the months ahead held for any of them. It was kind of exciting.

Haima seemed momentarily stunned. She blinked and tried letting the pieces fall into place. 'But doll . . . you love work. Like, *really* love it.'

'I know. I do. But there are things back home I love too. And I just . . . want to make room for them.'

'Damn.' Haima fell silent again, still working on those falling pieces. She squinted Nancy's way. 'Has this got something to do with the guy you were complaining about the night you nearly died in the canal?'

Nancy stilled, then slowly pulled the little bamboo ice-cream spoon from her lips. Haima was being dramatic again, but, 'The guy?'

'Come on, Nance. The fella with the grandad name. Clifford or Cecil or something.'

Nancy felt the heat in her face. She laughed to herself. 'Clarence. So I mentioned him already?' Haima had kept that one up her sleeve. Sneaky.

'That's the one. He's not bad, you know, Nance. Didn't have you down for a groupie, but tall, dark and handsome, nice voice, great arms . . . I can see the pull.'

Nancy set her gelato tub on the tabletop, ever so slightly horrified, all of a sudden, at what exactly she might've divulged after that heavy session with Dodgy Roger. Haima grinned, flicked her dark fringe from eyes sparkling with superior intel. 'He's in your history, doll.'

'What?'

'At the office. I stumbled across him in there when I was looking for an old proof of concept Noah said he'd left on your hard drive when IT were running the great purge. I was not expecting to find what I found, I can tell you.'

Nancy cringed. Her browsing history. A snapshot of the inner workings of her mind, at a time when her mind probably wasn't being all that kind to her. She braced herself. 'Go on. What did you find?'

'Only that my most level-headed friend and colleague turns out to be a closet *fangirl*. I thought, *They must be good if Nancy's on board*, so I googled them. Saw one of them hailed from the same neck of the woods as you. Figured you probably knew him at least, hence all the replays. I think I prefer his solo stuff, if I'm honest. I'm guessing you do too, given the trail of vids. But they're good together too. Have they played in town?'

Nancy shook her head to herself. There were no secrets at work. They were going to need more than non-disclosures and a decoy campaign to keep the lead protected from gossips and spies.

'Not yet. They might, if they stick together. They almost let him go.' Nancy allowed the thought to slide over her. How anyone could think of letting Clarence go. How Mol had always had the good sense to keep him close.

Haima lunged forward, something juicy on the table. 'Why? What did he do? Sex? Drugs?'

Nancy smiled and looked out over the park. Strangers going about their business, each quietly carrying their invisible hopes and dreams and worries. 'Nope. Just . . . *life*, Haima. He was doing life. As best he could. It's not always compatible with other interests.'

Haima dipped her chin, disappointed. 'You sound like you know a lot about it.'

Nancy shrugged. 'I know what he's worth. And I think his band are smart enough to know it too.'

'I'll bet you do,' grinned Haima. 'Poor old Cecil. Well, good for him. I'm sure he'll make it on his own if he ever has to, right?'

'Clarence,' corrected Nancy. 'And he's not on his own.'

Chapter 35

'I'm telling you, Ray, it was a big deal back then and I've heard your school friends talking about it when they get off the bus. The higher you get your name up this sycamore, the higher up the pecking order you'll be at school.'

'That's stupid, Nancy,' frowned Ray. 'And immature.'

'You make a valid point, but I'm telling you, this tree is like . . . a *thing*. Whittacker would've chopped it down years ago just for poisoning his horse, but even Beth wouldn't let him chop it and it was her horse that ate the seeds. Trust me, we need to put your name on this thing, Ray.'

Nancy balanced herself on the first branch of the sycamore and held her hand out for him, but Ray's feet were rooted more firmly to the ground than the tree was.

'But you said not to climb any higher than the dodgy heart.'

Nancy looked at Clarence sitting next to her on the bough, then up to where Lucy Hemmings had scratched out that heart in the tree bark. It did look a long way up.

'I did say that,' she admitted. Plus, she had seen Ray drop like a rock from these branches once already. She tapped a finger on the branch anyway.

Ray cocked his head and squinted up at them. 'Couldn't you just put my name up there for me? You're a better climber than I am, and no one would know.'

Clarence turned his baseball cap back to front and shrugged. 'I won't tell if you won't?' There was a strict code about this sort of thing, but there was also a code about letting sods like this Oliver kid get away with picking on your squad, and that was what they were now, Ray said, a squad. The four of them, Annabel on the merits of her cooking, and Ernie because, well, just because he was Ernie. Clarence was about to earn his spot too.

Nancy straightened up, took another look up there and felt some of Ray's reluctance. 'Are you coming, Ludlow?' she asked, before she lost her bottle.

'Sure.'

Clarence smiled up at her from beneath his cap and she was instantly affected. It had got worse, this affliction of becoming instantly undone by Clarence Ludlow, it was like having water in her ears all the time or walking in too-high heels, the near-constant threat of overbalancing. Not good when you were about to scale an epic tree.

'Ready?' he asked, reaching upwards. His hoodie rode up over his hip. *Concentrate*, Nancy warned herself. She nodded. She felt her legs liquefy the higher they managed to haul their adult bodies up through the branches of their old tree, but it felt familiar too, like the steps to a dance you used to know, or the words to a song. Plus, the threat of Annabel arriving any time now with flasks of tea was enough to make her get a wriggle on. Her heart felt the healthiest it had in a long, long time, but just because she was unlikely to have a palpitation up here, there were no guarantees Annabel wouldn't if she caught her kid too high up.

They made it up past Lucy Hemmings' faded efforts, past some of the marks they recognised and others they didn't. Clarence checking, always checking, that Nancy's feet and hands were where they should be. And then they were nearly as high as they could go.

'Are you OK?' he asked. He grinned then, a broad smile that belonged to his younger self. Nancy felt a thrill ripple through her but couldn't decipher if it was the fear of falling back to the earth or the promise of Clarence's gravitational pull. Best not to think about either just now. She nodded and found a comfortable position against the trunk. The yoga she'd swapped her runs for was working, the breathing and stillness and calm had started to root inside her. Annabel had joined in in front of the living room TV and had already signed up to a class in town, a class she really would go to, ready for when Nancy went back to the city, which she would soon enough. Haima had agreed the hybrid arrangement, hoping the office would seduce Nancy all by itself. But honestly, she wasn't so sure it would. And there was still all that holiday time to get through first.

Clarence touched her on the ankle. 'This has got to be high enough to last him all through high school. His mates aren't getting up past here,' he said. Nancy breathed in and steadied herself. She looked out through the changing leaves and clusters of helicopter wishes all about them to the views of Mistleton's finest landscapes. She turned and took it all in, Whittacker's rolling fields, the autumnal light through the valley, their furlong snaking all the way down to this one tree like an inevitability.

'They're brave little buggers if they can,' she said.

Clarence took out his penknife and set to scoring Ray's name into the trunk. 'So what are we thinking? Just *RR*?'

'How about *RAY*? So there's no disputing it?'

'Roger that,' said Clarence.

Nancy watched him for a while before letting her eyes wander. Molly's name was up here somewhere. Nancy had never seen it, but there was no doubt Mol had gone as high as she'd said. But it was a long time ago, and trees were like people that way, not changing much through the decades, but not unchanged either. Perhaps the bark had healed itself, or Mol had climbed up through the other side. But then . . . she saw it. Faded, but there.

She swallowed. 'She went higher.'

Clarence slipped his penknife back into his pocket and straightened up so his shoulders were level with Nancy's feet. He pulled himself up onto the next branch beside her and looked up. He laughed to himself.

'She went higher, Clarence.'

'Of course she did. Wait, Nancy, what are you doing?'

Nancy found her next footing, then a handhold. Then another not-so-sure footing. Clarence followed her. 'You don't have to,' she said.

'Are you kidding me? Ray's watching. I'll never live it down if you leave me behind.'

Nancy smiled.

'Hey, if it's a hero you're holding out for, I'm definitely not your guy.'

'No?' she asked, feigning shock.

Clarence pulled himself closer. He pressed a kiss to her lips. 'I can't promise to catch you, Nance . . . but I will fall with you. Happily.'

It was more than good enough. Clarence didn't know that he'd broken her fall already, they all had in their own way. Maybe even Ginny.

Nancy took a few last tentative stretches and reached the place Molly had climbed to all on her own before hacking her name into the leaderboard. She reached up and traced the letters Mol had managed without losing her grip. *Molly was here.* Yes, she definitely was. And the world would never be the same again.

Clarence held out his penknife. 'Would be rude not to. Seeing as we're up here.'

Nancy looked at the mark Molly had left behind. One of the many, many indelible marks she'd left.

'Don't suppose you've got a Sharpie on you instead?'

Clarence shook his head.

Ray wanted to see photographic evidence when they returned to earth. He was still marvelling at his name up in heights on the picture on Clarence's phone when the barking floated across the meadows. Fig strained forwards; from here she looked like a horizontal birdbath with her funnelled collar fixed to her head. It was a strange feeling Nancy met with now each time Fig waddled her way. The same old trepidation of being flattened or drooled on or covered in dog hair . . . but also relief. Gratitude that Mol's dog was still here to make mischief.

'How long is she going to wear that thing?' asked Clarence.

'Until she has her stitches out,' replied Ray. 'Then when her fur has grown back, Annabel said she will go back to sleeping in the kitchen instead of by the log burner.'

Nancy shook her head. 'She'll never go back to sleeping in the kitchen. Fig's going up in the world. Speaking of which, my mum doesn't need to know I was up the tree, Ray, *comprende*?' Ray held his finger to his lips and made a turning-key gesture. They were pals, Ray and Nancy. Unlikely, solid pals.

A way further behind Fig, Annabel and Ernie trailed the other end of the very long lead Ernie had fashioned from an old washing line he'd had in his shed. Annabel was taking no chances with sheep, or guns or badger setts.

'Sorry we're late!' she called, waving a flask at them. 'We've had a brush with the law!'

'What?' asked Nancy.

'Tell them, Ernest,' Annabel said. 'Henry Locke has been talking to us, hasn't he? I remember pulling a bee sting out of his thumb when he was this big,' she added, jabbing her knee. 'I should've left it in there.'

Henry was the local bobby now. He and Nancy had been in the same school year. He'd turned eighteen, gone bald almost overnight and still hadn't left home, Beth said, after telling Nancy about the last time Henry had gone up to the farm to talk about her dad's gun licence.

'Everything OK?' asked Clarence.

'Oh, he wasn't so bad, Annie,' said Ernie, laying out the picnic blanket. 'Just doing his job. He said that would be the end of it now, so there's no need to worry.'

'What job?' asked Clarence.

'You haven't been back up Cranton Woods, have you, Mum?'

Annabel ignored her, instead exchanging an innocent look with Ernie while she dipped in and out of her basket. 'He just wanted to know if we'd seen anything. Someone's bike was misplaced last week, he said. Just wanted to know if anything suspicious had caught our eye.'

'Was it Oliver's bike?' asked Ray. 'Two burglars stole it last week but his dad made their neighbours all show him their CCTV and they saw it being taken into the park. Is that what they were asking you about, Grandpa?'

Nancy's back straightened. Ray had recounted her story to them over Sunday lunch, Annabel flushing red with shame while the account of Molly's renegade justice with Freddie Blumfield's BMX had fallen animatedly from Ray's mouth.

She watched her mother settling herself on the blanket, twisting off one of the flask lids. Ernest gave Annabel another furtive look. Nancy looked to Clarence to see what he was making of all this.

'The park pond's always been a popular destination for boys' bikes,' he said, making himself comfortable.

'Well, maybe they should be kinder boys. Or at least not leave their expensive bikes on their driveways in full view,' breathed Annabel, unboxing cheese scones now.

'Oliver said his dad said the police would track them down easily because they left so many clues. He said they were the sloppiest thieves his dad has ever seen, even more sloppy than America's Dumbest Criminals.'

'Sloppy?' blustered Ernie.

'One of them was wearing a bad fake moustache, Grandpa. And the other one had bright orange Crocs on. And they're on the park cameras too. They didn't even want to keep Oliver's bike. They just pushed it in the water.'

Annabel cleared her throat. 'Tea, Clarence?'

'Thanks.' He gave Nancy a side-eye.

'So what have we all been doing then?' asked Annabel brightly, sitting back and crossing her ankles. Nancy looked at her mum's baked bean gardening clogs.

'I climbed the sycamore and put my initials in the trunk,' lied Ray.

'That's my boy!' exclaimed Ernie. Nancy gave Ray a hard look. Why was everyone suddenly behaving like pathological liars?

Clarence passed Nancy her cup of tea and let Fig settle down between him and Ray. The scar across her hind was going to be a good one.

'The wind's getting up, Nance,' he said. 'Are you warm enough?'

'Perfect, thanks.' She touched his finger next to hers on the blanket, just enough to let him know. Then she lay back on her elbows and looked up at the sycamore.

'Yep,' agreed Ernie, 'soon be time for trick-or-treating and Bonfire Night, hey, Ray?'

'It's only just October. There's still time to enjoy the

415

autumn,' said Annabel. Helicopters spun steadily down to the earth around them. The leaves had already started to turn on the sycamore. They flittered above their heads like a great yellowing umbrella. Soon the tree would be ablaze with colour, a last encore, wishes by the thousands all set in flight. And then the snow would come again to the furlong. Another winter. Another New Year. And it would be all right. And they would be lucky to get to see it.

'Goodness, it's beautiful down here in the autumn, isn't it? No wonder you kids loved it so much.'

'Under the cool shade of a sycamore, I thought to close mine eyes some half an hour,' said Ernest.

'Goodness,' repeated Annabel.

Ernie shied like a schoolboy. 'Don't be too impressed, it's the only Billy Wigglestick I ever remembered. They are magnificent, though, aren't they? Sycamores. Not least for their ability to grow in the shade of their own parent. Now that *is* impressive.'

Annabel smiled at him, but Ernie didn't shy away this time. She cleared her throat. 'So what do you think, Ray?' she asked, nodding towards Nancy and Clarence. 'Would you go gambolling down a near-vertical hill, chasing a rolling cheese? Or is it just these two who think that sounds like fun?'

'How about it, Ray?' rumbled Ernie. 'We do like our cheese.'

A brown moustache sat over Ray's top lip from the hot chocolate Annabel had passed him. He watched a helicopter wish spin its way down onto his knee.

'The golden wheel spider can roll downhill on sand dunes in the Namib Desert at more than thirty . . .' he frowned and cocked his head, 'no, forty rotations per second. When there's a wasp trying to lay eggs in them. It's a lot of cartwheeling, but they're OK.'

Ernie's eyebrows rose appreciatively for his grandson.

'They aren't thinking of going to the Namib Desert, though, Ray my love,' said Annabel. 'Nor do they have wasps on their tail. And you can buy cheese from the supermarket.' Something like worry moved over her face.

'Mum. We're not going until next summer. We haven't even looked at camper vans yet.'

'Good. Because I'm doing super with my piano lessons, aren't I, Clarence?'

'You're a natural,' Clarence smiled.

'So you can hold off breaking his ruddy neck, please. I'm already having to share him with his bandmates. Nipping off for weekends here and weekends there. We all need you in one piece, Clarence.' Yes, they did. But life could get messy sometimes, and it was all right. Nancy would take Clarence as he came. She would take any of them in their many, complicated, precious pieces, and hold on tightly to all of them.

'We're just going to watch, Mum. There will be no cartwheeling, trust me.'

'Yes, that's what your sister said when she first put those pins in the map, like anyone was convinced!'

Clarence had spotted their map on the back of the downstairs loo door. It had been his idea, to take a road trip sometime. A few weeks away when there was a break in his schedule, ticking off some of the places Mol had put her stickers to. Clarence had started sticking a few pins of his own too. There had been some talk of taking Molly's ashes along the way, but this was where Molly Woods belonged. This was where she had rooted and flowered. This was her home.

'I've told you before, Mum. Not many people are as brave as Mol.' Although Nancy had just made it all the way up the sycamore as high as Molly. Not bad for a mere mortal.

'My grandpa says bravery wears different coats,' said Ray.

'Yes, it does,' agreed Annabel. 'And sometimes it dresses as a complete lunatic with no sense of self-preservation . . . or gravity.'

Nancy laid her hand over her mum's. 'No cartwheeling. I promise.'

The wind picked up again. 'Hold onto your hats, we might be in luck!' Clarence nodded at the crop along the ridge, the wind pushing a current through it like underwater weeds, rippling and undulating all down into the valley, somewhere an octopus might hide.

'Mum, ready?'

Annabel nodded. Ernie patted her hand before she slipped a deceptively unremarkable cardboard tube from the backpack Nancy and Clarence had carried here. Precious cargo, making one last trip across the furlong. Clarence kissed Nancy's head before she got to her feet. She helped her mum to her feet too. Annabel reached for Nancy's cheek, gave it a quick touch and turned away, leading.

'You guys stay here, watch the show. It's a good 'un,' Nancy smiled. 'See how many of them you can catch, Ray. We won't be long. Fig? Come on, girl.' She took Fig's lead and followed Annabel to the other side of the sycamore, where the wind and sunlight flowed down the valley and hit the tree head-on, from where Nancy knew Molly's ashes would be scattered the furthest. She breathed in the scents of the cool earth beneath their feet, the sweetness of the afternoon air tumbling over the meadows, the smell of their mother's hair.

'Look up, Mum. Isn't it beautiful?'

Annabel lifted her chin, taking in the views up through the boughs too, to the low sun bending and breaking and re-forming its light again between the gaps in the leaves above them, as high as they could see, until the wind reached down into the valley and the sycamore on the furlong, sending the first great flurry of helicopters spinning down over them like sylvan confetti. Annabel carefully took the lid from their precious consignment, and with Nancy's help, let Molly's ashes go. And in a heartbeat, she was gone. In the only way a person can ever really be *gone*.

Nancy felt her mother's hand in her own. Felt Fig's considerable bulk against her legs. Felt her sister, safely there in every beat of her complicated heart.

It was a force of habit, making wishes under the sycamore. Nancy tried to think of one now, but actually, she was OK. Annabel was OK. For now, she'd leave the wishes for someone else, someone who needed them more than they did.

She watched the fluttering seeds falling around them, around her squad, huddled at the base of the sycamore. Some other kid would climb as high as Molly one day. Maybe another pair of sisters, harvesting helicopter wishes, or hiding from the boy whose bike they'd slung in the duckpond, or just trying to out-brave the rest and get their names nice and high. Maybe they wouldn't be brave at all, but just trying to find out if you really could get to Heaven if you just had the right tree. Or it could be that they would be looking for something, or someone, they couldn't always find closer to the earth any more. But what they would find for sure, if they climbed high enough, was what a girl named Molly Woods had carved into this tree years before she'd become lost for a while, and what her sister had carved into the same spot when she'd found her again.

Molly was here . . . with Nancy.

Acknowledgements

If writing a novel can be likened to running a marathon, there are many folks to whom I owe my deepest gratitude for coming out during the winding course of this book, to stand on the sidelines offering sustenance and that most generous and transformative of gifts . . . encouragement.

Looking back, I began writing this novel in the foothills of what felt at the time to be a fathomless personal shift, when I wasn't in the best shape for marathon running. It took a long time before the views started to open out again and a clear path began to take shape. Not everyone has the stamina to jog alongside you on all those empty miles while you find your way back on track, inevitably some will fall away, but my exceptional publisher HarperCollins never did.

I cannot thank them enough for patiently waiting for this novel, or for the wonderful editors they sent my way to nudge me from those first difficult foothills to clearer, sunnier ground. Heartfelt thanks in particular to Cicely Aspinall for graciously tolerating the many bumpy miles I dragged her through, and later Cat Camacho for expertly taking the baton and proving to be the best running buddy a writer could hope to cross the finish line with. A huge thanks also to Kate Byrne for the warmth and enthusiasm shown for this book and for her hard and fastidious work nudging it out into the world.

This novel is about the gift of loving and of being loved, so I'll take this opportunity to remind my friends and family how much I love them, how lucky I feel to have had them shaking their pom-poms my way, reliably cheerleading from the sidelines all these years, and how very grateful I am for them.

Jasper Knight, it feels only right to give you a nod for the many hours of impeccable company you afforded me while this story took shape and for all the walks over our beloved Cannock Chase to work out the plot kinks together. The conversation could be a little one-sided but you were always willing, with not a single word of complaint. You've been the very best of friends.

And finally, to Annisa. I have borrowed from you, my wise pal. That place you found for the safekeeping of lost and precious things . . . thank you for sharing it. I hope you don't mind my sharing it within these pages.

ONE PLACE. MANY STORIES

Bold, innovative and
empowering publishing.

FOLLOW US ON:

@HQStories